Shinobi:
SAMURAI for MI6

Agent Samurai, Vampire-Hunter
Book 7

by

D.C. Rhind

Also by D.C. Rhind

Agent SAMURAI, Vampire–Hunter Series:
Once A SAMURAI…
…Always A SAMURAI
Immortal SAMURAI
Ronin: Outlaw SAMURAI
Daimyo: Lord SAMURAI
Maha-ka: Sorcerer SAMURAI
Heart of a SAMURAI

Calebra Fantasy Series:
The Warlord's Blade
The Wizard's Quest
The Sorcerer's Gambit
Revenge of the Wolf
The Pirate's Nemesis

"Shinobi: SAMURAI for MI6," by D.C. Rhind.
ISBN 978-1-62137-608-8 (softcover).

Published 2014 by Virtualbookworm.com Publishing,
P.O. Box 9949, College Station, TX 77842, US.
©2014, D.C. Rhind. All rights reserved. No part of this
publication may be reproduced, stored in a retrieval
system, or transmitted in any form or by any means,
electronic, mechanical, recording or otherwise, without
the prior written permission of D.C. Rhind.

"Friendship multiplies the good of life

and divides the evil."
— Baltasar Gracián —

"A hero is one who knows how to hang on
one minute longer."
— Novalis —

"The noir hero is a knight in blood–caked armour.
He's dirty and he does his best to deny the fact that
he's a hero the whole time."
— Frank Miller —

For Carol,
my Carrie,

For Sean,

and

for all those who've stuck by me on this
amazing journey.

Beware; They are among us!

Preface

Chester Basin, NS, March 16, 2014

When I first set out to write this book, I had my mind on Russian prisons, so I started researching famous and infamous prisons: Butyrka, Lubyanka, and Lefortovo.

Then a news story caught my ear: The Russians, in gearing up for their Sochi Olympics, were worried about terrorism. Time to Google. What terrorists could be bothering the Russians?

Next thing I knew I was sucked down the rabbit hole — Chechens — then the Putin nightmare began. Putin has always, for me, triggered a gut–reaction of mistrust. I started digging into his history. Did he have a dark side? Next thing I knew I was up to my neck in an article by Scott Anderson, a book by Alexander Litvinenko, and another by Masha Gessen, stories by Oleg Kalugin, culminating in a CBC National News piece in April, that featured all of the above.

Before I knew it, I decided that Michael's perception of the situation, as well as the mission, had to be much bigger than a simple rescue and exfiltration. I felt a need to remind the world of Mikhail Trepashkin and Alexander Litvinenko. Then, the character of poor damaged Natasha Cherninova began to evolve, until she took me completely by surprise.

D.C. Rhind, Chester Basin, NS, 2014

Prologue: *Michael*

Chester Basin, NS
November 15, 2013

*C*onfined, unable to move.

Of course! He realized that, just emerging from vampire sleep, from the void, there might still be a certain paralysis. No — it was more than that; the air was stale.

Then — too strange to explain — his face feeling like it didn't belong to him — like he was wearing someone else's skin! He was! So was Carrie, so was Tony. They were all wearing someone else's skin, and about to venture out into unknown territory.

Urge to panic — his innate warrior nature immediately suppressed that.

So I'm about to advance into unknown territory wearing someone else's skin. Get over it!

His eyes snapped open and he sat up, Kato grumbling a complaint at having to relinquish possession of his shoulder and upper chest.

Was that a dream? Dreams almost never intrude on vampire sleep — well, there was that time in Romania when Carrie was in trouble, but that was more clairvoyance than dream.

He got dressed, glanced at Carrie, still comatose, Teila curled up in the crook of a raised arm.

Take a walk, he decided. *Check on the boat — it's been windy the past few days — make sure it has nothing to do with the boat — What could feeling trapped, stale air, and wearing someone else's skin have to do with the boat? Okay, so check on the boat and think while you're walking.*

1: *Mason*

Vauxhall Cross (SIS Headquarters), London
November 14, 2013

C aptain Bruce Mason finished reviewing the latest batch of field test results for a group of *Double–0* agents for whom recertification had been due. He placed the pages in a file folder, then locked the folder in his top drawer.

Cynthia can file that when she comes back in tomorrow morning, he told himself.

He was about to leave when the phone on his desk rang. He answered it to find nothing but silence on the other end. Frowning, he repeated his *Hello* twice, then hung up. Then his cellphone, a smartphone, did the same thing.

It was beyond curious — such events were becoming more common. At his flat he routinely found long silent messages on his answering machine. He'd had his phone line checked, had the answering machine checked — even gone so far as to replace the device. Caller ID was blocked, and even experts from Q–branch were unhelpful — no way to trace the caller.

Rising from his desk, he glanced out the window, his gaze coming to rest on Thames House, the home of MI5, across the river. He'd come close to passing the mysterious phone-call issue on to them, but had balked — he could just hear *C* making his usual fuss about giving MI5 another chance for a botch-up — *C* was a tad elitist when it came to the sister branch of the *Secret Intelligence Service.*

Bloody Hell, Mason thought, *5 would have solved the mystery by now — this sort of thing is their daily fare, after all.*

There had been hope among some, himself included, that the MI6 and MI5 apparatus would have been housed together in Vauxhall Cross upon the building's completion, making better cooperation possible. MI5 dealt with domestic intelligence, whereas MI6 was responsible for foreign intelligence. Knowing from more than forty years of experience how many grey areas there were, Mason had been of the opinion that housing both SIS agencies under one roof might have helped, but bureaucrats on both sides had other views. MI5 had its roots in Military Intelligence, whereas MI6 stemmed from Naval Intelligence.

Maybe you should have stuck with Naval Intelligence, old boy, he mused; then, *No, if you'd stuck to Naval Intelligence, you'd never have met Tony or Sam or a host of other friends.*

He shook his head, got up, grabbed his topcoat, and exited his office.

"I had no idea you were still here, Cyn," he announced to Cynthia, his secretary, still at her desk.

"I was just about to leave," she admitted with a smile. "It's just after 7:00."

Mason nodded. "Oh, by the by, there's a file in my top drawer that needs filing first thing in the morning. *C* might also want a copy."

She smiled again. "Why don't I just look after that now, then it's done, just in case Sir John wants to peruse over morning tea."

Mason easily read from her demeanor that she wasn't as eager as she might seem to add more to an already long day.

"Off you go," he insisted. "It'll still be there in the morning. By the way, did you put a call through to me a few minutes ago?"

Cynthia frowned, then shook her head. "No, sir; there was a call — I saw the line light up — but I assumed it was personal to your direct line, since it went straight through."

Now it was Mason's turn to frown. "I suppose it could have been personal — I really can't say. In fact I have no idea who it was; there was no one on the other end. In fact, I've been getting a few of those lately, always a blocked number."

"Well, that is odd," Cynthia commented.

"Indeed," Mason agreed. Then, musing aloud, he added, "I've gotten the same at my flat, including long blank messages on the machine, even after replacing the bloody thing.

"Well, that's enough for tonight. I'm off to the club for a Scotch, then dinner, then home to sleep before it all starts again tomorrow.

"Here, let me help you with that," he offered, quickly grabbing her coat and holding it for her.

"Thank you, Captain," she said, flashing him a more radiant smile.

"Not a bit, Midshipman," he returned.

"Your car should be waiting down front" she added. "I knew you'd forgotten again, and took the liberty of having Robert stand by."

Chagrinned, Mason commented. "It was infinitely easier when I was a *Double–0* and drove myself. Lots of things were easier, including remembering trivia."

Cynthia frowned. "I know for a fact, sir, that you *never* forget the important things. Besides, I should have buzzed you about arranging your driver."

"Nice try, Cyn," Mason admonished from the doorway, then headed for the elevator.

───────

As promised, his car was waiting for him in front.

"To the club, Robert," he told his driver as he entered the back of the classic 1962 Bentley S2.

Robert nodded, started the engine, pulled away from the curb, then headed south the short distance to Vauxhall Bridge, turned right onto the bridge, then proceeded across the Thames, then left onto Grosvenor Road. They hadn't gone far south of the bridge before Robert pulled over.

"Sorry, sir; I've got a warning light on the instrument panel — shouldn't take but a moment."

He got out, raised the engine bonnet, checked a few things, frowned, seemed about to lower the bonnet — He suddenly went rigid, raised a hand to his chest — it came away bloodied — Then he slumped against the car.

Mason pulled his Walther PPK and reached for the door handle.

The door locks clicked down.

The front–rear divider window elevated into place.

There was a hiss of escaping gas. Instinctively he took a deep breath and held it, trying unsuccessfully to find a way to escape the car.

Within ninety seconds, he started to blackout from holding his breath. Whether he wanted to or not, he was about to start breathing in whatever gas had been released into the car. It had a sour smell at first, then he couldn't smell anything. Everything faded to a foggy blur. The foggy blur faded to black.

2: *For MI6*

Chester Basin, NS
November 15, 2013, 3:00 PM

*I*t was a cool afternoon, cooler than usual for mid–November in Lunenburg County. Some yellow leaves still clung tenaciously to a few oaks and maples about the new house. Mike had awakened — he still called it that, though he no longer thought of it as sleeping — he passed out for about three–and–a–half hours each day, from anywhere between 11:00 and 11:30 AM, until about 2:30 PM. Most of his kind seemed doomed to remain incapacitated from sometime after full sunrise until shortly before sunset, but Mike functioned reasonably well until closer to noon, when the deadly sun was at its zenith. Of course, Mike had also proved that, for him, the sun was no longer as deadly as it was for most vampires — well, those that weren't sorcerers as well, or blessed with ancient blood.

As he walked back from the boatyard, enjoying the fading feel of fall and the whispering warnings of winter's approach, he felt *Myrddin* in his mind.

Something troubles you, Michael.

He nodded. *Yes, Myrddin, but I have no idea what. The boat's fine, all covered up for winter — I thought the wind might have damaged one of the tarps.*

He told Myrddin about the bizarre images and feelings that had come upon him just as he was emerging from the void.

Something of consequence must have caused your instincts to intrude on your consciousness while still in vampire sleep. Your Wiccan powers are more profound than you accept, Michael. You've honed your warrior skills, and embrace those aspects of your Wicca nature that contribute to them, but, despite your declaration in Austria nearly three years ago, you still haven't completely embraced what you think of as sorcery — what makes you, as your Japanese friends call you — Maha–ka. Perhaps — Have you checked on all your friends? Tony? Jonathan? What about Heather in Scotland — I really liked her, you know.

Mike smiled, remembering how much joy meeting Merlin had given the elderly witch that Mike and Carrie had originally met in Rostock, Germany as Madam Olga. She and her son, Alex, had been posing at Gypsies, using that as their cover while, as agents for the *Scholomance*, they surveilled a particularly sadistic and bloodthirsty vampire.

He glanced at the angle of the sun.

It's just after three, Merlin said in his mind, then, *I'm sorry; you were probably about to judge that for yourself.*

Once more Mike flexed the corners of his mouth into what passed for a smile on most introverts. He left the road and stepped into the trees at the edge of his property, passing through the outer pines and firs until he was beyond the inner ashes, birches, oaks, and maples. He walked the broad slope to the side deck, then wended his way down the rocky slope to the back and the entry door into the basement, a simple turning gesture of his hand causing the door to unlock.

Inside, he continued past the nearly–finished guest bedroom, past the red velvet curtain that marked the entrance to their home theatre, then on toward his office, immediately after the door to the downstairs bathroom.

The door looked like the door to a castle dungeon, complete with barred inspection portal and even a stone surround trim. Mike opened the door and stepped in, turning on a wall cresset that looked early Victorian. The walls were covered in stonework wallpaper, except for where two large bookcases, painted black, housed Mike's library from their former house in the city.

He turned left past one bookcase, rounded the corner of his desk, which was hidden behind that shelf, flicked the switch that lighted another antique replica, this one a Georgian hanging lantern, dangling by a chain from the ceiling.

He turned on his desk lamp, then collapsed into his office chair.

"*Raowrrrr*," Kato yowled, announcing himself as he stomped his way down the stairs. He appeared around the corner of Mike's desk, and uttered another long–drawn–out complaint.

"I'm sorry," Mike apologized, seeing in Kato's thoughts the image of the Siamese cat waking, not knowing where Mike had gone or when he would return. "It's getting cold out; you wouldn't have liked it. Besides, Wayne's dogs are out, and the big one barks at everything — well, not me so much."

He continued to pet Kato, who purred and settled into his lap, paws against his chest, then reached to the button at the back of his iMac, booted the machine, and waited for his word processor to load. He was reviewing his efforts to outline a new novel, when his desk phone rang. Caller ID said *CSIS Halifax*. Mike frowned. Charbonneau would have displayed as *CSIS Ottawa*, but Jean always called Mike on his iPhone, which was encrypted and much more secure than any landline. In fact, there'd been very few calls from

Charbonneau since Mike's adventures in Austria back in 2011.

Mike answered the phone, to be told that he would be getting a call on his iPhone almost immediately from the Director of CSIS. Mike acknowledged receipt of the information, then hung up, immediately removed his iPhone from his pocket, and placed it on his desk. He frowned — the director was supposed to field all contact through Charbonneau. It was part of the price of Mike remaining in active service after being wrongly declared a rogue agent four years before — *Ronin* was how Mike usually thought of it, falling back on the Japanese term for a rogue *Samurai*. He'd gotten tired of the director pestering him at every turn, constantly trying to armchair–quarterback his fieldwork. He'd been close to resigning, a fact that had brought the director near to panic, especially with his predecessor backing Mike, and Sam Larkin smugly declaring how the CIA would snatch Mike up in a New York minute, with a substantial increase in salary. The director had relented.

CSIS just didn't have the straight–forward view of things that CIA and MI6 had. It probably stemmed from their confused origins — CSIS had been formed in the mid–1980s to replace a former RCMP body, initially a counterpart of Britain's MI5. Mike's role in CSIS was an anomaly, much closer to that of an MI6 *Double–0* asset. His official title was *special agent*. He was CSIS's only special agent, recruited soon after agreeing to help Tony Dewhurst deal with an Interpol case. HRM PD, Mike's godfather in particular, had been baffled by a string of murders that looked like vampires on a murderous rampage.

More than two years before, Mike had climaxed his CSIS career by destroying the last holdouts of the elitist group that had hoped to establish vampire dominance over humans. He had almost been burned to death, surviving an entire day in the sun. That, plus identifying a terrorist bomb–maker with links to Al-Qaida, had granted him extended leave from CSIS.

Indeed, over the past year, he had had very few cases, and almost all were mundane, most having almost nothing to do with vampires. He'd spent much of that year doing, almost single–handedly, all the work needed to finish more than three–quarters of the basement. He had done the framing, drywall, and finish trim. Carrie had done the drywall mudding, sanding, and all the painting. She'd even wallpapered his office with the amazing *dungeon* wallpaper.

With most of the construction work behind him, Mike had finally turned his thoughts back to writing. CSIS consistently interrupted his attempts at writing. His revenge: fictional versions of selected cases.

Now, as he glanced at his iPhone lying on the desk, he awaited yet another CSIS interruption.

The sound of clashing swords emanated from his phone, and the CSIS emblem appeared on the screen. Mike took the call on speaker.

"Yes, sir," he greeted.

"*Samurai*," the director stated without preamble, "I just got a call from the head of British Intelligence, concerning your friend Captain Bruce Mason."

Mike frowned, suddenly wishing that the director used FaceTime. It was easier to read facial expressions than rely on vocal nuances for what a person *wasn't* saying.

"Mason, sir?" Mike prompted.

"Has gone missing," the director finished for him, "and, well, *Samurai*, to get to the point, MI6 has officially asked to borrow you. No, that's not right — there's nothing official about it. By the way, his designation isn't *M*, it's *C*. Anyway, *C*, who is actually Sir John Sawers, personally asked me to lend you to him. As far as we're concerned, if you honour the request, you'll officially be on paid leave. I can only assume they'll also be funding you in some way. What I do know is: if you do accept, there's a ticket waiting for you at Halifax International Airport for an 8:00 PM *British Airways* flight. And, *Samurai*, it would be a considerable coup for us to have MI6 owing us a favour for a change."

"Is Jean in the loop on this, sir?"

"Charbonneau? No; I can't see how he could be. *C* called me on my private line, and I immediately called you — well, not immediately; I called the Halifax office first to have them give you warning of my impending call."

Mike smiled — he'd hung up on the director a few times after the *Ronin* incident. "So what other facts do you have, sir, aside from Mason being missing?" Mike asked. *No wonder I woke up so unsettled! This must be what I sensed.*

"No idea," was the director's curt response, "well, not much. We picked up some chatter from the Americans, including what might be circumstantial evidence that's led to speculation that he's passed sensitive information to the Russians."

Mike's mouth tightened to a rictus. "Then it looks like I'll be heading for London, sir."

As Mike ended the call, he glanced at the clock on the credenza shelf above his desk — 3:40. He reached out with his mind. Carrie was still asleep — she rarely awakened before 4:00.

He activated his phone again and called Sam Larkin, Assistant Deputy Director: Operations, CIA.

"Hey, kid," Sam greeted. It used to annoy him that Sam insisted on calling him *kid* — Mike was older than Sam, but, even before his change to vampire, looked several years younger.

"Hey, Sam. What do you know about Mason?"

There was a sigh, then Sam said, "Not much, but he's missing, and circumstantial evidence points to suspicious links to the Russians."

Mike frowned, shaking his head. "I don't buy it," he insisted. "It seems *C* wants to borrow me."

"Yeah, I don't buy it either" Sam acknowledged, "We got a whiff of that MI6 request less than an hour ago. That must have stuck in *C*'s craw. You going?"

"I think I'd better," Mike said. "Okay, thanks, Sam. I guess I'd better give Tony a call. He'll want in on this. He and Mason have considerable history."

"Tell me about it," Sam retorted. "Back in the days of the Cold War, we crossed paths on so many cases that I started to feel like Felix Lighter, with Mason as James Bond." Sam sighed, obviously reminiscing about his friendship with Mason. "Anyway, good luck, Mike. If you need anything..."

Mike rang off, then called Tony, who answered on the second ring.

"Michael..."

"Switch to FaceTime, Tony" Mike cut across his greeting. When Tony's face appeared on the screen, he wore a perplexed frown.

"What is it, Michael? You seem perturbed."

"*C* of MI6 called my director personally. Seems he wants to borrow me. He said nothing about it except that Mason is missing. However, according to Sam, Mason is not just missing; there's circumstantial evidence linking him to Russian contacts."

Tony let out a whistle that trailed off. "*Please* say you're going," he said, almost in the same breath.

"Apparently a ticket awaits me at the *BA* desk, for 8:00 PM," Mike replied. "I was just about to throw a few things in a bag and grab my passport. Carrie's still asleep, so I'll wait for her to emerge from the void."

"So, you spoke to Sam?" Tony mused. "And he didn't have anything else to offer?"

Mike shook his head.

"Well, then, I'll pack a bag, too. If you can swing by here on the way, we can take my car to the airport. I'll just make a quick call and make sure I can get booked on the same flight, even if I have to pull a few strings."

Mike smiled, knowing that, for *Lord* Anthony Dewhurst, getting a seat on a *British Airways* flight might not be too difficult, even if it meant bumping a less well–connected passenger from the flight.

"*Raowrrrr!*"

Mike was just pocketing his phone. Kato stared into his face, brilliant sapphire eyes expressing concern, even worry. Mike gave a tight smile and scratched the side of his friend's furry face. "Sorry, buddy, but it looks like I have to go away for a while" he said, whereupon Kato reached out a paw to his chest, then butted his head under Mike's chin before rubbing his head against Mike's face several times. Mike smiled, then gathered fourteen pounds of purring Siamese into his arms. Almost immediately there was a tiny *mew*, and Teila, Carrie's cat, now about three-quarters Kato's size, but still very much a kitten in her demeanour, appeared around the corner of the desk.

"Is your mummy awake or are you just getting independent?" Teila looked at him with wide eyes, then left, heading for the stairs.

"I think that's our cue to follow," Mike commented to Kato. Kato hopped down to the floor and followed Teila, allowing Mike a moment to open the credenza cupboard to his left and remove his Walther PPK and shoulder holster. Looking at the boxes of cartridges, he ignored the boxes of holly rounds with Osmium core, selecting lead hollow-points instead.

As he closed the cupboard, he glanced to the curved wall behind his desk chair. Atop his file cabinet was a stylized rack, each side carved from wood in the profile an oriental dragon. An ivory-hilted katana rested on the dragons' claws, while *Mountain Wind*, the katana made in the 14th century by legendary master *Muramasa Sengo*, rested in the mouths of the dragons. For a prolonged moment he stared at the sword, debating whether to take it. If this mission didn't involve vampires — and there was no reason to think it did — then he wouldn't need his katana. But then, it would the first time he'd ever set out without it.

He closed his eyes, trying to reach out into the void for some sense of the future, but nothing came. He shook his head, then triggered a shutdown of his computer and departed his office, the katana left behind.

Kato was waiting for him at the bottom of the stairs, head cocked to one side. When Mike was just two paces away, he turned and leaped over the first four steps, trotted up to the turn, and paused, waiting for Mike to catch up. Teila was waiting at the top of the stairs. *Mew.*

Bright afternoon sunlight filtered through the window of the front door, illuminating the varied colours of the foyer's stone–tiled floor. Angling right, he followed the cats past the broad entrance to the combined living room and dining room to the left (the architect called it a great room). To the right, across the hall, an opening almost as wide provided entry to the kitchen, floored with the same stone tiling as the foyer.

Teila and Kato were hunched before the tray for their food dishes, looking expectantly at Mike. He resisted the urge to chuckle. Going to the fridge, he took out a can of *Friskies* (fish, of course). Kato attacked his dish with the ravenous attitude of a starved wolf, compared with Teila who sampled hers for a bare second, then went into a hunch to watch Kato.

Mike opened the pantry cupboard and extracted a tall plastic container of dry food, putting a handful in each larger pet food dish. Before putting the food away, he paused to cup Kato's face in his hands.

Slow down, he projected. *There's no panic. She barely eats her own food; she's certainly not about to eat yours.* Kato hung his head for a second, then started in on his dry food, albeit a bit slower than usual.

Mike extracted two bottles from the upper left corner of the wine rack built into the end of the kitchen island. Most of the bottles were red wine for guests; these were an O–positive for Mike and an A–positive for Carrie. The rest were in the fridge, but Mike had found that he and Carrie could keep a bottle out for a day or more before the blood cells began to deteriorate significantly, and it made warming it much easier. In this case, Mike retrieved two ceramic goblets, warmed them in the microwave for a ninety–seconds, then poured some blood into each.

Continuing down the hall to the master suite, he set the goblets down on Carrie's nightstand, then walked to the other side of the bed, removed a small kitbag from his closet, set his Walther and the box of cartridges into it, then retrieved his wallet and passport from his nightstand. Two pairs of black jeans and his new black Otomix sneakers went into the kitbag, then he went through his bureau, gathering two black turtlenecks and an assortment of socks and underwear. He'd wear a suit and his Tony Lama boots on the plane. *If I need anything fancier, I'll have to buy it over there*, he thought, then replaced the turtleneck he was wearing with a clean one in dark royal blue.

Next he unplugged his iPad from the charger, unplugged the charger from the wall, and put those in the ballistic nylon case for his iPad, along with the charger for his phone. Pulling the velcro flap on the front of the case, he transferred his passport to the large pocket under the flap. There were additional pockets and holders for everything from business cards to pens, even spare change. *No novel writing this trip*, he thought, and removed the Bluetooth keyboard and set it in the basket on the bottom shelf of his nightstand, *though being a semi–obscure fantasy novelist is a good cover for this trip, especially after having attended that convention in Austria.*

That's got to be enough, he told himself, looking at the scant handful of luggage. It seemed so small compared to the arsenal of weapons he'd gotten used to hauling around the globe — *sgian dubh* (small Celtic daggers), his *shirasaya* hiking stick with it's hidden katana blade, and, of course, *Mountain Wind*.

He was still pondering all of this when Kato and Teila entered. Teila hopped up onto the bed and settled on Carrie's pillow, next to her face. Mike forestalled Kato as he tried to climb into Mike's bag.

"Not this time," he whispered, cuddling his friend, whereupon Kato rubbed his head and uttered a plaintive sound.

Mike was just setting him down when Carrie stirred. Her eyes flashed open, scanned left and right, looked confused, almost feral, then she struggled upright, looking about the room until her gaze came to rest on Mike. The feral look softened, then she smiled. The smile immediately faded to a frown when she noticed his kitbag and iPad bag.

Walking around to her nightstand, he sat on the bed, and passed her a goblet.

"The director called," Mike said, which caused Carrie's frown to deepen.

"And you didn't hang up?" Carrie commented.

Mike gave a slight nod. "The Halifax office called to warn me. It's about Mason: he's missing, suspicious circumstances raising a buzz. I spoke with Sam, but all he can gather is inferences to passing information to the Russians."

"That's not the Mason we know," Carrie insisted.

Mike nodded his agreement. "*M*, who, it turns out, is actually *C*, called the director and asked to borrow me. Tony insists on coming along, too. I'll drive the Solstice to his place, then we'll continue to the airport in his car. Apparently MI6 has a ticket for an 8:00 PM *British Airways* flight waiting for me at the *BA* desk. Tony's flexing his considerable diplomatic muscle to get a booking on the same flight."

"And me?" she asked, making a pout. "Am I stuck here looking after the babies?"

Teila nuzzled against her cheek. *Mew?*

"Well, just one baby," she amended, "and one big boy, accept that he turns into a big sook whenever you even leave the house."

Kato flopped between Mike and Carrie, stretching a paw up to Mike's arm, then let out a mournful yowl.

Mike sighed and petted Kato once more.

"At least the director was agreeable about lending me to MI6 — that's gotta be a first," he said, "both for CSIS and, I'm sure, for MI6."

"Maybe that's why he was so agreeable," Carrie suggested. "It's a major feather in their cap for CSIS to have to lend one of their agents to MI6."

Mike nodded. "I suppose. The director did say something to that effect. Anyway, I'll be glad to have Tony along. I expect to feel out of my depth on this one. I got used swinging a katana and killing vampires for a while. Though, there have been smaller missions, like raiding CIA files so our government would know to back away from that terrorist who was trying to hide behind Canadian Citizenship."

"You'll do just fine," she assured him, placing a hand on his shoulder. She then pulled him into her embrace, kissing him hard on the lips.

"Keep your phone charged," he teased. "I'll be calling."

"So, you're off to play ninja?" Carrie asked.

"I suppose," he replied, then, "Actually, the original word was *Shinobi*. The term *ninja* didn't appear until the advent of movies, when some American producer decided *ninja* was easier to pronounce. We've been stuck with the term *ninja* ever since.

3: *Flight to London*

Mike set his meagre luggage on the passenger seat of the Pontiac Solstice, started the engine, then pulled out of the yard. As he drove through the dwindling daylight, the uneasy feeling crept back over him, mostly concern for Mason and how the case would play out. He'd left Carrie searching for the cat carrier amid the accumulation of stuff she'd pulled out of the soon–to–be guest room. That prompted a wistful hint of a smile, knowing that she'd eventually find a way to join him. The thought both comforted and troubled him. He didn't like going off without her, and knew deep down that they made a good team, but he instinctively feared for her safety, even after her indispensable assistance in Korea.

After forty-five minutes he exited the highway onto Joseph Howe Drive and worked his way toward the MacKay Bridge over the northern end of the Narrows, then onto the Circumferential Highway. He took the Micmac Mall exit, made his way through the twisting and turning maze of residential streets to Hawthorne, and caught a green light to continue across Prince Albert Road, and pulled into Tony's drive less than a minute later.

Tony glanced up from lowering the trunk lid on his Cadillac, parked to one side of the drive, leaving room for Mike's Solstice. As he pulled up beside Tony, a wan smile told Mike that his friend was possibly even more concerned than he. Mason and Tony had a history that dated back to the 60s.

"Pull up around the back," Tony suggested. "It'll be safe behind the house. We'll take my car to the airport. Just stow your kit in the boot."

There was almost an awkwardness to the silence as Tony made his way to Woodland Avenue, which became the highway to the airport.

"I assume you have your Walther," Tony commented, to which Mike nodded.

"MI6's Q-Branch would have issued you another," Tony mused, "but a familiar weapon is better."

Mike could relate to that. Even with his Zen ability to make anything feel like a natural extension of himself, his stubborn preference of his *Muramasa* katana over any other sword was testimony to how important ingrained familiarity with a weapon could be at a crucial moment.

"Have you spoken to Nigel?" Mike asked.

Tony's nod was almost imperceptible. "Just before you pulled in. Not much really: Phone LUDs show frequent calls from a *London Daily Examiner* reporter's private line and home phone — most from her end, only a few originating from Mason, and then only over the last couple of days. Nigel is still trying to get his hands on Mason's actual phones."

"Nothing to his cell phone?"

Tony's frown deepened. "Nigel found something puzzling. Mason's cell called the reporter's number a few times, but his last call was to a number in Moscow that looks like it could be an *FSB* number."

Mike frowned. "*FSB* — Why would Mason be calling Russia's secret state security police? Aren't they the new KGB?" He shook his head.

"So the Director actually called you?" Tony asked, his face showing his surprise.

"At least he had the sense to call me on my cellphone, though he did have the Halifax office call ahead on landline."

This prompted a grin from Tony. "That explains why Carrie almost always answers your home phone. 'He's in his dungeon; better try his iPhone' is what I get from your charming bride whenever I call."

"There's a phone on my desk," Mike shot back, a tad defensive, then, grinning, "though I do check caller ID before deciding whether or not to answer. But, yes, I usually ignore the landline and let the machine take it. I figure anyone with a serious reason to call me has my mobile number."

"Coming back to Mason," Tony remarked, "according to Nigel — he hacked into MI6 reports to *C* — There's also a file folder missing from Mason's desk drawer. It's presumed to be a set of training reports — recertification tests." Tony paused, his brow still furrowed, then added, "The odd thing about it is that he told his secretary it was there, and asked her to file it first thing in the morning, and to copy it to *C* before filing it."

"Why is that odd?" Mike asked, catching himself almost immediately. "He wouldn't do that if he was about to abscond with the file. She'd miss the file the moment she went looking for it first thing in the morning." He paused. "You got all this from Nigel?"

Tony nodded. "Our friend might as well be head clerk for MI6 the way he passes straight through their firewalls. Q must be paranoid of him by now."

Tony parked in the parking garage opposite the terminal, and they walked briskly across the walkway, into the terminal, and walked southwest away from the entrance with its bookstore and newsstands, Tony leading the way straight to the *British Airways* desk.

They spoke to separate clerks, Mike smiling at the way the clerk fell all over Tony — "Of course, Lord

Dewhurst, there was no trouble obtaining executive seating."

Mike's ticket was also first class, though he realized it probably had more to do with getting a seat at short notice than any desire on the part of MI6 to cater to him. Once the two clerks realized that Mike and Tony were traveling together, Tony's clerk took over seat selection and seated them together.

Airborne, Halifax, NS – London, UK

"So, after two years in MI5, what took you back to MI6?" Mike asked. They were an hour into the flight, and Tony was explaining how he met Bruce Mason.

"Simple, really, Michael; The war was taking a turn against us, and *C*, as the head of MI6 was known at the time — *C* for Mansfield Smith–Cumming, the first head of Intelligence back before the First War. Then, after the Kim Philby fiasco, they changed it to *M*, out of some notion of amusement, based on Flemings books. Anyway, *C* wanted someone who could get into Germany and look into the rockets that had started descending upon us — not all the nightly bombs were dropped from aeroplanes. I'd been part of MI5's *Operation Double-Cross*, feeding misinformation to the Nazis, and had even couriered several dispatches to the other side. So, while the nature of my condition was not known, it was known that I could manage a fair bit of skullduggery in dodgy locations, and make my way back to hearth and home to report about it.

"I met Mason in the fall of 1960. The Russians were experimenting with space rockets — mostly getting our attention with a lot of explosions in the Kazakh area, now called Kazakhstan. My job was to go and see what they were up to, and they gave me this fresh-faced youngster from Naval Intelligence as a helper for the mission." Tony grinned. "Gad, he was young — green, the Yanks would have called him — couldn't have been any more than seventeen or eighteen — at least, that's what I thought at the time."

Mike's smile faded to a frown as he did the math.

"Wait a minute, Tony — I always thought Mason was barely sixty. If he was seventeen in 1960, he'd be nearing seventy by now. How can he still be active in MI6 at that age?"

"Mostly because he's very good at what he does, but partly because, as you just implied, he looks younger. And, just between you and I, dear boy, he wasn't seventeen, he was fifteen — lied about his age, joined the navy, then got pushed straight into naval intelligence — his test scores were unparalleled. He was sixty-eight last August — his birthday is six days after yours. Of course, it wasn't until the mid–sixties, after eliminating a spy uncovered in his section, that they upgraded him to *Double–0* section."

"Eliminating?" Mike asked.

Tony nodded. "Shot him. The fellow was trying to make a break. He pulled a gun, shot one poor chap just he was drawing his sidearm, then grabbed a young woman as a shield. Mason was just entering. He sized up the situation, made a dive for the fallen agent, snatched up his pistol, and aimed it at the infiltrator. The young lady in question was just tall enough to block the heart shot all agents are trained for, so Mason shot the blighter through the throat, severing the spine — cool as can be through the whole adventure, according to all the witnesses. Amazing for a genius cryptologist — is there such a term as *decryptologist*?

"Even saved my life a time or two over the next few years. Finally, in the spring of '66, nagged by curiosity about your father, I talked *M*, as we were now calling the director, into lending me to Interpol for a nasty case that took me to Sydney, where I not only met, but got to work with, your father — that was the time of your unfortunate bicycle accident."

"How long after that was it before you went over to Interpol permanently?" Mike asked.

"About three years," Tony replied, a tinge of sadness in his tone. "It was time — too long in one place doesn't bode well for our kind." His raised eyebrow, and his pointed glance carried the unspoken warning that, Mike, too, might soon have to make changes.

"Did *M* ever know the truth about you?" Mike asked, then, his memory supplying an echo of Sam Larkin's comments at Heathrow Airport years before, answered his own question. "Of course he must have. Sam knew about you — he even knew about me when I barely knew myself. I can't imagine the CIA knowing too much about you that the SIS didn't."

"*M* knew — it reached a point that I had to explain the situation. And, Michael, there's something else you should know..."

"Mason has some of your blood in him, but not enough to turn him," Mike finished for him. When Tony seemed surprised, Mike made a disparaging grimace. "Come on, Tony — he's sixty–eight, yet he looks barely early–to–mid–fifties. I assume Mason got seriously wounded during a mission?"

"It was a bullet through the — the large artery that exits the heart, branches upward, then curves downward below the heart —," Tony paused, clearly waiting for Mike to supply the name.

"The descending aorta," Mike provided.

"Anyway," Tony resumed, "the puncture of the aorta was clean, leaving Mason hemorrhaging internally. We were a long way from medical assistance, so I did the only thing I could — I bit into the edge of my palm and made a brief stream of my blood squirt into the wound. Within seconds he seemed more stable; in a few minutes he could to stand with my assistance."

"Who shot him?" Mike asked.

"A KGB agent who'd been chasing us." Tony replied. "A hardliner from their *SMERSH* program, designed to root out and eliminate spies. That would have been spring of 1972."

Mike came out of revery — his mind had lapsed into a meditative state — and glanced at Tony, now immersed in the *London Times*. With nothing else to do, he let his mind drift through the cabin, sampling the thoughts of the passengers. The flight was little more than half–full, so there wasn't much to sample.

Tony gave him a gentle nudge. "That fellow standing at the curtain between first and coach seems unusually interested in us," he pointed out.

Mike turned his head just enough to register the man in his peripheral vision, then reached out with his mind. "He's an air marshall. Seems someone told him we're with Interpol and CSIS."

"Of course; someone would have to explain why we bypassed security," Tony commented, nodding.

"I'll see what he wants." Mike added, then, catching the marshall's attention, he gestured to the vacant seat across the aisle, whereupon the man strolled casually forward and sat down.

"I'm Bryan Marshall," he introduced himself in a British accent, prompting a grin from Mike.

"Is that your real name? Marshall Marshall?" Mike asked, suppressing the urge to chuckle.

Marshall frowned. "So you know I'm an air marshall; and yes, it's my real name." His rictus of a smile implied that he'd heard enough jokes on the subject.

"I'm Mike Cameron, and this is Lord Anthony Dewhurst," Mike said by way of introductions. "So what's on your mind?"

"Are either of you armed?"

"Sorry, old boy, but our luggage is *packing heat*, as the Yanks like to phrase it," Tony replied with a smile, leaning forward to speak across in front of Mike.

Marshall hesitated, then explained, "I'm a bit concerned about four passengers: all in coach, not seated together, but evincing awareness of each other; two obviously Arabic, the remaining two not so obvious. In fact, one might even pass for European or American."

"But there's been enough subtle communication among them for you to suspect that they're together, but trying to appear as if they aren't together," Mike suggested, to which Marshall nodded.

"Why don't you head back to your seat. I'll be along in a moment," Mike promised.

"Shall I follow along, just in case?" Tony asked.

"Not sure," Mike mused. *Stay tuned; I'll keep you posted*, he added, communicating telepathically.

Mike got up and strolled casually back to coach, pausing to chat with a female attendant, then continued back to where he spotted Marshall.

"Bryan," he greeted as if they were well–acquainted, then took an empty aisle seat across from him. "Heading home?" he asked. "Why didn't you tell me you were in town? I'm just heading over for a conference, myself."

He then leaned toward Marshall and let him point out the four who worried him. Once Mike had them pinpointed, he went to work, subtly accessing the thoughts of each, which immediately troubled him. They were thinking in Farsi — Mike had a smattering from his Afghanistan mission. Almost immediately, one relocated to sit next to another — the two more darkly–complexioned, both seemingly older than the other two, about five seats further forward.

These two were now whispering together, becoming increasingly animated, casting glances back at the darker two. When one of the younger, light–complexioned, possibly Arabic, men showed signs of getting up, one of the dark pair signaled for him to remain seated, tapping his watch.

Mike decided not to wait any longer. Focusing on the one who'd just commanded the restless one to stay in his seat, he forced his way into the man's mind, ordering him to remain immobile. Instantly the man went rigid, whereupon Mike did the same with his neighbour. In another moment he had all four incapacitated.

Come on back, Tony, he projected. Dewhurst strolled back less than a minute later, taking the seat in front of him. Mike took a moment to bring him up to speed, then indicating the darker pair, said in his mind, *I'll take the one on the left; you take the other. Meanwhile, Marshall Marshall* (he smiled) *can watch the other two.*

Getting up, Mike leaned toward Marshall and said, "You were right, but it's all under control. You keep watch on the other two while Tony and I deal with the swarthy pair."

Marshall started to argue and question, but Mike fixed him with a stern look and compelled him to agree. Tony had just taken an empty seat in front of one of the deeply–tanned Arabs when Mike arrived next to him.

Speak to me in English, Mike commanded in Farsi, then forced his way into the man's mind. The Arab, an Irani national, tried to resist, arrogantly assuming that this infidel couldn't possibly hold power over him.

Mike formed the image of fire. The man was about to scream aloud until Mike silenced him, leaving him screaming in his mind, while his body fought to writhe and squirm, perspiring profusely.

Shaytan awaits you, Mike intoned in the would–be–terrorist's mind. *No paradise, no virgins, just eternal fire. Who made you think Mohammed would forgive you for creating even one orphan?*

The man responded with a name Mike had heard in a news report. Tony nodded — he'd made a mental note of it.

Describe your plan of attack, Mike commanded.

The man resisted, but Mike forced deeper, squeezed, and made the fires larger and hotter. Almost immediately he got images of four kitbags in overhead compartments. In each was a small, innocuous container of liquid — two with pink liquid labeled as shampoo, two with blue liquid labeled as mouthwash. The man then pictured gathering all four together, giving a pink and a blue to his partner, whereupon each would go at the same time to opposite airplane lavatories. Once mixed into empty water bottles and well–shaken, the combination would explode after ten to fifteen minutes.

Mike checked the seat pocket in front of the man and, sure enough, there was the empty water bottle, given him by an unknowing attendant, completely ignorant of the deadly use to which it would be put. Leaning further in, he located a similar bottle in front of the other man. Invading this man's mind only served to confirm what he'd learned from the first man.

Angry, Mike locked eyes on the second, a Syrian national, treating him to the same mental anguish of fire that had loosened his accomplice's tongue. He left both men frozen rigid, yet trembling and perspiring, as if in the throes of some sort of fit.

Let them sweat it out for a while, he told Tony, not a trace of remorse or pity in his demeanour. *The Syrian had a head full of rhetoric about something called*

'Islamic State' — *another Al Qaida wannabe?* He shrugged.

Mike walked forward, and paused to examine the minds of the other two conspirators. These two, however, were just unknowing stooges. They were student radicals, possibly doomed to someday escalate into full–fledged terrorists unless someone found a way to defuse the anti–Western rhetoric of which their heads seemed full. The swarthy pair, having contacted them through a fundamentalist blog, had waylaid them in the terminal and given each an innocent–looking bottle to put in their carry–on.

Produce the bottles, Mike commanded.

Wide–eyed, the two complied immediately, placing two bottles of blue 'mouthwash' in Mike's hands.

Harmless, innocent mouthwash, Mike pronounced in their minds. *Mix them together with the two bottles of shampoo carried by your two new acquaintances, wait fifteen minutes, then BOOM! — This plane falls out of the sky in pieces, your mangled bodies falling with the wreckage, heroes to the cause.*

"Who are you?" one of them asked in a whisper, horror blatant in his expression.

"Just a representative of the evil, decadent West," Mike whispered back. "How do you feel about your down–trodden Islamic Extremist Brotherhood now?"

"F**K That!" the other blurted.

"I can't help but observe that they didn't even have a completed pair," Tony mused as they made their way back to Marshall.

"I'm not sure what to make of that," Mike replied. "Were they trying to make sure the recruits couldn't steal their thunder or making sure that the components were kept as separate as possible?"

Mike then shrugged, adding, "Either way, it worked out well for the plane, and for the other passengers."

When they reached Marshall, Mike quietly explained what he'd learned, gave Marshall the two blue bottles, then helped him find the pink bottles in the terrorists' carry–on luggage in the overheads.

Marshall looked puzzled as he applied zip–tie restraints to the swarthy pair, eying their ague with suspicion.

"They're contemplating Hell," Mike remarked without further explanation.

"What about the other two?" Marshall asked.

Mike shrugged. "You're the air marshall, but my guess is they might be well on the way to being de–radicalized. Perhaps holding them for lengthy questioning might drive the point home better, but I'd be wary of anything that feeds into the notion of making Western governments look like the bad guys."

Marshall pondered that, then gave an understanding nod. "I suppose I could point out the fine for accepting anything from a stranger into your luggage, then reluctantly agree to wave the fine. Of course they'll spend some time on a few watch lists."

Returning to their seats in Executive, Mike put his head back and let his mind loose to wander until the feel of the plane descending for a landing at Heathrow brought him back to reality.

———

"*C* should have a car waiting for us," Tony mused as they were deplaning. Then, as they were approaching the first checkpoint for Customs and Immigration, he added, "I say, old man, now that's a familiar face."

Mike glanced toward the booth and spotted Wentworth Pennington–Smythe, the MI6 analyst that they'd met in 2011 in Bischofshofen, Austria. *Hopefully this is a bit more his speed than playing spy amid a coven of vampires,* he projected to Tony. The latter just smiled and nodded.

Pennington–Smythe waited until the immigration agent made as if to beckon them from beyond the red line, then flipped open his ID folder and whispered to the officer, who nodded, then beckoned them forward, whereupon Smythe stepped forward.

"Wentworth," Mike greeted him, then shook his hand.

"*Samurai*, Lord Dewhurst," Smythe declared in an eager tone, pumping Mike's hand several times before shaking Tony's. "I have a car to take you directly to Vauxhall Cross."

Mike nodded. "The sooner we can get all the facts of the case, the sooner we can begin."

Damn, he confided to Tony, giving his upper arm a rub, *must he insist on priming the pump with every handshake?*

Tony had to turn his head to hide his broad grin.

4: At MI6

It was almost 3:00 AM when Pennington–Smythe escorted Mike and Tony into the SIS Headquarters Building, then up to the top floor offices of *C*, the Director of MI6, where they were greeted by an attractive woman in her mid–forties.

"Thank you Mr. Pennington–Smythe," she said. The tone was pleasant, but it could not be taken for anything less than a dismissal. Smythe seemed disappointed, almost hurt, but he made a quick exit.

Mike set his bag on a chair and stood motionless, Tony at his shoulder. Neither reacted to the secretary's apparent lack of acknowledgement of their presence.

I'm sorry, old man, but I've been out of the loop too long to know this secretary — don't even know C, Tony projected to Mike. *She's hardly Moneypenny, I must say. Ahh, those were the days — not that her name was an actual Moneypenny, but Fleming did base her on a real person.*

She frowned as if sensing she was the object of their thoughts, then, in a defensive tone, offered, "Mr. Pennington–Smythe has a tendency to hover and attempt to be flirtatious. His grasp of what we do here seems acquired from the Bond films. He's harmless enough, but..."

"Wentworth's enthusiasm sometimes get the best of him," Mike suggested.

"That's right;" she said quickly, "you met Pennington–Smythe in Austria almost three years ago. Was he helpful?"

Mike shrugged. "We have our own man for research and IT work," he explained. "However, he did assist Nigel, especially at one point, when Nigel had been compromised and was somewhat indisposed."

Her frown told Mike that she knew almost nothing about that case. *C* apparently kept her out of the loop more than *M* did Moneypenny in the movies. Rising, she came around from behind her desk, offering him a cool hand.

"I'm Penelope Daniels, *C*'s receptionist and executive secretary, just in case you, too, were expecting Moneypenny."

"I try to never anticipate or assume," Mike replied. "Besides, Lois Maxwell passed away some time back. I am, however, surprised that *C* and his executive secretary would be here at this hour."

"Special circumstances," she replied, releasing his hand. "Mr. Pennington–Smythe had instructions to bring you directly here, *Samurai*."

She reached for Tony's hand. "Lord Dewhurst," she greeted. "*C* thought you might want to tag along. I might even suggest that he hoped you would."

"If I might interrupt your speculation, Mrs. Daniels, perhaps you could send agent *Samurai* and Lord Dewhurst right in." The voice came from the high–tech intercom on her desk.

Mrs. Daniels' instant grimace showed her chagrin at being eavesdropped upon and caught in the act of inappropriate gossip. She recovered immediately and gestured toward the padded door to one side.

"*C* will see you now," she said, adding, "You can leave your bags."

Mike, however, grabbed his bag as he turned toward the door.

The office was more spacious than Mike expected, the decor a tad more modern than the woodgrain panelling of the older movies, yet none of the ultramodern exemplified by more recent films, no doubt reflecting the mood of its owner.

C was also not what Mike was expecting, though he had come across some info about him, like the scandal around the time of his appointment — his wife had posted pics on *FaceBook* of him playing *Frisbee* on the beach. Mike guessed his age as mid– to late–fifties. Three hours after midnight one might expect shirtsleeves, loosened tie, or even tie removed and stuffed in a jacket pocket. *C* had his jacket on, and his tie up snug against his collar.

He's concerned about making a good impression, Mike decided, puzzled by that fact. *Is it for Lord Anthony Dewhurst, erstwhile 006 from MI6's Cold War era? Certainly not for me.*

When *C* glanced up from the spread of papers before him on his desk, he blanched noticeably, stared at Mike, then at Tony. He seemed to require a moment to recover composure.

He knows we're vampires, Mike transmitted to Tony, *and he's nervous.*

"Ah, *Samurai*," *C* greeted. "I'm so glad your director was willing to allow us to borrow you. Our own people are spread rather thin, and, well, with this issue already garnering attention in the press, I was hoping your unique talents might unearth something useful, and that your friendship with Mason might motivate you." He stood, hesitated, then came around the desk, hesitated again, then extended a hand to shake Mike's.

He was quite tall, taller than Tony.

Scanning his thoughts further, Mike confirmed his awareness of Tony and he being vampires, as well as fear of how to behave toward them.

Relax, Sir John, Mike projected in a compelling manner, addressing him by his name — and *C* did.

"And, you, of course, must be our erstwhile 006," *C* said to Tony, shaking his hand. "Good to meet you Lord Dewhurst."

Tony simply nodded.

"Thank you for meeting with us this late," Mike said, then, "So what case facts do you have?"

C gave a nod and immediately launched into the particulars: "Mason had been under no discernible duress; he completed a standard work day, running a bit overtime, but not unusual for either him or his secretary. He alerted her to a file of papers in his desk that would require filing in the morning — reports from duty–fitness tests on field agents. He even suggested that I should see a copy before she filed it. When she looked in the morning, there was no file.

"Mason's car was found abandoned near Gatwick Airport. His driver's body was concealed in the boot — dead from two bullets through the heart. Mason's gun, an older MI6–issue Walther PPK, was on the seat in the back. There were traces of an aerosol anesthetic gas. Q–Branch is still hoping to isolate the specific agent and determine who might have supplied it."

Very concise, Mike thought, *just as one might expect from someone trained in the sciences.* He interjected, "So, what about the — Sam Larkin of CIA mentioned 'suspicious links to the Russians'?"

C glared. *"You spoke to someone at Central Intelligence about this?"* The previously suave voice had gone cold, acquired an edge.

Mike just went silent, waiting it out. *C* seemed to alternate from rapid breathing to holding his breath and turning more livid. An artery in his neck was pulsating, as was one in his left temple. Mike frowned, wondering what had happened to the man who had majored in the sciences in university, notably physics.

Clearly, he's a thinker, but this is the reaction of a feeler. So, like me, he probably became a thinker in his early teens. Stress brings out the submerged feeler. And, no doubt, the past few days have been stressful in the extreme.

"Will you be alright, sir?" Mike asked patiently.

There was further silence as *C* seemingly tried to force himself into some semblance of calm.

"You're not precisely a team player, are you *Samurai*?" *C* asked.

Mike frowned. "Team player? Which team might that be, sir?"

C puffed himself up, seemed about to explode, then declared in a carefully controlled delivery through not–quite–clenched teeth, "Agent *Samurai*, here at *SIS*, we pride ourselves on staying within the ranks. We don't make a point of crawling to MI5, much less *the Americans*, every time we're at a loss for intel."

Mike felt anger and resentment of his own begin to grow, and forced it down, but his tone became icy.

"Of course not, sir — and yet, at your request, here I am, almost three thousand miles from home.

"As for *the Americans*, as you put it, Bruce Mason and Sam Larkin have sufficient history that, when the director of CSIS relayed your request, I called Sam to make sure he knew his friend might be in trouble, and to see what he knew or might be able to learn.

"Since I also number Mason among my friends, I'll use whatever resources I can to determine his whereabouts and affect his rescue, including my friendship with the CIA's Assistant DDO. If that labels me as not being a *team player*, then perhaps you should try recruiting from another team — or consider broadening your views to include a more modern, more global, dare I suggest *less xenophobic* definition of teamwork. Besides, isn't one of the attributes of a *double–0* agent the ability to work without a team?"

Mike decided to punctuate his rebuke by sucking as much heat out of *C* as he dared. It not only recharged his taxed system, but the chilling effect on the head of MI6 was obvious. *C* swallowed hard and took an involuntary step back away from him, fear showing in his eyes.

Mike's eyes felt hot — a sign that they were glowing with the same lethal combination of chi and spiritual energy that could readily become flame. He eased in a slow, deep breath, calming himself, but kept his eyes fixed on *C*. The ball was in his court.

C, for his part, regained some composure, then frowned. If he'd been puffed up before, he was considerably deflated now. He took a breath.

"My apologies, *Samurai*," he said. "You're quite right. Look at me; you'd think I'd never been posted to the UN. I made some bad assumptions about you after reading your file, which dates back to '06 and your overextended visa in Bhutan — due to illness you claimed at the time."

Mike remained silent, still offended by *C*'s previous attitude. He'd run into the same notions among certain British teachers in Bermuda, who'd looked down their noses at anything not of UK origin, making cracks about Americans and their *Rambo* mentality, somehow lumping him into the same group. *Oh, look! The colonial calls biscuits cookies!*

C, however, seemed waiting for a comment from Mike. *He knows he was in the wrong, but he's too proud to admit it. He needs a concession from me, like the answer to this unspoken question, to reestablish a sense of peace between us.* He finally relented: "I'd spent eight months at a Shaolin temple in Loyang, Henan Province, expanding my knowledge of Kung Fu — an area of study I'd begun in my teens."

"And from October '06 to May of '07?" *C* prompted. He seemed relieved, almost as if he thought he was successfully defusing a bomb that he feared might have blown up in his face.

"Studying aspects of mind–control from a Tibetan Tulku in Lhasa," Mike said.

C nodded pensively. "A region also controlled by the PRC. Of course, there was no difficulty in backtracking through records to see that, prior to China, you had spent eight months at the *Yagyu–Shinkage Ryu* in Kyoto, Japan, — Did I pronounce that properly? — before traveling to China. No doubt that explains the origin of your codename within the Canadian SIS."

"Not entirely," Mike replied cryptically, causing *C* to frown again.

"So there may be something to the theory Mason penned into your file — that you are the reincarnation of a 17th–century Samurai?"

"*Bushi*," Mike corrected. "*Samurai* is a derogatory term invented by those jealous of the elevated status of the *Bushi* class. It amused certain peasants and non–*Bushi* to refer to samurai as *servants* because we served the Shogun."

"And yet you've adopted this term for yourself."

Mike gave a wan smile. "Jean Charbonneau, my section supervisor at CSIS, chose the term." He shrugged. "I, too, serve — my country, my friends, those in need, and, as much as possible, my own sense of justice and morality."

"Hence the havoc you created in almost every intelligence agency's computer network back in 2008." *C*'s expression seemed torn between admiration and disapproval. It reminded Mike a little of Monahan, now four years dead.

"Actually," Tony interjected, "it was my man, Nigel, who disseminated that information in such a manner. Mike merely expressed the desire to make sure every agency would do their part."

"It was the right thing to do," Mike added, the edge creeping back into his voice. Then, "If we might return to the case at hand, and Mason's alleged 'suspicious links to the Russians, sir?"

C glanced at a large antique wall clock and sighed. "Quite right — *tempus fugit*. According to phone LUDs, Mason had far too much phone contact with a reporter from the *Daily Examiner* — one Brenda Peters, a known associate of certain Russian nationals that MI5 have tried, somewhat unsuccessfully, to keep under surveillance. Most of the calls originated from her, but, on the day in question — the last day — there were two calls to her from one of Mason's numbers, culminating in a call to a Moscow number that traced to Lubyanka, but we couldn't determine to what specific FSB office."

Mike frowned. "Which of Mason's numbers, sir?"

"Does it matter?" *C* challenged.

"It might matter a great deal," Mike replied.

"It was his cellphone: an iPhone, or one like it."

"Which, sir? An iPhone or one like it? It makes a great deal of difference. For example, a lesser phone might be a lot easier to hack than an iPhone, though SIM cards can be cloned."

"Yes, our people in Q–Branch suggested that very thing. Perhaps you should meet with them for that information. I'll see if I can't make Q available.

"Oh, and, *Samurai*, if you can put a lid on any parts of this, —" he held up the most recent copy of the *London Daily Examiner*. The headline read:

High Level Traitor at MI6?

The brief article beneath promised to reveal more over the next few days.

With that, he picked up a phone and made a call.

"Mrs. Daniels will have someone escort you. Oh, and, *Samurai*, —" A pained look crossed *C*'s face. "I really do apologize for earlier. I'm very glad you could come, and, well, welcome aboard. You really do have a reputation for achieving the impossible, and in a short time. In this case, a short time may be all we have. The press are all over this, especially certain tabloids, all trying to exploit the worst possible scenarios, as if determined to embarrass us." He huffed — "Of course they do. God forbid that the SIS be permitted to protect the UK and its allies from foreign threats or espionage, never mind tarnishing the reputation of a brave man who's given fifty years of service to his country and this service."

"About those missing files," Mike mused, "did anyone question the cleaning staff of the night before?"

Sir John nodded. "Those we could were questioned, but one man in particular seems to have disappeared."

"Convenient for him; inconvenient for Mason," Mike commented. "I would think *that* might ease suspicions against Mason considerably, especially if the man in question should prove to be even remotely associated with anyone Russian. Can someone provide me with a name and address?"

C gave a curt nod, pressed a button on his elaborate phone system, and said, "Mrs. Daniels, would you see to it that Agent *Samurai* has the name and address of the missing nighttime cleaner? Then escort our guests to Q–branch."

Mike was about to take leave of *C* when *C* turned to Tony and almost blurted, "Forgive me, Lord Dewhurst, but, I assume that you were — during your entire tenure with us — well, I mean —"

He seemed completely flustered.

Mike smiled. He was no stranger to the trouble a thinker can get himself into when he lapses into feeler mode — *especially when the introvert behaves as an extrovert in the same instance.*

"I had more than a century of experience in, shall we say, *controlling my urges*, before joining the Service, just shortly after Georgi Rosenblum changed his name to Sydney Riley. In fact, it was Riley who initially recruited me."

"But that was before even the First World War!" The fact that *C* barely whispered it did nothing to hide his blatant amazement.

"And, Sir John," Tony continued, "While his killer instinct is far more defined than my own, Michael's control is nothing short of amazing. In many ways, he is vastly older than I."

"If I may interject," Mike commented, "Tony is probably hoping to convey that we feed from the bottle, and hardly ever from the vein."

Just then the door opened to reveal Mrs. Daniels, a printed file card in her hand.

MI6, Quartermaster Branch

"This intricate little device is what made Mason's driver stop the car," Q explained, holding up a black plastic casing with a trailing wire harness. "It tapped into the instrument panel and the electrical system, activating several warning lights at once, triggered by remote control, possibly even a smart phone." She tapped the tiny antenna that stuck out from one end. "The assassin could trigger the device, then await his chance for a clean shot."

The head of Q–Branch was female, early forties, and with an IQ Mike quickly surmised was somewhere beyond genius level. He needed only a cursory examination of her thoughts to recognize the storehouse of knowledge of physics, chemistry, and electronics that greatly surpassed his own understanding.

"There was a similar device attached to a canister of gas — tests show it's a derivative of *fentanyl*, making it most likely Russian in origin. The canister was in a backseat door, hidden behind the liner panel.

"Also, these are the LUDs that pertain to Ms. Peters, and the Lubyanka number," she added, holding up a list. "The calls from Mason's cell to her number are suspect, especially the one to Moscow," she commented. "His home machine has lengthy messages from her that contain no message — at least not on the surface. At first glance, it was as if she might have hoped to create suspicion by how many times she called and how long, from a straight–forward scanning of the LUDs, she appeared to have remained on the line. Look here, for example, at this four–and–a–half–minute call. One would think that Mason had indeed spoken with her for almost five minutes. In point of fact, Mason's machine took the call. Peters said nothing, but there is a faint hint of static. Computer analysis, however, reveals an underlying data transmission, a bit like a fax, though nowhere near as audible. It took a few tests, but experiments finally showed that, when Mason called home, via his iPhone, to check his machine and played back the recording, it required less than a minute of playback for the underlying code to program his cellphone to call her number the moment he rang off from his home machine. Whoever programmed the worm had to know the specific iOS version of Mason's phone."

Tony removed a card from his wallet and passed it to her. "Could you send the relevant data to Nigel Worthing? He's my IT tech at Interpol."

She smiled and took the card. "Nigel and I are well–acquainted. It'll be nice to send him something before he can nick it for himself — assuming he hasn't already," she added with a trace of chagrin. "It was Mr. Worthington who discovered and alerted us to the underlying software worm in the recorded phone message."

As if hoping to mask her embarrassment, she quickly added, "By the way, *Samurai, C* has authorized me to replace your older model PPK with our new PPK/S 9–millimeter. You may find the grip a tad more to your liking." She cast a glance as his hands. When he didn't respond immediately, she added, "Though technically a short cartridge, we've managed to squeeze in just a bit more powder, improving the penetration. And, of course, the increase to .38 caliber from your .32 means the projectile will hit with a bit more impact. And we also have a supply of your unique ammunition requirements." A puzzled look crossed her face as she referenced his holly–and–Osmium bullets.

Seems she has no idea why I might need holly rounds, he projected to Tony.

The vampire situation is highly classified, Tony replied. *No doubt Mason kept it to himself and C. It's clear that C knew about you, especially in light of how he backed away when you got agitated with him.*

"So?" Q prompted, catching Mike off–guard. "*Samurai* — the PPK/S?"

"May I see one?" Mike asked, then followed her over to a counter, where she pulled two graphite cases closer, opening one for Mike to inspect.

Mike took a moment to examine the weapon. Sure enough, the grip felt just a bit more natural to his wide palm and thick fingers. He looked at the back of the slide, noting the absence of the three LED indicators he'd seen in the last Bond film.

"I guess it can't be coded for my palm print," he quipped, prompting a smile from Q.

"Sorry, *Samurai*; that particular model went to Daniel Craig. It is something we're considering, though. If you like, I'd be happy to let you see a demonstration of the difference. We have a target set up with a piece of eighth–inch steel plate. As you can see —" She fired the PPK/S at the plate, punching a neat 9–mm hole in it, "— the PPK/S has no trouble penetrating, whereas —" She picked up an original PPK and fired, but the bullet ricocheted off, "— bullets from your PPK bounce off."

Mike reached into his bag and pulled out his own PPK, relaxed, summoned his chi, and felt his eyes get warm as he focused just to the right of the hole made by Q's bullet. As he fired, he launched the built-up burst of chi with the bullet, propelling it beyond it's usual muzzle velocity, so that it, too, punched through the plate.

Q frowned. "*That* should not be possible," she insisted, shaking her head, clearly puzzled.

"Let's just say that I cheated," Mike said. "In my work, there are cases when improved muzzle velocity is more liability than asset. In fact, I mostly use my silencer to reduce the velocity."

Mike pulled his shoulder holster from the bag and slipped the harness about his shoulders. He noticed Q's eyes widen in alarm at the speed with which he moved as he holstered the weapon.

"So, while I complement SIS on your progress with the 9–mm ammunition, I'll stick with 7.65–mm."

"I notice you're lacking the silencer pocket next to the spare clip holder," Q commented. "May I at least replace your shoulder holster harness? Do you prefer ballistic nylon or would you like leather?"

Jeeze, Q, determined to give me something? "Nylon's fine," Mike answered.

Q left the room, returning moments later with a grey box. "You're in luck. I feared we wouldn't have one. The new model has all but totally replaced the older models, though there are a few older .38 caliber models still in use."

It took but a moment for Mike to slip into the new harness. Locating his silencer, he slid it into the pocket next to the clip holders, holstered his PPK in the new holster, then transferred his clips.

"I can also offer you two boxes of your special rounds — we still have a few boxes of 7.65–mm stock. May I ask why you need such unusual ordinance?"

Mike gave her a stern glance, then, with a hint of a smile, said, "You can ask,..."

"Actually, my dear," Tony spoke up, "that's as highly classified as anything gets around here. And, if I'm included in *C*'s largess, I wouldn't mind trading in my old PPK for a newer one, especially since mine is from the 1950s. I prefer leather for the holster. And I would also appreciate a supply of the holly–and–Osmium rounds."

She responded by quickly pushing a graphite case toward him, a box of hollow–points, then got up on tip-toe to extract a brown–labelled box with its leather holster harness. "There you are, 006. I'll be back in a moment with the custom ordnance."

While she was gone, Mike made a point of pulling his weapon a few times to get a feel for the new harness. It needed some adjustment, but he knew he'd adapt to it just fine. Meanwhile, Tony took a moment to don his new holster harness, load and holster the PPK/S and clips, then slip the silencer into its holder. He was just slipping his suit coat back on when Q returned with four blue boxes.

"I'm afraid I only have two for each of you," she commented. "More are being manufactured. I can let you know as soon as they are completed."

Tony just smiled, took all four boxes from her, put two in his case, then set Mike's ammo in his bag.

In Pennington–Smythe's Car, after MI6

"So, what have we got?" Mike summarized: "He was gassed, his chauffeur shot — and his own sidearm was left on the backseat of the car. And there's this reporter, Brenda Peters, hounding him with phone calls, and the elaborate lengths to which someone went to make it look like Mason was calling her. There's also the missing file, though I think it's safe to assume that the missing cleaner lifted that."

"Speaking of the missing cleaner," Tony observed, "his address requires a detour of only six blocks, though in the opposite direction." He handed the page with the address to Pennington–Smythe, adding, "if you could pull up half–a–block away..." Then, to Mike, "you were right about him being Russian — well, Ukrainian, maybe. I think Kovanyuk is a Ukrainian name — Boris Kovanyuk."

————

Mike and Tony got out of the car on opposite sides, Mike heading for the shadow of an ancient stone building. Reaching out with his senses, he located two men — he presumed they were MI5 spooks — watching the building that housed the cleaner's apartment. Across street, in the shadows between adjacent buildings, he located an older man, also watching the building. This one was consumed by fear.

Steeling his resolve, he willed the watchers to not see him, then tore across the street in a blur, to appear out of nowhere in front of the older man. The latter turned with surprising speed and tried to bolt but, with a *whoosh* of wind, Mike was in front of him again. A gentle, yet irresistibly firm hand pressed the man against the building, pinning his back to the stone blocks.

"Who told you to take the file folder from Mason's desk drawer, Boris?" he asked in a low tone.

The man started to hiss a protest, but Mike stopped him with an icy stare, making his eyes glow with preternatural light.

"Answer the question, Boris — *now*."

"Brenda Peters. She is from the old country. She knows about my mother's illness. She said she'd help with the doctor's bills."

This guy has a living mother? Mike thought, amazed. Then, "Where is your mother?"

"In a nursing home in Severnyy, near Moscow," the man replied, terror evident in his voice. "She has a rare heart condition. They could not help her in Luhansk or Donetsk, and Kyiv seemed too far and so expensive, then Brenda Peters offered to have her flown to Moscow. Doctors treated her — it was like a miracle — then they transferred her to the home in Severnyy."

Suddenly he stared at Mike. "Who are you? *What* are you?" It came out as a hiss.

"Something from a nightmare," Mike replied, resisting the overwhelming urge to feed. "Tomorrow you will explain everything to your supervisor at SIS. I hope you don't get fired. Perhaps they will take your mother's illness into consideration.

"In the meantime, I need to know what you did with that file."

"I delivered it to a man at Brenda Peters's office." He removed a slip of paper from his pocket and gave it to Mike.

On the way back to the car, Mike stopped at the surveillance vehicle. Tony was already chatting to the men inside, showing them credentials, seemingly oblivious to the drizzle that was just beginning.

Mike stuck out a hand. "Agent *Samurai* of the Canadian SIS, on loan to MI6. Kovanyuk will be reporting to his supervisor first thing in the morning, with a full confession. Please convey to your boss that the leverage concerned an elderly, infirm mother — he couldn't afford her care. Perhaps your boss can convey some notion of compassion to the appropriate people at MI6. More comprehensive health benefits might go a long way toward improving security.

First things first, though, he projected to Tony, *as soon as I've rested, I need to pay a visit to —* he consulted the slip of paper Boris had given him, — *Max Cochrane — I have a hunch he's Brenda Peters's editor.* Boris handed over the MI6 file to him.

———

With Mike and Tony returned to the car, Pennington–Smythe pulled away from the curb, windshield wipers flapping at a moderate pace, and set out, initially en route to a hotel, until Tony rejected that in favour of his own London flat. *It's not much further than the hotel, has two spare rooms, and has the added security of Nigel regularly sweeping it for electronic surveillance,* Tony explained.

What about Nigel? Mike asked him. *Any chance we can put him onto a few things before sunrise?*

"It's after 5:30 AM now," Tony mused aloud, glancing at the time. "I suppose I can wake him up."

Or we could wait until we're at your place, Mike projected, casting a meaningful glance at Wentworth Pennington–Smythe.

Not a problem, Tony said in Mike's head, then triggered a call to Nigel.

With the phone pressed hard against Tony's ear, the Cockney's groggy tones, while plainly audible to Mike, were clearly not heard by Pennington–Smythe.

"Dreadfully sorry about the time, old man, but, if you could pop by the flat ASAP, we'd greatly appreciate it. And, Nigel, a few bits of gear might be appropriate."

Mike grinned. He could hear Nigel putting in a breakfast order for lots of black coffee, crispy bacon, toast, scrambled eggs...

"He'll be around by 6:30 AM," Tony said as he pocketed his phone.

It was 6:00 when Wentworth Pennington–Smythe left them, after having been assured by both Mike and Tony that there was absolutely nothing more he could do for them.

5: Nigel On the Case

Tony ascended the front steps of what appeared to be just another three–storey townhouse on the street, opened the front door, and walked in.

Mike was appalled. "My, God, Tony, you didn't even have to unlock the front door!" he exclaimed.

Tony's response was a smile. "And, for that you can thank our dear talented Nigel," he replied. "There's a facial recognition sensor built into the pane of the door. Poor Mrs. Snell, my tenant on the first floor, was forever losing her keys. Now she doesn't even have to remember to lock the door. The sensors read the face as you approach the door. We're hoping to eventually incorporate finger– or palm–print reading into the handle, as a final security precaution."

Once inside they proceeded up a narrow flight of stairs to the next floor. Tony was leaning heavily against the rail as he ascended, and Mike, his legs feeling stiff and reluctant, felt a need to do the same.

"It's much the same here as at the entrance," Tony added as he stopped at the only door on the second floor landing. "Hidden cameras read faces on the way up the stair, and, since the door handle's reading of handprints isn't fully up–to–snuff — MI6 are still working on the hand–recognition you quipped about when you referred to Bond's new PPK/S in *Skyfall* — a bit more dodgy than anticipated — trouble locating the battery to power the microcircuitry." As he said this, he touched a section of wood panel to the right of the door, whereupon it slid to one side and a hand–reader flipped up. The moment Tony laid his hand on it, the door clicked open.

The interior was spacious, decorated in much the same manner as the house on Hawthorne Street in Dartmouth — a mix of Georgian and Victorian furniture, with a large unused desk in a corner. A narrow stair against one wall led to another floor.

"The first door at the top of the stairs is your's," Tony told him. "My room is in the back, on this floor. Feel free to freshen up while I check my bloodstock and arrange a fresh delivery, including your O–positive. I haven't been here in almost year, so I doubt if anything is drinkable, except, of course, the Scotch."

As he said this, Tony gestured with a crystal decanter filled with pale amber liquid. It only took a trace of a smile from Mike for him to pour an ounce into a highball glass of matching patterned crystal.

Mike accepted the glass then raised it in salute as Tony finished pouring one for himself. He let his glass clink against Tony's, then said, "To finding Mason."

He peeled off his suit jacket, shook the worst of the rain off, then hung it on an antique wooden coatrack near the door. "Is it always this gloomy?" he asked, peering out at the rain still falling from a leaden sky.

"Welcome to London, dear boy," Tony said with a grin. "Blame it on the Gulf Stream — That's what the weather lass on Channel Two always does."

"*Oi! An' no' even a po' o' coffee for me!*" Nigel called out as he came through the door to the flat. Breaking into a grin, he ran to Mike and hugged him enthusiastically, somewhat to Mike's embarrassment, though Mike was acutely aware of Nigel's gratitude for having saved him from an extremely powerful vampire–witch.

Glancing at Tony over Nigel's head, which only came up to his chin, he asked, "Is there coffee?"

Tony broke into a grin. "I imagine the beans are in the freezer. I'll get a pot going. Meanwhile, Michael, you can set your bag in your room, while Nigel sets up and gets his system activated. I'll warm some blood for you the moment it arrives. I'm sure you're in need of something after your hyper–speed exertions with the elderly janitor coming on the heels of jet–lag, not to mention some of *C*'s nonsense — I saw how he stirred you up with that crack about team players."

Mike's response was part nod, part shrug. "So what's the source of his mistrust of MI5?"

"Surely you must know that MI5 evolved out of Section 5 of Military Intelligence," Tony explained. "And MI6, might more properly have been named *NI*6 — Section 6 of Military Intelligence was actually a branch of Naval Intelligence."

Mike sighed and rolled his eyes. "So it all comes back to army vs navy?"

Tony nodded. "Alas, dear boy, yes."

Nigel went back to the apartment door and returned with a system of connected boxes and cabinets that reminded Mike of the way rock bands pack their gear, then set to work unlatching and removing covers, pulling out components, and began setting up on the empty desk. Mike recognized the first bit as an Apple LCD screen that was larger than his iMac screen.

"How did you get all that up the stairs?" Mike asked. "It must weigh a ton!"

"Wiff no lift, it weren't easy!" Nigel declared, still huffing a bit, "bu' i's no' even a hundred kilos." He then proceeded to set up a cpu tower, printers, scanner, and a few peripherals that Mike didn't recognize.

Mike sat in a padded chair, leaned back, and soon felt himself drifting.

"Almos' done," Nigel chirped. "Coffee on yet?"

Nigel's system turned out to be a state–of–the–art Mac Pro tower with a 32–inch screen, a scanner, two laser printers, and a few other bits of hardware.

"Nigel," Tony called from the kitchen, "Q should be sending you data concerning Mason's phone calls." His announcement was punctuated by the whirr of what Mike recognized as a coffee grinder.

"You mean 'is LUDs an' stuff abou' the software worm 'idden in 'e long silent messages left on 'is answering machine? I go' oll 'at a day or two ago — cyber–nicked it, analyzed it, ffen sent 'er an 'eads up abou' ffe nature o' ffe worm." Nigel beamed like the metaphorical cat who swallowed the canary. "Clever bi' o' work, 'at was — serious 'igh grade — I mean, we're talkin' top shelf.

"'Ooever ffis Brenda Peters is, she's got some major–league 'acker talent at 'er beck an' call."

"The question is," Mike offered, "just who precisely is Brenda Peters."

"I'm workin' on it, an' so is my mate Gregory. We go' an 'unch, ffough — mostly based on 'ow our friend Mason was nicked. It 'as ffe earmarks o' someffin' 'e Ruskies use' to do back in 'e cold war days."

"Are the Russians seriously messing with MI6?" Mike asked. "I thought all that was over with."

Tony appeared from the kitchen alcove, taking a tentative sip from his Scotch, and shaking his head. "Putin's behavior at every relevant venue says otherwise. He makes a point of obstructing every move the West tries to make. The Russians have always been that way — look at Viet Nam."

Mike frowned. "I thought that was Communist China propping up the Viet Kong," he said. "I know the US were wanting to show the Soviets that they'd go all out in a war, *without* resorting to nuclear weapons."

Tony looked weary as he shook his head. "The Kong were armed with AK–47s." His voice was noticeably more subdued — the vampire need to succumb to the void seemed almost upon him.

Mike suddenly realized that he felt the same. He gave a slow nod. "Kalashnikovs are only made in Russia. I thought Putin's seemingly obsessive need to obstruct the US in foreign affairs was to cover his covert arms deals — with Saddam Hussein at the time, and, lately, with Iran and Syria."

"It goes deeper than that, I'm afraid," Tony replied. "Nothing overtly antagonistic, just a kind of resentment for Communism failing. There are even those who think he might have played a part in the current economic decline in Europe, especially its associated backlash against the economies of Canada and the US."

"Anyway," Mike resumed, "what exactly do we have on Ms. Peters, other than the fact that she works for the *London Daily Examiner*? And what about the number called from Mason's cellphone — the one that MI6 seems to think is an FSB number?"

"What we 'ave, mate, Ms. Peters, first, is a woman 'oo, according to computer evidence, didn't bleedin' exist before 2006," Nigel replied. "'Ow she conned ffe *Examiner* into 'irin' 'er is a mystery. I mean, ffey're not ffe *Times*, but ffey do seem to check out ffe creds o' ffeir employees before actually 'irin' 'em — at leas' ffat's 'e rep. Even ffe birff certificate she used for 'er bleedin' passport application looks a bit dodgy."

"Dodgy?" Tony queried, "How so? Is there a copy there? Does it look like a forgery?"

"No, gov'nor, but, if you go straight to ffe birff registry, she's not ffere. *But*, if you go at it from a different direction, ffe certificate *is* ffere, jus' no' indexed — like it weren't ffere to begin wiff, but got filed later. I mean, it's as if some bloke said, 'Oi, ffis one's not on file; I better file it!' — a case of bureaucracy at its sloppiest, if ye're askin' me. An' it just opens an even bigger can o' worms. It says she were born at Great Ormond Street Hospital for Children, but, ffere was a fire in 'e records room in 1991, so ffere's noffin' before ffat!"

"Ormond Street — Ormond Street —" Mike muttered the phrase over and over until it fell into place. "Peter Pan," he mused. "Barry donated proceeds from Peter Pan to the Great Ormond Street Children's Hospital. Now why do I know that?"

Nigel grinned. "Because Maggie Smith told you — in 'e movie *Hook*. Shame Sean's not 'ere; 'e'd 'ave pulled that out of an 'at quick as Bob's–yer–uncle."

Mike smiled. "No doubt. For that very reason, Ormond Street might be a favourite choice for forgers looking to place someone born before 1991."

Nigel kept digging.

"Well," he said, "seems she 'ad an uncle already workin' for 'e paper — one John Kessler —" after more fingering over the semi–silent keys, he continued, "— 'oo turns out to be Ivan Kesslov, jumped ship from a Russian freighter in 1968, claimed asylum in Sweden, got a job as a typesetter in a newspaper, ffen came here in 1973 an' go' a job wiff 'e *Examiner*. 'E may have vouched for Peters as 'is niece, but, even wha' little I can get on 'im from 'acking 'e Russians, says Ivan were an only child."

"You'd think MI6 would have picked up on that," Mike mused.

Tony shrugged. "Perhaps, but failing to mention it to us isn't proof that they didn't find it. Besides, MI6 is more focused on the outside, not what's already inside. That's 5's job, and *C* no doubt gave you a hint of how upper level personnel view the sister branch."

Just then a chime sounded.

Tony aimed a remote at a small screen by the door, displaying a man in courier uniform with a clipboard in his hand. "Yes?" Tony spoke in the direction of the screen.

"Perishable delivery for Lord Anthony Dewhurst," the courier announced. "Two crates, signature required."

"If you'll watch the door for me, dear chap —" he said to Mike, "— I shan't be able to access the hand–pad to get back in."

Mike stood by the door, watching on the screen as Tony went to the front door, signed, then gathered two heavy–looking crates in his arms and headed back up.

Mike met him at the door, taking the top crate from him. Moments later, Tony had removed the lids from both crates, revealing a styrofoam lining and twelve wine bottles in each.

"That's your O+, Michael," Tony said, indicating the crate he was examining. "I should imagine you're ready for a glass by now — if not an entire bottle."

Mike managed a wan smile. "You're not too far off, though, my intake is still about half what it once was. Ever since Myrddin—" He left the rest unsaid. He'd met the ancient sorcerer–vampire, known to the world as the legendary, if not mythical, Merlin, immediately after surviving exposure to the sun for most of a day. Myrddin had given Mike a more than generous infusion of his blood, making him so much stronger, and making him seem even more ancient in terms of his vampire powers.

"I'll open these and warm us up some breakfast," Tony said, taking a bottle from each crate and adjourning to the kitchen alcove. "As for you, Nigel, I rang the grocers with an order that should appear directly."

He returned a few minutes later, a warmed goblet in each hand, passing one to Mike, who, with a nod of thanks, proceeded to sit in an armchair near Nigel. He took a slow sip of the blood, paused to allow his fangs to resume normal size, then took another sip. As his system assimilated the blood, the overwhelming fatigue began to recede. He polished it off and headed to the kitchen for a refill, returned after warming the remains of the bottle, and collapsed into his chair.

"Nigel," he mused, "presumably, Ms. Peters must have had some other credentials before being hired by the *Examiner*."

"Oi, yeah — courses in journalism from a college righ' 'ere in London. She seems to 'ave at least done 'e final course, which required takin' four ovvers firs'— whot ye call prerequisites —"

"Thereby creating the plausible assumption that she has accreditation for the prerequisite courses," Tony offered.

Mike nodded, then, taking another sip, he pondered, "Assuming forged transcripts are involved, who does such work locally? They may have provided her with her identity as well."

"Vasily Boronovich would be ffe best bloke for a job like 'at," Nigel suggested, bringing up info about the man onscreen.

Mike saw a round face with jovial features framed by short grey hair. "Interesting," he mused. "He effects a friendliness in his face that's belied by a hint of coldness in his eyes. Got an address? Maybe I should have a chat with him."

"Less'n 'alf an hour by cab," Nigel said, then tapped the keyboard until a page spewed out of the laser printer. "An' ffat ovver number — 011-7-495-224-1897 — 'e firs' bit's direc' dilin' codes, but ffe res' tracks to ffe top floor o' ffe Lubyanka Buildin', meanin' full colonels an' up, bu' ffat's where it stalls out — no directory. If yer callin' in, 'e switchboard'll direc' yer call. Ovverwise, ye'd 'ave te know ffe precise number." He passed the printout to Mike, who read it, then passed it to Tony.

"The Lubyanka Building," Mike mused, "That used to be KGB Headquarters. And I think, from what I've read, they had a prison of sorts in the basement."

"Well, detention areas and interrogation facilities," Tony corrected. "It's the headquarters of the FSB now, though, since Putin's rise, the FSB is almost indistinguishable from the former KGB, though, by some estimates, they're considerably more ruthless."

Mike frowned at this, read Boronovich's address from Nigel's printout, then passed the page to Tony. "I'm not long from slipping into the void but, as soon as I reemerge, I think I should pay this guy a visit, in addition to the offices of the *Daily Examiner*. It's your town, Tony; since I don't know my way around, care to accompany me?"

"Absolutely, Michael," Tony agreed. "It's been an eventful night and morning, beginning with your mental tasks for the air marshall during our flight."

Moments later the door chime sounded again.

"Oi," Nigel chirped, "I bet ffat's me tuck!" Bolting out of his chair, he raced for the door.

———

Mike opted for trying to reclaim Mason's stolen file before visiting Nigel's forger. At 3:15 PM they pulled up in front of Suttcliffe House on Fleet Street, all concrete and glass, with a clock mounted like a business shingle a couple of storeys above the street. Mike looked for a sign to confirm that it was, in fact, the offices of the *London Daily Examiner*, but found nothing.

"It's the correct address," Tony commented. "I'm sure there'll be a directory inside, dear boy, which should lead you straight to this Cochrane chap."

Sure enough, in the main foyer, close to the elevator, was a large display board behind glass. The offices for the paper were on the third and fourth floor.

At the third floor, another directory referred them to the fourth floor for Max Cochrane's office.

Wait here, Mike projected to Tony, as they were adjacent to rows of plush chairs, occupied by people seemingly awaiting appointments.

At Cochrane's office, he ignited his eyes with Wiccan power and riveted the secretary with his gaze, projecting: *Max Cochrane is expecting me. Carry on with your work. I can see myself in — we're old friends from college.*

She just sat there, staring straight ahead.

Max Cochrane looked about forty–five, but his face had a bloated look and an excessively ruddy complexion, matched only by his curly head of fiery red hair. *If he doesn't ease off on the booze, he might not see fifty*, Mike decided.

"What's the meaning of this?" Max blurted, rising from his chair, then fell silent as his eyes locked onto Mike's glowing ones.

I need the folder Boris Kovanyuk gave you, Mike directed.

Max hesitated, then Mike forced deeper into his mind, and gave a slight squeeze. Yet, surprisingly, Cochrane resisted, his respiration accelerating, his heart pounding, as he retreated a half–step.

This clown's half in the bag! I don't have time for this, Mike thought, and focused more energy to his eyes. He advanced to the edge of Max Cochrane's desk, took a determined stance, and leaned forward, the splayed fingers of both hands coming to rest on the desktop. With a surge of effort, he went into

Cochrane's mind until he found himself looking at the office through Max's eyes. Cochrane had been drinking. *Now show me the file.*

Max turned to the file drawers behind him — the top drawer had a combination dial. He turned the knob until the latch opened, then extracted the MI6 *Eyes Only* folder and set it on the desk.

Glancing up, Mike was shocked to see his own body standing at the front of the desk, legs apart, fingertips braced against the desktop. The glow of his eyes was gone, leaving them pale and lifeless. *I've never gone astral with my eyes open*, he realized. *I didn't even intend to go out–of–body. Is that what it looks like? My God; I look like a corpse!*

Mike withdrew from Max, then staggered a step as he came fully back into himself.

I never thought of that — I just astral–projected into Cochrane, while standing in front of him, and left my body on its own, on its feet. It's a wonder my body didn't collapse to the floor! Some part of me must have remained behind. No; I was braced against his desk. Did I know to do that? Was it just luck? I'll have to tell tell Carrie about this, as well as Anil.

Sit, he commanded Max, then examined the file, pulling out his iPhone as he did so.

He snapped a hi-res photo of each page, then texted them all to Nigel, before calling Nigel on the phone.

"Nigel, I need you to use the photos I just texted to create fake copies, with all the names and data altered. Then I need the new docs sent back in a format that I can print here from my phone."

"I'm on it, gov'nor," the Cockney chirped. "It's a standard duty fitness assessment report. I may even 'ave one on file to work from. If not, well, MI6, 'ere I come, 'acking ffrough yer firewalls again."

Mike grinned, as he heard the sound of Nigel's typing over–layered by a constant stream of Cockney banter, mostly a confusing garble of rhyming slang, until — "Ffere ye go, gov'nor. It's comin' at ye now by eMail, as a multipage PDF file. Go te yer settings app, check wifi, an' look for 'is wireless print router."

Mike did as directed and read off the offered results, until Nigel said, "Ffat's 'e one!"

Mike selected it, then selected the attached PDF from the eMail. Detecting a printer attached to the router, the iPhone, in addition to options for opening the file, offered *print file*, which Mike did. Seconds later a laser printer whirred to life and spat out several pages, which looked identical to the originals, except for the change in names and stats. Some of the names amused him, for example: Pennington–Smythe seemed to have been promoted to *Double–0*, while other names were recognizably fictitious, like Harry Potter.

Mike smiled as he put the papers back in the file and folded the originals, tucking them into an inside pocket of his jacket.

"That was quick," Tony said when Mike returned.

Mike grinned. "No, Nigel was quick. MI6 should treat him to something special, maybe a nice vacation somewhere with his wife." He then explained what he had accomplished with Nigel's invaluable assistance.

Tony smiled, then it broadened into a grin. "So, when the *Daily Examiner* goes to press with their exposé on MI6 incompetence — and they will — it will start out as a huge embarrassment for MI6, but will eventually backfire, as news of the false nature of the file becomes apparent. *Sink me!*, Michael, you're a genius. It's brilliant — simply brilliant!"

Mike, with his usually dismissive air, shrugged off the praise, commenting, "I think we should continue on to the workplace of Nigel's forger."

Once in the car, he called the offices of MI6, and got put through to *C* immediately.

"I have Mason's missing file," he reported. "I replaced it with a fake, all false names and data. When the *Examiner* runs with it, don't react. If you can swallow a little public embarrassment for a bit, once someone tries to vet the info, they'll see it for what it is. MI6 will be exonerated, and the *Examiner* will be the ones with egg on their face. Just to give you an idea, early in the list is 00–agent Wentworth Pennington–Smythe, who didn't fare well. Nearer the end, though, Harry Potter received a glowing report."

———   ——   ———

They found Vasily Boronovich at 3:45 PM, in Tottenham, in a dingy little shop, in an equally dingy alley off a side street. The door was locked, which slowed Mike for all of half a second.

"Eh! I vork here! My door vas locked! How you get in? Vhat you vant vit me? I call police!" It came out of him in a rapid–fire burst.

Mike stood still, arms folded across his chest, Tony just behind his left shoulder.

"The phone's right there," Mike said in a low voice, gesturing to an old phone on the desk. "What are you waiting for?" He opened his CSIS ID folder and tucked it into his belt, the way he'd seen TV detectives display their badges. He then made a show of unholstering his Walther PPK and screwing the silencer into place, all the while trying to look cool, professional, and entirely menacing.

The Russian's eyes widened in alarm, then fixed themselves on Mike's eyes. A moment of full eye–contact was all it took. Mike surged into Vasily's mind, searching for images of Brenda Peters. He found it all — forged transcripts for courses never attended, forged identity, right down to a false birth certificate listing Great Ormond Street Children's Hospital as the place of birth.

What's her real name? Mike asked in Vasily's mind, but encountered major resistance. Using his chi, he took a grip and squeezed, making Boronovich's eyes bulge, but he still remained silent.

He squeezed harder.

Nyet, Nyet, Boronovich muttered in agony.

Mike focussed his grip on Boronovich's heart, forcing it to slow, but, again, to no avail.

Fear and pain aren't working, he observed. *Perhaps I should try the opposite.*

Mike projected chi outward, creating a luminous aura about himself, then filled Boronovich's mind with a sense of euphoria. As the Russian's eyes widened in glazed rapture, Mike probed deeper.

There was a gasp from Tony.

"Brendu Petrova," Boronovich murmured. Mike then steered Boronovich toward his desk. "I want copies of everything," he insisted.

His face still in the throes of rapture, Boronovich nodded, then turned to a back wall lined with filing cabinets, rifled through one, and came back with a file folder, about one–half–inch thick. In it were a copy of Brendu Petrova's Russian passport, her original birth certificate from the USSR, a number of photographs — some with very straight black hair — and copies of Boronovich's forged documents. The new document photos showed Brenda Peters with the same wavy brunette hair Mike had seen on Nigel's computer screen.

"I'm not sure what use it will be, but at least we know that Brenda Peters was born in Vyazma, USSR, as Brendu Petrova," Mike said.

Tony gave Mike a pat on the back. "You've done a profitable hour's work. I dare say, after your mental efforts with Vasily Boronovich, you must feel either warmed up or exhausted. What's next on the agenda, old man? If it were the old days, I'd be thinking about a visit to —"

"Mason's apartment," Mike finished for him.

Tony grinned. "Conveniently enough, it's about two blocks beyond my flat, in the direction of Vauxhall Cross and MI6."

Once clear of the shop, Tony stared at Mike.

"I have to ask, dear boy, what did you do back there? You looked — well, *sink me*, but *angelic* is the only thing that comes to mind."

Mike shrugged. "That's sort of what I was going for. It's hard to explain, but, well, Boronovich is Russian Orthodox — I'd have thought, being from the Soviet era, that he'd be atheist. Anyway, it occurred to me that Vasily might fear angels more than devils."

——— —— ———

Mason's apartment was similar enough to Tony's for Mike to wonder if it had been designed by the same architect.

"Was there ever a Mrs. Mason?" he asked.

"Once," Tony replied, a note of sadness to his tone. "Her story bears striking resemblance to Bond's marriage at the end of *On Her Majesty's Secret Service*, though, in Mason's case, it lasted maybe three years before she was killed by a car bomb meant for him."

Mike was making a thorough search of cupboards and drawers. He found Mason's passport in a locked desk drawer and, after a cursory look at the stamped pages, pocketed it.

By the time another ten minutes had passed, Mike decided there was nothing further to be learned from Mason's apartment.

"We should head back, in case Nigel has unearthed anything else," he said with a sigh. "I'm anxious to get after Mason. My gut tells me that, by now, he's probably somewhere in Russia."

———

Mike sat in an armchair, sipping at a goblet of O–positive, then realized he hadn't spoken with Carrie since departing Chester Basin. A glance at his watch showed him — well, it showed him that his watch was still on Atlantic Standard Time. He made a rueful smirk and pulled his iPhone from his pocket — London time was 5:35 PM, which would be 9:35 in Chester. He tried mind–linking with her, but what he got was chaotic — bright store lights, people pushing shopping carts —. He tried calling, but it went straight to voicemail. *If that glimpse I had was Walmart in Bridgewater, there'll be no cellular signal more than twenty feet inside the entrance.* Giving up, he took a moment to reset his watch, then glanced across to where Nigel still poured over the file Mike had lifted from Boronovich's file drawer.

"Oi, gov'nor — still chuggin' along over 'ere!" Nigel chirped, turning to notice Mike. His eyes had the hyper–alertness of an advanced a caffeine buzz.

Going to the kitchen alcove, Mike rewarmed his goblet of blood and noticed that the previously full coffeepot was now down to a quarter.

"Maybe you should ease up on the coffee or switch to decaf," Mike suggested, prompting a guilty grimace from Nigel.

"Busted," the Cockney joked, then added, "Bu' decaf tastes like de'idrated camel dung!"

Mike raised an eyebrow. "Much experience with camel dung?" he asked, smiling. "Try to find Colombian beans decaffeinated by the Swiss water process. You're comparison to camel dung probably means you're sensitive to the ethyl–acetate used in the standard decaffeination process."

Approaching the desk, he sipped his O+, then leaned over and picked up Brendu Petrova's USSR birth certificate. It listed her father as Anatoli Petroff. As he read the name something flashed before his mind's eye — *Mason running through trees on a hillside somewhere — someone pursuing, shooting at him. Mason drops to one knee, takes careful aim, and fires. The first shot grazes the pursuer's knee, spinning him sideways. The next shot passes through mid–thigh, dropping the man. Then Mason turns and continues his dash down the hill.*

"Take a break, eat something, then see what you can find out about her father," Mike suggested.

Nigel nodded. "I rang 'round for take–away a while back — gotta show up soon, ffough traffic can be bleedin' murder ffis time o' day."

Mike then sensed Tony's mind from the back bedroom, pondering something about Mason. He decided to warm him a goblet of O–negative. His timing was perfect. Mike exited the kitchen just in time to put the goblet in Tony's hand as he was rounding the corner from his bedroom.

"Why, thank you, Michael!" Tony said, beaming a smile. "So how's Nigel progressing with the file you gave him."

"He's on an enforced break at the moment, sending out for some food, I hope — too much caffeine.

"However, when I was reading her father's name off her real birth certificate, it triggered what might have been a vision of the past. Do you know anything about an Anatoli Petroff?"

Tony muttered the name a few times. "*I say*, I believe I've heard that name before — Mason telling me a story about some adventure or another, but that was years ago."

Just then Nigel reappeared, forking bits of cake into his mouth. "Got Chinese take–away coming, but I found ffis in 'e freezer — ffirty seconds in 'e nuker, an' it's good to go."

Mike frowned.

Nigel flashed a sheepish grin, and declared: "Oi, I need someffin' to counter ffe caffeine."

"Like a sugar rush?" Mike commented.

"Nigel," Tony suggested, "I rang up the grocer for what I thought would be several days' worth of provender. Wasn't it enough?"

"Sorry, gov'nor, but, when I ge' focused —"

"You can't tear yourself away long enough to actually cook anything?" Tony suggested, prompting another sheepish look from Nigel.

"Well, since you already have take–away presumably en route, perhaps, in the meantime, you might see what you can unearth about Anatoli Petroff, Brenda Peter's father. I know the name, and I think it relates to a story Mason told me some years back. Also, Michael seems to think it triggered a psychic glimpse of some past event."

Nigel's face took on a serious look. With a brisk nod, he returned to his desk and began a fresh search, this time hacking the MI6 database.

"And, Nigel," Tony added, "Look into coffin purchases in the past week. In fact, check airports for someone shipping a casket out of the country since Mason's disappearance."

Mike frowned, but Nigel just grinned and went to work on it.

"Coffins?" Mike inquired, recalling his own trip in a coffin. They'd anticipated Stanislaus Mihilache's goons watching the airport for his arrival. He'd travelled from Halifax International Airport to a funeral home in a casket, in the back of a hearse.

Confined, unable to move. The feelings tied to the dream he'd discussed with Myrddin flooded back.

"Mason was in a coffin —" he declared. "I felt it, emerging from the void on the day the director called."

Tony nodded. "A premonition intruding when your mind was the least distracted," he suggested.

"Myrddin said something about checking on my friends," Mike added, then, to explain, "Sometimes I can talk to him in my head."

"Back in the day," Tony elaborated, "the use of coffins was an industry trick for smuggling people out of Russia. It worked brilliantly for defecting scientists — a coffin can hold reams of research notes, as well as their disillusioned author."

"And it would work just as well for spiriting an uncooperative captive out of England and into another country," Mike mused aloud. Then, "Nigel, can you access coffin arrivals into Russia?"

"I'm on it, gov'nor."

6: *From Coffin to Cell*

Mason's first sensation was pain. It was several minutes before it receded enough for him to recognize it as a headache — *No — a migraine* — the worst migraine he'd ever had.

The after–effects of some narcotic, he decided, then remembered the hiss of gas coming into the back of his car, wondering what gas they'd used, recalling Q once assuring him that there were few reliable knockout gases. *Well, someone found one.*

Poor Robert, he thought next, as his mind replayed the scene of his driver jerking a hand to his chest, and the hand coming away covered in blood. Robert had just slumped against the car when Mason's world started to fade.

Now, as feeling began to spread to the rest of his body, he tried moving his arms to bring his hands up to his head, the center of his pain nightmare. The effort only increased his agony, but it did reveal how confined his space was — he could barely move his arms at all. There was almost no space between his arms and the smooth sides of wherever he was — he could gently flex his arms about an inch, then they came up hard against a padded wall, covered in something that felt like satin.

There was a little more room once he worked his arms up onto his abdomen and chest — maybe an extra inch or two, but that was all. He persevered until he could touch his head, but it meant pressing his elbows hard against whatever wall was in front of him.

He tried raising his head, but he only made it two or three inches before his head came in contact with more satin and padding over a hard surface. He eased his head back down — *the last thing I need, with this bally headache, is to thump onto another hard surface* — and was surprised to feel softness — *a pillow?*

Well, that was considerate. Then, *wait a minute — pillow, narrow confines, satin lining —*

He froze, refusing to give way to panic. *Stay calm. It's a casket. Okay, you're no stranger to this — we brought Kandinsky over the border into West Germany using a coffin. As long as you don't run out of oxygen, you'll be fine. Relax; discipline; control your breathing, and, above all, conserve oxygen. Ignore the nausea; there's no room to vomit in here, anyway. In fact, you may as well try to sleep.*

When he awoke next, he sensed motion and a dull muffled droning sound. The headache had receded to a dull memory. After an interval, there came a measured *hiss*. It stopped, then was repeated. Then again. He counted until he had the pattern: *Hiss* (count of three) — stop for a count of six — *hiss* for three seconds, then stop for six seconds. He followed this pattern through six or seven repetitions, then his awareness faded.

Returning consciousness brought another headache, though not as bad as the first. The sense of nausea was also less than the first time. There was a change in movement — a sensation in the pit of his stomach of descending altitude. It ended abruptly — a feeling of cushioned impact accompanied by something that reminded him of screeching tires, like in the movies. It was the roaring sound immediately after that triggered memory of these identical sensations — a jet airplane had just landed.

He must have drifted off again. This time the motion was different — more personal. *The coffin is being unloaded from the plane.* Minutes later, there was another *hiss*, a pause, then another *hiss*. This time it only made him drowsy, not unconscious. Painfully blinding light — A pinpoint of pain in his neck triggered a feeling of panic — Numbness spread out from his core, turning his arms and legs to jelly. Someone closed his eyes — His heartbeat getting slower — slower —— slower.

——— —— ———

Muffled voices — *Russian* — Platitudes, condolences? — Death of someone's uncle?

Another sharp pinprick to the neck — warmth returning — Something different — Something he heard? — Something he felt — *Heartbeat!* He could hear and feel his heartbeat! *Why do I find that so exciting?* he wondered.

The lid lowered, returning him to darkness.

More motion, being wheeled along a relatively flat surface.

——— —— ———

His eyes opened abruptly, then squeezed shut immediately — too bright a light after so much darkness. He tried to raise an arm to shield his eyes, but, while there was some movement of his fingers, the arm refused to respond.

"Hello, Mason," a female voice said, the tones musical, friendly, but with a practiced sincerity he found phony. "Welcome to Russia. You haven't been here in a while, have you? No, of course not — not since you crippled my father and left him for dead."

He tried to place the face leaning over him — brunette, wavy hair, pretty features, but the cold, cynical smile didn't reach the eyes. He judged her age as early– to mid–thirties.

It was the voice of the woman who kept calling, leaving messages. Could she also be responsible for the long silent messages?

Crippled her father and left him for dead? He couldn't even imagine who that might have been. He'd never intentionally crippled anyone in his life. Quick, clean kills had always been more his style.

"We're not sure how to repay that favour," she mused. "Perhaps we'll let Papa decide. We're on our way to see him." She punctuated this by closing the lid, plunging him into darkness once more.

———

More motion — scraping sounds, as if the casket were sliding around in — the back of a truck? It got worse, more bumpy, then he felt the casket slide until it impacted against something that banged with a hollow metallic sound, causing his body to lurch and slide inside the casket, until his head came against the padding at the upper end. More rattling and clunking, then the lid of the casket opened, and two men seized him and hauled him up, then dragged him across the bed of a pickup, over the open tailgate, then dumped him off the back to sprawl onto rocky, dusty ground.

One, with a wavy head of medium brown hair, contrasted to the other's almost shaved black buzz–cut, questioned his partner as to whether or not *that* had been necessary. Buzz–cut sneered and responded with what Mason decided might best be translated as *wimp*.

Before he could get his bearings, they had jumped down, seized him up again, and began dragging him toward the entrance of a cinderblock building, built on a foundation of mortared stones, *rather like cobblestones*. The broad steps to the entrance were of the same rounded stones as the foundation — *river stones, not quarried*, he mentally catalogued, *worn round and smooth by current erosion. So where's the river?*

One — two — three — four — counting the steps was easy; his feet dragged up and over each and every step, slid along the top until his toes collided with the next row of stones.

They paused at the doors, leaning him against one while Wavy–hair fumbled for keys in his pockets. There was a whiff of perfume — he knew the fragrance, though its name escaped him — *1971 — a female Soviet factory worker he'd been — well, it had been part of a — why is that mission coming back to me now? — The Czarina's Bouquet, that was the name of the fragrance —* He shook his head, trying to dispel the memory and clear his thoughts. The woman let out a gasp of exasperation, seized the keys from Wavy–hair, then unlocked the door, launching into a spiel of abuse in Russian about how useless the man was. *What a charming girl!* he thought.

Inside was institutional — painted cinderblock — it looked like the entry to a factory: outer waiting area in front of offices, the bulk of the factory floor dominating the rest of the building. He smelled old leather, chemicals, and a hint of — old blood? They dragged him to a large locked door. There was no fumbling with the keys this time — Buzz–cut had taken over the keys and had the key ready. He opened the heavy war–era door, revealing a stone stairway. The top steps had been mortared over to smooth them, but, step by step, as they dragged him down into darkness, the mortar became more chipped and fragmented until it disappeared entirely.

One, thump — two, thump — three, thump — it took fourteen thumps to reach the bottom. Crude lights came on — feeble bulbs in cages attached to the ceiling joists (*floor joists for the floor above*, he reminded himself, his thoughts still meandering haphazardly.) *It's got to be aftereffects of whatever narcotic they gave me.*

Czarina's Bouquet assailed his olfactory organs again — cloying flowery aroma with an underlying alcohol base. The brunette who seemed to think he had crippled her father — she passed them, casting an icy glare at the men dragging him until they stopped, allowing her to pass. Wavy–hair moved out of courtesy, but Buzz–cut gave almost a sneer of distain as she pushed by. *Does Buzz–cut know something my angelic hostess doesn't?*

She jerked her head, as if ordering the men holding him to follow her, then led the way down a dark grey hallway, past several heavy–looking doors, until they came to a particular door — the only one so far with a small barred window, more or less at eye level. Here she unlocked and opened the door, whereupon the two men dragged him inside and dumped him unceremoniously on a narrow iron–framed bed.

Chains ending in 18th century manacles hung from eyebolts mortared into the stone walls. Mason was still disoriented and confused, fighting to clear his thoughts, when Buzz–cut abruptly jerked his arms out in front of him, and Wavy–hair closed the manacles about his wrists and fastened them with padlocks.

This done, they stepped apart sideways, making it possible for the woman to approach, then stood, menacing, Buzz–cut's hand resting on the butt of his belt–holstered pistol.

The woman stepped up before Mason. She moved her left hand as if reaching for something at her right hip, then smiled a small, cold smile. Instantly the hand lashed at his face in a backhand blow, her fist closing just as it hit his cheek, splitting the skin and drawing blood.

He had just enough time to steady himself, relax his neck, and close his eyes, before the right fist drove a punch into his nose, breaking it in an explosion of blood. He forced himself to retain composure as rage surged through him. *Well, that cleared my addled head,* he thought, *though I can't say it did much for my headache — or my sinuses.*

He rattled his shackles and asked, "Could I trouble someone for a handkerchief or a tissue? I seem to be experiencing sudden sinus trouble."

The brunette laughed heartily, kicked him in the shins, then spat on him.

"There's for your sinus trouble," she declared, then, turning, she strode out, still repeating the phrase *sinus trouble* and laughing.

Wavy–hair picked up a rag from under the bed, held it to his nose, and said, "Here; blow."

From where he sat at the edge of the bed, the chains barely allowed Mason to reach his nose, but he managed to blow a fair bit of blood loose, then laid back, keeping pressure on both nostrils, and making an effort to reposition the nasal septum straight.

"Lie still," Buzz–cut commanded, jerking his legs into a bent position, and fastening manacles to his ankles the moment Mason's legs maintained the position. He then promptly cuffed Wavy–hair in the back of the head, and berated him for *mollycoddling* the prisoner.

The door slammed, deadbolts clicked into place, and Mason was left alone. He struggled to sit up, barely succeeding — partly from weakness, but mostly from the limitations imposed by the chains manacled to his ankles. The best he could manage was an angular sideways recline against the wall, his legs pulled up close. *No doubt one of Caligula's favourite positions*, he thought, comparing it to the cliché Roman recline.

He had no idea what day it was or how much time had elapsed since he'd been taken. He was weak from lack of food, thirsty in the extreme, and the state of his beard implied several days of growth.

His next task was to study the details of the room about him, taking in anything that might help with an eventual escape. The room was small and almost unfurnished. Indeed, aside from his bed — *WWII army issue, I should think* — there was little space for much else in the three–by–five–meter cell. The door looked to be about five centimeters thick — hardwood, he surmised, with bars — iron, by their look — set into a fifteen–by–twenty–centimeter aperture. He recalled noticing the inspection window as his captors were dragging him to the cell.

The only source of illumination was a single incandescent bulb mounted to a brace between ceiling joists. There wasn't even a barred window in the outer wall, assuming one of his walls was an outer wall — *No — three cinderblock walls and one stone wall. The foundation was mortared stone. The stone wall is an outer wall.* His bed was against the stone wall.

The manacles were tight — not so tight as to bruise — they were too ancient to allow for adjustment. He experimented with deforming his hand by compressing the thumb and little finger toward each other, then tried pulling his hand out of the manacle. The effort only further taxed his already drained strength. The manacle itself was of iron, about eight millimeters thick, between four and five centimeters wide, and left very little room for wrist movement. The one about his ankles was about the same.

How did they know how to size these so precisely? Did someone infiltrate my flat while I slept and measure my bloody wrists and ankles? And these bally things are antiques — why, these iron chains must be two hundred years old!

His senses reeled and a wave of nausea hit, forcing him to clench his teeth and compress his abdominal muscles. It helped — *thank God* — *if I'd vomited, they'd probably have left me enjoying the aroma of that misadventure.* He was now flat on his back, legs drawn up. His head gave a few more spins, then consciousness faded.

7: *Into the Unknown*

London, Sunday November 17

Tony was reading one of Nigel's printouts, sipping a goblet of blood.

"*I say*, Nigel, old toff, have you accessed Mason's old case files for Anatoli Petroff yet?"

"Any chance, Yer Lordship, remembers an Oleg Penkovsky?"

Dewhurst's lips moved and Mike heard him repeating the name in his mind, then Tony explained: "In 1961, Penkovsky persuaded Grenville Wynne — a section 2 spy, not *double–0* — to arrange a meeting between CIA and MI6 people in London — well, not to belabour the details, it led to passing intel on to the Yanks about Krushchev's plans for Cuban missile bases. They captured Wynne, interrogated him to find who leaked the information, but Wynne spent eighteen months in Lubyanka rather than expose Penkovsky."

He took a sip from his goblet, then focussed on Nigel, clearly waiting for him to continue.

"Well, while your pal Wynne were luxuriatin' in Lubyanka's posh accommodations, Pentovsky eventually introduced Wynne's replacement, a *double–0*, our boy Mason, to one *Anatoli Petroff*. Ffen, in

1969, Petroff decided it were time to say farewell to Muvver Russia an' 'ello to ffe decadent West. It were into 1970 when MI6 sent Mason over to fetch 'im an' escort 'im over ffe border into Finland.

"Bu', as luck would 'ave it, ffe 'ole ffing were a cock–up — Mason were never certain if Petroff chickened out or if it were all a ploy to nick *'im*. Ffey were just about to cross over in a desolate region between Russia and Finland when Petroff ups and shoots at Mason — Mason never un'erstood why. Anyway, Mason ends up pluggin' yer boy Petroff in 'e leg and gettin' away into Finland wiff little more ffan a clipped wing.

"Petroff's history gets a bit vague af'er 'at. Seems 'e Ruskies weren't too trustin' of 'is version o' ffings. Ffey ffrew 'im into a cell at Lubyanka fer a spell, ffen an even more charming accommodation called *Butyrka Prison*. Seems 'e 'ad a nasty time of it in 'ere — ffey amputated boff 'is legs — ffe why of it seems a bit dodgy — Mason reported a clean shot to one leg — Petroff collapsed — ffe dogs were closin' in, an' Mason didn' feel too keen 'bout tryin' to drag ffe bugger into Finland any more."

Mike mused: "I had a vision of Mason being chased down a wooded hillside, someone shooting at him. Mason grazed his pursuer in the knee, then shot him mid–thigh, just as your report says. Petroff was standing side–on; it's possible that the bullet went through both legs. If that were the case, and the bone damage was bad enough, or the legs went septic from rotten cloth — pieces of the clothing invariably get carried inward by the bullet — his people might have opted to amputate both legs, especially if they were upset with Petroff's handling of the assignment.

"Where was Petroff born? What city or town?"

"Um —same as 'is daughter: a cattle farm on 'e outskirts of — it's called Vyazma," Nigel read from the file on his monitor. "It's a small industrial center no' far from Moscow — leather, mos'ly, but it's a major railway 'ub, too. Anyway, e' were ffe youngest o' five, wiff four older sisters. In fact, e' KGB weren't all ffat comfortable wiff 'at for some reason.

"Psychology," Mike suggested. "Five brothers might have toughened him up; five sisters implies the opposite."

"An', comin' back to ffe great coffin query, I go' a bit o' someffin' 'ere — several coffins left London, several entered Russia, but only one left 'ere *and* entered Russia in 'e last few days, an' 'at were Saturday and Sunday — out o' Gatwick on Saturday, an' arrivin' at Sheremetyevo — *Oi!, say 'at fast ffree times, I dare ya* — Anyway, ffat's 'e airport a bit norff o' Moscow, as opposed to Domodedovo, ffe bigger international airport — some might say ffe main airport, a bit souff o' Moscow."

Mike pondered this, then mental images began to form — *Mason in a casket — Mason being removed and dragged toward an old industrial–looking building somewhere in a rural setting, though he got a sense of a more urban sprawl not far away.*

"How do I sneak into Russia, not far from Moscow?" he asked Tony.

"You? Sorry, dear boy; I'm sure you meant to say *we*. As for how *we* sneak into Russia, tourist visas with a plausible cover story has supplanted black parachutes of late. In your case, you could flash your cards about and claim to be researching ideas for your next novel — plot locales or whatever — you'd be the best judge, dear boy, of how to make that credible."

"And where does that leave you?" Mike asked, just a little amused.

"Why, *sink me*, dear boy; you know how you get when you're focused on a new piece of fiction — Why, you couldn't find your shoes without your dear Uncle

Anthony, and I shall tell them as much. Of course, you'll be expected to roll your eyes a lot and snarl under your breath." Tony concluded by beaming at Mike in the most innocent way.

Mike restrained a chuckle. Then, "My impression of Russia is that tourist visas take time and involve reams of red tape."

"Actually, gov'nor, technically you 'ave to be invited," Nigel interjected.

"Normally," Tony resumed, "one applies to one of several sanctioned agencies for the invitation, some of which are approved Russian travel agencies, but, yes, the wait can be lengthy. The best we'll get is about thirty days, though I'm hoping two weeks will be enough. After all, if we haven't found him by then —" His face took on a concerned look. "I think we'll let MI6 take care of the details. I'll call *C* in a moment. Also, if we give the appearance of staying at only one hotel instead of moving around Russia, it will attract less suspicion."

"What about firearms? Do we go in unarmed or do you have a plan for smuggling our sidearms in the luggage? I doubt Russian Border Control will be too interested in your Interpol credentials."

"Minor bother," Tony assured him. "Since you don't speak Russian, it must fall to me to compel the appropriate officials to ignore scanners and not search our bags."

"By ffe by, Michael," Nigel announced in an amused tone, "It took a bit for ffe *Examiner* to get back to ffe story, but ffey released two names today. Did you know MI6 'ad two *Double–0* agents named Pennington–Smythe an' Burkhardt, an' ffat ffey boff failed ffeir reassessments?" Nigel chuckled, then added, "O' course, ffe *Times* remains mum on 'e subject. Waitin' for ffe *Examiner* to tighten ffe noose aroun' ffeir own necks?"

Tony chuckled, then projected to Mike: *Kurt Burkhardt is a new clerk* (he pronounced it 'clark') — *not even an analyst.*

Mike grinned. "Excellent, Nigel. And now, if you'll excuse me, I'm heading up to my room for a bit — I really do need to get Carrie on the phone."

When Mike finally got through to Carrie, she was in the midst of packing, and sounded harried. He tried to explain that they were about to head to Moscow, undercover, but she uttered a quick, "Love you; gotta go — I'll text soon," and rang off.

By the time he returned downstairs, Tony was just putting his iPhone away. "That was MI6," he explained. "It's all arranged: We're booked to fly out late tomorrow night, arriving in Moscow early Tuesday morning."

—— —— ——

Domodedovo International Airport, Moscow
Tuesday, Nov. 19, 6:00 AM

"**T**he purpose of your visit to Moscow, Mr. Cameron?" The Border Control officer, who, Mike noted, spoke relatively unaccented English, was studying him. He looked to be in his late–twenties, his hair buzzed in a military style. Mike noticed a scar on one side of his head where the hair didn't seem to grow. The name tag read *P. Cherninov.*

Mike didn't hesitate. "I'm a novelist — I write fiction. I want to use Moscow and surrounding areas as a location for parts of my next book, and I need to see things first–hand to get a feel for how to describe the locale — I have a bit of an obsession for accuracy." He paused, pulled his card case from his back pocket, and fished out one of his colourful *author* business cards to give to the officer.

"You write fantasy and spy novels?" the officer asked, seeming perplexed.

"Frankly," Mike responded with an abashed grimace, "my espionage novels aren't too far–removed from fantasy. The main character is slowly becoming a vampire." He lowered his voice for the last comment, as if fearing being overheard.

"Vampires as spies? That would be something. Are your books available in Russia?" The officer was chuckling. "Most of our Western visitors these days have something to do with our upcoming Winter Olympics at Sochi. Perhaps you can work something about that into your novel."

Mike was tempted to quote J.K. Rowlings' comment: *I don't take dictation,* but opted instead for an arched eyebrow, as if intrigued by the idea. "I must admit, I've been so removed from world events and the news — focused on my writing — that Sochi and the upcoming Olympics hadn't even crossed my mind. Most of my ideas revolve around Moscow. Sochi is to the south, on the Black Sea, isn't it? I could take a look, but I'm sure, with all the final preparations, the area must be restricted.

"As for my books being available in Russia, I have no idea. You could try Amazon — I heard that they are trying to set up here. Barring that, eBooks are available from my website to anyone with a PayPal account, as well as via most eReader accounts."

The officer nodded, still studying the card, pocketed it, then leaned in to Mike, and whispered, "A friend smuggled me an iPad from Germany."

He then cast a glance at Tony, and added, "And this man is your uncle?"

Mike nodded. "On my mother's side. He helps me with peripheral and superfluous details."

The officer frowned as if puzzling through what peripheral and superficial details might entail.

Tony piped up: "When Michael sets his focus on a new book, he can't see much else. I help with mundane day–to–day trivia. He alluded to not being up-to-date with the news? Most of the time, when he's wrapped up in a new story, he can't even keep track of where he left his shoes." He grinned, which was Mike's cue to sigh and roll his eyes.

"Unfortunately, it's all too true," Mike confessed. "He also keeps me from eating all the things my doctor insists I shouldn't."

Cherninov grinned, "Perhaps you should stick to a diet of blood like a good vampire," and gave Mike a quick wink.

"You are booked at the *Radisson Slavyanskaya* for three weeks, so that's the length of your visa," the officer commented, then, frowning at something on his computer screen, asked Tony, "Have you ever been to Moscow before Mr. Dewhurst?"

"No," Tony responded slowly, pursing his lips and shaking his head. "Before I retired, my work took me to several countries in more western regions of Europe, but never to Russia, not even back when it was the heart of the Soviet Union."

"Apparently, there was an agent of MI6 with your name back in the '40s and into the '60s. There's also an Anthony Dewhurst who works with Interpol, as if the systems suggests they might be the same person."

Tony smiled almost to the point of grinning. "Good heavens, dear chap — *'40s and '60s?* — is your computer suggesting that I'm over ninety?"

Mike rounded on Tony. "MI6, Tony? Interpol? — *Really?* Have you been holding out on me? I mean, no kidding, Tony; if you know anything at all about MI6, you need to give me all the details. Can you imagine what that could do for the authenticity of my work?"

Mike seemed focused on Tony but, all the while, his peripheral vision was fixed on Cherninov.

Officer Cherninov's frown faded and he shook his head. "It must be another Anthony Dewhurst," he suggested.

"There most certainly was," Mike pointed out. "Lord Anthony Dewhurst was one of the recurring characters in the *Scarlet Pimpernel* books by Baroness Emmuska Orczy — They even made movies based on some of them."

Cherninov pondered this, then a smile curved his lips, bringing a twinkle to his eyes. *"They seek him here; they seek him there,"* he quoted in a whisper.

Mike grinned. *"Those Frenchies seek him everywhere* — You've got it. Leslie Howard played him in the old black-and-white movie, then went on to play Ashley Wilkes in *Gone With the Wind.* I love those old films."

Still smiling, the officer gave them each another glance, then — *stamp, stamp.* "Make sure you carry your papers whenever you go on excursions."

He tucked the visitor cards into their passports, then returned them, saying, "Enjoy your stay, and good luck with your new book. Maybe you can write me into your story somehow?"

Mike pulled out his iPhone, opened the *Voice Memos* app, tapped *record* and murmured: "Russian Border Services Officer: a lieutenant, perhaps? Tall, ruggedly handsome with cleft chin. Very slight slavic accent, as if educated abroad. Army influence — should have trained as a commando, maybe Spetsnaz. Research Russian Special Forces."

The official's eyes widened, he beamed, straightened his posture, adjusted his tie, then burst into a bout of hearty laughter.

"I thank you very much for the promotion," he declared but," — he tapped a shoulder epaulet — "I'm just a sergeant, and only recently a senior sergeant." The laugh faded to a chuckle, and he glanced about as if to make sure no one saw him laughing. "There are three more ranks between me and lieutenant second class." He regained composure and tried to look more stern as he beckoned to the next in line, but he did give Mike a sly wink.

Once they exited the customs control area, Mike paused and leaned against the wall, head back, eyes closed.

"I say, dear boy, are you quite alright?" Tony asked, sounding anxious.

Realizing that Tony was staring alternately at his eyes and his ears, Mike concentrated on the glamour he'd been projecting, making his eyes appear normal again, then used his fingers to brush his hair over the tips of his pointy ears, extending his glamour to those as well. He gave a quick nod. "Fine; just tired," he said after a moment. "Need nourishment and a rest."

Tony frowned. "I had no idea you weren't wearing your contacts. I'll get you out of here and to the hotel posthaste." Moments later they were on a train headed for their hotel, southwest of the center of the city.

Mike leaned against the window and turned just enough that, opening his jacket, he allowed Tony a glimpse of the shoulder holster of his Walther PPK.

Consternation showed on Tony's face. "You wore that through all the metal detectors and X-ray machines?" he hissed.

Mike blinked and made a slight nod. "I had an inexplicable concern about being caught unawares coming out of the airport, my piece still in my luggage. Of course, why I should feel so dependent on it after all I've learned and managed over the past few years, I can't fathom." He shrugged. He could see the next question forming in Tony's mind and, too weary for further speech, he projected, *X-rays, sonograms — they're all about energy. I just projected enough energy of my own to mask everything but what I wanted the sensors to see. It's exhausting work — I may have tried too hard, unsure of how much effort it would take.*

Anyway, it's done; I'm here now, and, after an infusion of O–positive and a nap, I'll be fine. I also need to get in touch with Carrie. We had a hurried chat yesterday — she was packing. She promised to text me, but hasn't. I think she's about to pack the cats and follow me — she's done that before, and with dire consequences, you'll recall.

Tony nodded in sympathy. *Perhaps you should try her now — text her if you're too weary for speech. But, really, Michael, I'm sure there's no chance of that Venice incident being repeated. After all, my dear chap, who could possibly think to target her?*

Carrie responded immediately to Mike's text with a phone call, launching into a stream of chatter that all but overwhelmed him the moment he answered. Even Kato was *yowling* in the background.

"Oi, gov'nor; 'ow's ffings on 'e ground ffere in 'e ol' former U.S.S.R.?" he heard in the background.

It took a moment for everything to sink in.

"Nigel?" he blurted, the shock shaking him out of his stupor. "Carrie, where exactly are you?"

"At Tony's apartment in London," she replied. "I gave up on trying to get you or Tony on the phone, so, right after the plane landed, I called Nigel. He gave me the address to Tony's *flat*, as he calls it, and I had the taxi bring me here. Are you really in Russia? Kato's fine but, as you can hear, he really misses you. I think even Teila misses you; I know I sure do.

"Hey, what's that noise in the background? Are you on a train?"

"It's an express line from the airport," he explained, hearing the exhaustion in his voice. He let her rattle on some more, his head resting against the window, his eyes closed, his mind already starting to wander.

"My mind feels like mush at the moment," he finally said. "I need to crash at the hotel, then we'll start exploring the surrounding area for inspiration. I need to get a feel for the locale before I can plot out my next move. Mostly, though, I'm just craving a nice warm breakfast."

He could hear Nigel in the background explaining Tony's suggestion for Mike's cover story.

Carrie went silent, then: "I'm a distraction, right now, aren't I? But I can't stay here, and I've already come too far to think of heading back home. Besides, I can help you, Michael; I've helped you before."

Mike reached out with his mind and connected with her, feeling her emotions and sensing her thoughts better than he could interpret through the phone connection. *We can hang up now and save batteries*, he projected. He read nothing but sincerity, yet her innate stubbornness was there, already brewing just under the surface.

Just stay there for bit — maybe just a few days, he replied. *You are a distraction, albeit a very nice one. I think I need to focus on the mission until I know more. So far it's been nothing but improvisation — winging it — but I need a more concrete plan. I need to get a feel for where Mason is, who has him, and why. And, frankly, I can't imagine you trying to get into Russia with two cats in a cage. I certainly don't want to run the risk of them being impounded or whatever.*

But he could already see her shaking her head. *It's not a problem, Michael. I inquired at Heathrow when I arrived. As long as you have all the paperwork — and I have a whole ream of it — it's easier to bring pets into Russia than it is into England. And, my sweet man, in case you hadn't noticed, we made it into England without one single problem.*

Mike gave a pensive nod, but quickly countered with, *what about your own visa? MI6 had to create ours. I can't see C instructing Q–branch or anyone else to come up with something. In fact, let's hope he doesn't even know your in England.*

But Carrie countered with: *Actually, Nigel already has that covered — He hacked into MI6 computers and did something, whistling and grinning the whole time.*

Mike sighed, then, *You simply must thank Nigel for me* — he made sure to sound ironic. *Okay, just give me two or three days to get a better handle on things.*

You seem exhausted, she observed. *Has anything happened?*

Just overuse of energy, he explained. *I thought I could simplify things by using Wiccan skills to fool the airport scanners. Also, I got tired of wearing my contacts, and have been using glamour to disguise my eyes. I have new respect for what Torok managed on a mass–level at that gathering at the Chateau Laurier in Ottawa four years ago — My God! Has it been that long? Anyway, it all worked, but I really need to feed and rest. Then I have to get out and see what I can reconnoitre about Mason. Tony has us booked at the Radisson Slavyanskaya, towards the western outskirts of central Moscow.*

Tony, meanwhile, was doing a search on his phone, then placed a call. Mike heard him requesting a delivery of both O–positive and O–negative to a suite at the hotel.

———

Mike came-to with a start, his eyes snapping open to find Tony sitting on the edge of the bed, leaning over him, concern in his demeanour.

"It's 9:00 AM, dear boy," he explained. "We're in a suite on the sixth floor. You made it here under your own steam, then all but passed out, much to the bell hop's consternation. When I assured him you had an extreme case of jet-lag, he just gave a sympathetic nod, and departed.

"Here; I think this is what you need — it arrived about twenty minutes ago, maybe ten minutes after we did." He held out a heavy ceramic mug. The copper–and–iron tang of the aroma triggered a reflex, extending Mike's canines.

Tony helped him sit up enough to take a generous quaff. By the third swallow, he'd rallied, and Tony stood, making room for him to achieve a sitting position at the edge of the bed. Then, taking the mug from Tony, he finished it off, holding it out for a refill.

Dewhurst smiled. "By all means, my dear chap," he assured him, then picked up an unlabeled wine bottle from the nightstand to pour another mugful.

The rooms are undoubtedly bugged, Tony projected, *so we'll be safe if we just communicate this way. If you think you might be up for an excursion during the roughly two hours we both have before our enforced resting periods, Nigel has pinpointed Mason's location for us on our GPS apps. Apparently, a few years back, it became standard SIS procedure to implant GPS micro-transmitters in all their top assets. Of course Nigel hacked the MI6 computer for the tracking info on Mason's implant, then routed the necessary particulars to both our phones. Oddly enough, despite Nigel having located the Petroff family farm just west of Vyazma, according to his implant, Mason seems to be a few kilometers west of Sheremetyevo Airport.*

Mike stood, moved a little to take stock of his balance and strength reserves, then nodded. *Another train ride?*

Tony shook his head. "What you need, dear nephew, is a car ride in the sunshine — I booked a car while you were napping — a Volkswagen Golf." *Rentals have come along way since the last time I got stuck with a post–War vintage ZiL. Anyway, it's just a bit more than forty kilometers to the airport. Mason seems to be on or near a secondary road to Vostryakovo — maybe five kilometers west of the airport.*

Mike did the mental math and said, "Let's do it."

——— ——— ———

There, across the street, at ten o'clock, Tony projected, indicating a man in a nylon jacket and baseball cap, leaning against a car. He was smoking a cigarette, and seemed committed to ignoring another man, similarly dressed, also smoking, who pretended to study a car parked on the street. Both looked in their mid– to late–thirties.

KGB? Mike asked, then corrected it to, *FSB?*

Well, the tactics are certainly old school KGB, Tony replied. *They were either KGB–trained, or the FSB never wrote their own tactics manual.*

Mike pretended to laugh, pointed to a few things, then snapped a picture of the front of the hotel with his phone. Even when they were in the car and heading out, Mike made Tony stop while he got out and took another photo.

——— ——— ———

"Well, *dash it all*, it's supposed to be here," Tony declared, clearly frustrated.

They'd arrived at the location indicated on their iPhones, but there was no sign of Mason.

Mike frowned, then went rigid, sniffing the air.

Seeing his reaction, Tony did the same. "I smell blood," he observed, "but not fresh."

Mike was already moving toward the bushes to one side of the road. Within moments he reached under a bush and extricated a tiny micro-transmitter, barely larger than a grain of rice, with one of the smallest hearing–aid batteries Mike had ever seen, all coated with dried blood.

"It seems someone was privy to MI6 procedure," he mused, holding up the tiny device. "Where would it have been located? My guess is that they cut it out, probably in a hurry, and certainly not under hospital conditions."

Tony frowned. "*Sink me!* According to Nigel, they like to insert them between the shoulder and the neck." He tapped the center of his own trapezius.

"Just under the skin?" Mike asked.

"I suppose so," Tony replied. "In Mason's case it would most likely be the right shoulder, Mason being left-handed — less irritation after the implantation."

Mike frowned, pocketed the micro-transmitter, then checked the time. "It's almost 10:00 AM," he pointed out. "If our next step is to reconnoitre the Vyazma area, it'll have to wait 'til after 2:30. Then at least we'll have more than twenty hours to work with."

Still frowning, Tony gave a reluctant nod, then tossed Mike the car keys.

"I say; would you mind driving, old man?" he asked, leaning heavily against the car door as he eased into the passenger seat. "I dare say it's all starting to catch up with *me* now."

"We'll need an exit strategy," Mike commented while driving back toward west–central Moscow. "What's the border like between here and Ukraine?"

"Sorry, old man; it's been so long, I'm sure I'm woefully out–of–date on that topic. Why Ukraine?" Tony asked.

"An old school friend of mine, whose parents were from Ukraine, spent a number of years working with a Christian Ministry group there, and did a lot of traveling back and forth as recently as last year,

including some trips to Russia for the same group —
apparently they broadcast some TV shows out of
Russia." Mike shrugged. "I guess I just got the
impression that travel between Russia and Ukraine was
pretty easy. It made me wonder about trying to slip
Mason over the border somewhere near Kharkiv or
Donetsk. Or maybe in the mountains — the hilly
region toward Belarus?"

"Ukraine's in a spot of turmoil at present," Tony
pointed out. "Their president, very pro–Russian, and
from Donetsk, which is about 60% Russian, had been
working on a deal with the EU, then suddenly backed
out, in favour of a deal with Russia. The ethnic
Ukrainians are rather upset about it, and have begun
protesting in Kiev, or Kyiv, as the Ukrainians prefer it
be named. But what about after Ukraine?"

"Romania is south of the western portion of
Ukraine," Mike replied. "I guess, having been there
before, sneaking him into Romania seems more
comfortable. Besides, Radu is there to lend a hand."

"That's one idea," Tony agreed. "There's also
Finland to the north, though that takes us past the old
capital at St. Petersburg. We could even consider the
longer route through Estonia to Latvia, then Lithuania,
and into Poland. I'd think twice about Ukraine, though.
I don't know when your friend was last there, but
they're planning a major antigovernment protest for
Kyiv's Maidan Square, aiming for November 21st.

"Coming back to Mason and getting him out: it's
too bad we don't have a passport for him..."

Mike smiled. Reaching to an inside pocket of his
jacket, he pulled out Mason's passport and showed it to
Tony. "I took the liberty of lifting it from his desk
drawer — small locks like that are a cinch to
manipulate after getting used to heavy door locks."

Mike drove fast, arriving back at the hotel by
10:30, just in time to race in a blur up to the suite.

8: An Old Adversary

Mason awoke to lethargy and confusion. The pain in his head had subsided, but he was even more weak from what he could only assume was low blood sugar, having no idea how long it had been since his last meal.

There was a mix of pain and itch above his right shoulder, between the shoulder and neck. Reaching his left hand to the area allowed him to feel something under his shirt, stuck to the skin atop the trapezius.

Feels like a bandage of some sort, he mused, *but why —?* It took a few more seconds for the dull ache to trigger the memory of someone from Q–Branch inserting a GPS micro-transmitter under the skin in that area, back in the mid–1990s. *I guess MI6 won't be tracking me this trip*, he decided.

He checked his shackles once more, hoping there might be a way to pick the locks, then checked his pockets. *When you're the supervisor for double–0s,* he mused, *I guess that reduces the odds of carrying stray paperclips. And judging from the size of the iron eyebolts to which these chains are attached, they'll be set too deep into the masonry to be pulled out by anything less than heavy machinery.* In fact, a glance at where the shaft of an eyebolt entered the mortar, gave the impression that the bolt holes had been drilled, then filled with fresh cement before inserting each eyebolt.

There was an odd sound in the hall outside his cell, then the rattling of a key in the lock. The door swung inward, and a man wheeled a wheelchair through the doorway, turning to push the door shut before wheeling the chair back around to face Mason.

He was heavyset, slovenly, and in need of a shave. The hands manipulating the wheels of the chair were large — the broad hands of someone who'd grown up used to manual labour. Both legs had been amputated, leaving six to eight inches of stump to each leg, and the legs of his trousers were pinned to close off the ends. The arms were long enough to imply that, with intact legs, he might have been a shade taller than Mason's 5'–11". He looked vaguely familiar — maybe fifteen years older than Mason. He glared at Mason, his expression conveying anger and resentment. Then, quite suddenly, a sly smile formed. The smile seemed to take a few years off the man's face, though the lines were still there. It was the slyness of the expression that helped trigger recognition. Without it, he doubted he'd ever have been able to place this man who, while just two or three years younger than Mason (he now realized), looked closer to eighty.

Petroff — Anatoli Petroff. Mason stared in amazement. It all began to make sense: *Brenda Peters — she would have been born Brenda Petrova. 'Welcome to Russia. You haven't been here in a while, have you? No, of course not; not since you crippled my father and left him for dead.'*

"Anatoli Petroff," Mason pronounced. "Brenda Peters is your daughter."

"Brendu Petrova," Petroff corrected.

Mason nodded. "So how did you end up in the wheelchair? I shot you in the leg — remember, you were shooting at me —. And why was that, anyway?"

"I was trying to bring you down to take you back to Moscow. I decided that I couldn't face the thought of leaving. The KGB might not have paid much attention to me, but would MI6 be any better? Besides, you were already showing up on our radar, as the Americans used to say. If I brought you in, it would have brought me to the attention of my superiors."

"Petroff, I shot you in the leg — in *one* leg," Mason argued calmly. "How could that have crippled you?" His frown turned to a gape of amazement as Petroff exploded in a tirade.

"Because your bullet went though both my legs!" Petroff bellowed at him, then, with more of a snarl through clenched teeth: *"It took me more than a week to crawl to where I could find help. And, before I even reached St. Petersburg, I found a SMERSH team waiting for me."* As he continued, his voice escalated once more. *"I spent a year in Lubyanka — They not only wouldn't repair my legs, but they tortured me by repeatedly—"*

He stopped and took several deep breaths, seemingly in an effort to regain composure. When he continued, his tone was more even, but still fierce, icy.

"They took the left leg first. It seems that big artery in my thigh was severed — I'd tied that leg off with a tourniquet — apparently too tight. They weren't clear whether it was your bullet or the shrapnel it made of the thigh bone as it blasted its way through. So much for bragging about the superiority of Soviet medicine!

"Then, during my two years at Butyrka, it was too late to save the other leg," he hissed. "A doctor at Lubyanka had removed your bullet — it had lodged in the right thigh bone. He did some suturing, but nothing more," Petroff growled, then, "I guess he missed the pieces of trouser leg that went into each leg with the bullet. Then the festering began — the rot..." By now he was hyperventilating, a look of madness in his eyes.

As his breathing slowed to normal, he looked on Mason with less rage, more vindictive stare, but Mason could tell that the madness was there, just under the surface.

"They decided that you'd turned me — made me a double–agent," he continued in a raspy tone, not much more than a whisper. "No matter what I told them, they wouldn't listen. They insisted that I'd been trying to defect and lost my nerve, forcing you to shoot me." He huffed an ironic laugh. "They couldn't even hear how they contradicted themselves."

Mason frowned. "Anatoli, that *is* what happened, except that you were the first to shoot. Why can't you just admit that you —?"

Before he could finish, Petroff went into another snarling rage. He pulled a handgun. *Tokarev, .22– calibre, an assassin's weapon,* his mind couldn't help but process. In the confines of the room, the roar seemed deafening — huge sound from such a little gun. Fire burned through Mason's left thigh — fire and the feeling that something in there had somehow exploded. Mason grunted in pain and shock, clenching his jaws to keep from crying out. He'd be damned if he'd give Petroff the satisfaction.

But, while he struggled to retain composure, Petroff wheeled his chair more to Mason's right, came in closer, took aim, and shot him in the other thigh. This time, though, it didn't catch him by surprise, and he was able to hold his breath and keep his jaws clenched. He experienced once more the feeling of a small explosion inside his leg. The ache in each leg felt bone–deep. Feeling the opposite side gave no indication of an exit wound on either leg. *So Petroff's warped sense of justice requires that I experience a bullet through each femur, just as he did.*

"Any chance of some form of pressure bandage?" Mason asked. It took all his willpower to maintain his typical British stiff–upper–lip attitude. "It'd be a bloody shame if I were to bleed out before having an opportunity to starve to death."

Petroff's smile was vindictive. "You know, I wondered that very same thing during my first week in Lubyanka," he said. "They started to bring some disgusting form of gruel during the second week. Butyrka's food, by comparison, bordered on fine dining."

He blew at the end of the still–smoking barrel of the Tokarev, then, with that same perverse smile, probed the wound in Mason's right leg with a thumb, as if hoping to locate the bullet and push it deeper. Then, turning his wheelchair about, he rolled toward the door. After opening it, he paused just long enough to glance back and add, "Who knows? Maybe I can arrange a bit of cold gruel for you sometime tomorrow — maybe swill — How do you feel about swill?"

Once more the sly smile leered from his unshaven face, then he began an almost maniacal chuckle as he he departed, closing the door after he was through.

Alone in the cell, Mason did what he could to examine each wound, starting with the left. Blood was still flowing, but not the unstoppable flood associated with a severed femoral artery. Further examination showed the same with the right leg. He kicked off his shoes, then managed, with much struggle, to tear his trouser leg, starting at the small hole left by the bullet.

There'll be fabric in the wound, he mused. *Nothing for it, old man*; he thought, forcing himself to remain stoically calm, *it's not as if there's a surgical nurse at your disposal. What made Petroff's other leg fester was wool fabric rotting in the wound — Russian wool —.*

He looked closely at the cloth of his trousers, then sighed in relief — the fabric was polyester/nylon, promoted for never requiring ironing. *At least the fabric bits won't rot in the wound, though I can't imagine they'd do me much good hanging about inside the wound track.*

It took perseverance, but he stubbornly persisted until he tore the resistant fabric all the way around his leg, then slid it down and off. Tearing it lengthwise was easier. Soon he had two strips, each long enough to encompass his thigh. He tied off the left leg first, then proceeded to examine the right.

He'd been tired before. Now, with blood–loss and shock from two bullet wounds, he could barely tear the second trouser leg at all. He settled for tearing an opening large enough to examine the wound.

The level of bleeding was about the same as for the other wound, yet something felt different — a bit more painful deeper in. He reviewed his memory of the two gunshots, surprised that his recollection of the first shot was as good as it was. MI6 had trained him to observe, even under duress. The shot to the right leg was more deliberate, more studied, more likely a direct hit. He had no idea of the calibre of Petroff's marksmanship; he'd been more interested in his spy–craft and knowledge base.

His vision was starting to blur, his focus drifting. He settled for folding the torn section of trouser leg inward, away from the wound, and tying the second strip of fabric about his right thigh outside the trouser leg. Collapsing back on the bed, he felt the world spinning away from him.

———————

When Mason awoke again, a fog clouded his thoughts and made the least movement seem nigh onto impossible. It seemed to last for hours. Finally, after what seemed a frustratingly long time, he managed to struggle onto his back. Moving his arms was exhausting.

Imagine that! he joked to himself. *I actually turned onto my side and moved my arm!* As he explored his left thigh, he noticed the improvised bandage was caked with dried blood. As gingerly as he could, he loosened the knot, then slid his fingers between the bandage and his leg, shifting along in tiny increments, in an effort to separate the bandage from his wound. He tried using saliva to wet his fingers, but he had almost no spit at all. Still, after what seemed an exhausting effort, he managed to expose the wound.

As near as he could tell in the poorly lit room, the wound showed so sign of infection, and no desire to continue bleeding.

And it doesn't stink; that's got to be a good sign, he mused, recalling a time he'd rescued a senior British SAS officer from the IRA. That one had a bullet wound in the upper arm, near the shoulder, that had become infected, and smelled like something had crawled into the wound and died. By the time Mason got the major to Larne, north of Belfast, and the boat that would take them to Scotland, the stench was almost unbearable. The arm had to be amputated almost as soon as Mason got him to medical care at Carlisle, before both could be flown back to London.

Mason lay still, eyes closed, fighting to remain awake. He'd gotten the bandage retied, careful not to make it too tight, but knew he was drifting back toward unconsciousness. He continued to remain motionless, hoping to recover some energy.

If I keep on like this, I'll be dead soon. No — banish such thoughts, you blighter. You're Mason of MI6 — must trudge on for Queen and Country! This last thought brought a feeble chuckle out of him. *Stiff upper lip, my arse! Stiff upper leg, maybe — stiff upper legs, make that!* The chuckle continued until it was almost a laugh, then faded.

Opening his leaden eyelids seemed to require almost a heroic effort. *Time — What's the time?* Another heroic effort brought his arm close enough to note his lack of wristwatch. *Did I know that?* he asked himself. *When did they take my watch?* He tried to remember when he'd last looked at it. The answers that came were ludicrous — in the club a week or two ago — in the office when they first brought him the new field assessment reports — no, as he finished with the last report. *Oh, give it up, old man — your bloody watch is gone. No bloody wonder — it was a Rolex Mariner. God only knows what these villains will get for it on the black market — probably not a fraction of what it's worth.*

He shifted onto his back and collapsed.

Sometime after that, there was a rattling of the door lock, the door opened, and Wavy–hair appeared, gave a curt nod, and tossed a bottled water, landing it on the bed, just inches from him.

Mason picked it up, removed the cap, and tried to mutter a coherent, *"Spacibo,"* but the door was already closing. Reminding himself not to drink to quickly, lest his unused stomach reject it, he sipped just enough to wet his mouth, then swallowed carefully, making a point of doing even that small chore in two increments. He then waited what might have been another minute before trying again with a slightly larger amount. *Woah; that was almost two tablespoons,* he joked to himself. *If you don't get yourself under control soon, you'll be gulping entire mouthfuls!* He smiled at his brave attempt at gallows humour, recapping the bottle after drinking about a third, careful to lay it where he could easily find it.

His head felt clearer, his mind a little sharper. Still, the water had done little to restore his strength. *Need food for that,* he reminded himself, — *even if it's swill.* He doubted Petroff would come up with swill. What little he'd seen of the place upon arrival had conveyed the idea of some kind of cattle processing facility — there'd been a lingering smell of cows and cowhide, but no smell of pigs. *Mind you, Petroff might go to great lengths to be demoralizing. The bastard wants revenge — revenge for his failure, his cowardice, and a host of other shortcomings. Funny how weak–minded, narcissistic blackguards can restructure the reality of their past so easily, blaming everything on someone else, then rant about what the world owes them.*

9: Vyazma

Mike came out of oblivion as he almost always did: alert and raring to go. He bolted upright, and checked his watch — 2:20 PM — *about usual*, he observed to himself. He'd removed only his jacket, draping it over the back of a chair, leaving his shoulder holster on. Out of habit, he checked the small of his back for his *sgian dubh*, then remembered he'd chosen to forego all that this mission.

Out in the living room, he picked up his iPad, was about to activate FaceTime, then remembered Tony warning that the rooms would be bugged. *Tony, and certainly Nigel will know more about finding bugs than I, but Tony's still out of it, and discussing this with Nigel in a bugged suite makes about as much sense as planning a bank robbery at a police station. Come on, think — they use batteries, hearing aid batteries, NiMH? Lithium-Ion? And there'll be a micro-transmitter.* He smiled, reached out with his senses, expecting a static sound, and in no time at all he'd located two in the living room, two in each of the two bedrooms, even one in the bathroom. *Focus, find the frequency ranges, match it with a massive chi burst, and — overload.* He projected a burst of energy, sensed an abrupt end to the static sound, smiled, then sat down as a wave of dizziness overtook him. *No problem; just warm some blood and feed.*

He was halfway through his first half–mug when Nigel's face appeared on his iPad screen — he seemed engaged in trying to clean or dry a large cast iron skillet. Mike couldn't help but smile at the Cockney's antics with the heavy implement.

"Anything new, Nigel?" he asked, waiting while Nigel set the skillet aside, then disappeared offscreen.

"Oi, yeah," he declared enthusiastically from somewhere offscreen, then reappeared and set down a plate with what looked like a toasted bacon sandwich, dripping with ketchup.

"Ffe proverbial *Two Bob Bit* 'as 'it ffe bleedin' fan," he continued, chuckling. "*Former MI6 Double–0 Agent Proves Traitor!*" he quoted, "An ffat's just ffe 'eadline. Ffe story identifies our missing Mason, claimin' as 'ow 'e delivered a top–secret file to a Russian agent, ffen took off, 'ightailin' it for parts unknown. Ffey don' splain 'ow a senior reporter o' ffe *London Daily Examiner* go' 'is mitts on said file, jus' ffat ffey plan to release jus' a sample o' ffe juicy bits in tomorrow's edition. Ffey did release ol' Pennington–Smythe's name — Imagine ffat! Mason gets labeled a bleedin' traitor if 'e passed on ffe name, bu' ffe bleedin' *Examiner* is an 'ero for printin' it on page four an' announcin' it to ffe bleedin' public? *Bollox!*

"Anyway, I also go' a bit more on 'e two blokes what made ffe trip wiff Brenda Peters an' ffe coffin: Pietro Androvich an' Leon Koslov. Leon is a Spetsnaz reject — insubordination and just plain mean, from 'e amount o' time 'e spent in 'e klink, but ffat didn't keep 'im outta ffe bleedin' FSB — I ffink 'e's jus' a private — no' much more 'n an 'ired ffug.

"Pietro Androvich, on 'e ovver 'and 'ad ffe required term in 'e Russian army, ffen mustered out 'n' went back to bein' a baker's 'elper." Nigel shrugged.

"Ffe only property associated wiff Petroff is 'at ol' cow 'ide place to ffe sou'west o' you. In fact, I'm findin' 'ints 'at ffe ratbag bastard might o' killed 'is own parents sometime after joinin' ffe KGB."

Mike frowned. "Hints? What sort of hints?" Then, gesturing to the sandwich on the desk, said, "Don't let me keep you from your lunch."

Nigel's face brightened. "Ffank you, gov'nor!" he chirped, then attacked his awaiting sandwich, eyes bright with anticipation. Mike suppressed a smile, then warmed a second half–mug of his own breakfast.

"Well," Nigel resumed, then proceeded with an incoherent dissertation, his usually crippled diction muffled by a mouthful of sandwich.

"Why don't you take a moment to chew and swallow that before continuing," Mike suggested.

"Yeah; right–you–are, gov'nor," Nigel agreed once he'd swallowed at least half of the mouthful. "well, as I were tryin' to say, seems 'is folks — well, 'is mum more ffan 'is dad, got linked to some kind o' dissident movement. It's no' clear 'ow or wha' it were abou', bu' ol' Petroff took it upon himself to sort it out. An' 'at were 'is first time on 'e carpet wiff 'is bosses. Ffey only wanted Petroff to observe 'em an' identify ffe leaders. Well, Petroff jumped ffe gun, eliminated ffe leaders, ffen executed boff 'is parents! All I can get from a seriously redacted file — an I'm serious, Michael, ffere's more blackout ffan words to ffis ffing — is a reference to Petroff bein' —" he paused to read from the computer screen — "more concerned wiff 'is own embarrassment–by–association' ffan wiff ffe good o' ffe state, an 'e word *narcissism* did get used."

"You said he executed his parents. How?" Mike asked. He returned his ceramic mug to the microwave, heated it for two minutes, then poured a third helping of blood, waiting a few moments for it to absorb heat from the mug.

"Ffeir skeletal remains were found in a burned out shed on ffe edge of ffe property, each wiff a nice, neat bullet 'ole ffrough 'e back o' ffe skull. *An'* according to records, 'e were *constantly* tryin' to get assigned to ffe KGB's *bodyguard* unit — assassins. FFat's why 'e likes 'e .22 Tokarev so much."

Mike nodded, musing: "A .22 slug will pass through the skull at close range, but ricochet off the inside, unable to get out, destroying the brain as it bounces around." He took a sip from his mug, decided it was warm enough, then asked, "When was this?"

Nigel consulted an adjacent screen. "Early in 1970, possibly righ' after New Year's," he supplied. "It were in 'e followin' March when 'e 'ad whot you might call 'is *episode* wiff Mason."

Mike nodded. "So the ploy with Mason was an attempt to get back into his superiors' good graces, assuming he'd ever been there. And all this happened, including the amputation of his legs, before he managed to father his daughter."

Just then, Tony entered, passing behind Mike, giving him a pat on the shoulder as greeting, then proceeding to heat a mug for himself.

"Oi, Yer Lordship; top o' ffe afternoon to ye," Nigel greeted.

Tony just smiled. "Yes; Hello — I'm sorry, Nigel; by all means, carry on. I was hoping to not interrupt. From the look on your face, you were about to say something in reference to Michael's comment about Petroff fathering his daughter after the amputation of his legs — certainly no great hardship. After the major conflicts of the century just concluded, scads of war veterans returned home legless to father families."

"*But*," Nigel countered, "in 'e case of our man Petroff, ffere seems some doubt — at least according to medical records referring to loss of — well, let's just say ffere were some problems makin' 'e pipe 'ard after gettin' 'is legs whacked. *And*, Brendu Petrova were raised by 'er dad an' ffe youngest of 'is sisters. An', I foun' a notation by some bloke — wai' a mo' —" He scrolled down through pages on the adjacent monitor unit until he found what he sought "— Two bodies were found no' too far from Petroff's former flat in a poor Moscow suburb, also shot execution–style, jus' like Petroff's poor mum n' dad. One bloke in particular — a toff named Illya Markovich — ffought ffey were Petroff's wife an' a bloke 'e fancied was 'er lover."

Tony's brow furrowed. "I knew Illya Markovich," he mused. "As an analyst, he was not only thorough, but, I dare say, rather insightful. If he surmised that Petroff's wife was seeking her comforts elsewhere, then, no doubt, he had good reason. Either way, it doesn't paint a glowing portrait of Anatoli Petroff. And, in light of her role in our current investigations, Brenda can't possibly know about the truth of her parentage or her mother's death."

"Considering the dedication she put into going after Mason, there's no way she sees her father as anything but a victim," Mike agreed. "So Petroff killed both his parents, because they were connected to a dissident movement — professionally embarrassing to Petroff — then did the same with his wife and her lover. I see a pattern here — Petroff is a narcissist, Tony. It also explains his current outlandish plan: He sees everything in life as a personal affront.

"Remember Stavros Soutzos from our first mission together? His jealousy of you drove him to elaborate lengths in concocting that complicated scenario."

He set down his empty mug, then asked, "How soon can you be ready to roll, Tony? We've got about twenty–one hours — more than enough time to drive to Vyazma and reconnoiter."

Their two chain–smoking shadows were in suits today. Mike went into their heads and compelled them to study the upper windows of the hotel instead of watching them.

It proved a 210 kilometer drive from the hotel to the outskirts of Vyazma; it took more than twenty kilometers to escape Moscow's sprawling environs. Mike found himself comparing Moscow to Halifax and Toronto, though he decided Toronto was more relevant — an urban sprawl that had overgrown its boundaries, eating up adjacent suburbs in its need to expand. An inner beltway encircled the city's denser *inner city* to a radius of roughly ten kilometers from the center. But the outer twelve–to–thirteen–kilometer band beyond this mixed urban and industrial with splashes of rural, almost as if the city was clinging to itself, reluctant to let go. It wasn't until after the MKAD, a second beltway confining this last quasi-circular band at 20–23 km from the heart of Moscow, that the view on each side of *Minskoye Shosse*, the E30, finally looked rural. Even then, the patches of farmland were occasionally forced to give way to random suburbs and what looked like industrial parks. Just past the exit to Yeremino, Mike began to hope that they might at long last have escaped the clutches of the Greater Moscow Metropolitan Area.

I swear cities are all the same, he thought. *It's just like Halifax: even when you think you're done with it and finally on the way to the South Shore, you still have the lingering industrial and urban sprawls of Bayer's Lake and Chain Lake Industrial Parks.*

"Despite your roots of growing up in Sydney, then moving to Dartmouth, you really aren't a city boy at heart, are you, dear boy?" Tony commented, offering a sympathetic smile.

Mike frowned. "You read my thoughts just then?"

"I dare say, you were rather loud with your mental assessment," Tony explained with a chuckle.

By six o'clock they were seeing increasingly industrial–looking buildings — the outskirts of Vyazma. Mike found an exit road that took them through the western edges of the town, then continued southwest, to connect with the P134, which would take them to the property Nigel had pinpointed.

The rural nature of the scenery had increased dramatically. In fact, the countryside looked almost desolate — once green grassland was now yellow, turning to brown. Even the trees seemed unhealthy, almost defoliated, making Mike frown. *They've ravaged the soil and not replenished the nutrients?*

"There should be a road turning off to your right just around this turn," Tony advised.

Sure enough, an unpaved road did exit just where Tony had predicted. This, too, was lined with trees that looked to be dying, their yellowed foliage either still clinging to withered branches or having already fallen to the almost barren ground.

After driving another fifteen minutes, they encountered a roadblock.

Mike got out of the car slowly, sizing up the two men manning the sawhorse–style barrier, illuminated by the VW's headlights. Both were armed with what he categorized as some form of modified AK-47, and their eyes had the hardened, steely, disciplined look of military or ex–military. Their eyes were all he could see through the ski–mask–like balaclavas. Hands raised and offering a tentative smile, he approached slowly.

"Do either of you speak English?" he asked, then, "*Parlez–vous français?*" Their blank stares remained unmoving, even after his feeble attempt with his extremely limited German.

Then he heard the sound of the passenger door opening, and Tony joined him, rattling off a stream of

Russian at the two men. One continued to fix his blank stare on them, but the other voiced what sounded like an abrupt and concise reply.

Tony continued to speak. Now it was two blank stares, causing Tony to frown. Then, with a shrug, he turned and commented *soto–voce* to Mike, "Seems the road is closed. He also added something vague about a gas leak, but I think it's all a sham. What do you want to do, Michael?"

Mike glanced about. Through the barren trees, his vampire eyes made out hints of distant buildings. "Plenty of trees to obscure secured bodies," he observed. "I'll take *Happy*, there to the right." *Happy* was the more burly of the two, and certainly the more surly, since he'd not voiced so much as a syllable.

In a blur, Mike was behind the man, pinioning both arms with his right arm, his unrelenting pressure across the man's elbows forcing a mild paralysis into the hands, while his left hand encompassed a pincer grip on the throat that suppressed the carotid arteries. He held it patiently. Almost immediately the hands released their grip on the Kalashnikov, but it took two minutes before the man went limp.

Tony had opted for cold–cocking his man to the side of the head with his Walther.

Mike dragged his man into the trees until he was a dozen feet in from the road, propped him against the bole of the tree, tore off the balaclava, then pulled a pair of heavy zip–ties from a utility pocket in the leg of the soldier's combat fatigues.

"*I say, old man*, with the thickness of the trunk and the girth of these chaps' biceps, neither man's arms are going to reach around any of these trees," Tony pointed out, but Mike was already removing his man's belt.

He zip–tied one wrist to the belt, brought that arm around the bole of the tree, then zip–tied the other wrist to the belt before pulling on the belt and buckling it at the last notch. When the prisoner regained consciousness, the most he would be able to manage was about four inches of slack between his back and the bark of the tree. Two rolling hitches took care of the remaining tail of the belt.

"Brilliant," Tony commented.

Mike positioned Tony's man against the next tree, and secured him in the same manner, making sure that neither man could reach either of the belt buckles, even if he managed to undo the rolling hitches. He was ready to leave when he thought better of it and, squatting again before his man, began slapping him on the cheek until his eyelids fluttered, then opened.

"Ask him about Petroff," Mike said to Tony. The moment Dewhurst acquiesced, Mike steeled himself to the effort, and pushed into the man's head, forcing him to respond. The result was a lengthy stream of Russian. Whenever the man stopped or hesitated, Mike generated visions of flame and resumed squeezing. Soon the once taciturn thug was gibbering in fear, his eyes awash with tears.

"Odd," Tony mused, "They're road security for a drug–dealer — crystal–methamphetamine — though, from the way he regards their boss, and their own military bearing, he seems more like a commanding officer. I think they're both FSB, though they seem highly reluctant to discuss it."

Mike focused, made the flames rage, and squeezed harder.

"Yes; he's FSB," Tony asserted. "In fact, despite the lack of insignias, they're both sergeants. Their boss seems to be an unnamed general. As to methamphetamine, I would have thought some form of opiate more likely, with the easy access to poppies."

"What about Petroff?" Mike asked, but Tony shrugged. Mike persisted: "He knew the name — I could see it in his eyes."

Tony asked again, then shrugged. "You're right. He does seem to know of Petroff, but he insists that Petroff isn't part of the narcotics operation, and isn't at any of the properties reached by this road."

"We'll see about that," Mike commented. He took a moment to resume carotid pressure until the man lapsed into unconsciousness once more, then began arousing the other prisoner, but interrogation of this one brought no different results.

He passed one of the automatic weapons to Tony. "What do you make of this? It looks like an AK, but it's not like any AK–47 I've ever seen."

Tony looked at it, pulled the curved magazine, and examined a bullet before returning it to the magazine and reinstalling the magazine. He located a release button where the stock joined the weapon, pressed it, and demonstrated how the stock could be folded out of the way, looking as if it had been removed, "It's an AK–103; they came out in 1994. The army replaced all their AK–47s with 74s, but, as far as I know, these are pretty much limited to Special Forces and the FSB. They also have an AK–105 now." He passed it back to Mike.

"So, these guys and the two clowns outside our hotel are the successors to the KGB?" Mike queried.

"As Nigel implied, dear boy," Tony replied, "the FSB *are* the KGB. Putin even controls major corporations like Gazprom, through exKGB colleagues that he's installed at their helms."

Mike let out a whistle. "No wonder the Russians came up with the term *Kleptocrat*. It fits."

Returning to the road, Mike pivoted the barrier to one side, then moved the car beyond it, pausing just long enough to return the barricade to position. A glance toward the trees showed no evidence of the secured men.

They got back in the car, and Mike continued driving, until, at a fork in the road, Tony instructed: "Take the right." Tony was studying the GPS app on his iPhone. "We're less than a kilometer away."

Moments later, Mike pulled the car off into what appeared to be a long–deserted cattle farm, frowning even before he stopped the car.

"He's not here," he commented, then exited the vehicle.

"There's no one here," Tony agreed; "and I don't think there has been for quite some time."

Mike studied the ground, all senses questing for traces about him, as he walked toward the largest building. "Someone was here more than a week ago," he pointed out. "Look here — wheelchair marks in the dirt. I don't think they were here for very long." He went to the nearest door, and found it weakened by dry–rot, its hinges severely rusted. Even the framing of the structure looked sagged. "It wouldn't take too much of a storm to finish off this place," he observed.

"But why leave those two thugs back there?" Tony asked. "As a diversionary ploy, it seems useless. It would have made sense if the drug lab had been here, but, since it obviously isn't..."

Mike shrugged. "They're someone's stooges. Who knows? — Maybe our meth dealer is cooking up his product in the next farm complex, like that one over there." He gestured to a similar distant property.

Tony shrugged. "It's dark, and will be getting cold soon. I dare say it might even snow tonight. Should we free those thugs back there?"

Mike shook his head. "Not yet. I think I want to press on and check out that place." He gestured to the barely visible set of buildings. "Something is nagging at me to keep going along this road."

"After confiscating or at least disabling their weapons?" Tony suggested.

Mike nodded and gave a brief half smile. "One of Sun Tzu's rules: Never advance with an armed enemy at your back."

It took another fifteen minutes to reach the next property. The gate was closed and manned by two more armed guards, powerful flashlights mounted on their weapons.

"I can smell the iodine and acetone from here," Mike observed, then blurred into motion, vaulted the gate, and struck his man with a series of punches, culminating in a *shuto* to the occipital region. He snatched the AK–103 away from the unconscious man as he was collapsing to the ground.

"I'm afraid this one had better reflexes than your chap," Tony commented. "Either that or I'm a lot slower than I used to be. I had to break his neck — he was trying to shoot you."

"I appreciate that," Mike thanked him. "Healing during sleep doesn't fix bullet holes in clothing. And, Tony, I haven't seen any evidence of you slowing."

Mike restrained his victim and secured him behind a small outbuilding, then, picked up the AK–103 from the dead guard and tossed it to Tony. A quick movement made sure Mike's weapon was cocked and ready.

"Shall we?" Tony asked, gesturing toward the buildings before them. Mike nodded, then blurred forward until he was at the door to the facility.

He paused, focusing his senses on the door mechanisms, realized the door was locked from the inside, then manipulated the lock until it was opened. The interior was dimly lit — Mike had a memory flash of a similar, though smaller, operation in Halifax from years before. This place reeked of volatile fumes just as the other had. *It's a shame I didn't bring a flare gun*, he thought. *Why must these parasite always seek to live of the exploitation of people's weaknesses? They're no different than the vampires I end up destroying.* He shook his head, dispelling the distraction. All villains were predators, from schoolyard bullies to drug dealers to ripper vampires. Ultimately it was a form of laziness — it's easier to take than to work.

Before him were maybe a dozen or more workers in lab coats, processing crystal–meth. Ignoring these, Mike moved quickly and silently toward the back, where, similar to the place in Halifax, there was a two–storey section with a gallery overlooking the work area. He knew there had to be stairs somewhere but, rather than waste time looking, he launched himself upward, clearing the rail to land in a crouch.

He straightened, then flattened against the wall next to a window. A cursory glance into the office revealed three men with shoulder holsters, seated at desks and going over paperwork. A fourth paced near the back, smoking a cigarette, and staring at a page in his hand, muttering in Russian. He couldn't understand the language, but he could read the ruthlessness in the man's soul. All had the hardened look of men who were experienced in taking life.

Reaching out with his senses, he found no others, just this group. Tony was circling the lower level. Mike hung the Kalashnikov on his shoulder by its strap, drew his PPK, and attached the suppressor. Fifteen feet further along, in a narrow corridor between offices, he found doors. Trying the relevant knob, he found it locked, and used his Wicca talents to silently move the tumblers. PPK at his side, he opened the door and stepped inside.

He had qualms about killing such men, even though their activities might justify it, so he allowed them the first move, and shifted his PPK toward the back of his leg, out of view of the men. The three seated men kicked their chairs back, got to their feet, and drew their pistols, firing the moment they saw him.

The one at the back was slower, no doubt enthralled by what he was reading.

Mike blurred to the left, evading the hail of bullets from three Makarovs — each of the three seemed on the way to emptying his clip in an effort to drop Mike. He raised his PPK. Three spitting noises — Three neat holes dead center of three foreheads.

As the corpses dropped to the floor, number four at the back finally looked up, his expression one of annoyance. A fierce gleam came to his eyes, then they narrowed in what Mike decided must be a mix of frustration and rage. There was no fear. In fact, what he sensed from the man was a form of ruthless entitlement — the kind of attitude that makes certain movie thugs say, "Do you have any idea who I am?"

Mike let a hint of a smile flicker about his lips as he tucked the Walther into his belt. The man grinned, pulled his Makarov, aimed it at Mike, and, with a short speech in Russian, fired a single shot — a shot that missed when Mike blurred to the left.

This time the man took a two-handed grip, steadied his aim — Mike saw in his mind how he was preparing for another dodge to the left. He fired four shots, tracking a fraction more to the left with each. Mike blurred right, then fired a single shot, also dead–center of the forehead.

He took a moment to check on Tony, who had the workers downstairs covered with his Kalashnikov, then he walked over to his last victim and removed the paper from his hand. It was in Cyrillic, unintelligible to Mike, but, knowing Tony would be able to read it, he folded and pocketed it. A cursory search of the office revealed nothing of particular interest to him.

"I'll be down in a moment," he called from the rail, then checked the other offices. The one at the back was the neatest and most impressive, clearly that of the boss. In a desk he found and pocketed an old address book. The computer offered nothing that caught his attention or interest — just a lot of files related to methamphetamines and opiates. Then he found a folder of files related to MI6 and the KGB, with one file simply entitled *Mason* and another labeled *Petroff.*

Accessing the mail app, he created an eMail to Nigel, headed "From *Samurai*," attached the folder, and sent it. He then tore open the tower casing, extracted the hard drive, and pocketed it.

He was about to leave when a photo on the wall caught his eye: a stern–looking middle-aged man, wearing the muddy green military uniform of the former USSR. He was shaking hands with a man in a dark suit, whom Mike recognized as Leonid Brezhnev, a former Chairman of the Presidium. Beneath this was a framed clipping from *Pravda*, showing the same officer, and naming him General Nikolai Alexei Kemedov, KGB.

A table lamp on a side table went out. Mike's Walther was in his hand in a flash. He frowned, then noticed a timer behind the lamp — it was set to come on and go off at certain times. *To create an illusion that the boss is in the office?* Mike wondered. It gave him an idea. Removing the lampshade, he unplugged the timer and carried the lamp and timer with him. Just past the office, he located the stairs to the lower floor.

"Any thoughts on what to do with this lot?" he asked Tony, indicating the lab workers, who had stopped working and turned off their various flame sources, mostly single burner stove-type devices.

"According to their spokesman, the bus that brings them here and takes them home daily is around the back," Tony explained. "The man with the keys was one of those you dealt with upstairs. I suppose we could send him up to look for the keys. I'm sure one of them would be more than happy to drive everyone home."

Mike frowned, remembering the four Makarov automatics lying on the floor in the office alongside the dead bodies of their owners. He gave a tight smile and a shake of his head, flashing Tony a mental image of the weapons. "I think I should get the keys. No sense in potentially arming anyone who might feel disgruntled at the loss of his job."

He set the lamp and timer on one of the work tables then, turning, he launched himself upward again, clearing the gallery rail, to a chorus of gasps from the lab workers. The man with the keys was one of the three who'd been at a desk. While Mike found car keys in everyone's pockets, this one carried a larger set, with one that looked so different that Mike decided it had to be the bus key. He also found an FSB officer's ID on each body in the office, pocketing them out of instinct.

While the workers, under Tony's supervision, located and donned their coats, Mike plugged in the timer and set it to come back on in ten minutes. Seeing that Tony had the workers assembled just outside the door, he flicked a finger at the lamp bulb, shattering the glass but leaving filament intact. He set the lamp on its side very close to a gas burner, turned on the gas, then went from burner to burner, turning them all on.

He shut the door as they left the building, then they marched the lab workers around the back to what looked like a small school bus. Mike handed the keys to the man Tony had indicated as the spokesman, who, in turn, after a brief discussion, relinquished the keys to another lab worker who went to the driver's seat and started the vehicle, while the remainder boarded the bus and took their seats. Moments later they watched the tail lights of the bus recede as it continued out the road. There was an explosion, then the roar of flames consuming the building that had housed the meth lab.

"I say, dear boy, you really do have a profound hatred of the drug trade. This is the second meth lab you've blown up in — what? — five years? That time you used a Very pistol. How did you manage it this time?"

Mike shrugged. "I jury–rigged a timed explosion." He headed toward the car.

"Do you have any knowledge of a General Kemedov?" Mike asked Tony when the bus was gone from sight. "I have the impression that this operation is run by General — no doubt former KGB General — Nikolai Alexei Kemedov."

Tony mused the name Kemedov over and over, nodding slowly. "We crossed paths a few times back in the day. He started out in the army, became attached to the GRU — Military Intelligence, then the KGB took him in. He ended up in counter–espionage under General Kalugin. And you think he was running this?"

Mike nodded, then told Tony about the photo and *Pravda* article on the office wall. "I also forwarded to Nigel a folder of documents from Kemedov's computer," he explained. "Aside from files concerning MI6, he seems to have a specific interest in both Petroff and Mason."

He watched as Tony's brow furrowed. "I hope he won't be able to track that eMail and know that we're onto him — especially since it traces to Nigel."

Mike cracked a half smile and pulled the hard drive from his pocket. "They won't be tracking anything without the hard drive," he explained. "Besides, I think his computer is toast.

"And," he added, setting the four ID folders on the dash, "Not only were his stooges at the roadblocks FSB, but the thugs in the office were FSB officers."

"Hmm," Tony stopped the car to look at the folders, "Two Warrant Officers and a Captain. That's quite a day's work, Michael."

"What do you make of this?" Mike asked, handing Tony the paper he'd ben unable to read.

Tony glanced at it and shrugged. "It's a schedule of which customer wants how much and when. Unless you plan on taking over the operation, it's useless."

"Unless we come across someone wanting to shut down the operation," Mike rebutted.

10: Out of the *Frying Pan...*

*F*lames were visible in the windows of the meth–lab as they pulled away. They were backtracking to the *Y* in the road when another, more deafening, explosion erupted. Mike delayed just long enough to release the captured guards before continuing. His instincts were pulling him to an unknown property just another mile or so to the west. He pulled over.

"Tony, can you drive? I think I want to go out–of–body to reconnoiter. All I have is a compelling premonition, and I'd like something more substantial, more firsthand."

"Of course, Michael; whatever you require," was Tony's only comment before exchanging places.

Once settled into the passenger seat, Mike relaxed his mind and drifted into the meditative state that allowed him to separate his consciousness and certain aspects of his energy, then pushed out, traveling over the countryside. A mile ahead he came to the edge of another former cattle farm with what he assumed was a tanning facility. This one looked in much better shape than the Petroff property. Inside a farmhouse he found the bodies of a man and a woman slumped over the kitchen table, each showing a single bullet wound to the head. Mail lay scattered on the counter. It took some effort to move papers and envelopes enough to read addressees, but he read the name Vasily Banderovsky, which struck a chord in his memory. There was a smaller envelope addressed to Natalia Banderovskaya.

He raced back into his body, his head giving an abrupt jerk as his eyes opened.

"Vasily Banderovsky," he said. "There are two bodies at the kitchen table in the farmhouse where we're heading. I read the name on envelopes lying strewn on the counter. I've seen the surname somewhere in connection with this case. Does it mean anything to you? There was also a smaller, greeting–card–sized envelope addressed to a Natalia Banderovskaya."

Tony mused the name, but shook his head. "Not a jot, Michael."

Mike began sifting through visual memory, deciding to focus on having been in the office of the forger Vasily Boronovich, eventually coming to the original birth certificate of Brendu Petrova — Father: Anatoli Petroff — Mother: Tatyanna Banderovskaya. "Petroff's wife was Tatyanna Banderovskaya," he announced. "I read it on Brenda's birth certificate. Perhaps Vasily and Natalia are relatives."

Tony was nodding his head. "Banderovskaya is the feminine form of Banderovsky," he mused. "Vasily and Natalia are probably brother and sister — Russian women don't typically take their husband's name. And it wouldn't be unusual for Petroff to have married someone from a farm similar to the one where he was raised. In fact, back in the day, it might have been expected, though his time with the KGB might have displaced such notions in his mind."

"I sensed the presence of people in other buildings — residual presence — as if they'd been there recently and left or —" he shook his head, uncertain of how to express it, "but I had no compelling sense of Mason still being there."

Mason stirred, his peripheral vision barely catching the opening of his cell door. He lay perfectly still — easily done, since he could hardly move. Aside from the ache in his legs, which, remarkably, seemed to be fading, he was so restricted by his chains that he couldn't achieve a comfortable position.

He watched a head of wavy brown hair appear — the more hospitable of his two jailers — carrying a steaming bowl. Once through the door, he turned and closed it carefully, then brought the bowl to Mason.

Mason waited patiently for eye contact. "*Spasibo*," he said, then made a futile attempt to sit up, exaggerating the effort to accentuate his helplessness. "Do I have to wear these leg irons?" he asked. "Isn't it bad enough that I have a bullet in each leg? Both thigh bones are undoubtedly shattered. I'll be crippled for life. Perhaps, if I live long enough, Petroff will have your surly partner amputate my legs. Maybe he'll find a second wheelchair for me. Either way, my days of dazzling crowds with my speed in the hundred–meter sprint are over," he declared, all the time gesturing with his right hand — to the wounds in his legs, to the shackles about his ankles, then ultimately rattling the fetter about his right wrist. "And, unless you're planing to spoon–feed me, you may as well take that away." Dropping his head back onto the mattress, he made one last gesture with his right hand, then turned his gaze to the wall, focusing his hearing on the young man for any sound of movement.

He heard the *clink* of the bowl being set on the floor, then the metallic jingling of keys. Fixing a look of shock on his face, he turned back to observe the rear of the man's head as he unlocked the fetters from about Mason's ankles. Wavy–Hair next unlocked the manacle from Mason's left hand, then proceeded to ease him into an upright position before lifting the bowl and placing it in Mason's hands. From the breast pocket of his heavy flannel shirt, he removed a spoon and set it into the stew, the aroma of which was so tantalizing that it took all Mason's willpower to remain complacent.

"It's from a can, heated on the stove," Wavy–hair muttered, as if ashamed that it wasn't homemade.

"*Spasibo* —," Mason said again, then, "I'm sure it will be wonderful. — I don't even know how to address you. You've been so kind." Mason offered his most sincere smile — he'd practiced it in the mirror most of his life, to make sure it never lost it's charm.

"Pietro —." It came as a low, hesitant reply. "Pietro Androvich."

"*Spasibo*, Pietro Androvich," Mason offered once more. "Thank you for not prolonging my torture, and thank you for bringing me this. The lack of food was beginning to wear on me."

It was like pulling teeth, but, little by little, he got Pietro to talk about himself. His parents had been bakers. He'd been raised in a kitchen to the smells of baking bread. Food was the focus of his upbringing. He'd become a baker's helper at a young age, before being inducted into the army for his years of compulsive service to the state.

Mason applied every subtle ploy he knew to keep the young man talking. Pietro was twenty-eight years old. His companion jailer was Leon Koslov. Koslov had applied for Spetsnaz training but had washed out of the program, and was bitter about it, blaming everyone but himself. He nodded, "So he rejects all forms of humanitarian kindness as indications of weakness. He thinks cruelty is an indication of strength," to which Pietro nodded.

"Now he is FSB," Pietro whispered, "which, under Yeltsin, was much better, much less like old KGB, according to my parents. But when Putin got in, he turned the FSB back into the KGB, replacing moderate or liberal officers with former hardline KGB, and replacing lower level soldiers with thugs."

"According to some interviews I've seen," Mason commented, "Putin refers to himself as having been a thug in his youth."

It took Mason what seemed like almost an hour to eat half of the stew. He had Pietro set the remainder on the floor by the bed, assuring him that, even cold, it would be welcome once Mason had rested enough to be able to consume more. He then made a show of struggling to ease back into a reclined position, his head falling back against the mattress. He even expelled the the air from his lungs in an exaggeratedly slow sigh of exhaustion before closing his eyes and pretending to drift off to sleep.

Once Pietro had departed, he listened for any hints of sound from outside his cell door, then sat up again. Steeling his nerve, he gripped his right thumb and deliberately wrenched it back and to one side, clenching his teeth and grunting in a barely audible growl as he dislocated the digit. Now, still grimacing against the agony, he could slowly extract his hand from the manacle. Gripping his thumb again, he pulled until he felt it re-articulate against its seat. Agony discouraged further movement of the digit.

Getting to his feet, he paused, waiting for a wave of nausea and vertigo to pass, then, with a hand on the edge of the bed, collapsed to the floor. He picked up the bowl and took a moment to polish it off. He retained the spoon, then struggled to resume his seat on the edge of the bed. He looked about for his shoes, but couldn't see them. He tried under the bed. *I guess someone made off with them. Petroff isn't taking any chances with me, is he?*

Trying to stand had been excruciating, but not nearly as bad as he'd expected.

With a bullet in each femur, possibly through one, I shouldn't even be able to stand, he thought.

Gripping the shaft of the spoon as close to the bowl of the spoon as possible, he used the last three fingers of his right hand to grip the bowl and bend it at a right angle, then bent it back. He continued this, making the motions faster until the bowl snapped off. Now he felt ready. Getting back onto his feet, he lurched left to the wall, and, with his left hand against it for support, struggled cautiously to the door. It was locked but, with his years of training and experience, that didn't deter him. He patiently scraped the broken end of the spoon shaft against the wall next to the door, first on one side, then the other, until he had sharpened the tip enough to suit his purpose. It was time now to relax against the wall to the right of the door — the side with the doorknob.

He continued to scrape the tip of his improvised *shank*, improving the sharpness. Picturing what he would have to do, he felt uncertain enough about his stamina to worry about it slipping in his grip. He slipped the butt end into the door jamb and bent the last few millimeters at a right angle. Now he could brace this part against the first metacarpal of his little finger, giving a more secure grip. There was nothing left for it now but to wait. He leaned his head back against the wall, closed his eyes, and listened.

The joint of his right thumb, where it joined to the metacarpals, was now swollen half again as large.

His legs ached and remaining on his feet was excruciating. It might have been an hour before his patience was rewarded by the sound of approaching footsteps. He recognized the gate — not Pietro's more relaxed tread, but the almost Prussian marching step of Leon Koslov. *So much the better*, he thought, knowing killing Koslov would trouble his conscience much less than killing Pietro. Steeling his nerve, he double-checked his grip on his weapon, pictured the target in his mind, and tensed for action.

The moment the door opened, he pivoted at the waist, seized the neck of Koslov's shirt with the fingers of his right hand — he almost cried out at the agony it produced in his thumb — and pulled him in, driving the tip of his weapon into Koslov's unprotected throat, aiming for the right carotid. A gout of blood spurted out past the blade, telling him he'd hit the bullseye.

Kicking Koslov's feet from under him, Mason dumped him to the floor on his face, gave his shank a twist and pulled it out, then placed a foot on Koslov's head, just behind the left ear, and bore his weight down. He hoped the pressure to the mastoid region was more excruciating than the femoral agony the application of pressure was causing him. Koslov's futile struggles only accelerated the hemorrhaging, bringing death faster. After about twenty seconds Koslov's fingers gave a few last spasmodic twitches, then nothing. Mason took a moment to wipe his bloody left hand on the clothes of his victim, then rifled him for keys and weapons, helping himself in particular to the handgun. He was expecting a Makarov, but it turned out to be a post-war vintage Tokarev TT-33. *A weapon is a weapon*, he told himself, then inspected the weapon, pulling the clip. It was well-oiled, though the magazine showed a few rust spots.

He left the cell, locked the door, then, Tokarev secure in his left hand, lurched off, looking for a way out. For Petroff to have made it down in his wheelchair, there had to be an elevator, but Mason preferred a stairway, and eventually found one. He was looking for a backdoor when he heard sounds of a commotion at the front of the building. Two gunshots rang out, then a voice issuing commands in Russian rose above the dwindling sounds of chaos.

"Search the premises and find Mason," the voice ordered. It was an older man, educated, from the style of his Russian. "He'll, no doubt, be in a cell on the lower level." Someone snapped their fingers.

Mason struggled to the rear, found a back door, and slipped silently out of the building. He immediately jerked his head around, shutting his eyes tight, and waiting at least a minute before looking through squinted eyes. The late afternoon sunlight told him the sun would be setting in an hour or so, yet, after innumerable days in darkness or dim light, the illumination overwhelmed the optic centers of his brain. Still squinting, he adjusted his grip on the Tokarev, then forced himself to continue. The discomfiture of his sock–feet on the almost frozen ground helped distract him from the agony in his legs.

He'd only lurched twenty feet when a soldier armed with an AK–105 stepped from around the corner. He was about to raise his handgun, but the intruder merely shook his head, swinging the automatic rifle into lethal position. He was dressed in blue-and-grey camouflage, with a black military–grade bulletproof vest. There was no insignia on the front, but Mason knew that the rear would display the Cyrillic characters for the FSB, Russia's federal security service. Sure enough, the shoulder epaulets were those of an FSB senior sergeant.

Mason expelled a heavy sigh, then flipped the Tokarev in his hand and offered it to his new captor.

The soldier tucked the pistol into his equipment belt, and, jerking the barrel of his Kalashnikov for emphasis, and commanded: "Predshestvovat' menya." (Precede me.)

"Very well, but I shan't be sprinting," Mason assured his new captor, then staggered off, grunting with almost every agonizing step.

The soldier steered Mason around to the front, where the door looked as if someone had kicked it in. Pietro Androvich lay just inside the doorway, shot through the forehead. There was just enough powder trace blackening the edge of the bullet wound to indicate he'd been shot at point–blank range.

Sensing the proximity of the soldier behind him, he decided that the man expected him to pass through the doorway, so he stepped past Pietro's body, then noticed another body to one side. It was the trim form of Brenda Peters, also with a single bullet hole in her forehead. Anatoli Petroff sat in his wheelchair, fuming helplessly, bordered by two soldiers, each armed with ubiquitous Kalashnikovs.

They were in what might once have been the foyer to a large postwar leather facility, from the lingering smell of — stale tea mixed with paint thinner? — knowing Petroff's family history, Mason assumed it was tanning fluids. To the left was the door to a large office but, beyond Petroff and his guards, the rest of the immensity of the building faded into shadow. He had a vague impression he'd seen this part of the building upon arrival, but the memory was clouded, *no doubt by lingering traces of narcotic*, he decided.

To the right of Petroff, and a few steps closer to Mason, stood an older man — late sixties, maybe even seventies — wearing a drab green uniform. The oak leaf pattern at the collar and the two–star–on–black insignia of his shoulder epaulets marked him as a lieutenant–general.

"Captain Mason — I'm delighted." He broke into a grin and extended his hand as if to shake Mason's.

"General..." Mason prompted, hoping to ignore the offered hand, since the throb of his own was merciless.

"Kemedov —" the other responded, "— Nikolai Kemodov, just in case you were tempted to confuse me with the Dashiell Hammett character given brief mention in *The Maltese Falcon*." He added the latter with an amused chuckle.

Mason processed the info. *Nikolai Alexei Kemedov — KGB two–star general in Counter–Espionage, under General Oleg Kalugin, at the time of the fall of the Soviet Union.* "You'll have to excuse my appearance," he said, offering his own smile in return. "I've been away without a suitcase for far too long — how long I'm not sure." He made a haphazard effort to brush his hair into place, paused to fight the encroaching dizziness, then offered his right hand to Kemedov, grimacing at the effort to extend his swollen thumb out of the way. He relinquished the General's grip as soon as possible.

Kemedov glanced at the now–bleeding bullet wounds in Mason's legs, then at his right hand, and smiled, commenting, "So you dislocated your right thumb to escape a manacle. No sign of a lingering handcuff, so that hand must have not been manacled at the time of your escape." Then a glance at Mason's feet brought on another chuckle. "No shoes? And, what have you done to your trousers?"

Then, glancing in Petroff's direction, he added, "Really, Anatoli; shooting him in both legs, just like he did to you all those years ago wasn't enough? Did you think he might try to hang himself with his shoelaces? If he were determined to hang himself, he would have torn away and shredded his other trouser leg." Once more he chuckled.

Turning back to Mason, he said, "Someone find this man's shoes; they must be here somewhere."

Almost immediately, one of the FSB soldiers brought them and, at a gesture from Kemedov, set them on the floor before Mason, who promptly slipped his feet into them, giving silent thanks that they were loafers — he couldn't bare the thought of trying to tie laces with only one functioning thumb.

"We were discussing your thumb, I believe," Kemedov prompted, now lapsing into English.

Mason nodded, not sure how much to say, then explained, "The body of Petroff's more sadistic henchman, one Leon Koslov, — though perhaps it was really his daughter Brenda's henchman — lies dead in the cell I recently departed."

Kemedov tried to hide a scowl at the mention of Leon Koslov. *Koslov was FSB — One of your men, Kemedov? Why would one of your FSB men be with Brenda Petrova or with Petroff? Did someone already find his body?*

"Pietro, lying there near the door," Mason resumed, "was kind enough to be persuaded to undo all but the right handcuff — I succeeded in convincing him I was right-handed. Petroff had me manacled by both wrists and ankles — he seemed interested in maximum discomfort and inconvenience. It's a shame Pietro had to be shot."

Kemedov gave a disinterested nod and a shrug. "Expedience," was his only comment. "Now, if you two will oblige me, it's time to depart for Moscow. Prison awaits you both." He gave a brief smile, then, with a nod to one of the soldiers flanking Petroff, he turned and walked out.

Mason's guard gave him a gentle nudge in the direction of the door, and herded him toward one of several official–looking vans. Another soldier opened the back of the van, then Mason's escort helped him up into the back, settled him on a rear–facing bench, then removed zip–ties from a pocket on his pant leg.

"Just the left hand," Kemedov commanded; "He's already dislocated his right thumb, but you can secure his right ankle as an extra precaution. Petroff should be manacled to the frame of his wheelchair, just in case he's lost little of his former conniving trickiness over the years — wheelchair arms are often removable."

Two soldiers hoisted Petroff, in his chair, up into the back of the van, then, using hardware mounted to the floor, locked his wheelchair in place so that he faced Mason. Mason's guard then shifted and settled onto the floor against one side near the rear. Once the rear doors were closed, he relocated to a corner, from which he could watch both prisoners.

Moments later the van started, as did the others, and they set out down the bumpy road from the farm. The light had been fading as he'd gotten into the van, but he had the sudden instinct that the sun had just set, as if he could see it in his mind. *Curious*, he thought.

Before long the road became smoother and he could close his eyes, ease his head back against the back of his seat, and succumbed to the urge to doze.

———

It was pitch black when a change in motion awakened him. The van had come to a stop. The rear doors jerked open, jolting the soldier in the corner awake. He scrambled to his feet as two soldiers hopped up, crouching immediately to free Petroff's wheelchair from its restraints. The moment they had Petroff removed, Mason's guard cut his zip–ties, and helped Mason to his feet.

Mason reeled, not sure he could walk unassisted, but the soldier just took a backward step and leveled his Kalashnikov. Moments later, Kemedov appeared at the back. He seemed about to say something, then frowned and gave commands to two other soldiers who appeared at his shoulder, then entered, taking up positions on each side of Mason, each gripping an arm, and escorted him out of the van.

Mason felt as if his heart had shifted lower inside his chest. Before him, just past the sidewalk, was a ten–step flight of steps — two sets of five steps with a lengthened landing at the top of the first five, before continuing on to the second set. A globular lamp post at each side of the landing lit the walkway leading to the entrance of what might have passed for an innocuous red brick building, unless one read the blue sign to the left of the entrance, at the height of the transom window above the doors. Beyond, lit by spotlights, was an ominous circular tower. At first glance, one might not even notice that the red brick structure was attached to the left side of a much larger edifice.

The circular tower was just part of the massive sprawl of buildings beyond. Mason had seen aerial photos several times. It looked remarkably like an out-of-date industrial facility, but it was one of the most notorious prisons in Russia, it's reputation so brutal it was still used in modern movies. This was Butyrka Prison.

11: *Disappointment*

*I*t was almost 8:00 PM when Tony eased the rental car to a stop under the cover of foliage to one side of the road, about seventy-five yards out from a large factory-style building. Mike exited the vehicle and spotted the farmhouse where he'd seen the corpses, just to the left of and maybe fifty yards beyond the processing building. The whole complex was almost identical to the Petroff place, except that this property had been better maintained. As expected, reaching out with his senses toward both buildings, revealed no evidence of life, just residues to indicate that people had been there recently. There was also the smell of drying blood, but the worst assault on his senses was the stench of advanced decomposition from the farmhouse.

By the light of the rising moon, amplified by his vampiric vision, he identified the tire tracks of at least four vehicles — *large vans*, flashed in his thoughts.

"What do you make of all this?" Tony asked. He was just straightening up from having squatted to examine the tire tracks. "And I smell blood from the building ahead of us."

Mike nodded. "And the remains of the Banderovsky couple are in the farmhouse beyond," he murmured. He paused near the entrance, squatting to examine tracks — sock–feet followed by well–treaded boots. He closed his eyes, reaching out with his senses, his nostrils flaring.

"Mason," he murmured, "and in sock–feet." He motioned for Tony to go left, while he went right.

He backtracked the spoor to where Mason encountered the soldier. His mind formed images of the events, interpolating from the evidence on the ground. In another twenty feet he found where Mason's spoor left the back door. He met Tony again at the rear.

"Nothing my way but footprints reminiscent of SAS–style special–forces boots," Tony commented.

Mike nodded. "Mason left by way of the back door, then met someone about twenty feet further on, who, from the way the bootprints remained behind him, must have escorted him to the front entrance. Blood evidence implies that Mason has bullet wounds in each leg, which began bleeding more from his efforts to walk, then seemed to ease off as he progressed. And, Tony, he was without shoes — insult to injury."

Tony frowned at that. "Petroff must have tried to duplicate his own wounds on Mason! It's hard to accept that he could even walk! Well, at least he's still alive," he offered.

Mike frowned. "Knowing he has vampire blood in him..." he speculated, "Well, I keep thinking back to that Afghanistan/Tajikistan mission, and how fast I kept healing, especially when epinephrine kicked in."

The front door had been forced open. They found the body of a young man just past the doorway, and a slim, dark–haired woman just beyond.

"Brendu Petrova," Tony mused, "You'd know better than I, but I think she died more than an hour ago — probably not the end she foresaw for herself. I assume this one by the door helped bring Mason here."

"Pietro Androvich," Mike pointed out, recognizing him from the photos Nigel had displayed with their background info. "They were shot about an hour–and–a–half ago, probably while we were at the meth–lab. We'll no doubt find Leon Koslov elsewhere on the premises."

"I smell blood, but at a distance, possibly the floor below us," Tony commented. "Some of it is new, but the smell of Mason's blood is older, not recent like what you found leading from the back door to here."

Mike placed a palm on Brendu's forehead, cleared his mind, and reached out, capturing her last visual impressions:

The door bursts open and — a soldier enters — Pietro looks shocked — an officer brushes past the soldier — the swagger of the older man shows confidence to the point of arrogance. A voice calls out from elsewhere in the building — The officer scowls, then snarls, — Mike transmitted the phrases to Tony, who translated:'First my phone number, and now this? Friend of yours?' *— Then he pulls his Makarov and shoots Pietro, who collapses just past the doorway. Brendu's last images were of the officer's face turning to her father's to gauge his reaction — shock on Petroff's face — then a leering smile on the officer's face becomes a cold, vindictive smile — a muzzle flash, and the image fades.*

Mike knew the face from the photo and clipping he'd seen on the wall at the meth–lab — General Nikolai Alexei Kemedov. He caught Tony's eye. "It's Kemedov — the commander of the soldiers was Kemedov."

Tony cocked an eyebrow. "Shall we proceed to the lower level?" he asked.

Mike nodded.

Finding stairs to the lower level took a while. The upper level was huge. Mike guessed the basement area would be much smaller, since no one would want to dig out anything the size of the upper level. Once below, it took but a moment to find Mason's cell, with a modest blood trail leading away from it.

"Koslov," Mike commented as he stepped over the corpse just inside the doorway. "Mason got his revenge on at least this one." Even in death Koslov was scowling.

He glanced at the empty bowl on the floor, then examined the manacles, paying particular attention to the one still locked.

"He'd have to have disarticulated his thumb to get out of that," he offered.

Tony nodded. "It was standard training back in the day, though there was a time when agents were taught to amputate the thumb if possible."

Mike arched an eyebrow. "A bit extreme when disarticulating the first phalange will do it."

He reviewed what he'd obtained from Brendu Petrova, and projected a Russian phrase to Tony, what someone had called out from further away.

"Koslov is down here. He's dead." Tony frowned. "It makes sense: Kemedov heard that, and said, 'First my phone number, and now this?'"

Mike nodded. "He next asked if Pietro was a friend of Brendu's, then shot him."

———

The buzz of flies was audible from outside the farmhouse. The scene inside was sad and brutal — the bodies of a man and a woman, both in early stages of decomposition, seated at a kitchen table, slumped on the tabletop where they'd collapsed after each being shot in the head.

The distressed look on Tony's face said that he was offended in the extreme by the smell. Leaving the door open wide, Mike heaved up the sashes of two windows, then found two more windows in the next room, which he also opened.

"They're remarkably well preserved, most likely due to the cooler weather and related lack of humidity. You could wait on the porch," he suggested, but Tony shook his head.

"I know you assisted at the odd postmortem back in the day, but this reek is positively ghastly. How on earth do you tolerate it?"

Mike shrugged, saying, "Probably the same way I avoid the flood of negative brainwaves when I have to terminate a villain; I just block it out. I also breathe more shallowly. Back in the day, Vicks up the nostrils helped, too, but I doubt if there's any handy."

Going to each, in turn, he placed a hand on the head, closed his eyes, and tried to read what lingering images might remain. It was deteriorating, a lot like looking into a house through very dirty, grimy windows.

A knock at the door. She opens it, surprised at having to look down — a man in a wheelchair — Petroff's face. Puzzlement mixed with curiosity, then anger as she recognizes the face, then shock — a pistol in his hand.

Koslov, brutal–looking with his perpetual scowl and close-cropped hair, wheels Petroff into the kitchen, then stops, folds his arms, and stations himself by the door, as if making sure no one can escape.

Her brother is seated at the table – she'd just scooped the last two fried sausages from the iron skillet onto his plate before answering the door. His reaction is one of outrage that Petroff would dare to even show his face at their door. He'd always suspected Petroff's guilt in the death of their younger sister. Petroff then forced — Natalia — Banderovsky's older sister's name was Natalia — to sit at the table, then shot her.

"Petroff," Mike announced. Noticing Tony staring at him, a frown on his face, and trying, with the aid of a handkerchief, to shield his nose from the odor of decay, he added, "The man is Vasily Banderovsky, Petroff's brother–in–law; his sister's name is Natalia — There's a small envelope on the counter addressed to Natalia Banderovskaya. Tatyanna was the youngest of the three siblings."

"I say, dear chap, must we linger? These two aren't getting any less ripe."

Mike started to frown, but managed to mask it with a smile. "I think we can go. These two have been dead for weeks — at least a week before Mason was taken.

"Now what?" Tony asked.

Mike, still looking at the deceased couple, shook his head. "I don't know. I don't think Brendu Petrova or her henchman, Androvich, recognized Kemedov, but, from what Brendu saw of her father's reaction, Petroff did — my gut tells me Petroff knew Kemedov. They seem to have packed Mason and Petroff into one of the vans before driving away."

"But to where?" Tony asked.

"We could try following the convoy tracks," Mike suggested, "but, since Kemedov was in uniform, and accompanied by an official FSB team, I'm going to go with *back to Moscow* as their intended destination."

The tire tracks of the vans were easy to follow. They backtracked to the meth lab, stopping along the way where Mike had left the sentries tied up. At the actual facility, three of the vehicles had remained outside the gate, parked to one side. The fourth had continued in toward the building. Footprints showed how one occupant had exited the van, gone closer to the now–burnt-out building, stood a moment, then returned to the van. The returning strides were longer.

The van tracks left the property, the three companion vehicles falling into line behind it, then all four continued back out toward the highway, disappearing the moment they reached pavement.

"You were right, dear boy, Kemedov is taking Mason and Petroff to Moscow," Tony mused.

"What's in Moscow, and why would Kemedov be taking them there?" Mike frowned, accelerating. He wanted to get back to the hotel and contact Nigel. "I know nothing about the man, except that he's about Mason's age, a former general in the KGB, presumably still a two–star general in the FSB. Would he take them to FSB Headquarters?"

Tony was nodding. "Possibly; that would be Lubyanka, the old KGB Headquarters. I heard something a few years back about the FSB being handed over a prison facility in Moscow as a detention center. Nigel would know."

Instead of continuing on the highway, Mike exited before the MKAD. He felt uncomfortable with the notion of giving anything but the appearance of having wandered just outside the city limits. They had passed several cameras at intervals, leading Mike to wonder just how much might be known of their travels outside central Moscow.

Weary, he pulled over soon after leaving the highway, leaning his head back against the headrest.

"Try a quaff of this," Tony offered, handing him a stoppered wine bottle. "I'm afraid it's not warm."

Mike could smell the distinct aroma before even releasing the lever of the stopper. Two swallows did much to revive him and help clear his head. Dawn was brightening the sky ahead. He took two more pulls, then noticed that Tony was doing the same from a similar bottle, *O–, no doubt*, he mused.

He stoppered the bottle and passed it back to Tony.

"Thanks for thinking to bring that. I wonder if the opened bottles would arouse police interest here like it would back home," he added with a hint of a smile.

"*Jesus!*" Mike blurted as an eighteen wheeler tore by, barely missing sideswiping them.

"If the actions of that driver are any indication, I doubt if suspicion of drunkenness is even a crime in Russia, " Tony suggested. "If a policeman took any notice of our bottles, I dare say it would more likely lead to a suspicion of us being deranged psychopaths." He ended the comment with a grin.

Whoom! Mike actually jolted away from his car door as a car tore past, again missing by only inches, and at probably twice the posted speed limit.

He frowned, then commented dryly: "Driving is much more peaceful in Chester Basin."

———

The sun was well above the horizon by the time they were back in the hotel. Mike linked with Nigel on FaceTime, while Tony returned the rental car.

The first thing Mike noticed when Nigel's face came into view was how worried he looked.

"Sorry, mate, but yer lovely immortal bride is no' 'ere any more. She packed up ffe kitties an' 'eaded for ffe airport ffis very mornin'. I ffink she's on 'er way to join you, Michael."

Mike sighed. *Maybe she'll make it without incident. Who knows, she might even be an asset in finding and rescuing Mason,* he tried to convince himself, in an effort to overcome his innate, if sexist, sense of — chivalry, over–protectiveness?

"What about the files I sent you?" he asked, aware that his tone had become more stern. *Relax; Carrie will be fine*, he told himself again.

"Fascinating readin', ffat lot. Seems Kemedov 'ad Petroff pretty much pidgeon–'oled. An', 'e were rapidly workin' 'is way to bein' 'e number one drug kingpin in Russia.

"As for yer concerns about ffe Ruskies trackin' yer movements while gaddin' abou' ffe countryside, fear not, Nigel is on 'e case." The sound of his typing came over the FaceTime link.

"Okay, mate, I've 'acked into ffeir system an' scrubbed all data between Moscow an' Vyazma during ffe time period o' your little excursion. Not, I gotta mention, before notin' ffe movements of a certain convoy o' vans whot might be of interest to you," Nigel punctuated his dissertation with a whistle. "You're no' gonna like where ffey dropped off Mason an' Petroff — well, Petroff, maybe; but no' Mason."

"*Nigel!*" Mike growled, his mood not up for the Cockney's vocal meanderings.

"Oh — Sorry, Michael — Butyrka Prison. Boff Mason an' Petroff showed up on 'e roster for Butyrka Prison las' night. It looks like Kemedov is credited for ffe apprehensions or wha'ever ffey're callin' it.

"Anyway, gimme a mo — tell you whot, Michael — it's gettin' close to your daily nap time, why don' you go get some kip, an' I'll 'ave wha'ever I can 'ave when ye wake up. Ol righty, mate? An' Michael, try no' to worry abou' Carrie. She's one sharp bird, ye know, *an*' can take care o' 'erself in a pinch."

Mike sighed and nodded. He could sense that he was close to fading, even though it wasn't even 10:00 yet. He was just about to reach out to Tony's mind to see if he was uncharacteristically fatigued as well, when the door to the suite opened, and Tony entered.

"I exchanged vehicles, Michael, though, I dare say — What is it dear chap? You look positively ghastly." He closed the door, tossed keys on the table, a look of deep concern on his face.

Mike frowned. "Carrie is on her way here, cats and all." He shrugged as soon as the words were out. "She has a stubborn streak. I just hope she makes it through the bureaucracy at the airport okay."

Tony gave a sober nod, then stared fixedly at Mike again. "There's something else."

"Mason is in Butyrka Prison — Kemedov took both him and Petroff there. Why would he do that?"

But Tony just shook his head. "I haven't the foggiest, but it is certainly puzzling. Let's hope Nigel unearths more information."

"He hopes to have more by the time we're awake," Mike said. "I do feel unusually tired."

"You look positively done in," Tony declared. "You've done a lot with minimal rest, especially considering what you pulled off at the airport. After all, Michael, even vampires can be victims of jet–lag — the sun's schedule is quite different here from Chester Basin. You've done an out–of–body search —"

"I get it, Tony; I'll crash early." Mike cut him off before he could summarize Mike's activities of the past twenty hours. He gave a hint of a smile then headed for his bedroom.

Once composed on the bed, he reached out to find Carrie.

I'm in the air, en route to Moscow, she informed him. *We should be landed by 5:00 PM your time.*

Try to rest, he warned her. *That's dangerously close to your normal wakeup time. You don't want to be stuck in a vampire coma with an attendant trying to arouse you upon landing.*

He could sense her concern — she hadn't thought about that anymore than he had during his own flight.

Before giving in to the void, he reached out over the city with his senses. The chain-smokers still loitered outside. It took a while to notice an oddity, so different from any city he'd ever explored at night: an almost complete lack of cats. Mangy half–starved dogs practically ruled the night. *Do the dogs attack and eat the cats?* he wondered. *Kato won't be going out into that.* Then he gave in to the void.

12: *Carrie Arrives*

C arrie's eyes opened. As usual, there was a brief moment of confusion, the inner beast of the vampire not completely in check. She forced herself to remain rigid until she could see something to tell her where she was, that she was safe. The beast, after all, was a senseless predator.

Then the smiling face of a flight attendant came into focus.

"We're here at Domodedovo Airport, ma'am," she advised. "You still have a moment before we actually begin deplaning. Have you filled out your entry documents?"

Carrie hesitated another moment — *don't snarl, don't show fangs; we're on the ground in Russia. Michael is here* — then she recognized the flight attendant and smiled. "Entry documents? — Yes; they're in my purse with my passport and the cats' documents. What about Kato and Teila — my cats?"

"They're fine. I have them up by the exit. They'll be ready to deplane with you."

When her turn came, she exited with the carrier, found her suitcase at the baggage carrousel, located a cart, then made her way to the end of the line to await her moment of inquisition.

I'm here, Michael, she called out with her mind, hoping that Michael would read her.

I'm here, came the immediate reply. *Look for a guy with a crewcut — his name-tag says P. Cherninov. He has a scar, identical to Sean's — he must have acquired it in childhood, and the hair never grew on the scar tissue. He'll remember me.*

Carrie scanned all the officers in the various cubicles, then spotted the one who fit Mike's description. *Got him,* she projected.

Good. Now focus your mind on him until you force him to look at you and become aware of you. That's it, he's looking right at you. Now compel him to call you.

It worked. Cherninov frowned at first, then forced a puzzled smile. "You brought your cats?" There was incredulity in both his tone and expression.

"The little one has a fit if I leave her behind, and the bigger one is an absolute sook when my husband is out of his sight. Michael will be so surprised when I catch up with him at his hotel — he's here researching a new novel. He got here a day or two ago with Uncle Tony — Tony helps out when I'm not around — Michael gets *so* wrapped up in his focus when he's writing."

The officer, Cherninov, smiled. "Yes, I remember your husband and his Uncle Tony. Mr. Cameron writes vampire fiction — he gave me his card. So he doesn't know you're arriving?"

Carrie made a guilty grimace, then beamed a radiant smile. "I couldn't help it. I missed him and got the sudden urge to surprise him. Oh, and I have all the required documents for both cats, including the serial numbers of their implanted chips. You can scan them and verify that their shots are all up-to-date."

After a careful perusal of her paperwork, he stamped everything. "The scan won't be necessary; I'm sure I can trust you." Then, pulling Mike's card from a pocket, he whispered, "I used my PayPal account to download the first book from his website. I read the first seven chapters last night. I'm looking forward to reading more tonight, right after my wife falls asleep." He gave her a conspiratorial wink.

"The train will take you directly to the hotel where Mr. Cameron and his uncle are staying."

———— —— —–

I did it! she almost screamed in her mind as she settled into her seat on the train.

I know; I was watching it all through your eyes, Mike's voice said in her head, *I'll be waiting for you where the train stops. Remember: it's the* Radisson Slavyanskaya. *It'll be on a big sign, in large red letters, to the right of the tracks.*

True to his word, as she exited the train, carrying the cat carrier and dragging her bag by it's extended handle, there he was, smiling, albeit looking concerned, as if worried about something.

He took the cats from her, set the carrier down, and seemed about to throw his arms about her, but she grabbed him, pivoted, and slammed him against the back of the shelter.

"You're not going to cut me out of this, Michael," she started in, all her pent–up anxiety flooding into her voice. "I was almost as much a part of Torok's destruction as you were! Remember Korea? Morgan Price and all those soldiers out to kill you? And what about Austria? Prince Vincent and his sick *Brat Pack*? You can't keep playing this game of lone —" she hesitated, searching for the words, "— I don't know — this Lone Ranger crusader–knight thing you've got going on. We're supposed to be a team!"

She expected him to argue, forcefully and persuasively — he was good at that. Instead, his brow furrowed, his mouth tightened to a rictus, and he nodded in agreement, then the left side of his mouth cracked a weak smile.

"Been saving that up since I left last week?" he asked, still seemingly trying for what she decided was too cute of a grin.

I knew from the beginning that you'd get away with a lot on how cute you can look! she thought.

"I love you," he murmured, "almost more than I can get a grasp on in my mind. In two lifetimes, those I've loved this way have died. I seem driven to protect you from what I've begun to view as some sort of curse haunting me through my incarnations."

Seeing the reality of it in his eyes, she pressed him against the glass, herself against him, aware of how her breasts pressed against his chest, and knowing how aware he'd be of the same. Then she lurched up onto her toes, her lips coming hard and firm against his, feeling the tightness of his jaw relax as he kissed her back. He clung to her, his mouth on hers, their tongues doing that spiraling dance that they seemed to do of their own accord.

"I'm glad to see you, too," she exclaimed as they finally subsided into a hug.

Kato's harsh *yowl* and Teila's meek *mew* brought them both back to reality.

As she pulled away, she noticed that his frown had returned. "I'm sorry," he said, "— for everything."

But he was still frowning, still troubled. She studied his face, frowning herself, then got a glimpse in his mind of a confused jumble of images.

"It's about Mason, isn't it?" she said.

He nodded. "He's in Butyrka Prison, shot in both legs — It's a HellHole even by Russian standards!"

Another throaty *yowl* from the carrier, followed by a smaller but just as insistent *mew*, made it known that the carrier occupants had been ignored long enough.

"Hey, buddy," Mike said into the cage after raising it to eye–level. "And hello to you, too, little peanut." Then, to Kato, "You'll have to be patient just a bit longer — I can't let you out here; it'll have to wait until we're in the suite. You won't be playing nocturnal detective in Moscow, buddy. You might survive the cold, but the place is overrun with near–feral dogs. There are almost no cats in Moscow!"

———

The moment Mike ushered Carrie into the hotel room, Kato insisted on an immediate release from the cage. Not only that, but he quite determinedly settled on Mike's shoulders, about his neck, and began pawing at his arm, wanting his thumb. Even Teila insisted on squirming into Mike's arms for a quick snuggle, purring loudly, then moved to Carrie and assumed a similar position around her neck.

"I'm sorry, my dear," Tony apologized, passing Carrie a goblet of warmed O–positive, "but this will have to do until the delivery of A–positive arrives. I called the moment Michael knew you were coming, but this isn't London, and I fear the network is less efficient.

"And I procured a litter pan for Kato and Teila, which I placed in your en–suite bathroom."

As if on cue, the door chime sounded to announce the delivery of Carrie's blood supply, immediately followed by a FaceTime chime on Tony's PowerBook. Kato and Teila, also took off at a dash, as if they'd understood Tony's every word and were in desperately need of their potty.

Mike tapped the touchpad to accept Nigel's FaceTime call, and Nigel's face appeared on the screen. He looked about to say something when he noticed Carrie looking over Mike's shoulder.

"*Oi*, Carrie — great, you made it ffrough ffe airport alrigh'? — even wiff 'e kitties? I bet yer relieved, Michael.

"Anyway, about Kemedov — ffere's a lorry–load o' deleted files, an' even more whot's been redacted to ffe point ffey migh' as well a' been deleted.

"Not only is 'e FSB full o' former KGB, but, according to *Spiegel Online International*, ffe Academy of Sciences claims 'at — le' me read ffis — *Four ou' o' five members of Russia's political and business elite have a KGB past.* An' 'oo do we 'ave to ffank for 'at? — Vladimir Vladimirovich Putin. Seems 'e orchestrated it soon after comin' to power in 2000. In fac', during a visit to Lubyanka, ffe former Central Moscow Headquarters o' ffe KGB, that very year, numerous media reports 'ave 'im announcin' to 300 Generals ffat, *Instruction number one o' ffe attainin' o' full power 'as been completed.*"

"So," Mike declared, "the main issue is, with Putin being who he seems to be, why is Kemedov still around. Was he an approving pal? Does he flood Putin with campaign contributions — do they have that here yet? — Does he have something on Putin?"

I ffink it's go' more to do wiff Putin's attachment to ffe KGB, an' whot some folks call his *Cold War* 'atred o' ev'ryffing Western," Nigel opined. "It were KGB involvement in ffe coup whot led to 'e final fall o' ffe Soviet Union, ffat made Yeltsin decide to disban' ffe KGB, separatin' it's powers between ffe FSB and ffe SVR. But ffe moment Putin became President, he began undoin' or softenin' mos' o' Yeltsin's reforms. Little by little, he seems on a mission to revive ffe old Russia o' ffe Soviet era, an' drugs or no drugs, Kemedov is 'is kind o' bastard."

Mike pondered all of this, staring off into space, then abruptly said, "Nigel, dig into Putin's activities between '98 and '99. What did he do to go from relatively unknown to the hero of the people who won the 2000 Presidential election?

"Oi, ffa's easy, mate — ffe Chechen terrorist bombings. If 'e Chechen rebels 'adn't blown up ffose apartment buildings — 'e firs' was a barracks for Russian soldiers an' 'eir families. It were 'is aggressive action on ffat whot made 'im an 'ero in 'e public eye."

Mike frowned. He was in his head, rifling through memories of news broadcasts, headlines he'd read — becoming increasingly suspicious.

"Take a close look at 1998 through 2000, anyway," he told Nigel. "How did he go from retired KGB colonel to obscure politician to director of the FSB? And why would Yeltsin step down and pave the way for him?"

Nigel immediately started typing rapidly.

"Lemme ge' an 'old o' Gregory to 'elp wiff ffis, ffen I'll ge' back to you quick as *Bob's–yer–uncle*. I can give you one bi' of ffe puzzle, ffough: why Yeltsin gave 'im ffe presidency on a silver platter, so to speak. Yeltsin were bein' prosecuted fer corruption. Putin's firs' act as Acting President were to issue Yeltsin whatcha call a *ge'–outta–jail–free card*: complete amnesty from prosecution."

With that, Nigel ended the FaceTime session.

"That's looking like a rather large can of worms, Michael," Tony commented after Nigel disappeared, "but I can't see what it has to do with the mission."

Mike frowned, shaking his head, "I don't know Tony; I honestly don't know. I just know that's it's nagging me in the back of my mind and in the pit of my gut, and I can't let go of it."

"Too much politics for me," Carrie declared. "I'm going to take a shower. I'll run you a hot bath when I'm done, Michael. Perhaps that will help."

Tony looked lost in thought, then a hint of a grin slowly formed. "I'll see if I can't scrounge up some candles," he announced, "maybe even call room service and see if they can provide any from the hotel gift shop. Perhaps your talent for sorcery will find something, like Mason's cell in Butyrka. By the way, Michael, I found a few of the bugs, but they seemed duds. Did you do something?"

Mike nodded. "Sort of a chi–zap." Then, "I think I'll head up to the roof for a bit of fresh air before my bath. Perhaps it'll clear my head and help me see past this quagmire of distractions."

———

Mike squatted at the edge of the hotel roof and looked out over the Moscow skyline. The view from his seven–storey perch was spectacular. In the distance he could make out the glowing minaret–like domes of Saint Basil's Cathedral, part of the Kremlin, lit up like a Disneyland castle.

He sensed he was being observed — vampire presence on another, taller rooftop, maybe a hundred meters away. He stood, gauged the distance, then launched forward in a burst of speed, hurling himself forward and upward, becoming airborne. He felt gravity overcoming his momentum, defining the apex of his arc, and forced chi downward, adjusting his height, then unleashed another burst to his rear to increase the force carrying him to the new rooftop. *Who says vampire's can't fly?* he thought — *Well, okay — sorcerer–vampires can fly — well, sort of.*

He landed with surprising grace, pulling the corner of his mouth back in the barest hint of a smile. *I half expected to sprawl on my face*, he mused. *I guess I'm getting better at this.*

Several dark figures converged on him, surrounding, yet keeping a cautious distance. Many were snarling in guttural tones.

"*Vi litali*!" several declared, followed by a voice saying, "You flew!"

The chorus of snarls dwindled, drowned out by murmured declarations, which sounded like, "*Glaza!*"

Focusing his mind on the nearest, one of those who had spoken in English, Mike probed and saw that his eyes, sapphire cat's eyes, their vertical pupils no longer masked by glamour, were also glowing, radiating energy — what Wicca called *magick*.

One of the snarlers made a lunge at Mike with extended fangs and talons.

"*Nyet, Boris!*" the nearest vampire shouted

Mike wheeled into a zen stance, and focused his eyes on Boris.

Boris froze in place, immobile, unable to even snarl. Mike held him there a moment, watching as Boris's eyes widened in shocked alarm, his lips trembling as he fought to breathe, but was helpless against Mike's grip on him.

The abrupt warmth in Mike's eyes warned him that the glow was on the edge of erupting into flame. He glanced from face to face, the soles of his Otomix combat sneakers shifting, lifting his arches and taking his weight more on the balls of his feet.

He reached out to assess the positions of those about him, gauging their mood and readiness to attack. "You may think you can take me by numbers," he said, "but, trust me: you can't. If you try, many of you will die in the first second."

"*Otdykhat*; *On ne predstavlyayet opasnosti*," the shorter Muscovite he'd already marked as possibly a leader ordered in a commanding tone. Immediately those around Mike seemed to stand down and shift from behind him to in front.

Mike released Boris, who bent over, hands on his thighs, and continued to gasp for breath, as if he'd just finished a marathon.

The leader resumed speaking. "I told them to relax, that you are not a danger," he explained, then, "You must be the von they call *Samurai*. Ve know you travel vith Lord Dewhurst, and that he arrived in *Mockba* — Moscow — and ordered a delivery from our network. I considered that you might be vith him and have been vatching your hotel. Ve hear things about you, like vhat you did in Austria almost three years ago, and to Count Torok in the Carpathians a year before that.

"They fear you. Vord of you has been spreading since you killed Von Strelitz in Germany. Ve heard of your prowess vith a sword, as vell as your unusual powers as a vampire. Then ve began to hear stranger, more terrifying things, mostly from to the vest, out of Moldova and Romania. Is it true that you can summon fire? Many of us thought it vas exaggerated, a dramatic embellishment."

Mike took a moment to study the vampire before him. He was shorter than most of the others, with handsome features — Mike smiled at that thought — had he ever even seen an ugly vampire, except for Torok, who had chosen to look like a monster?

"Your English is very good," Mike complimented.

"I vas once Aleksandr Nicholaiovitch Romanoff," he explained. "I vas the youngest brother of Grand Duke Alexi Alexandrovitch. I vas born in 1855, and brought over in 1874. I vas vell–educated, and continued to travel and learn. I was fortunate to be in Vienna vhen the Bolsheviks overran my country. Most of our kind vere destroyed vhen they slaughtered the nobility. The peasants had no idea of vhat they vere doing vhen they torched coffins found in the crypts under certain palaces, thinking, no doubt, that they vere merely the remains of honoured ancestors."

Mike nodded. "I'm Michael Cameron, the one you know as *Samurai*," he said. "What you heard was less exaggerated than you thought. As for handling fire—"

He decided a simple demonstration might save him the trouble of having to convince lingering doubters, and prevent further unnecessary violence and injury on their side. He held out his hand, and a gout of flame burst into being, raging upward more than a foot before easing back to a few inches, then dying out.

The Muscovite vampires leaped backward, all except Aleksandr, though he was clearly startled.

"You can hold fire in your hand and your vampire tissues are not consumed!" he gasped. "Ve also heard that you survived a day in the sun, another impossibility, yet it must be so; your skin is darker, human–looking, like Russians from the south near the Black Sea."

Mike nodded, then reeled as a wave of dizziness all but overwhelm him.

Aleksandr leaped forward and grabbed his arms to steady him, joined by one of the braver of the Muscovites.

"Thank you," Mike breathed. "I'll be fine in a moment. I just need —"

"You need blood," Aleksandr insisted, and looked about to tear into his own wrist.

Mike forestalled him, pulled his stainless steel flask from his back pocket, and drained it in two quaffs, feeling the blood restore him. *Serves me right for showing off so soon after propelling myself up here*, he chided himself.

"I've been studying at the *Scholomance* — the new one, in Scotland," he explained. "Apparently some of my ancestors were gifted in areas of so–called magic." Then, seeing many still showed signs of anxiety, he added, "I mean you no harm. Nor do the *Scholomance*. They watch and observe, keeping a watchful eye on the predators. I seem to have become their enforcer."

Aleksandr nodded. "Ve, too, mean you no harm. Vhat you do is good for us: You veed out the bad vons, removing for us the danger of being exposed by their villainous ways. And, you have done much to improve our situation, like vhat you did in Austria. Ve even have a blood netvork in Russia now, as your Lord Dewhurst clearly knows, though —" he spat at the rooftop, "— Vladimir Putin vould destroy it if he knew. He'd probably vant to be von of us, and force us to be like ve vere a century ago."

Mike pondered this and commented "You don't like your president very much."

"He is just another Bolshevik," Aleksandr said, then, "No; he is more like the vons who took over from the Bolsheviks, the Stalinists. The Bolsheviks merely vanted to improve their lot from how oppressive the Tzars could be, but the ultimate leaders, people like Stalin, vere villains, who saw that they could pervert Marx's principles and make themselves the new Tzars. Putin is von of these. The Presidents before him vere no different. They, too, vere autocratic tyrants. *The People's this, and the People's that,*—" he spat again at the roof. "Nothing vas the people's.

"And, as for the people, most feel the same distrust of this Putin, but, under him, Russia has been a bit more prosperous for some. It is easy to be blinded by hope of a return to the so–called glory of former days vhen Russia vas a Soviet power, but it is all an illusion: power and glory for those in charge, somevhat shorter breadlines for the new proletariat."

Mike nodded, then said, "I'm here to locate and rescue a friend — a human who was kidnapped from England. I have evidence suggesting that he may have been captured by the FSB and taken somewhere."

"Then he vill be in Lefortovo," Aleksandr said. "Lefortovo vas given to the FSB for their use. And, Michael Cameron, your friend's situation could not be more hopeless. The FSB are no less ruthless than the KGB before them."

Mike frowned. "Thank you, Aleksandr." He offered his hand to the vampire, who hesitated, as if expecting it to be hot from the flame he'd conjured earlier, then took it in a strong grip.

"Good luck vith your mission, Michael Cameron, good luck with rescuing your friend," he said. His coven of vampires all nodded and murmured, "*Udacha,*" which Mike decided was probably Russian for *good luck.*

Since the return to the rooftop of the *Radisson Slavyanskaya* was all downhill, Mike found he only had to control his direction of motion and slow his descent before landing.

———————

Once back in the suite, Mike grabbed a bottle of blood and headed for the bath, laying it in the tub while he ran more hot water. After ten minutes, he uncorked it and began drinking straight from the bottle. Soon he was luxuriating in steaming hot water, surrounded by lit candles, and still drinking from the bottle.

As his mind reached out over the hub of central Moscow, he wished he could speak Russian enough to better sample the thoughts of those he encountered.

Finding Butyrka took some time, and what he did find was worse than a zoo. It was overcrowded and, as near as he could tell, the guards were brutal. Exploring from cellblock to cellblock became an exhausting headache that produced no results. The water was going cold, the candles burning low, when he came across a simple mental image that transcended language. A handful of guards had done a double–take on two escorted prisoners who had come through the main entrance, been signed in, then whisked off down corridors and out a side exit. One had been moderately tall, aided on each side by two FSB soldiers, and bleeding from both thighs. The other, more burly and as slovenly as a homeless person, had been confined to a wheelchair.

The images allowed Mike to tune in to Mason's residual spiritual energy enough to try to track him as he left, but the trail faded until he had nothing left but a vague sense of direction.

Mike sat up in the tub. *Perhaps Tony and Nigel can help,* he thought, then, arising from the tub, he grabbed a towel and was starting to dry himself when a slender pair of arms encompassed him from behind. It brought a warm smile to his face.

"I surrender," he declared, raising his arms above his head. Then, turning slowly about, he brought his arms down so that they were about Carrie.

"Were you too focused on the case to miss me?" she asked, making a pout.

Mike felt guilty. It was true, though there were many times during the past several days when his thoughts had turned to her. "Not all the time," he claimed, then his lips sought hers. He swept her up in his arms and carried her to the bed.

"Oo," she cooed; "I like your outfit."

"You're bad," he teased.

"I try to be," she replied in a coquettish manner, "— just for you."

Slow embraces, exploratory fondles, and random kissing soon gave way to unabashed passion.

Afterward, holding her against him, Mike noticed that her breathing returned to normal almost as fast as his, proof that she'd been continuing the training exercises he'd taught her.

"You've been practicing Wing Chun?" he asked.

She gave a tiny nod, then giggled. "Every day until I left to fly here," she assured him. "You might need to repair the dummy — it's cracked in a few places — well, broken more than cracked. I snapped off the two outer arms, and one of the extended legs is sort of, well, um — shattered."

"Sort of shattered?" he echoed.

"I think I got carried away," she admitted in a meek tone, causing Mike to break into a grin.

"Don't worry; if I can't fix it, I can arrange for parts to be sent out, even if they have to come from Hong Kong or China."

She smiled at that, then her face became more somber. "What did you learn about Mason?" she asked.

"I still don't know where he is," Mike replied. "I need to talk to Tony, and see if Nigel can dig up something — maybe track the van via traffic–cam."

He told her about the vampires he'd met on the rooftop, including how he'd foolishly drained himself of energy, hoping to spare them unnecessary violence, then explained Aleksandr Romanoff's unique place in Russia's history.

"Aleksandr told me the FSB use a prison called Lefortovo. I should tell Nigel about that," he said. "I'm sure he can unearth a ream of information about the place. They also offered a curious perspective on President Putin." He frowned. "I've always felt that Russia's new president had a darker side, but everything I've learned here points to him being more of a concern than most of the world might realize."

"Oh, I almost forgot," Carrie murmured to Mike, "I have almost a week's worth of newspapers in my suitcase — mostly that rag, the *Examiner*, but a few copies of the *Times*, as well. What the *Examiner* is saying about Mason is awful. *The Times* makes a slight effort to defend him, commenting mostly on MI6's lack of response, and how they should be silencing the *Examiner* — something about an Official Secrets Act?"

Mike smiled, and kissed her. "Not to worry," he said. "It's all in hand, and will soon blow up in the *Examiner*'s face."

13: *Lieutenant Cherninova*

Natasha Cherninova, *Tasha* to her one or two close friends, stared at her reflection as she adjusted her bra — not as delicate or as flattering as many in the shop, but the nicer models had exceeded her budget, as well as the strict uniform guidelines of the FSB. She'd been looking for wider shoulder straps, when she found this one, more feminine than the old industrial models. She couldn't have handled a 12–hour shift on one of the more expensive frilly numbers, with their stringy straps biting into her shoulders. Besides, she was reluctant to reward her breasts with special privileges.

It had taken most of her life to accept them as being part of her. At first, when she was fifteen, new to the Russian National Swimming Team, she was almost proud. Her mother, who claimed Romanian ancestry, had had an amazing figure. But Natasha's breasts not only decided to grow, but seemed determined to grow faster than all the other girl's, threatening to slow her glide through the water. And then there were the reactions: first the other girls whispering and giggling, then the boys on the men's team ogling and leering at her like hungry wolves. The thought triggered the recurring nightmare — the Seoul Olympics, 1988 —

Locker room — two burly swimmers from the men's team grabbing her, dragging her to a bench — the men's captain leaning against a locker, instructing his confederates to hold her down — her legs flailing and kicking — two others grab her ankles — then the captain, Grigori, on her, inside her —

She squeezed her eyes shut, forcing the memory back into the deep, dark closet where she'd been locking it away for years. When she opened her eyes, her arms were trying to hide her bosom. *Not so big*, the lingerie clerk had teased, *barely more than C–cup. You should have seen the lady I served yesterday — surgically enhanced, Oo, la–la. Of course, with your pronounced pecks, latissimus dorsi, and more powerful than usual trapezius muscles, it just draws the eyes upward — You were a swimmer, mishka? But, of course you were! I remember you, Natasha Cherninova.*

Natasha hastily pulled on her uniform blouse and buttoned it, directing her eyes away from the mirror and onto the two faces in frames on her bureau — framed newspaper clippings. She'd even written *Enemy of the State* across the visible portions of the articles under each photo, a ploy designed to throw off suspicion should her apartment ever be searched.

At forty–two years of age, with more than twenty–five years in first the KGB and then the FSB, she knew all about the paranoia needed to survive in the job. No one could ever know that the round, pleasant face to the right of the mirror was her father, or that the one to the left, recently deceased, was a friend and former colleague of her father's. In fact, one of her last assignments, before being reassigned to Floor One, Special Wing, at Lefortovo, had been to keep her father under surveillance — that is until he finally backed away from all investigations, anything to do with the FSB, and seemed to drift into obscurity — a disgraced FSB colonel, turned lawyer.

He and her mother had been teenagers, experimenting with their young passions — her mother sixteen, her father unbeknown to her mother at the time, not quite fifteen. Natasha's mother was horrified, filled with shame when she learned Mikhail's age — when she found she was pregnant — but was soon ushered off to a special home to have the child. Then, in his twenties, now a young KGB agent, her father met and married a woman and had a son, ending forever any access to his name. That mattered nothing to her, though; her mother's name had been enough. Her mother had proudly drawn Tasha's attention to her father's every success and promotion.

Pride and shame. It wasn't until her own puberty became so blatantly evident that her mother told her of the tragic story of her conception, warning her to be chaste, to be careful.

"I thought they would throw me in a prison for being some kind of slut and daring to ruin Mikhail's future," her mother had declared. "Why would I want to ruin his future? I thought I loved him; we both thought we were caught up in a fairy tale love story."

That was when Natasha was thirteen, the same year everything changed for her. The school swimming coach discovered Natasha had just broken a school record in the distance freestyle. After that, it was a military–style regimen of training, controlled dietary regimen — To finance it all, she was inducted into a cadet program — *junior KGB*, they joked.

By sixteen she was a low level KGB operative, given language training, and enrolled in Moscow University — *Listen carefully to all they say, Natasha. You never know what might be useful, Chat with the American girls, the West German girls, the Canadian girls, the French girls, the Finnish girls... And not just the girls — when you're around the men, stick out your chest a little more, and smile.*

That was how it had all started. She seemed to always make the National Team, and then the Olympic Team, though there were times (*and they got really mad*) when she barely qualified. When she was fifteen — a difficult year for her: her chest had slowed her time by the barest fraction of a second — an official from the Russian committee had taken the coach aside, had a quiet chat, after–which the lowest ranking girl was bumped from the team to guarantee a spot for Natasha. The girl wasn't KGB.

It wasn't until years later, after the KGB had become the FSB, when she found herself spying on her own father, that her discomfort and discontent grew beyond tolerable, but she had to hide it. With the advent of the Putin regime, discontented people were no longer safe — they had a way of becoming mysteriously injured or even disappearing. Some had been gunned down in broad daylight in front of their own homes, and before witnesses too shocked and frightened bear witness.

She glanced at the face in the frame to the left — the other *enemy of the state*. They'd assigned him to assassinate her father in 1995, right after pulling him off the Soldi Bank Investigation, where corrupt banking deals involving the Russian mob, crooked banking officials, a confusing mix of the Chechen mob and Chechen rebels, proved to be what her father had decided was a hotbed of FSB corruption. Faced with intimidation and a fear of assassination, he'd almost resigned. Then, in 1999, the very assassin assigned to kill him in '95 requested him as special investigator for the September Bombings, blamed on Chechen separatists. Mikhail found abundant evidence, all pointing to the FSB, including several of the same characters from the Soldi Bank Case. He wrote a letter to the Director of the FSB. Then the persecution escalated. He resigned, falling back on his recently–

earned lawyer's license. He continued to fight, drafting an open letter to President Yeltsin, and filing a lawsuit against the FSB.

Once more the FSB called upon Colonel Litvinenko to rid them of this troublesome do–gooder. But the more Litvinenko looked into her father's acts, the more he liked him. Not only that, but the FSB hardliner General kept tacking more names onto the hit–list. So, Alexander Litvinenko stalled, then, knowing that everything her father had been claiming was true, to the FSB's shock and dismay, he went public at a Moscow news conference.

Then his own troubles began.

She smiled at the face with it's movie–star looks — that is until the ravages of radioactive polonium had destroyed his beauty, until he ultimately died in a London hospital, another retired exile.

Retired, she thought, annoyed at the cruel irony of the word. *Yes, he retired from public life — fired from the FSB on trumped up charges, after daring to levy accusations against the country's heroic President. Retired — yes, the FSB retired him, alright.* Retirement was even a euphemism for assassination here in Russia, copied from American movies.

Her blouse tucked in and declared wrinkle–free, she tightened her belt, tied her tie and fastened it with the tie clip, then donned her uniform tunic.

She picked up the holster belt, buckling it about her waist, then pulled her tunic down to eliminate wrinkles. She scowled. The very uniform code that demanded perfection, seemed also designed to draw attention to her chest.

Pulling the Makarov PMM from its holster, she pulled the clip, then ejected the chamber round. Returning the bullet to the clip, she reinserted the clip, then snapped the muzzle slide back to cock the weapon and chamber a round, then, holding the hammer with her thumb, she squeezed the trigger and eased the hammer back into place before holstering the weapon once more. It felt heavy in her small hands. Rumour had it that, in the forces of the West, women were often issued lighter sidearms. Not so for the FSB. In the FSB a woman had to be a man. Women had to be as ruthless as men. *And all because they wanted more rounds in the magazine, and higher muzzle velocity. For me, this thing kicks like a mule!*

Picking up a small swatch of polishing cloth, she wiped at her name–tag, making sure there were no blemishes. *Lt. N. Cherninova* — finally a First Lieutenant. How long had *that* taken? *Too long*, she told herself, knowing that she'd have been a major by now, if only she could have been more ruthless.

If only she'd *been more ruthless.* If the KGB had been more ruthless, they might have done something about how the men's swim team had gang–raped her that day after practice, but, hey, they were KGB, too. And the team captain had been a senior sergeant, about to become a sergeant major. *You are just a lance corporal, Corporal Cherninova, and barely sixteen*, the officer had reminded her. *And who are your* alleged *attackers?* (he gave special emphasis to the word *alleged*) — *two corporals, two junior sergeants, and a soon–to–be sergeant major.*

She'd been forced to knuckle under. She'd stood in front of the mirror that night, crying her eyes out, clutching a butcher's carving knife in her fist, determined to cut off the offending breasts that had betrayed her so ultimately, but, in the end, she didn't have the courage.

Instead, she made a point of avoiding the men's team for the rest of her swimming career. But their horrid captain had become the bane of her existence. Even now, the major who had officiated over her final interview before allowing her promotion to first lieutenant, had been that same self-important, entitled asshole who had led the assault on her that day. Grigori Dyatlov — how she wished she could take a carving knife to parts of *his* anatomy. He'd even smiled at her through the whole interview, enjoying her discomfiture. In the end, it was almost as if he'd finally taken pity on her. Maybe it was the faint burn scar on her face, just before her left ear — hot wax, thrown in her face by this very bastard, two years after she left the national swimming team. *No, General Kashirin had whispered something in his ear, something that had made him blanche.*

She clenched her jaws, grinding her back teeth in frustration as she gave her tunic one last downward tug. Grigori Dyatlov hadn't been motivated by lust; it was all about control and domination. He'd seen her as a looming threat that had to be subjugated, at least that was what the therapist had insisted.

Still, the hate lingered. She hated Major Grigori Dyatlov. She hated the FSB. She hated the government that was ruining her country — but what could she do about it?

Go to work, she admonished herself. *Go to work and bide your time.*

Lefortovo, Special Section, Floor One

She'd barely settled into focusing on the routine tasks at her duty station when a general appeared. She snapped to attention the moment she saw him approaching, followed by a small gang of FSB privates, with a few lance corporals, some surrounding a pathetic–looking ruin of a man in a wheelchair.

Two more burly soldiers were supporting a moderately tall, ruggedly handsome man, who looked as if he couldn't stand unassisted. His trousers were a ruined mess, one leg torn off above the knee, with two salvaged strips acting as crude bandages at mid–thigh. This one forced a weary smile, then straightened his posture, as if embarrassed by his appearance, and wishing he could make a better impression. He reminded Natasha of a lion: still regal, even in captivity.

The other, the one in the wheelchair, was a slovenly beast. He had untrustworthy eyes — he was a predator — not something noble and courageous like a lion, but more devious, slinking — *hyena* was the distasteful image that came to mind.

She took all this in with a few quick glances, just as her training had drilled into her.

She was ready for the general — *General Kemedov* she read from the name–tag. This was the general who had arranged the assassination of her father's friend and former colleague, possibly even the several failed attempts on her father.

She snapped to attention, gave a brisk salute, then reached to take the transfer papers from him.

"Two transfers from Butyrka," she stated blandly. "Any special considerations or attributes I should note in the log — anything that might affect cell consideration?"

"Well," General Kemedov offered with a wolfish leer that sent a chill down her spine, "since our friend in the wheelchair — a former KGB operative from *the good old days* — is the one who shot our other friend in both legs, I think making them roommates is highly inadvisable." He barked out a roar of laughter.

She made sure not to smile. She knew enough of this general's reputation to know better. His cruel attempt at humour had probably been designed to trick her into that very lapse. He was known to be not just cruel, but corrupt — he was also known to live beyond his means, but no one knew how he managed it. And, when you're an FSB General, it took an order from Putin himself to launch an investigation.

"There are two available cells, without shifting other inmates," she stated, rotating the monitor to show him. "36, an isolation cell, and 19, here, down this corridor which got all new beds this year. Other than that, if you had specific locations in mind, I could arrange relocations to make those cells available."

Kemedov was now eying her up and down. She had a mental image of him licking his lips, and steeled herself to avoid an instinctive shudder.

"Very dedicated of you First Lieutenant Cherninova — very dedicated. I must note that in my report. Hmm, yes, Cherninova, our darling Olympiad." Again the leering smile.

Then, "Let's give the more comfortable bed to Captain Mason — he's a senior MI6 man, and I suspect his visit to our fair country was not of his own choosing, though I leave it to others to have the last word on that. No doubt the man at the top will revel in parading him on the news as a captured spy, seeking some long–sought–after British embarrassment. In fact, I'd even suggest letting a doctor have a look at him — perhaps in a week," he added with a cruel smile.

She pulled the in–house radio from her belt and spoke into it. In less than ten seconds, two soldiers with keys appeared on scene, prepared to escort the prisoners to their cells.

Before departing, Kemedov shot back over his shoulder, "I'll see if I can't arrange interrogations for next Sunday, the 31st. How about we schedule Petroff for 10:00 AM?"

Then he was gone.

14: *Mason & Natasha*

Mason groaned and struggled to sit up. He felt stiff, and his leg wounds, though somewhat scabbed over, still wept some blood and tissue fluid whenever he moved his legs.

So don't move them, he reprimanded himself.

The guard, an FSB private, was standing just inside the door. The sleeves of his blue–and–grey camo fatigues were rolled up to the elbow, an FSB logo being the only marking on the rest of the sleeve. He looked barely more than twenty.

"Has he eaten yet?" a woman's voice asked in Russian, from just beyond the doorway. He decided it was a pleasant voice — *pleasant? Delightful, almost erotic voice. Probably has the face of a bulldog.*

The guard took a step forward and pushed the door further open, then snapped to attention. "I was just about to give him his tray, sir."

Sir? The woman who now stepped just into the doorway was hardly a *sir!* In England, *Ma'am* might have been considered appropriate, though political correctness was forcing a trend toward calling women officers *sir*, even in his own branch of service.

This one, though, was strikingly good to look at, and pleasingly well–built, too — clearly an athlete.

There was a childlike petiteness about her — he decided it was the combination of her slim, athletic build, and her height of maybe five–foot–four. He guessed her age at mid– to late–thirties.

"Forgive my not standing in the presence of a lady," he said, flashing his most charming smile. "I'm afraid recent events have left me at a bit of a disadvantage where such courtesies are concerned."

She offered the barest hint of a smile in return/ Stepping completely into the cell, she pulled a small wooden table up in front of where Mason sat at the edge of his bed, then retrieved his food tray from a stand just inside the door, and set it before him. She gave him much more radiant smile, then stepped back to the doorway.

"Since the General saw fit to give him the nicer of the two cells," she announced to the guard, "let us also make sure that he doesn't starve to death. I'm almost off–duty, so I'll see that he eats. I'll mention to Lt. Rosikoff that you should see that he also eats lunch."

Then, almost as if in afterthought, she added, "maybe we should mark this one as deserving of special meals, rather than the usual slop that passes for food, though this facility is actually quite good for its meals. I hear that what passes for food at Butyrka would choke a pig."

The guard shot an apprehensive glance to the adjacent corner, where a dome–shaped housing marked the location of a surveillance camera and, most probably, an associated microphone.

"This is Lefortovo, an FSB facility;" she reminded him, "I hardly think they'd be interested in my opinion of the food at Butyrka."

And yet, you lowered your voice and maintained a careful lack of modulation, Mason thought.

It was apparent from the guard's fidgeting that he wanted to leave, but seemed awkward about how to make it happen until the lieutenant showed a hint of a smile, then stepped clear of the doorway and into the room, stopping directly under the camera housing.

"Let me know when you're ready, sir," he said just above a murmur, "and I'll be back to open the door."

She nodded, touched a finger to the antenna of her radio and held up two fingers. When he looked confused, she rolled her eyes and gave the call button two rapid presses. His radio responded immediately with two pops of squelch.

His eyes showed understanding, then he nodded, said, "Yes, sir," and left.

Mason lifted the hard plastic warming cover and found a bowl of beef broth, an elongated dinner roll (he decided it was rather like a small baguette), and a cup of black coffee. He was surprised; he'd expected tea.

"Is it permitted to ask the time?" he asked as pleasantly as possible. "I mean, is this meant to be breakfast, lunch, or supper?"

She looked as if a sarcastic retort was about to come, then murmured in English, "Around here we just call it *food*. However," she glanced at her watch, "since it is after nine o'clock — 9:00 PM — you can regard it as dinner or supper. You've probably been asleep for most of the day. The guard brought out your lunch untouched."

"Your English is very good," Mason offered. "You could probably pass for American or Canadian." He sampled the broth, than raised the bowl and drank off several ounces.

"Or maybe even British," she responded, giving him a version of his own Oxford accent so flawless that he reacted in a burst of laughter, causing him to almost gag on his soup, which burst forth in a spray.

He floundered for a napkin, then found the most absurd excuse of a flimsy little paper napkin he'd ever seen, more suited a small roadside restaurant.

"Bravo!" he rasped, still coughing a little. "I could take you home with me — you'd fit right in."

"At MI6?" she asked, raising her eyebrows, her tone still humourous.

"Heaven forbid!" he declared, still keeping his voice barely more than a murmur. "They'd monopolize your time with a myriad of questions about military strength, missiles, etc. No, if I truly took you home, I'd probably put in for the retirement I've been avoiding for the last thirteen years, so I could be free to show you around to all the beauties of the British Isles."

"Such as..." she prompted. "Missile silos? Military bases? Naval shipyards?"

He frowned, giving a sad little shake of his head. "Alas, I fear *C* and the Minister of Defense would have firm opinions about that. No, my dear, I was thinking more along the lines of Hyde Park in London, the coast of Cornwall, the Dover cliffs, the forests of Wales, Hadrian's Wall, and beyond that, the unending grandeur of the Scottish Highlands. In fact, just two years back, because of a friend, I had occasion to visit a charming old castle in the town of Anstruther, where they actually claim to teach some form of Wicca — witchcraft."

She fell silent, staring at him as if in shock.

Good lord, old man, you've actually gone too far. She either thinks you're half serious or, more likely, full barmy.

Picking up the roll, he nibbled a little at an end, then dipped it in the broth.

"Of course, you'd probably have to clear it with your husband," he added with a shrug.

A musical laugh burst out of her so fast that her hand shot up over her mouth with an audible *smack*. She fought to recover, looking guiltily up at the camera, though the merriment never left her eyes, she seemed to be fighting back further laughter.

So beautiful, yet so inhibited, he thought. *What happened to break your spirit?* He glanced at the rank markings on her epaulets — lieutenant first class. *So why isn't she at least a major or colonel?*

"Just as, I'm sure, you'd have to overcome your wife's objections," she riposted, the light of humour still dancing in her eyes.

Mason drew a breath, took an experimental bite from the broth–soaked roll, then set it down.

"That won't be necessary," he explained, trying to keep the sadness out of his voice, but it came through anyway. "She died rather suddenly almost thirty years ago." The show of sympathy in her eyes surprised him.

"Suddenly?" she prompted in a hesitating tone,

"Did you see the James Bond film, *On Her Majesty's Secret Service* — with George Lazenby?"

The life seemed to leave her eyes. "She died in an explosion — a car bomb?"

"I'm sure it was meant for me, but I wasn't the one who started the car, hoping for a simple trip to the apothecary." He lowered his eyes. "I came close to packing it in after that. It took a dear friend named Tony to pull me through. One doesn't make a lot of friends in this business — well, at least *my* corner of it, assuming you're not being groomed for the SVR."

"There was a time," she mused, "but not so much anymore." Then, "I'm sure you have a lot of friends..." She stopped, a puzzled look crossing her face.

"So what brought you to Russia, Captain Mason? General Kemedov suggested that — how did he word it?— that your visit might not have been of your own choosing?" she seemed cautious, trying to make it sound like a casual conversation.

"I owe it all to a former opponent from the Cold War. He had his daughter kidnap me and smuggle me out of Britain in a coffin, all so he could dump me in a cell and shoot me in both legs.

"You see, my dear — I'm sorry — Leftenant —"
he paused to read her name–tag "— Cherninova.
Calling you *my dear* is a typical British slip of the
tongue when speaking to a beautiful young lady. I'd
hate to add a charge of sexual harassment to whatever
charges your government is compiling, stemming from
my unannounced presence in your country."

She seemed curiously amused at his last joke. *Is
sexual harassment even an offense over here? No, it
goes much deeper than that — she's made complaints
in the past and they've been ignored, or worse. And I'd
wager that burn scar on her face is somehow involved.*

"Anyway, you see, Leftenant, some years back,
this former rival convinced me that he wanted to
defect. I came over to smuggle him out. I think he lost
his nerve at the last moment — we were just crossing
over into Finland.

"Well, the blighter pulled his weapon and tried to
shoot me. Got me, too — well, not much more than a
graze, really — not a very impressive marksman, our
Mr. Petroff. He'd already turned away from me, to run
back across the border into Mother Russia.

"I meant to shoot him in the leg, mostly to keep
him from coming after me. Apparently, the bullet
passed through both legs from the side. The rest is the
result of whatever he put himself through getting back
to Moscow. But, when he finally arrived — he
apparently felt he couldn't call for a ride — someone
was waiting to arrest and question him.

"They questioned him for a while in Lubyanka.
The KGB must have been upset with him. They were
more interested in torture tactics than any kind of
medical care. Eventually, at Butyrka, a doctor felt
obliged to amputate his legs.

"So, Anatoli felt it was the height of fair play to
shoot my driver, have me gassed in my car, and
smuggle me into Russia. In fact, he didn't even do it

himself; he brainwashed his daughter — she was posing as a reporter for a London tabloid — into doing it all for him. She seemed convinced that I was the author of all her father's problems. Aside from recognizing the inside of a coffin, I never even knew where I was — somewhere rural, eventually, whereupon Petroff made his entrance, shot me in each leg, then left me in a cell, shackled, barely able to move, with what might best be described as medieval shackles.

"I had just finished escaping — part of that involved disarticulating my right thumb —" he held up the hand, the thumb still swollen, "—fortunately, as you may have noticed, I'm left–handed.

"I managed to kill the nastier of my two guards — a sadistic brute, I dare say — and was just lurching my way out into the unseasonable cold, when I heard gunshots and practically ran into the arms of an FSB soldier. He escorted me back into the building, where I met General Kemedov. He, or perhaps one of his men, had shot everyone but Petroff: his daughter, who had masterminded my abduction and tried to make me look like a traitor — even the one humane jailor."

Mason felt like he'd talked enough for one day, so he shrugged, picked up the coffee and sipped, putting it down immediately — it had gone cold.

He shifted himself back onto the bed so he could lean against the wall.

"You never did respond to my hint about a husband," he reminded her.

A curious, almost pensive, look came over her, which softened her entire demeanor, giving him a hint of how pretty a little girl she must have been. Even with the burn mark on the side of her face, she was still extremely attractive. "I am not married," she said finally, as if admitting it caused some form of pain. He decided to change the subject.

"Well," he said, "that meal was so wonderful that I can hardly wait for the next one."

It brought a glimmer of a smile back to her face, and she suggested, "You should probably rest, and I must return to my station before anyone notices I'm not there — though it's not as if the upper hierarchy would inconvenience themselves by visiting us at this late hour. In fact, my relief should arrive in five minutes — a better reason for me to hurry back to the duty desk."

She tapped the call button on her radio twice.

"Perhaps I'll check on you after I'm back on duty tomorrow — sometime after 10:00 AM."

Mason smiled. "I've been away from my desk at MI6 for God knows how long, but I'm sure my social calendar is quite clear for the next day or two."

———————

Mason awoke to a darkened cell. He was about to roll onto his side and sit up, but something was restraining his arms — no, more than that — there was a broad hospital–style restraining strap across his chest, and restraints on his arms as well.

It puzzled him. At some point someone had added the additional features to his narrow bunk.

He also felt more groggy than he had when he'd last awoken. *So what's this about? Is someone keeping me drugged? Lt. Cherninova? — Surely not — Steady on, old man; don't jump to her defense too eagerly. After all, she's Russian and FSB, and you know next to nothing about her.*

Yet all his training and experience in making assessments about people, *profiling, as the Yanks now called it*, told him she was trustworthy. In fact, there was something vulnerable about her — he'd been good at spotting that in women — something that made her ripe for just the right kind of subtle persuasion. It would take time, but time was what he had in surplus.

So, what's with these restraints, old top?

His mind felt clearer now. He could move his legs, though they were still uncomfortable. *If only someone would remove the confounded bullets!* He then noticed something amiss with his right hand — Someone had set his thumb into proper position, using two wooden stir sticks for splints, taping the whole thing with medical tape.

"Lt. Cherninova," he murmured aloud. *So it was you after all. You probably didn't dare to remove the bullets — Kemedov may have even specifically ordered that they be left alone — but you took it upon yourself to repair my thumb and make sure I remained quiet and still until everything settled.*

His stomach was rumbling but, with no idea of the time or when someone was going to bring food, he composed himself to drift back to sleep.

———————

He awoke abruptly to the rattle of keys in the cell door and the *clank* as the deadbolt withdrew, and was pleasantly surprised when Lt. Cherninova entered bearing a food tray.

"Did you do this?" he asked, trying to gesture with his taped hand.

She smiled and gave a quick nod, then sidestepped to her corner, out of the camera's line of sight, and passed the tray to the guard, who set it on the table, now moved against the wall. He then released the restraints confining Mason, and helped him to sit up before moving the table into position in front of him.

She fixed the guard with a stern glare that made the young soldier straighten, salute, and leave, closing the door behind him.

"It was the least I could do — Kemedov's orders, while implied, were somewhat specific — that you could probably wait a week before the bullets were removed." She made a grimace. He decided that she didn't like Kemedov very much, but, recalling what he knew of Kemedov's reputation for brutality, especially with women, he wasn't surprised.

"You're very kind," he said, offering up his most charming smile, and getting the reaction he hoped for: a hint of a blush and a more bashful smile than usual.

"And you're very stubborn," she replied. "I had to sedate you to do anything, and, even as the sedative was taking effect, you were still trying to tear off the splints. Restraining you seemed essential to your healing. So how does your hand feel today?"

The thumb was totally immobilized — she'd even used an aluminum finger splint to brace across his hand sideways. He could wiggle his fingers. He loosened the tape just enough, and found he could wag his thumb a little within the confines of the loosened splint.

"I dare say it'll be quite functional soon enough," he said, then, "Again, I really must thank you, *Leftenant* Cherninova."

He was hoping the exaggerated formality might spark a desire for informality on her part, and make her reveal her first name.

There was a moment of hesitation, then an odd smile — rebellious? — then she murmured, "Natasha."

"Natasha," Mason repeated, then broadening his own smile, he added, "I bet your dearest friends call you *Tasha*."

"One or two," she conceded. "And you, *Captain* Mason?"

"Just Mason," he insisted. "My mother had a pedophile brother named Bruce, of whom she was inordinately fond — of course no one knew he was a pedophile. Apparently I was one of the first to learn of it, when I was fifteen and he decided to pay a nocturnal visit; I snapped, gave him a sound thrashing, much to Mother's horror, and left. I joined the Navy right after, and soon refused to be called anything but *Mason*."

She remained silent. "I, too, know something about such abuse," she said after a while, hesitating, but, once she started, it seemed to just pour out, until she'd told him a horrific tale concerning a Sergeant Grigori Dyatlov and the men's swimming team.

Now it was his turn to feel aghast. "And your superiors did nothing?" he asked.

"They were men, more important than I, and their captain was already looking at promotion to sergeant major." She shrugged as if she'd come to accept the insignificance of it.

"But you were only sixteen — I'd have horsewhipped the blighters, the whole bally lot of them!" Mason snarled, clenching his teeth in righteous fury.

She smiled unexpectedly. "I expect you would have," she asserted. "Are all the male agents of the British Secret Intelligence Service so staunchly chivalrous?"

He grinned, "Absolutely, m' dear; why, you have to spread a cape over a puddle for a lady just to be interviewed for application."

Natasha giggled. "Sir Walter Raleigh for Queen Elizabeth I," she acknowledged. "But, coming back to your name: you must have a middle name."

Mason made a wry grimace. "None I'd willingly admit," he declared. "I even had MI6 expunge it from my birth certificate. In fact, a hacker acquaintance assures me that there is no official record anywhere of my ever having had a middle name."

"Oh, my, that is serious," she chuckled. "Okay, then, *Mason* it shall be."

For the next several days their routine seemed the same. He began to fear she might get into trouble for the time she spent in his cell, always standing just out of camera view, but she never seem worried. Soon, he found he looked forward to her visits — almost always at meal times.

One Thursday evening — she not only told him the day, but also the date, revealing to him just how long it'd been since he'd been spirited out of Britain — she finally confessed to having used sedatives, not just to keep him quiet in the beginning, but to get his time turned around so that he slept during her off–shift and was awake for her duty schedule.

"Lt. Rosikoff is a fair–minded, and, I think, a kind man — he's young, very much in love with his young wife, and has a daughter, whom he considers to be an angel. However, he expects a promotion in the new year, and might be a stickler for the rules until he makes First Lieutenant."

Mason frowned. "How long have you been a first lieutenant?" Her repeated use of the word *young* made him question his initial assessment of her age.

"I got this last promotion eight months ago," she said with a sigh.

"Still," he offered by way of encouragement, "you're — what? — early–thirties? Surely you'll be a captain soon, and a major in another few years."

She glanced at the floor, then raised her eyes to meet his. "I turned forty-two last August." There was a hint of defeat in her voice.

Forty-two! I'd never have guessed that! Yet the thought of her being over forty actually made him feel better. *What are you thinking, you old dog?* But it was true: as impossible as the situation was, he was actually attracted to this woman that he'd been conditioned to regard as the enemy, though, at some point, probably before Petroff showed his true colours, he'd begun to think of Russia, at least, more as the opposing team, the competition.

"Tasha," he tried, hoping to console her, "I was a commander most of my career. I only made captain when I left field duty and took my current posting, which I can assure you, is a far–from–glamourous desk–job."

"Thank you for your attempted encouragement, Mason, but, do I really have to remind you that your MI6 rank is naval, whereas mine is army?" The smile was a kindly one. "You were actually either a major or a lieutenant–colonel for most of your career, lieutenant commander being the equivalent of major."

Mason sighed, then nodded. "Leftenant– commander from the moment I moved to *double–0* section, then full commander by the eighties.

"By the way," he added, anxious to change the subject, "depending on when in August your birthday is, I think we're both Leos. I dare say, though, that there's still a vast discrepancy in our ages, alas."

He was expecting her to laugh, her eyes reflecting the absurdity of the situation, but the smile never wavered; in fact, it seemed to broaden slightly.

"So, what? — you're over fifty," she countered, her tone skeptical.

"Alas, my dear, I was sixty–eight last August — the nineteenth."

"You must be a terrible torment to the young agents in the MI6 gymnasium!"

He wasn't wasn't sure which shocked him more: the admiring glow in her eyes or the glowing feeling it inspired in him.

15: *Finding Mason*

Thursday, Nov. 28

W hen Nigel finally reported back to Mike with an image of the FSB van passing through an intersection on the opposite side of the beltway labeled as *3-e Koltso*, he was exuberant in his excitement. "Your new friends, 'e Muscovite vampires, were right, Michael," he declared. "An', from whot I can gavver 'bout ffe FSB, ffat lo' are a bunch o' bleedin' buggers ye might wanna ffink twice 'bout messin' wiff, ffough I'm sure you migh' feel more sure o' yerself ffan I would — well, maybe even more so ffan mos' MI6 spooks."

Mike held his breath a moment, then, "*Nigel* — get to the point, please."

"Yeah, righ', gov'nor. *Anyway*, Lefortovo Prison, is jus' east o' ffe *3-e Koltso* — ffe second beltway from 'e center o' Moscow. Yer hotel, ffe *Raddison Slavyanskaya* is jus' off ffe west side o' ffe same beltway.

"Oh, an' Michael, remember wonderin' 'ow yer boy Putin got to be bleedin' Prime Minister o' ffe Russian Federation in 'e firs' place? Well, I go' it, an it's a doozy!"

"Try to summarize, Nigel," Mike admonished. "My mind is already planning to go out–of–body to find Mason."

"Right you are, gov'nor," Nigel said quickly. "Well, Boris Yeltsin were in a panic: ffe bleedin' Prosecutor General, a bloke named Skuratov, were investigatin' 'im for corruption, an' 'e noose were tightenin' 'bout 'is neck. Well, I go' video o' Putin's former top boss, General Oleg Kalugin, 'splainin' 'ow Putin 'ad a meetin' wiff Yeltsin, ffen invited ffis Skuratov to an FSB apartment, where 'e met up wiff two young Brass Flutes."

"Translate, Nigel, and please avoid further Cockneyisms," Mike said in controlled tone. "Mason still languishes in a prison cell somewhere."

"Prostitutes — 'ookers," Nigel translated. "Anyway, ffe 'ole place were wired — cameras 'n' sound. Next day ffe tape were all over Russian TV. A few days af'er 'at, Yeltsin appointed Putin as deputy PM. The PM, Primakov, weren't 'elpin' Yeltsin wiff gettin' rid o' Skuratov 'cause 'e were 'ead of a bleedin' anti–Yeltsin faction. So Yeltsin gives 'e boot to Primakov, ffen appoints Putin as 'is successor! Ffat were August. By September, —"

Mike nodded, finishing Nigel's sentence with, "— Putin was focused on the Chechen problem, bombing Grozny, and organizing the ground offensive in Chechnya, which cast him into the public eye as a hero, guaranteeing his victory in the presidential election the following January.

"Thanks, Nigel. Now, I really need to locate Mason — It's the real mission, after all."

"Jus' one more bit, Michael — it's abou' Kemedov. Remember you gave me ffat number Mason's phone go' 'acked into dialin'? Well, 495-224-2897 is Kemedov's direc' line at 'is Lubyanka office. Tracin' it wouldn' work, bu' it popped up ffe moment I did a deep search for dirt on Kemedov. I ffink Brendu Petrova di' a cockup when she plugged ffat number into ffe 'ack on Mason's phone."

Mike recalled the last image he'd lifted from Brendu's mind: the vindictive look on Kemedov's face as he pulled the trigger. *I guess he wasn't too pleased with her for pointing a finger at him*, Mike decided.

Mike arranged a horseshoe of candles — two–inch diameter Christmas candles, red and green, provided by the hotel gift shop, spreading out around him — then sat on the floor in the bathroom, his back against the bathtub, the steam wafting out of it attesting to the heat of the water. Carrie had also decided that the addition of the bathroom heater might also aid him.

In moments, he was out–of–body, out of the hotel, and pushing east across Moscow, beyond bends of the Moscow River. Crossing the river felt weird — breeze above the river, a slipstream of air created by the water's current, pulled at him, making it hard to navigate. He ended up hitching a ride across by clinging to a car. *Could this be the origins of the myth that vampires can't cross over moving water?*

A few blocks from the other side of the beltway, he realized he was looking down at Mason's prison. There was a sign on the outer wall but, to Mike, it was little more than gibberish. About three blocks worth of property intervened between it and the beltway. Drifting in over intervening properties was easy in his current form, but would be useless when it came time to free Mason — *I need a navigable path — I can't drag a wounded man, scrambling, through a maze of walls, fences, and barbed wire.*

A short distance to the south he found what he wanted — the printing on the sign looked like:

3HepreTN4ecKaR, the characters all the same height, the Ns and Rs backward. As he stared at it, he felt Carrie in his head, then Tony was there with her. The gibberish resolved into *Energeticheskaya Ulitsa.* In the third block, just past *Ulitsa Lefortovsky Val,* was a road that resembled a rounded rectangle, which turned in, travelled parallel to a tall brick wall, then turned back out. In the middle of the wall was a gated entrance, with a large sign — more Cyrillic. As he stared at it, the word *Lefortovsky* kept emerging, then Tony's voice said, *Lefortovo: the FSB detention facility.*

Looking to the northwest, he spotted two lanes coming in off *Lefortovsky Val* to two separate entrances. To the north was yet another sprawling brick edifice. He decided that his best choices when it came time to move Mason were *Lefortovsky* or *Energeticheskaya.*

He rose up, drifted over the wall, and immediately sensed Mason in one building — the nearest and most oddly shaped. It had an angular V attached to the back.

He found Mason in the southern portion of the V, which turned out to be two diverging corridors from a central guard station manned by a uniformed FSB man, whose shoulder epaulets displayed officer's insignia. Mike decided he was the duty officer for this part of the prison, and sensed agreement from Tony.

Second leftenant, Tony voice said in his mind.

Each corridor of the V had nine cells along the inner wall. Near the end of each corridor, opposite the line of nine cells, were three isolated cells. Mason was in the corridor that ran straight south, six cells after the duty station. A number plate labelled the room as *19.*

He passed through the door into the cell. Mason was asleep on his back on a narrow iron–framed bed; the mattress looked relatively new. The room was narrow, not much more than walking room between the bed and a wooden table against the opposite wall.

Someone had splinted Mason's thumb with wooden stir–sticks and medical tape. A void in the discolouring of the tape implied that some other form of restraint had been recently removed. *Deliberately disarticulated to escape his wrist manacle*, Mike thought, recalling Tony's comments, and admiring Mason's courageous resolve.

So who is the angel of mercy who fixed your thumb, but didn't dare remove the bullets — or perhaps didn't know how?

Whoever it was had given Mason loose–fitting prison–issue jeans and a similar denim shirt. His first thought was that removing the jeans might make it easier to extract the bullets from Mason's legs.

Stop thinking like a preMed student and think like a sorcerer, he chided himself.

Ignoring the pant leg, he reached into the right leg, wrapped his energy round the bullet that was just partially lodged into the outer layers of the femur, and began to pull it free. The bullet had flattened out as it passed through the skin and subcutaneous layers, flattening even further when it impacted against the bone. Mike tried to squeeze it into a more regular shape, but was unable. The best he could manage was to turn it and try to match parts of its shape to the mangled track left by the tumbling bullet — tedious, taxing work, forcing him to pause every time he elicited a groan from Mason, but, before long, he'd worked the slug free from Mason's flesh, and plopped it down between his leg and the inside of the leg of the jeans. A bit more chi guided the bullet down the length of the leg and out onto the mattress.

The left leg took much less effort since, having missed bone, the slug was less deformed. Soon, this too was lying on the mattress.

Mike now focused on the remaining damage. Removing the remains of what little material had travelled in with the bullets hardly taxed him at all, though, at this point, Mike was weary of remaining out–of–body. He connected with his body just enough to take more energy from the candles and the hot water.

He next reached into Mason's mind. *Mason — Mason — I need you to wake up.*

Almost immediately, Mason groaned, then his eyelids fluttered open. He stared about, wide–eyed.

It's okay, Mason; it's me, Mike. I'm here, but you can't see me. I need you to remain calm. The bullets are out of your legs, but you'll have to tighten your bandages. They came loose while I was extracting the slugs. The damage to your left femur seems minimal. You've sustained some muscle damage to both legs, but that should heal with time and rest. There's some fracturing of the right femur, but that will eventually heal on its own if you keep off that leg.

"Michael?" Mason whispered. "How is this even possible? How are you here? How do I hear you?"

Mike focused and made his energy coalesce into a ghostly image in front of Mason. *Tulku Anil calls it astral projection. It's kind of weird, though I got some serious practice in Austria, if you recall. Anyway, now that I know where you are, Tony and I will work on an extraction plan.*

Mason nodded, then whispered, "Natasha gave me proper bandages a few days ago, about the same time that she took away the tattered mess of my expensive dress trousers, and had the guard help me on with these denims."

Natasha? Mike asked in Mason's mind. *Did you find a girlfriend in here already? And, Mason, you don't need to speak audibly. In fact, considering this cell is probably monitored, you shouldn't. Just think what you want to say, and I'll hear it.*

Mason looked embarrassed. *I'll probably need therapy if I ever get back to Vauxhall Cross*, he declared. *It might be Stockholm Syndrome. Natasha Cherninova is a forty–two–year–old first leftenant in the FSB — the KGB used her as a spy during her teens, when she was on the Russian Swim Team.*

Mike smiled. *I'd love to hear it all over a Scotch sometime, maybe even meet the lady. In the meantime, continue to be a hero.*

Hero? Mason queried in surprise. *I'm no hero.*

Mike smiled. *That's where you're wrong, my friend. An 18th century philosopher and writer of hymns wrote "A hero is one who knows how to hang on one minute longer." Novalis was his pseudonym; his real name was much more long–winded. We performed a few of his hymns back when I was human and active in the choir. Anyway, I'm spent and have to get back to where I parked my body.*

He allowed himself to fade from view, then withdrew, lingering just long enough above the facility to double–check routes for getting Mason out and away from the area.

Moments later he was back in his body. His eyes snapped open to find not just Carrie, but an anxious–looking Tony.

"Mason is okay," Mike assured him. Then, to Carrie, "Did you call on Tony?"

Carrie nodded. "You got agitated and started muttering about not being able to read *Damned Russian* — your exact words."

"I'll warm up our beverages of choice, and await you in the living room" Tony said, then he *whooshed* out of the room.

A glance at the candles showed Mike that they were all burnt down to puddles of paraffin wax. He took a quick shower — extra hot, then grabbed Carrie — a quick kiss was all it took to get her started — but Mike quickly applied the brakes. "Sorry;" he apologized, "I didn't mean to start anything. In fact, I *really* need to feed. I found this last little excursion even more exhausting than our adventure in Austria, when I taunted d'Angelo and company into a quick resolution of that case."

Out in the main room, Tony handed him a warmed mug. He took a large gulp, then slowed, savouring the rest of the drink. He then located a pad of standard letter size paper and a pencil, settled onto the sofa, and began sketching.

"So he's in Lefortovo," Tony mused. "It's used exclusively by the FSB. What were your impressions?"

Mike noted the concerned look on Tony's face, and gave careful thought to all he'd taken in while there in his incorporeal form.

"Well, it was quiet — none of the noise one might associate with prisons — and, compared to Butyrka, it's a hotel. I think the area where Mason is held is reserved for special prisoners. He was the only occupant in his cell — it was too narrow for two beds, though they could stack two like bunk-beds."

He drew a rectangle in the crotch of the V, where the main building opened into the pair of corridors.

"The officer I saw was behind this desk, facing the opening. He had a computer, several security monitors, and a multi–line phone. His epaulets were black, with a blue line down the middle, and a gold star on the line, almost halfway to the button of the epaulet." As he described it, he drew it on a second page.

Tony was nodding. "FSB — *leftenant* 2nd class." Then, taking the pad, he marked two Xs in the space on either side of the blue line, closer to where the epaulet would attach. "If he's promoted to 1st class *leftenant*, they'll replace his single star with two, here, and add a small FSB crest here, just shy of the button, and the background will be light blue instead of black. Remove the crest, put back the original star, and change the light blue to gold, and you have a senior leftenant.

"Go back to black and add a fourth star and you have captain. Take away the line and make it two lines with enough room for a larger star in between, and you start again as a major." He then proceeded to draw the progressive changes in background colour, stars, and presence of the crest, to indicate lieutenant colonel through to general.

Mike committed it all to memory. Until he got Mason free and clear of Moscow, any officers he encountered were likely to be FSB, and it might prove useful to be able to recognize rank.

"Are you thinking of impersonating an FSB officer to get to Mason?" he asked Tony.

Carrie emerged from the bedroom, came over, joined Mike on the sofa, then, seeing his mug of blood, helped herself to a sip from it.

"I'll get my own and get you another at the same time," she said.

Tony gave her a smile, then frowned, pondering Mike's question.

"It's a possibility," he suggested — "Percy was the planner, but, over the years, one picks up on certain patterns. He liked things that were so daring that no one could imagine them being anything but what they seemed. Another ploy was leading the way as a decoy — he'd innocently pass through a city gate in disguise, making sure to draw lots of attention to himself, then we'd come along anywhere from ten minutes to half–an–hour later, dressed as soldiers, with a half–dozen *Aristo*s among us, and order the gates opened, reprimanding the sergeant of the gate, insisting that the cart he'd just passed through was indeed the Scarlet Pimpernel with the smuggled aristocrats. The latter often seemed the most guaranteed — Percy was the setup, and, of course, he had to put on enough of a show to be memorable. Then, when we swept down upon the gate, there was so much consternation and desire to appear guilt–free, that we were never even given a second glance. Of course, there was the time that Armand passed himself off as Chauvelin in order to whisk the young *Dauphin*, Charles, past Chauvelin's own guards."

Tony paused, his brow furrowing in thought. "*Od's fish*, old man, with some coaching in Russian, you could pass yourself off as Putin, though he is a bit more burly than you, and a few inches shorter — well, three or four— but I've seen you act. Remember that time Carrie dressed you up as an old man when we were trying to get out of Europe back in the days of — what was that blighter's name — Stan Michaels!"

"Stanislaus Mihilache," Michael said.

"Yes — Mihilache. *Od's Blood*, man, that was an adventure."

Mike looked at his friend, noting how his eyes fairly danced with enthusiasm, then recalled something he'd read in one of Emmuska Orczy's novels.

"Percy may have been, in your words, *the brains of the outfit*, but it was you and Sir Andrew who wielded the swords. The Baroness labeled Percy as an indifferent swordsman, while insisting that you were *one of the finest blades in Europe*. I wonder if that didn't make you a little reckless, hoping to cross swords with someone in the name of the cause." He stared fixedly into Tony's eyes, then saw a flicker of increased enthusiasm, followed by what might have been a brief blush of embarrassment.

Tony's grin faded to a smile. "I assure you that, with you and Carrie involved, I shall curb such outdated urges. Besides, there's Mason to consider. We can hardly have him struggling along while I'm dueling it out with a gang of FSB guards. Besides, I dare say, the blighters don't even carry swords!"

This latter brought a chuckle from Mike, a chuckle that faded almost as fast as it appeared.

Tony frowned. "What is it, Michael?"

"I did what I could with Mason while I was there," Mike explained, "but I think I should go back and cauterize his wounds so they won't bleed. I should also take a closer look at his right femur. I told him it would heal on its own if he stayed off it, but he can't stay off it if he has to escape Lefortovo.

"It might also be a good idea to see if we can determine what their plans for him might be. Why would Kemedov take him there anyway?

"By the way, Nigel told me earlier that the Russian number Mason's phone dialed was Kemedov's direct line at Lubyanka. And, from Brendu Petrova's last glimpse before he shot her, he was pissed at her."

"No doubt he felt she'd improvised too far," Tony commented, then, "What else did you see from her?"

Mike closed his eyes and revisited the image. "Kemedov's face and the muzzle of a Makarov — and a rank insignia on his shoulder epaulets — Black background, blue trim, no stripes or inner borders, two gold stars, close together, but toward the edge away from the epaulet button."

Tony shrugged. "That's a leftenant general."

Mike shook his head, murmuring, "and yet he's up to his neck in narcotics."

Tony shrugged. "I dare say, dear boy, for some, one source of power is never enough, especially once they get a taste of the money that corruption offers."

Carrie returned, looked in Mike's mug, and said, "Finish that and I'll bring you another. You still look drained — far too pale for my peace of mind."

Mike nodded, drained his mug, then passed it to her, mouthing a *thank you*.

Tony declared, "If Kemedov were at all worried about Putin — the man's position on the drug trade seems undeniably firm — well, I dare say Kemedov might like a distraction of this sort. As for Putin's hardline stance against the drug–trade, he'd say almost anything to look superior to the Americans, but he does seem to back it with action."

"So, if Kemedov fears Putin breathing down his neck, offering up a high–ranking MI6 officer is a viable distraction," Mike mused. "But what about the disgraced former KGB operative? Why would he take Petroff as well?"

"To look even more innocent and conscientious," Carrie said. She passed Mike his mug, and resumed her seat next to him. *"Hey, Putin, I found this guy being held prisoner by this crippled and somewhat deranged former KGB spy. I have no idea what's going on, so I brought them both in."*

"It works for me," Mike said, giving a nod, then planting a kiss on Carrie's lips. "Clever girl."

Carrie beamed.

"But why kill Brendu and the others?" Mike then mused. "He was mad at Brendu for using his phone number, but why Pietro?"

Tony nodded. "Valid point."

"He must have some agenda —" Mike continued to ponder aloud, "— something that others could argue and expose. This way it's his word against Petroff's, and who's going to credit Petroff, especially when he clearly murdered his own sister– and brother–in–law, just to have access to their property. He didn't even dispose of the bodies; he just left them there stinking up their own kitchen."

"Actually," Tony commented, "from the time Putin became director of the FSB, they've had a reputation for going in shooting, then questioning the survivors. "Pietro Androvich was Brendu's hired help. If Leon Koslov was Kemedov's man, and Kemedov knew Mason killed him, maybe he killed Pietro as payback for some perception of Brendu being responsible for his man's death."

He sighed, then added, "I'm concerned about the prospect of Mason undergoing an FSB interrogation. If he's as weak as you described, he'd be hard–pressed to not knuckle under."

"First things first," Mike announced, "I'm going back to cauterize his wounds." He emptied his mug, then passed it to Carrie. Cocking his head, his gave her what she liked to call his *puppy dog* look. *Please?* he mouthed, whereupon she smiled, took the mug, and went to refill it with warmed blood.

"Michael, I hope you're not planning to visit Mason until after you've had your sleep for the day," Carrie announced from the kitchen, but Mike was shaking his head.

"It's too important to wait," he insisted. "Besides, I mean to flood him with enough energy to aid him in case they decide to interrogate him today." Seeing the look of alarm on her face, he quickly added, "Don't worry, dear; I'll be surrounded by candles, and can draw on the flame for energy."

"*By Gadd*," Tony declared, "we'll have enough to threaten to burn the place down."

He went to a table near the door and produced almost a dozen of the same red and green candles. "And I can ring down for more. I dare say, the gift shop is all geared up for Christmas, *eh what?*"

Once more Mike was reminded of what young Lord Tony must have been like in the Pimpernel days. It set him laughing to the point that tears began weeping from his eyes.

"By the way, Tony," he finally got out once his mirth subsided, "it seems our friend Mason has a friend inside the prison — a girlfriend, in fact — an FSB first leftenant, no less. Her name is Natasha. She splinted the thumb he disarticulated to escape a one of his manacles." Glancing at Carrie, he added, "Another Leo, no less," to which Carrie gave a meaningful grin.

"I was in Mason's head long enough to gather much more than he'd want me to know. What started as flirting in an effort to possibly gain her sympathy, maybe even turn her —"

"Standard MI6 tactics, dear boy," Tony interrupted.

"Well, it seems to have worked, but on both of them. I think he's falling in love with her."

Tony frowned. "I hope that doesn't complicate matters."

Twenty minutes later, his third mug of blood consumed, Mike was back in the bathroom, cross–legged on the floor, his back against the bathtub, the tub refilled with the hottest water possible, and surrounded on the remaining sides by even more layers of candles.

In less time than it took his first visit, he was back at the officer's station at the V of corridors. The second lieutenant from his recent visit was scanning a screen of schedules. Mike immediately saw *Petroff, Anatoli, cell 36*, one of the three isolated cells near the end the opposite side of the V from Mason, and noted that he was scheduled for interrogation on the 31st, in two days' time, at 10:00 AM. There was no listing yet for Mason.

Then, just as Mike's essence was about to move away, an officer appeared — a captain, based on his insignia. The lieutenant snapped to attention, gave a brisk salute, accepted a slip of paper from his superior, then listened attentively, nodding, as the captain spoke briefly in Russian. There was another crisp salute, then the lieutenant began typing on his keyboard.

Mason, Bruce, MI6, scheduled for interrogation, Sunday Nov. 31st, at 11:00 AM.

He took off straightaway for Mason's cell.

Cauterizing Mason's wounds was a cautious endeavour, almost trial–and–error. He saw it as reaching an incorporeal pinky finger into a wound, focusing his energy as heat — not to the point of summoning fire — until he'd seared the few stubbornly weeping blood vessels shut. After the first wound, the other was easy.

Next he focused his attention on the spider cracking of Mason's right femur, where the .22 bullet hit. He used mild heat to partially fuse the fracturing, stimulating the bone cells into increased activity at the same time. What Mason needed now was enough energy to finish the job — that and more calcium in his diet.

He had acquired some experience in Austria with entering into other people — he'd plowed into Carmen leTrice, and become flame, incinerating her. *Okay,* he thought, *I'll need to be more gentle than that.* He pushed in slowly, then reached out, getting a feel for each and every organ system — the heart and lungs, the brain and nervous system — looking for where energy was needed, and then set about to deliver it.

He pictured reaching his hands toward the candles about him back in the bathroom at the hotel, knowing that his real hands would do the same, taking energy from the flames. He stretched his neck, feeling the heat of the water in the tub at his back, and absorbing that into his upper back and neck. All the while, he could feel the energy flowing into him, then out of his astral form and into Mason. He continued this for about a half–hour, until it became harder and harder to draw energy from his surroundings.

By now Mason's energy level was good — excellent in fact. He also noticed something else about Mason: He wasn't close to becoming a vampire — not the way Mike had been when he was on his first CSIS mission in Afghanistan, Uzbekistan, and Tajikistan — but he was certainly a step or two beyond human. *No wonder he managed to walk, albeit staggering, out of the cell where Petroff had been holding him.*

Mike's energy level, however, was far from good. Even in astral form, he was at a low ebb. He withdrew from Mason, left the cell, and found an incandescent lightbulb — rare in this bastion of fluorescence — and wrapped his essence around the bulb. It dimmed as he tried to suck the life out of it, then it flared bright and failed, the filament burnt out. He looked for another, but there were none.

The watch officer. He found the lieutenant, flowed into him, and absorbed energy until the officer reached a hand to his forehead and closed his eyes, leaning against the desk. He staggered a few steps, reached under the counter to the coffee machine, poured a mug, and drank it half down, waiting for the caffein to surge through him. *Odd — such a large amount of coffee in two quick swallows should have burned his mouth, yet it barely seemed warm.*

Mike's essence was grateful for the burst of warmth. He hovered in the thoughts of the officer, comparing images with the Russian thoughts that seemed to go along with them. After ten minutes of this, he felt like he'd just had his first class in beginners' Russian. He also knew where the officers' changing room was. Like most North American prisons, guards could arrive out of uniform and then change before going on duty. Also, should the necessity arise, they had a spare uniform on site.

16: *Uniforms*

*S*o, when do you get off duty? Mike wondered, still inside the body of the FSB lieutenant. He tried to remember the name on the name–tag — *Lt. D. Rosikoff.* He sounded it in Rosikoff's mind and got *Dmitry* in response. He rifled the man's happier images — *a pretty face* — *two pretty faces* — wife and young daughter? He focused on the faces. *Ylena and Anya.* He felt the lieutenant smile, then saw through his eyes as he checked the time on his watch — it was 8:47, the second hand about to make it 8:48.

There was a mental image of the watch hands at 10:00 AM, then a Russian phrase that Mike instinctively knew translated into something like *just over an hour to go.*

He decided to use part of that hour to look for Petroff. Leaving Rosikoff, he drifted down the opposite side of the V from Mason's cell. Near the end of the corridor, he found cell 36. Petroff was on his back on the bed, his wheelchair parked in a corner. He was staring at the ceiling, muttering in barely audible Russian.

What's the matter, Petroff? Mike asked. *Feeling ill–used? Imagine how Mason must feel? At least you weren't bleeding when they brought you in. Mason had been out in the cold, in shredded pants, on his sock–feet, staggering about with a bullet in each leg. You, on the other hand, were snug in that warm building — I never really explored the upstairs too much — did you have bedrooms upstairs? Lord knows you wouldn't want to sleep in the farmhouse, not with the stench of the corpses of your brother– and sister–in–law.*

Petroff's eyes darted about the room, looking for the source of the voice, but the voice had been in his head. He laughed, a nervous, irrational sound, then resumed prattling in Russian.

Mike went into his head. *English,* he commanded. *I don't speak Russian.*

"And what if I refuse?" Petroff demanded belligerently.

Mike formed flames in Petroff's mind. *Then I'll give you a preview of Hell before dragging you there.*

Petroff let out a scream, but Mike took a grip on his vocal cords and squeezed, throttling off the scream before it grew into anything that might attract attention.

He listened while Petroff blathered on about how unfair life had been to him — he should have been the eldest — he should have been treated better by his father, by his sisters — more appreciated by the KGB — more loved by his wife — it should have been easier to defect with Mason — when he lost his nerve, Mason should have just come back to Moscow — and that car bomb should have killed Mason, not the bitch he married —

A surge of rage tore through Mike.

You killed Mason's wife, trying to get Mason? You miserable, pathetic bastard! I should fry you right now! The world just owes you everything, doesn't it!

He took a moment to still his rage, lest he inadvertently destroy Petroff's mind. *Life should have been handed to you on a silver platter. Just how spoiled were you, the only boy with five sisters?* He shook his head. He'd known one or two people who thought along these lines — most of them had been on boats in the Bahamas, little more than floating alcoholics.

He spent another fifteen minutes terrorizing Petroff with fire — he even convinced him that his liver had caught fire, burning up from all the vodka it had absorbed over the years. By the time he tired of it, he felt confident that he'd so rearranged Petroff's notions of reality that any interrogator would find him just about useless. It had all been from his fear of the KGB ever learning that he'd intended to defect — Mason was the only one who could corroborate that.

They'll be here to interrogate you at 10:00 AM on Sunday, Mike told him, — *that's the day after tomorrow.*

He felt confident about Mason's ability to tolerate an FSB interrogation, but, if he had his way, Mason wouldn't be there when the interrogator or interrogators arrived to question him. In fact, if his plan worked, Mason might be free of Lefortovo Prison before sunrise.

He returned to the officer's station to await Dmitry's relief, hovering close to the lieutenant, careful not to spook him. He wasn't ready do go in and try taking over the guy just yet — not until he absolutely had to. Being able to say *Na Zdorovie, spasibo, da,* and *nyet* weren't going to get him past potentially suspicious FSB officers; he'd wait until the last possible moment.

Footsteps coming down the hall — the relief officer was approaching, and it was a woman. She was Carrie's size, perhaps a fraction taller, but similar in build. Carrie could wear her clothes, but they'd fit differently — Carrie's breasts were a bit larger, but this one had the *pectorals* and *latissimus dorsi* of an Olympic swimmer. *Is this Mason's Natasha?* She was a first lieutenant, senior to Mike's man. He could read the the officer's feelings as he watched her — he wasn't watching her legs, her face, or her chest as she approached, he was watching her epaulets. He couldn't translate the phrase that began repeating itself in the man's head, then he recognized the first sound as a crippled rendition of *three*, then something that sounded like *yanvar? Yanvar* — he repeated the sound in his mind — *January?* January was less than three months off — *Is that when your promotion is, Dmitry?*

As Dmitry's relief reached the desk, she smiled and made a comment. She'd seen where he was looking and seemed sympathetically amused.

The first lieutenant, *Lt. N. Cherninova*, according to her name–tag, grinned and repeated his recent mantra aloud — three months — whereupon she nodded, still smiling. She made a joke of saluting. He grinned and returned the salute in a less formal manner.

So you're Natasha, he thought, and he could see why Mason was so taken with her.

"*Lejtenants!*"

Both officers froze.

The newcomer seemed to have appeared out of nowhere, though Mike had heard his approach. This one wore captain's epaulets. Both snapped to attention and saluted. Captain A. Stepashin laughed, then spoke casually to both.

Mike's lieutenant relaxed, but Lt. Cherninova seemed very unsettled, as if some irrational reflex had been triggered.

Dmitry saluted again, turned, drew the first lieutenant's attention to some things on the screens, then, with a final salute to Captain Stepashin, left and headed into the section to which the V was attached, turning left, skirting a corner — *That's how the captain appeared so unexpectedly,* Mike decided.

To the right were several offices. A few looked like interrogation rooms. In the corner at the end of this corridor, Dmitry pushed on a swinging door and entered what looked like a locker room. Daylight came through windows covered by steel mesh, but it was a grey, overcast day outside.

Rosikoff opened a locker, peeled off his uniform jacket, put it on a hanger, took a brush from the upper shelf and brushed the jacket, then hung it up in the locker. There was another jacket next to it, trouser legs showing below the jacket, clearly sharing the hanger. The lieutenant kicked off his shoes, removed his uniform trousers and hung them on the hanger inside the jacket he'd just removed, then pulled on jeans and sneakers. Next he loosened and removed his tie, then the shirt, pulling on a sweatshirt, followed by a heavy nylon windbreaker, emblazoned with the FSB crest and second lieutenant insignia.

He was just about to close the locker door when Mike went into his head and took over.

None of the other lockers were locked. He quickly found the locker for Lieutenant Cherninova, whom he'd judged as being close to Carrie in size, and noted a spare uniform. Lastly he decided on a captain whose uniform looked to be Tony's size. He would have preferred a major or higher, but higher ranks either weren't stationed at the facility, or perhaps had their own offices and could change in private. Once again he wished he understood Russian well enough to get the info from the lieutenant.

He removed the appropriate uniforms from the lockers, including the second lieutenant's one fresh uniform. He carefully folded each on the bench in front of the lockers, placing the shoes to one side. In the captain's locker he found a uniform gun belt, complete with a holstered Makarov. *Well that's careless, Captain, but I thank you.*

It took some searching to come up with something to put them in. He went to the large garbage drum in the corner, lined with a black garbage bag, and was considering removing the bag, when images began flickering through the lieutenant's mind, barely conscious under Mike's domination. Mike looked up, his eyes coming to rest on the door to a larger locker in the corner, then decided to investigate. It contained a host of janitorial supplies, including a box of the oversize garbage bags. He took one, placed the three uniforms in it, added the shoes and gun belt, then tied the bag shut. A single heft of the bag told him that it's rating far exceeded the weight of its contents.

To the left, as they were leaving the locker room, Mike spotted what looked like two guards at a side exit, opposite the center of the bank of offices and what he surmised were interrogation rooms.

Okay — Now — Get me out of here!

He relaxed his control just enough to allow the lieutenant to think. *Never mind the bag you're lugging; just carry it,* Mike protested, forcing the lieutenant to maintain a tight grip on the bag.

He remembered the faces of the pretty little girl and the woman, a grownup version of the child, and made them appear in the lieutenant's mind. That did the trick: Dmitry set off in purposeful strides toward what looked to be a service entrance, out into a parking lot, got into a modest–looking compact car, then drove out of the main gate. Mike steered him around the beltway to the *Raddison Slavyanskaya*. He pulled up in front, dropped the bag inside the vestibule, to one side of the door, then got back in the car, and drove off. Mike waited until he was more than half a kilometer away before pulling out of Dmitry.

He gasped as he returned to his body. It took a moment to get his bearings — New candles sat next to the burnt–down remains of those he'd started with.

"Uniforms!" he blurted. "Garbage bag, just inside the vestibule, to the right of the front entrance."

Tony looked puzzled, but only for a moment, then got to his feet — he'd pulled a small chair into the room. "Fear not; I'll fetch them!" he declared, and was off, out of the room, and out of the suite.

Mike resisted the urge to laugh, wondering if this wasn't some kind of Pimpernel flashback for Tony, but Carrie giggled.

"Don't laugh," he warned Carrie. "You need to show respect; he outranks you. He's a captain; you're just a first lieutenant."

Still giggling, Carrie let his statement sink in, then asked, "And what are you, my love? A major?"

Mike made a wry face. "Sorry, dear; I'm just a lowly second lieutenant, who is almost my exact size, maybe an inch taller. I was hoping for a major's uniform for Tony, but, I was lucky to find a captain's."

They heard the door to the suite open and close, then Tony reappeared, bag in hand.

"We've no time to lose, Tony," he advised. "Mason gets interrogated Sunday morning." His eyes blurred briefly, and his voice trailed off.

"I can see by the look in your eyes that you're not going to last much longer," Tony said to him. "Let's get these spread out somewhere. We'll figure out our next move after we all awaken."

Carrie stood, turned, then reached out a hand to the doorway, bracing herself. "Oo —" she shook her head sharply — "It mus' be — close to —"

"It's nearing eleven o'clock," Tony finished for her, then helped her to a chair in the living room.

"We all need a cycle of vampire sleep," Mike declared. "Come on, Carrie." His own eyelids felt like lead, lethargy spreading, as he guided Carrie to bed.

——— ——— ———

Mike's eyes snapped open at 2:20 PM. Feeling thoroughly rested, he slid gently away from Carrie before arising, dressed in a hurry, then went in search of his blood supply.

He decided he could make do with just a half–mug, warmed to approximate body temperature, then grabbed a sketch pad. Sitting on the sofa, he studied the rank insignias on each uniform, then set to work sketching each, sipping at his O+ as he worked. The biggest problem was the background colours: both the captain and second class lieutenant had black with a central blue stripe, the stars making the only difference. First lieutenant had a blue central stripe on a light blue background.

He found Tony's sketches, and looked at the higher ranks. Major needed two stripes; Lieutenant colonel needed a white background. It also needed the FSB crest, but there was one on the first lieutenant epaulet, and it was a transferable pin. The stars were also transferable metallic pins. That got Mike thinking.

Stiff white material? The curtains were white, and they were fairly thick and stiff, reminding him of the fiberglass curtains his parents had back in the '70s.

Still sipping his blood, he walked over and felt them — some sort of polyester, but very much like those old fiberglass curtains. They reached almost to the floor, and were blocked by the desk; at the next window, they were blocked by the other sofa. The bottom hem was about three-inches — the epaulets were two-inches wide and just under six-inches long — *If I snip out enough for two epaulets, from the wall side of the hem, no one would notice for a while.*

He knew Carrie always carried a sewing kit, and went looking for it. It was a struggle for the tiny scissors to cut the fabric, but, soon he'd trimmed it exactly to size, then used chi to heat the material just enough to melt and seal the edges.

He opted for another half–mug of blood, then removed the first lieutenant epaulets and went to work. By the time he'd warmed and started sipping on a third half–mug, he'd sewn the white fabric into place, positioned the FSB crest, and drawn two blue lines in ballpoint pen. He was considering trying to embroider proper lines with a loop stitch, but the colour of the ink looked so good that he decided to go back over the lines, making them wider, then fastened two stars in their original first lieutenant position.

He compared it to Tony's sketch. The stars were smaller than those used for major through colonel, but he thought, *Let's just hope no one notices that. Besides, if the lieutenant colonel and the captain are intimidating enough, it should deflect scrutiny.* He smiled, picturing Carrie in uniform as a first lieutenant. *She can add to the distraction, especially if she acts all military and efficient — shoulders back, chest out — how dare you stare at my — I'm an FSB officer! And nothing is harder to avoid staring at than something you're not supposed to ogle.*

He attached the newly–fabricated lieutenant colonel epaulets to the captain's uniform, then relocated the captain's epaulets to the second lieutenant's uniform. Finally, he attached the second lieutenant epaulets to the shoulders of the first lieutenant's distinctly female uniform.

"*I say, dear boy*, you seem busily up to something," Tony declared as he entered, then made his way to the fridge and his bottle of O–. The puzzled expression still reflected in the furrows of his brow, told Mike that he had yet to notice the results of Mike's handiwork.

"Good morning Leftenant Colonel," he said, offering Tony a hint of a smile, and snapping him a salute, making a point of facing the back of his hand at his forehead.

Tony warmed himself a mug, took a sip, noticed the uniform with Mike's fabricated epaulets, then grinned.

"*Gadd*, Michael; it's brilliant. Wherever did you get the white material?"

Mike fixed his eyes on a curtain, and Tony, following the direction of his gaze, gave a chuckle.

"Resourceful as always. So you'll be my captain, and Carrie will be our first *lejtenant*," he commented, using the Russian pronunciation.

"I thought that, as a leftenant, she might add more of a distraction," he explained. "It's a bit sexist, but, if she masters the attitude, it will be tough not to stare, particularly if the dignified, by–the–book second leftenant is daring anyone to have the nerve to ogle."

"It's bloody brilliant," Tony declared, still chuckling. "I love it. Have you a plan for extracting him? I was considering declaring him as having escaped, then mounting a search, especially if we can come up with another uniform after we're inside."

Mike shrugged. "I was relying on mesmerizing guards to not see him or simply the notion that the leftenant colonel is there to affect a prisoner transfer. Whatever we do, you're the ranking officer, and the only one with a hope of passing himself off as being fluent in Russian.

"Mind you, Tony, during your days with the League, the French Republicans were expecting Percy. Sending soldiers off chasing after him was easier than it might be today." Mike was about to continue, then, as a new thought popped into his head, a small smile began to form.

"You have an idea," Tony declared. "Something worthy of Sir Percy's genius, I'll wager." He'd fixed onto Mike's smile and was now grinning, himself.

"More along the lines of Charles Dickens," Mike said, "in particular his *A Tale of Two Cities*."

17: *Into Action*

I t was a little after 4:00 PM when Mike heard the sounds of Carrie getting up, followed by the sound of a running shower. He carried her uniform and shoes into the bedroom, came back for his own, then made another trip to warm a mug of A+ for her and take it in. She was just getting out of the shower when he entered, smiled, and passed her mug to her.

"Your uniform awaits in the bedroom," he told her. "You will be a second lieutenant — I needed the original first lieutenant epaulets to make lieutenant colonel's epaulets for Tony. I'll be Tony's captain. As a lieutenant, you'd be Tony's adjutant. If the uniform fits you the way I expect, any men we encounter will be too busy staring at you to even notice us. We could speak Polish and get away with it."

She thought about it, paused, towel about her torso, and glanced in the mirror, her lips flexing into a mischievous smile. "And, as captain, you'd be — Tony's interrogator?"

"I suppose," he mused. "The interrogator isn't due 'til Sunday — Ask Tony; he's our point man on all things Russian, especially military matters."

"I can see you're in your head today," she offered, giving him a brief kiss. "So you spent your time after waking up making an insignia for Tony? How did you manage that?"

She listened, her eyes sparkling, while he explained about the curtain. She kissed him again. "You should have been around when Tony and the Scarlet Pimpernel were doing their thing, especially considering your other skills. Who knows? Maybe you were, and just can't remember."

Mike just shrugged it off, helped her towel dry, then watched as she dressed in Lt. Cherninova's uniform. He helped her tie the necktie, then, as she continued to adjust everything, he donned the captain's uniform.

"I'm not sure what to do about sidearms," he admitted. "I took the captain's holster belt and Makarov, but Lt. Cherninova, whose uniform I took for you, was on duty, and still wearing her sidearm. Tony and I might get away with carrying our Walthers, but I'm worried that shoulder holsters might be considered non-uniform."

Carrie finished tying her shoes, pulled on her uniform jacket, then belted the Makarov about her waist, over the tunic–style jacket. Lastly, she brushed out her hair, pulled it back in a ponytail, then donned her officer's cap, cocking it an a slight angle.

He adjusted his tunic over the shoulder–holstered Walther PPK. Leaving the top button undone allowed easy access to his weapon, but it looked sloppy by what standards he'd seen. He closed the button, then, in a lightning–fast move, undid the button and drew his weapon. He decided on a compromise: leave the jacket properly buttoned, then undo the top button once inside. After all, he was with a lieutenant colonel, and, having seen Lt. Cherninova's reaction to the other captain, he knew she wouldn't be challenging him.

He paused next to Carrie, glanced at the mirror, adjusted his own cap, then — *the face that didn't*

*belong to him — wearing someone else's skin — Carrie
— Tony — all wearing someone else's skin, and about
to venture out into unknown territory* — Memory of
the bizarre dream from weeks before came flooding
back. *So it was prescience.* He sighed, then gave a
quick, determined nod. *Okay, let's do this.* He adjusted
his tie one last time, gave his reflection a brisk nod of
approval, then smiled at Carrie.

"I'm Tony's bodyguard and interrogator. You're his
adjutant, but you're also lethal with a handgun and an
expert martial artist. Make it a part of how you see
yourself. Tap into the vampire predator inside you, and
channel a glimpse of that instead of suppressing it."

She straightened her posture and stared at him with
what was almost a predatory glare. It sent a chill down
his spine. She clicked her heels. "Ready when you are,
Captain," she said without a trace of a smile.

"*I say*, have a look at you two!" Tony declared
when they joined him in the living room. Lord
Dewhurst had transformed himself into an FSB
lieutenant colonel, complete with the, presumably,
spare ID he'd found in the inside pocket of the tunic.
Flashing the ID, he barked something in Russian. Mike
picked out the surname *Pitofsky*, but the rest was
incomprehensible.

He seemed totally in character. In fact, to Mike it
was almost an alarming transformation, from the
good–natured Lord Anthony Dewhurst to this new,
stern, no–nonsense FSB lieutenant colonel. A closer
look at Tony's ID revealed a *Captain* Pitofsky, who,
except for height and build, looked nothing at all like
Tony. Mike knew, though, that, with vampire glamour,
Tony could make anyone scrutinizing the ID see
whatever he willed them to see.

They went over the plan several times until, just as
the sun was setting, Tony pointed out, "Your plan only
falls apart at one point, Michael: Mason and I are,

more or less, of a height, while you and he clearly are not. If you've rejuvenated him as much as you think, he'll make a more convincing lieutenant colonel than I. His Russian is flawless, and he knows more about this current Russian Federation than I. Mind you, we only have to extract him from the building."

"So you'd take his place in the cell?" Mike asked.

"Well, only until you return by yourself to fetch me," he amended with a smile.

Mike thought it through and nodded.

"What about a car?" he asked. "Most of the ones I saw in the parking lot looked like private vehicles. But wouldn't a senior officer like yourself arrive in a marked vehicle?"

"Not necessarily," Tony replied. "Besides, you'll be driving; I'll be impressing them with my rank and arrogance." He smiled. "And you, dear Carrie, can distract them with your charms. By the way, you will be beside Michael in the front seat of the new rental, which is a black Russian–made sedan. It should look perfectly acceptable — more so than our erstwhile Volkswagen."

"Colonel," she acknowledged, and threw her shoulders back in an arrogant fashion, fixing him with an icy glare."

"You'll do just fine, *Lejtenant*," Tony approved.

Taking Mike aside, Dewhurst rested a hand on his shoulder, and said, "You seem uncharacteristically nervous, Michael, no doubt related to Carrie's role in all of this. You've prepared her well, especially that advice about tapping into the inner predator. Take a break and, remember the first rule of spy tradecraft: Look like you belong; act like you belong; and everyone will believe you belong. It's all in presenting a plausible deception. You'll be fine — you both will."

"And you?" Mike asked, looking searchingly into Tony's eyes.

Tony's half smile held a hint of mischief. *"Od's Fish*, dear chap, I was play–acting in France two centuries ago, with all of Paris looking for me. *Sink me!"* Then the smile disappeared, leaving behind the stern visage of Lt. Colonel Pitofsky of the FSB.

"There's something more," Tony ventured, staring into Mike's eyes.

Mike gave a nod. "When was Mason's wife killed, in reference to the botched Petroff defection?"

Tony pondered this, then replied, "Mason met her before that mission, married her maybe two years after he got back, then the car bomb occurred about three years later. Why, Michael?"

"So her death was five years after Petroff got shot and had his legs amputated," Mike mused. "Enough time for the KGB to have let Petroff go. Tony, Petroff arranged that explosion — I saw it in his mind. He wanted to eliminate Mason as the only one able to prove that he'd attempted to defect. He cursed her as a bitch for getting killed instead of Mason. I almost fried the bastard's brain in my anger."

Tony frowned. "We should probably keep this from Mason until we have him out of Russia."

"Agreed," Mike confirmed.

Mike parked the black Lada sedan against the curb on *Energreticheskaya Ulitsa.*

Excellent, choice, Tony said in his mind. *According to the sign, this is the interrogators' entrance. We will get out of the car here, and proceed inside.*

Mike exited the car, went around to the front passenger–side corner, and stood vigilant, his right hand conspicuously close to the top of his tunic, the top button of which he undid. He felt confident that he was projecting an intimidating air, that any onlooker would know a holstered weapon was just out of sight inside his tunic.

Carrie, meanwhile, opened her door and stepped smartly out from the passenger seat, shut the door, then opened the rear door for Tony, snapping to attention, and presenting a crisp salute as he emerged from the vehicle.

For his part, Tony's eyes made a quick scan of her profile from head to foot and back again, then ignored her entirely while he walked to where Mike waited.

Mike surveyed the surroundings once more, gave a nod, then let Carrie lead the way, while he walked at Tony's elbow, ever vigilant.

At the entrance, she displayed Captain Pitofsky's ID, cocking her head slightly to one side and arching an eyebrow, as if challenging the guard to question who the colonel was. Tony, of course, was projecting an image of himself as *Colonel* Pitofsky. Mike glanced at the guard's rank insignia: two gold stripes across the black epaulet, denoting a junior sergeant.

"This is my interrogator, Captain Minkin," Tony announced in what Mike assumed was flawless Russian, but, being privy to his thoughts, Mike knew he had the general gist.

You are interrogating someone this evening?

Tony mentally flashed the translation of the guard's question before replying in cool, almost menacing irony: "No; it's such a lovely evening, I thought I'd take my interrogator for a walk. He has a notoriously short temper. I hope he finds your inane questions less irritating than I," Tony snarked with an icy smile.

Mike fought the urge to smile at Tony's wit, masking it with what he hoped was an intimidating scowl. He fixed the guard with an icy glare, then reached out with his chi and drew heat from the man, making sure the sergeant felt an acute chill.

The guard snapped to attention, handed Tony his ID, and gave a salute that lasted until Carrie had opened the door and Tony had passed inside.

Mike immediately recognized where he was. Straight ahead of them were what he had previously guessed were interrogation offices.

Two more guards, both lance corporals, snapped to attention and waited for Tony to present his ID.

Tony looked so bored it reminded Mike of how the Baroness had perpetually described Sir Percy's affected foppery. Mike, on the other hand, used his position to scan, not just visually, but mentally, ascertaining the location of every guard or soldier on most of the first two floors.

This time Tony described him as, not just an interrogator, but his bodyguard. *A colonel with a bodyguard doesn't need a sidearm. Good thinking, Tony.*

Carrie was his adjutant. "But, don't be fooled by her looks," he insisted with a cold smile, "she's probably killed at least a dozen men, usually without recourse to her pistol, though she is the recipient of several awards for small arms marksmanship."

Carrie adjusted her posture subtly, as if unable to hide pride at Tony's praise, but, while the move accentuated how she filled out the front of her uniform, her hand noticeably slid along her belt a little closer to her sidearm.

Tony now beckoned for Mike to precede him though the corridors to reach Mason's cell. While they walked, Mike pointed out the changing room where he'd come upon the uniforms, then drew Tony's attention to the broad opening ahead, to the right. Beyond the aperture, the duty officer's station presided over the junction of the V of special cell corridors.

The moment he sighted Lt. Cherninova standing at her post, eying surveillance monitors and computer screen, he drew Tony to a stop, raised his hand meaningfully to its poised position of readiness to pull a shoulder–holstered weapon, his gaze panning to the right, and then the left.

Tony, that's Natasha Cherninova, Mason's new friend. Then, *Carrie, make a show of taking over my position.* He then fell back past Tony's elbow, looked to the rear, then once more to left and right.

"Lieutenant — *Cherninova*," Tony added the surname with emphasis, as if reading it off her name tag, and gave Carrie a glance, at which Carrie nodded. Mike remained stone–faced, despite his amusement at the obvious intimidation tactic — *if I don't remember your name, my adjutant will.*

Lt. Cherninova snapped to attention and saluted.

"Colonel —" she looked at his name tag, shook her head, blinked hard, looked again, then said, "Colonel Pitofsky, to what do we owe this honour."

Careful, Tony, this one has an unusually strong mind. I think she actually saw captain *on your name plate before you forced her to re–see it as* colonel. *We may have a witch on our hands.*

Tony gave her a charming smile, knowing that, in Russia, a charming smile from a high ranking officer could be as threatening as a scowl.

"I want to chat with Mr. Mason, our guest from MI6," Tony replied. "Captain Minkin, aside from being my bodyguard on occasion, is an interrogator."

She frowned, glanced at the computer screen and scrolled the screen a few times, then swallowed hard.

"I realize, *moy malen'kiy kotenok* (my little kitten), that we are not expected until Sunday at 10:00 AM, but," he gave her his most charming smile, "I am old, and old men get restless. I thought, *myshka*, I might have a preliminary chat with him tonight. I'm sure you understand, unless you'd feel better by calling General Kemedov. Perhaps General Bortnikov," he added, broadening his smile as he named the director of the FSB. "I can dial the number for you if you wish. Like me, he is an older man, though Alexander has a few years to go to catch me up. But, alas, he, also, is not given to sleep, especially so soon after supper." He continued to smile and, the more Tony smiled, the more uncomfortable Lt. Cherninova seemed.

A busty teenage girl, wearing a Speedo bathing suit — in a locker–room — screaming — four men holding her down, while a taller male... It all flashed through Mike's mind so fast that he found himself fighting to block it out, and angry to the point of near rage at what she had been forced undergo.

A snarl escaped before he could stop himself.

Cherninova started, went rigid, then stammered, "Certainly not; I'm sure, Colonel Pitofsky, your visit is no cause for disturbing General Bortnikov."

Mike caught her eying him out of the corner of her eye. Resisting the urge to calm her, he instead flashed a request to Tony for what words to use, then asked, "Is there something wrong lieutenant? Why do you look at me so?"

She immediately flushed scarlet from her neck to the roots of her hair, then stammered, "It is none of my business — I was merely wondering what happened to your regulation sidearm."

Faster than her eyes could follow, Mike pulled his Walther PPK. Once more, with Tony providing the Russian words in his head, he said, "I prefer this to the standard issue Makarov, and trust it more. I took it off a former — that is, recently deceased — MI6 agent." His lines delivered, he returned the weapon to its holster with what, in her mind, he saw as a blur. "But, you are right, *lejtenant*: It is none of your business," he added with a tight smile.

"Y–you —" she took a deep breath, "— will find Captain Mason down this southern corridor, behind me and to the left, on the lefthand side, just past the halfway point — cell 19."

Mike went into her head for about three seconds, hoping to calm her, then saw at a glance several things: She had a superb command of English, in fact, most of the major languages of Europe, and she was in–love with Captain Mason, whom she had determined she would never, ever address as *Bruce*.

Mike clicked his heels together, inviting a salute from her, then gave her a gentle smile, and locked his eyes onto hers, murmuring, in English, "Relax, Natasha Cherninova," which, under the influence of vampiric compulsion, she did.

Mike caught Tony's eye and gave a knowing nod, then the three continued down the hall.

It's a good thing she never noticed her own name on Carrie's name tag, Tony observed.

I was compelling her to see a different name, Carrie relayed.

Tony chuckled. *So was I, my dear. Pray tell, what name were you using? We must have been sending two different names, which would explain why her head was buzzing so much, and why she avoided looking at you, turning her attention instead to our very manly captain here.*

Mike shook his head. *She was fighting both your compulsions. As I said, she has a remarkably strong mind, and is probably Wicca. I suspect she's a witch who knows nothing of her innate abilities. That said, I think we can relax about her. Thanks to whatever charms Mason may have exerted in her direction, as well as a long list of traumas in her own past, a request from Mason might be all it takes to make her defect.*

Here we are, he projected as they reached cell 19. Almost immediately a soldier appeared, running after them, a ring of keys in hand. In a second he had the cell door unlocked and pulled open.

Mike's nostrils were assailed by a strong smell of disinfectant. Tony made a handkerchief appear seemingly out of nowhere, holding it over his nose, his expression one of distaste.

The soldier stationed himself to the left of the doorway, snapped to attention, and stood as if on stationary guard duty. Mike was concerned.

Carrie pushed past and into the cell.

Tony, Mike projected, *what do we do about this guy? I'd compel him to see and hear nothing from the cell, but I'm useless in Russian.*

Mike reached into the soldier's mind, took a grip, and was about to call on Tony for what Russian words to say, when he realized that the man had a rudimentary grasp of English. A moment later the guard was oblivious to their presence.

The cell door was still wide open, the key in the lock. *It's a prison cell; it's always locked,* he reminded himself. *The key opens it, pulling back the deadbolt, but the deadbolt returns the moment the pressure on the key is released. That's why he's here, at attention to one side; he's waiting to lock us in. He'll wait outside to let us out when we're finished.*

Mike entered the cell and pulled the door to, feeling unconcerned when the guard, his mind muddled by vampire compulsion, struggled to key the deadbolt back and close the door on them.

Tony was leaned over the bed, then stepped back to give Carrie room to play nurse, whereupon Carrie moved in, leaned over, and Whispered: "It's okay, Mason, we're here to help." Then, "Michael, help me lower these pants enough to examine his legs."

Mike slid a hand under the small of Mason's back and was about to lift his seat off the bed when Mason's eyes snapped open.

"*Samurai!*" he gasped, then fell silent, his eyes moving to Carrie, then to Tony.

He then sat up — possibly the most rapid move he'd made since shivving Koslov in his cell. The result was that, despite all the energy Mike had imparted to him, his eyes glazed over, and he started to keel over.

Mike's hands shot out and caught him.

Steady on, old man, Tony projected into his head. *This is meant to be a rescue. But first, Michael and Carrie need to assess the condition of your legs. In short, Captain Mason; rise up and drop your trousers.*

"*Da, Lejtenant Polkovnik,*" he acquiesced, then complied.

"You can sit and rest while I do this," Carrie suggested, then she began removing tape and unwinding gauze bandaging from his left leg. "Who did this, Mason?" she asked after examining the first wound. "The whole area has been disinfected. I'm surprised whoever tended to you couldn't have removed the bullets."

"It was Lt. Cherninova," Mike offered. "I'll hazard a guess that Kemedov gave specific orders for the bullets to not be removed."

"And you'd be right, *Samurai,*" Mason murmured. "Great to see you all, by the way. And, before I ask further questions, like how you came to be here or even knew that I was here, I should draw your attention to the camera and microphone, in that dome mounted to the ceiling, to the left of the door."

Mike found it quickly, then, reaching out with his chi, he created a power–surge in the circuitry, damaging the processors just enough to add a layer of static to both audio and video. He next followed the line back to the central server and it's hard drive, and altered his chi into something akin to a low level electromagnetic pulse, and corrupted the data.

"I doubt if even Lt. Cherninova will have any idea of what's going on in here," Mike suggested. "Speaking of her, did she find the bullets?"

Mason looked down at Carrie, still focused on the wound in his right leg, and said, "Left pocket of my denims."

Carrie frowned, dug a hand into that pocket, and pulled out two .22 slugs, one mashed almost flat, and displayed them on the palm of her hand.

Moving with a blur of vampire speed, Mike snatched them up and pocketed them, then glanced up at the camera. Even with the noisy image, his having become a blur might have caught someone's attention.

"If you're worried about Tasha, you needn't," Mason said. "She's a good officer, but there's been trauma in her past."

"*Tasha* is it?" Tony asked, grinning. "You've been busy. And, I must say, old man," he glanced about the narrow confines of the cell, "you didn't have much in the way of atmosphere on your side."

Mike frowned, and said: "From the flashes I saw in her head, I doubt if the leftenant is overly loyal to FSB command. I suspect she'd turn a blind eye to anything showing up on her monitor, unless she thought Mason needed her help." He linked with Carrie and shared with her what he knew and what he was surmising about Natasha Cherninova.

Carrie looked aghast when he displayed the images of her being gang–raped in a locker–room, then, still frowning, began replacing Mason's bandages.

"The wound is in an advanced stage of healing," she commented. "It reminds me, Michael, of nursing your your wounds back in Afghanistan — what was that place called? — Feyzabad? Someone had shot you in the back, not quite a through–and–through, so, being *Rambo*, you had to take your trusty *sgian–dubh* and dig the bullet out from the front. So, Tony, how long has Mason been carrying your blood inside him?" She cast a meaningful glance at Tony, though her expression carried no hint of recrimination.

"About forty years?" Mike suggested. "You were evading a *SMERSH* hit squad — around 1972?"

"That's right," Mason confirmed with a puzzled frown, "but how did you know about that? And what's this about Tony's blood?"

Mike explained, "During our flight from Halifax to London, Tony was reminiscing about the old days with you, and I put two–and–two together. I realized there had to be a reason why you look so much younger than 68 — yes, dear," he added, to Carrie, having seen her look of amazement; "he's 68 years old. In his case, however, advanced healing has a lot to do with things I triggered while influencing certain aspects of his physiology after cauterizing the wounds."

Carrie just nodded and continued her examination of his right leg. She was just replacing the dressing when he gave a slight groan and shifted position, jerking his head to face Tony. "Tell me the truth; how much time do I have?" He then shifted his gaze from Tony to Mike, as if waiting to see who'd answer first.

Mike shrugged. "I don't know, Mason — you're 68 — What do you think? Thirty years?"

Mason processed Mike's attempt at humour, then shook his head. "It's a serious question, Michael."

"Actually, old toff," Tony started in, but Mike forestalled him.

"I may be the best candidate for answering it, under the circumstances," Mike declared, whereupon Tony gave a confirming nod. "You've had Tony's blood in you for forty-one years — close to how long I'd been carrying it when you and I first met in Heathrow Airport. I was already photophobic, showing bursts of vampire strength and speed, super sensitive hearing, etc. Are you displaying any of those yet?"

Mason grasped the top of his pants, pulled them up, all the while clearly pondering everything. "I guess I'm unusually fit for my age,"he mused, "and have a somewhat younger appearance — just as you did back then, but, as to the rest: No, no symptoms at all."

"I remember that," Carrie commented to Mike. "Sam kept calling you *kid*, and it really got on your nerves."

"Mason," Mike resumed, "I was born with a vampire gene, possibly genes — Jonathan is still studying the specifics. While you clearly have accelerated healing, the rest of the expected changes just aren't advanced enough. It's possible that, under the right circumstances, like being frightened or startled enough to cause an epinephrine surge —"

"You mean an adrenaline rush?" Mason asked, to which Mike nodded.

"It seems to take a certain level of adrenaline to trigger the virus so that it focuses on rejuvenating the cardiac muscle and restarting the heart. But, if you slip away peacefully at the age of a hundred–and–four, then that'll probably be the last of you." He shrugged. "Of course, if you really want to change — and I don't recommend it — well, you have friends who can help with that."

"You regret the change?" Mason asked.

Mike shrugged. "Never had a choice," he stated flatly, "And I'm not referring to the state you're in, Mason; I'm referring to the prick who put a bullet through my right ventricle because Stanislaus Mihilache and Cesare Borgia paid him to do it.

"It was the same with Carrie. She never asked to fall from the roof of Torok's castle; she just wanted to get away from him."

Carrie nodded, sadness showing in her face. She straightened, took a deep breath, and forced a smile. "Maybe we should see if he's ready to actually use his legs. I mean, do we really want to hang around until Lieutenant Cherninova comes for a visit? She might want to check out the handsome British captain again.

"*Honestly*, Mason; here Michael and Tony have been searching over half of Russia for you — Michael, in particular — going out–of–body nightly for the past week — when all the while, here you were cozying up to a very attractive Russian FSB officer."

"She really is quite beautiful, isn't she!" Mason declared involuntarily, then his face took on a look of consternation. "What do you mean *cozying*? And how could you know anything about her?"

Tony spoke in Mason's head: *We're vampires, Mason. We read thoughts. Michael, though, can delve deeper than most, getting at things he doesn't even want to know.*

Mike backed up to the wall by the little table and held out his hands. "See if you can walk to me."

Mason did — cautious, almost lurching steps — then turned and walked back to the bed. He immediately turned right, went to the door, then turned and walked the twelve or so feet to the other end of the narrow cell. With every step, his gate became closer to normal.

"If I don't have to walk too far, and no one decides to chase me, I think I'll be fine. By the way, what time is it? Brenda Peters took my watch before I even made it to Russia."

Mike frowned. "It's just after 9:00 PM. Why? Are you expecting a meal delivery or something?"

"Tasha — Natasha — that is, *Leftenant* Cherninova, gets off at 10:00, relieved by Second Leftenant Rosikoff. If we can wait 'til after 10:00 PM, she'll be absolved of any responsibility."

———— —— ——

Natasha Cherninova stared at her monitors, her eyes darting back and forth from cell view to cell view, always coming back to cell 19. The view was severely pixilated, the image moving in glitchy jumps. She touched that square on the monitor, making it switch to full screen, which looked even worse.

Her eyes widened in alarm. *Those bastards!* she thought. *He's a colonel; he can do almost anything in here with impunity. Why would he need to interfere with the monitor? And how could he interfere with it? — some kind of electronic jamming device?*

She brought up the sound — the digital equivalent of static — the vocal tones were present, but it was nothing but a stutter of interrupted sounds coming in fits and hiccups. She killed the sound, then did a rapid pinch of her fingers and thumb on the touch screen, returning it to its normal multi–cell view. Her breathing accelerated; she shot a hand to her mouth.

Oh, Mason! What do I do? He's a colonel, with such a dark and terrifying feel about him. And that captain — he's a trained killer if I ever saw one.

Then the images of that terrible day in the Korean locker room returned, flashing through her mind. Then, — a few years later: *the men's team captain, now a lieutenant, asks her to his apartment — Asks? Lieutenants don't* ask *sergeants! They might sound like they're asking — Then, her refusing him, trying to escape, and him hurling the candle at her in a backhand motion — the melted wax splashing onto her face, the flame of the wick dying as the candle impacts, the skin of her cheek becoming the snuffer. No — NO!*

It became a scream in her head. Her hands shot to her ears to cover them and block out the screams, but she couldn't block out what was in her head.

When she finally calmed herself, the phrase remained — *In her head* — She touched her fingers to her forehead. There'd been a strange buzzing feeling — When? Why? Colonel Pitofsky — reading his name–tag, except it kept blurring into something else — there was a *Captain* Pitofsky here at Lefortovo —

Then there was Captain Minkin — his name–tag didn't say anything of the kind. The buzzing got worse. *I'm not supposed to see it.*

And the woman lieutenant — what was her name supposed to be? — the buzzing became like an hive of angry bees. *Come on, Tasha, relax — Relax, Natasha Cherninova* — it was in English, Captain Minkin's voice, then more buzzing.

Something is not right! This is incredibly wrong! she insisted, then buzzed a guard to come and cover her station.

18: *Surprised?*

Mike closed his eyes, letting images play on the mental screen of his mind: images Lt. Cherninova had unwittingly shown, as well as images he'd gleaned from Mason while in his head during two prior visits to the prison. Reaching out to both Tony and Carrie, he shared the horror of her gang–rape by the men's swimming team, led by their team captain, who Natasha initially labelled as *Sergeant Grigori Dyatlov*, then *Lieutenant Dyatlov*, and, more recently, *Major Grigori Dyatlov*. He then showed Natasha's mental images of Mason: how she saw him and how she imagined other things related to him. Next, he conveyed memories related to the man who carried the label *Father*.

"What do you think?" he asked, looking from Carrie to Tony.

"What do they think of what?" Mason asked, but Mike ignored him, continuing to watch Carrie and Tony's faces.

Do you know who this is? Tony projected the *father* face into Mike's mind as he asked.

Mike frowned. *No idea, but she keeps a framed newspaper clipping in her apartment, and her thoughts label him as her father.*

Tony's eyes widened. *A file on him crossed my desk at Interpol back in '02. He was an FSB colonel — part of their criminal investigations section. He was called in to investigate the '99 bombings that resulted in the second war against Chechnya. He claimed to have found evidence of FSB involvement. Next thing we know, he's spending four years in prison, charged with being in possession of sensitive documents. What caught my eye at the time was that he was released after two years, for good behaviour, but the FSB snatched him up that very same day, and hauled him back to his mountain prison in the Urals. They claimed the releasing judge had overstepped his authority.*

Remember what Nigel said, Michael? If the 'Chechens' hadn't blown up those buildings, inciting public outcry for hardline reaction, Putin might never have become the hero of Moscow, the public persona that got him elected President.

Mike glared. *Jeeze, Tony, this is one hell of a distraction right now.*

Carrie interjected, *Aside from her father and his troubles, it's blatant to me that Natasha is head–over–heels for Mason. Does he feel the same way?*

Mike replied, *As near as I can tell. He's trying to balance his perception of duty with his emotions. The emotions are winning, since he's already mentally composed his letter of resignation from MI6. He's also got a list of places he wants to show her. Would you believe Anstruther is one of them? He thinks she'd enjoy seeing Scholomance Castle, and he doesn't even know she's a witch.*

He glanced at his watch. "Okay," he said aloud, "we've got forty minutes before Lt. Cherninova goes off duty, and Dmitry Rosikoff comes on. Let's work this out. Tony, you and Mason change clothes. We need to be ready, no matter what. This could all come down to having to improvise without warning."

While Tony was removing his colonel's uniform, placing the components on Mason's bunk, then taking Mason's prison–issue denim shirt and putting it on, Mike's mind started to race, sorting through everything like pieces of a puzzle: Tony's plan to change places with Mason, letting Mike and Carrie walk him out. He then filtered through more of what he'd seen briefly in Natasha's thoughts — triggered by Tony's portrayal of the womanizing colonel, flirting with her in what amounted to sexual harassment — her father being imprisoned, released, then cruelly dragged back to prison — *That's nothing more than a demonstration of power.* He reached out into Tony's mind, rifling for images of him having scanned an Interpol file, until he found a name — *Trepashkin* — *Mikhail Ivanovich Trepashkin.*

Then he saw Tony sitting in the cell, waiting for someone, presumably Mike, to return and release him — *probably no big problem*, Mike decided... *unless...*

He glanced at Tony, in full prison denims, sitting patiently on the the bed. Mason, now dressed in the uniform of an FSB lieutenant colonel, complete with uniform cap, was pacing up and down the cell.

"Tony, you still have your watch on," Carrie pointed out. "You need to give it to Mason."

"Mason, quit pacing and sit down and rest," Mike commanded. "We need to figure this out, and I'm not sure you can be impartial about what's in my head. "

Mason looked indignant, but sat anyway, then began to fidget, clearly getting impatient and frustrated when no explanation seemed forthcoming. He was just about to get back up when Mike rounded on him.

"Mason, you're wounded. You're going to have to walk down this corridor, out to the entrance, past two sets of guards, then out to the car. *Please don't make me compel you. What's gotten into you? Where's the cool, resourceful 008 Tony told me about?"*

He sighed, then continued, "I think I'm onto an idea that will make everything fall into place. It still leaves us with no plan for the final exfiltration, but my instincts suggest that even that will work out fine."

He then joined minds with Tony and Carrie, deliberately leaving Mason in the dark.

The rattle of a key in the door lock announced that they were about to be interrupted.

———

Natasha Cherninova frowned at the guard who showed up in response to her summons. He wasn't the one who'd gone with *Colonel Pitofsky?* and company to cell 19. She now had serious doubts as to whether Colonel Pitofsky really was Colonel Pitofsky at all.

"Spell me at this station," she commanded. "There is something I must investigate immediately."

She ducked to the left and hurried off around the corner, but — there he was, the guard she'd expected, standing sentry outside the door to cell 19. Had the *colonel* ordered him to remain? *Of course he had; how else would he get out of the locked cell. Why didn't he have Mason conducted to an interrogation room?*

She quailed at the thought of what might happen if she burst in on them. Images flashed through her mind like pages in a child's flip–book — *Colonel Pitofsky leering, calling her moy* malen'kiy kotenok *(my little kitten) and* myshka (little mouse), *as if he could have her in his bed with a snap of his fingers — Captain Minkin drawing his pistol so fast that she hadn't even seen the hand move — Lieutenant — what was her name? — looking so challenging, a hand resting on her gun belt, in easy reach of the Makarov, and clearly not at all ashamed of the prominence of her bosom — all three were so intimidating —*

Further thought faded as —

— The men in the locker–room, tearing at the bottom of her prohibitively expensive Speedo suit — after their team captain had his turn, they held her in teams of three while a fourth got his turn until each man on the team — and all the while the team captain leaning against a locker, a sneer of smug arrogance on his face —

The door to cell 19 loomed before her. *Focus, Natasha! Get a grip on yourself!*

Unexpectedly her mind replayed a view of the female second lieutenant's name–tag, the name in startling focus — *Lt. N. Cherninova* — *her name–tag!*

"Guard, open the cell door!"

He stared ahead, seemingly oblivious to her.

"Guard! Open the door! Unlock cell 19!"

Still he stared blankly ahead.

She slapped him hard across the face, then snatched the keyring from him, found the key, and unlocked the door herself.

All the way down the hall she'd been running lines in her head about what to say to the colonel when she burst in. It all faded from her mind as she pulled the door open. There before her was the colonel, standing calmly, the captain to one side, the colonel's adjutant to the other.

She halted and stared, reality struggling to fight past the images she'd been expecting. *Mason! Mason in the colonel's uniform!* Glancing left, she was even more shocked to see the man who'd claimed to be Colonel Pitofsky seated on the bed, in prison denims. Her hand had shot to the Makarov at her hip, but the arm relaxed and fell to her side.

"I'm not sure what Kemedov has planned for me," Mason said in a gentle tone, "but my friends have strong opinions against me staying here to learn."

"Friends?" she echoed, then looked from face to face, suddenly seeing all the characters as if for the first time, that is, all but Mason. Mason still seemed the same man to whom she'd been opening up daily for a week — and that oh so charming smile —

"Mason, your legs..." She took an eager step toward him, about to place her hands on Mason's chest, then, uncomfortably aware of the presence of the others, she stopped herself.

Mason smiled. "Tasha, this is my friend Michael," he said, placing a hand on the shoulder of the man in the Captain's uniform. "I mentioned him — He's the one who introduced me to *Scholomance Castle,* in Anstruther, Scotland."

For the first time she saw that his name–tag really said *Lt. D. Rosikoff.*

"It's too hard to explain," Mason continued, "— I can't truly understand it myself, but Michael removed the bullets from my legs and cauterized the wounds."

The adjutant lieutenant declared: "You did a marvelous job of cleaning and disinfecting Mason's legs and dressing the wounds," and smiled sweetly.

"Tasha," Mason said, "this is Michael's wife, Carrie. She's a registered nurse."

Natasha's eyes shifted to her name–tag and, for the first time, was able to read *Lt. N. Cherninova* without a confusing blur and a buzzing in her head. *My name– tag — My Uniform? I knew it!* For a moment she could only stare. "But how? — When?..." Her head was starting to spin, the room spinning with it.

The captain — Michael— moved with the same impossible speed he'd exhibited with his Walther PPK. In a flash he had her, reaching a hand toward the wooden chair seemed to make it slide to meet the backs of her legs, and he eased her down onto it. *Relax, Natasha Cherninova,* he had said in her mind. Now he was saying, *It's okay, Lieutenant. Aside from rescuing Mason, we mean no harm to you or your country. With the exception of a few of the stooges who work for*

Kemedov in his part of the drug–trade, almost everyone I've met since arriving in Moscow has been very nice, especially that officer at the airport — P. Cherninov. Mason's friend Michael smiled. *So the P is for Pavel, and he's your cousin.*

She felt a pang of alarm. "How are you doing this?" she asked. "How are you in my head?"

"It's nothing to be afraid of — well, unless you're one of the *bad guys*. What I was about to say is that, on the whole, I've found the Russians to be a charming people. I have my doubts about your President, though — especially when I read about people like Mikhail Trepashkin and Alexander Litvinenko."

Michael was now giving her a fixed stare, eyebrows arched the way someone might if they were trying to coax — and images started flashing in her mind's eye: *Trepashkin — the clipping about her father, in the frame by her mirror, and the other of Litvinenko, who had become her father's friend before...*

"Before Andrei Lugovoy, former KGB "bodyguard" slipped him a lethal dose of radioactive polonium," Michael said, finishing her thought.

Her eyes alighted on the one person whose identity had not been explained: Colonel Pitofsky. "And who are you? You're wearing Captain Pitofky's name–tag."

He got to his feet and, with the type of bow she'd imagined the pre-revolution nobility having used, he said: "Tony Dewhurst, m' dear, at your service. Mason and I were colleagues for a number of years."

Mason recounting his wife's death — It took a dear friend named Tony to pull me through.

She stood and turned to face the one face she felt sure of, the one face for whom she felt the deepest trust — the depth of her feeling and trust for him was absurd, yet undeniable. She stared deeply into his eyes, but saw only concern, compassion, and an inexplicable affection for her. She inhaled deeply, held it a moment, then slowly eased it out.

"What can I do?" she said.

She looked to see the light of accomplishment in the eyes of the others, some sign of a sense of victory, of having *turned* her, in the parlance of the spy industry. But all she saw was patience and concern.

She was expecting Tony to take the reins at this point — there was something about him that spoke of a lifetime of commanding others, something that spoke of — inherited nobility — aristocracy? Instead, it was the captain, the one Mason had identified as Michael who answered.

"For the moment, I suggest you do nothing," he stated. "Return to your post; just lock us in and leave us. We really do have matters under control. Your camera for this room is permanently damaged and it's portion of the mainframe hard–drive corrupted. Don't ask how."

"He's a bit like Kulagina or Gradova," Mason offered, referring to two Russians with apparent psychic and telekinetic abilities, of whom the KGB had made use.

"But how did he get Rosikoff's uniform, and how did Carrie get mine?" She wasn't sure whether to be angry or just amazed.

Michael said, "That was Rosikoff, himself, though he probably has no memory of doing it."

"Who are you?" she gasped, turning to face him. "You don't sound British like Mason or Tony. Are you American? Just how big is this? Is it an MI6 operation or MI6 and the CIA? James Bond had his Felix Lighter in the movies..."

Michael smiled and explained: "Carrie and I are Canadian. I'm with CSIS; Carrie's civilian. *C* asked me to take this mission because of certain unique skills."

"Skills like reading minds and disabling electronics without touching them?" she remarked. "So I should go back to my desk, wait quietly for you, Carrie, and Mason to leave, with Mason posing as Colonel Pitofsky, leaving Tony to take Mason's place?"

"Actually," Tony interjected, "you'd be waiting patiently for Lt. Rosikoff to come on duty and relieve you. Then you go home, like you've done any other night. After that, we leave during Rosikoff's shift. You logged us in, leaving us still locked in the cell when you went off–duty — no fault to you, all perfectly by the book. Rosikoff comes on; you inform him that Colonel Pitofsky arrived with an interrogator to question me — nothing contrary to regulations.

"You can even suggest that there might be a problem with the surveillance feeds from cell 19, leaving it to Rosikoff to decide whether or not to investigate. Whatever the case, Rosikoff cannot be held responsible. Did I miss anything, Michael?"

Michael just shook his head.

"Oh, you have no idea what the FSB can do if they decide to persecute someone for making them look bad," Natasha declared.

"Like they did with your father?" Michael asked. "I'm starting to get an alarming picture of the FSB's capabilities in, shall we say, grey areas, even darker. If I have to, I'll go to great lengths to exonerate Lieutenant Rosikoff. But, for the meantime, we will not proceed until you've left the building."

"But how will you know I've left?" she demanded.

A half smile lifted the corner of Michael's mouth. *Don't worry; I'll know,* he said in her mind. "Drive home. If you want us to contact you when it's over, give Mason a phone number. I'm sure he wants it."

Turning to Mason, she gripped his arm with both hands, and whispered her address, repeating it, then the same with her phone number.

He placed a hand on one of hers. "Don't worry, Tasha, Michael will find a way to make it all work out. And, if you seriously want me to show you around those places I mentioned, we can make that happen."

She shifted her other hand so that it rested atop his, trapping it against her other hand. "And you'll retire from your dangerous work, so we can..." She was too afraid, too uncertain of her future and the intimidating power of the FSB, to finish the sentence — *This is just too crazy!* She merely looked up into his eyes and smiled hopefully. Men had only ever made use of her, abused her, victimized, making her feel helpless. This man had only ever been kind and understanding. *That could all be spy craft — the KGB taught me how to do all that* — yet something in his eyes said otherwise.

"I promise," Mason acquiesced in a low tone; "Besides, we'll have time to discuss all that."

"Do you have a car?" Mike asked, his brow furrowed as if there was something particular on his mind.

She shook her head. "I don't even drive." Seeing a look of amazement on Carrie's face, she quickly added, "Before the fall of the Soviet Union, I was denied time to pursue a driver's license — apparently there was no need; my transportation was always provided. The buses and trams here are very reliable, with new buses going wherever the trolly lines don't go," she paused, realizing how pathetic and defensive it all sounded. "My progress up the ranks was tediously slow. In fact, at every stage there was one particular superior officer who wanted to —" she swallowed hard. *Why is it so hard? And why do I even want to tell these people?* It was the look of sympathy in Carrie's eyes that made it easier but, even so, she had to blurt it out "— rub my face in the fact that he felt he could control me. I even suspected that he somehow knew who my father was and was trying to punish me for what certain officers have labeled as disloyalty to the FSB, but, the reality is that the FSB upper levels are almost entirely corrupt. It's a pack of beasts who truly run the FSB — and, indirectly, run this country."

She shut her eyes tight, ashamed of her outburst, labeling it unprofessional and unbecoming of a Russian officer. "I'm sorry," she declared. "The simple matter is that I do not drive; I rely on buses and trolleys. Why did you want to know?" She turned her glance to Michael, since he'd asked the original question.

"There are a number of ways I could get Tony out after Mason is in the clear," he said, "but one would make you look better, more on the ball, as we say in the West."

She managed a smile. "I'm familiar with the metaphor, originating from the design of movement for railroad watches. But what are you considering?"

"Could you leave and find a way to remain outside?" Mike asked. "Maybe walk a block or two away and wait." He paused, as if giving more thought to the matter, then said, "No, I think the best thing is for you to draw Rosikoff's attention to the situation with the monitors. Tell him you were about to come and check yourself. Then go home; follow your usual routine."

She nodded reluctantly. Then, looking at Mason one last time, "Are you sure you will be alright?"

He smiled. "I'm in good hands, my dear," he assured her. "— The best."

She called for the guard to open the cell, but he seemed slow in responding, looking dazed when he finally opened the door to let her out.

She hurried back to the duty desk, arriving just as Rosikoff was approaching.

"Ah, good you're here, Dmitry," she declared. "I was just about to check cell 19 — the monitor seems erratic. I suspect it's something wrong with the wiring.

Look; see for yourself." She drew his attention to the pixilated and intermittent picture and the sporadic unintelligible audio. She knew that Rosikoff was a technophile, and feared he'd see through the situation, but he was already nodding briskly.

"I'll look into it, Tasha," he assured her. "The microphone and the camera share the same circuitry, both digital, though hardly HDMI. Imagine this place having HDMI cameras!" he declared with a chuckle.

"Imagine me knowing what HDMI is!" she riposted, hoping to hide her nervousness with a chuckle. "What are you talking about, Dmitry?"

He smiled. "Just this, Tasha, whatever damaged the camera — most likely a power–spike — probably damaged the audio circuit as well."

Then, glancing at the computer monitor, he added, "Oh! The prisoner in cell 19 is getting an unscheduled interrogation?"

Natasha nodded briskly. "Colonel Pitofsky, with Captain Minkin, his interrogator, and the Colonel's adjutant, a female lieutenant second class."

"I'll go check right away," Rosikoff assured her. "I can use the excuse that the monitor seems faulty, and that I need the second lieutenant's name for the log. Now, I'm sure you've had a long enough shift — you must be tired to have missed the lieutenant's name for the log. Go on home; your day is done." And he buzzed for a guard before she even turned to go.

Natasha nodded. "*Spasibo,*" she acknowledged, doing her best to suppress the turmoil inside her, to act as she had any other night that week. Moments later she was outside and walking to her bus–stop. *Please be safe, Mason; Please be safe, Mason,* she repeated over and over again until it became a mantra, a mantra that she repeated over and over, fingers of both hands crossed, its rhythm matched to the rhythm of her footsteps.

19: *Escape*

The moment Natasha Cherninova left, Second Lieutenant Dmitry Rosikoff saw the guard approaching.

"Monitor this station until I return," he commanded, then he set a brisk pace to cell 19.

The guard at the door snapped to attention at his approach. "Be careful, sir;" he said in a whisper, "I'm not sure the Colonel wishes to be disturbed."

"Just open it," Rosikoff ordered, whereupon the guard rattled his keyring until he selected the appropriate key, then unlocked the cell.

The prisoner was seated on the small wooden chair, a captain standing before him, arms folded across his chest, legs in a broad stance. Everything about the captain seemed intimidating.

A man in the uniform of an FSB lieutenant colonel stood just behind and to one side of the captain, while an attractive woman in a uniform differing only in gender from his own, stood behind the prisoner.

The colonel raised his eyes to the doorway and fixed them on Rosikoff. "Yes? — Lieutenant Second Class Dmitry Rosikoff, is it? You thought I was hoping for an interruption, perhaps?" Rosikoff found the cool smile and challenging stare unnerving.

"I'm sorry, sir, but there is a technical problem with the camera and microphone in this cell. I merely wanted to ascertain that you were still here, and that nothing had gone awry with your interrogation."

The captain fixed eyes on him, and said, "I can't imagine what could possibly have gone awry, Lieutenant." It suddenly felt as if something had sucked all the warmth out of the room, turning it into a freezer. An icy chill grew inside him, making him feel desperate to get away from this cell.

He froze, suddenly unsure of himself, not knowing what to say. It was the chilling feeling from the captain — something about his mind, his — he shook his head, unable to even compose the thought, but some part of him intuitively knew that he'd somehow experienced this captain before, that the captain was not someone he dared even question.

"Perhaps," the captain said, nodding slowly, "you should make sure this anomaly has not occurred in any other cells."

Certain he'd just been dismissed, Rosikoff gave a sharp salute, turned, and left, casting an enormous sigh of relief as he escaped the captain's presence.

—— —— ——

Mike reached out with his mind and tracked Rosikoff as he went back to his station, then located cell 36, Petroff's cell. Petroff was still jabbering at the ceiling. Mike located the camera housing, wrapped his awareness around it, and projected his energy in the same pulse he had directed at the camera in cell 19. Then, for good measure, he went up a floor and did the same in the cell directly above Petroff, then the same in the cell directly above their own.

He smiled. "It seems that there are a few more cameras acting up, including two on the next floor."

Then, glancing at Mason, he asked, "Are you ready Colonel?" Then, "How about you, Tony?"

"Go ahead, and good luck," Tony assured him. "I'm actually surprisingly comfortable here, but I do look forward to your return. Alas, dear boy, I lack your remarkable skill with locks." He smiled.

Mike gave the door a thump with a fist, then whispered to Mason to call the guard in Russian.

Almost immediately, the keys rattled in the lock, and the door opened.

"You should assist the prisoner back onto his bed," Mason told the guard. "In fact, I recommend assisting him onto the commode — that is assuming that he hasn't soiled himself already."

Don't forget you're supposed to have a bullet in each leg, Mike projected to Tony.

Moments later as they passed the duty station, Mike overheard Rosikoff mutter, "Looks like cell 36 has the same glitch. I'd better call the other floors and make sure they check all their cells, as well."

He resisted the urge to smile.

One of the guards at the interrogators' entrance hesitated, staring at Mason, but an icy glare from Mike was all it took to get the door opened for them.

They got in the car, Mike drove half a block, then stopped and got out. It took just a moment for him to blur back to Lefortovo. He paused just long enough to will the guards at the door to not see him. They seemed startled when the door opened on it's own.

Passing the duty desk was simple, and soon he was back at cell 19. He focused his mind on the tumblers of the lock, gesturing with his hand as he projected chi and caused the tumblers to turn and withdraw the bolt.

"Let's go, Tony," he whispered and, seconds later, Dewhurst was with him.

Mike closed the door, smiling to himself as he pictured the guard discovering the prisoner missing, even though the door was locked. Then, as the thought occurred to him, he paused at the duty desk. A moment in Rosikoff's head was all it took to convince the lieutenant that the prisoner in cell 19 shouldn't have food until suppertime the next day. *Now Mason's escape won't be discovered until supper tomorrow, unless someone else comes up with a reason to check on him.*

Next, he detoured Tony into the locker room where, after looking at what sizes were available, he selected a junior sergeant's uniform and handed it to Tony.

When Tony showed surprise, Mike conveyed: *Glamour won't help us if a stray camera spots a man in prison denims walking out the door or down the street. The sooner you change, the sooner we can get out of here.* Tony agreed.

Passing the door guards was as easy as it had been upon entering. Tony could easily compel one or two people to not see him, but Mike, ever wary, compelled the guards to see no one.

They were on their way to where Mike had left the car when Tony said, "I can't deny being glad that's over, Michael. Now all we need do is spirit Mason into our suite and brainstorm how to proceed."

Mike nodded, adding, "And contact Nigel to have him delete all traffic–cam evidence of our rental Lada. The last thing we need is some keen FSB tech spotting that the black Lada leaving our hotel looks identical to the black Lada arriving at the prison. There's also the surveillance cameras outside the prison. I totally forgot about those while leaving."

"They were to your back, dear boy," Tony argued. "You would need eyes in the back of your head to notice them during our departure. Nigel will, I'm quite sure, remove any evidence. Meanwhile, there's the car, with Carrie and Mason waiting."

They *whooshed* forward and Tony got into the back with Mason, while Mike got behind the wheel, next to Carrie.

"Thank God!" Carrie exclaimed. "I was even thinking of getting into the driver's seat, just in case you needed a getaway driver."

"It's all under control," Mike assured her.

"Perhaps, but I'm not so sure about *her*," Carrie announced, looking ahead through the windshield. "In fact, *she* doesn't look under control at all."

Natasha Cherninova was standing in the shadows two poles away from the glass–sheltered bus–stop.

Mike pulled over against the curb and waited while Carrie lowered the window.

"As you can see, Natasha," he said, "everything has gone according to plan."

Natasha leaned in just enough for a view of the backseat, then heaved a huge sigh and beamed a smile at Mason, but the smile soon faded.

"Please, can you take me with you?" she urged. "I have this inescapable premonition that I can't go home tonight. I know it must seem foolish, but, no matter how I try to rationalize it, I can't make it go away."

"Get in," Mike said. "Ignoring premonitions rarely works out well."

Mason immediately slid over to make room.

In his rearview mirror, Mike spotted how Natasha automatically pressed against Mason until he raised an arm onto the back of his seat, then, as she snuggled against him in a manner Mike thought unbecoming of an FSB officer, Mason lowered his arm about her shoulders.

Tony had his iPhone out and was calling Nigel.

"Oi, I ffought I should be awake tonigh' jus' in case. I trust, Yer Lordship, ffat ev'ryffing went spit–spot. I mean, ye go' Mason outta ffere wiffou' no Barney?"

"I'm fine, Nigel; thank you for asking," Mason called out.

"Nigel, we need another bit of hacking," Mike explained. "It's the traffic—"

"Ffe traffic–cams between yer 'otel an' Lefortovo," Nigel finished for him. "Already done, *Samurai*. I'm on it now, messin' wiff each one as you pass ffrough on 'e way back. So, mate, 'owed it go? I mean, ye know, details?"

Mike sighed, then smiled. "Later, and more likely from Tony, Carrie, and Mason. In the meantime, there's the additional issue of the surveillance camera outside the interrogators' entrance to Lefortovo. Can we get that scrubbed?"

"You mean get *ffem* scrubbed, I'm sure;" Nigel corrected, "ffere's ffree of 'em. But, no worries! Our intrepid *Maha–ka*, agent *Samura*, 'as done 'is duty for tonigh', so, relax an' leave ffe rest to ol' Nigel.

"By ffe by, I looked into some o' whot you asked me to 'ave a dig into, an whot I unearffed is a can o' worms, make no mistake. Ffat bombin' business we were talkin' about, well, it even ties in wiff 'at bloke Litvinenko, whot claimed ffat KGB bloke Lugovoy poisoned 'im wiff someffin' radioactive. An' ffere's ffis ovver bloke, anovver FSB colonel 'oo Litvinenko got to investigate ffe bombings wiff 'im — anyway, ffis bloke left an' became a lawyer — Well, 'e spent fo' years in porridge on whot looks like —"

"*Nigel*," Mike interrupted, "*this is not the time.* Focus on the cameras for now, please. We'll go into all the rest later, once everyone is settled safely."

"Ah — Righ' — gotcha, Michael — I'm on it. Call me back when you ffink it's a better time."

Back at the hotel, Mike left the others in the car while he located and isolated their surveillance duo. Seeing an FSB captain approaching seemed to startle them enough. Mike decided it was time to make sure they saw nothing more. A simple compulsion had the two on a bus together, heading toward the Black Sea to visit one of the agent's relatives.

Mike smiled as he returned to the car, explained to Tony, who erupted into laughter, then he and Tony used more mesmerism to get everyone to the suite unseen.

"I'll put the coffee on," Tony announced, and began putting water into that device, then searched the cupboard until he found a small can of coffee and a box of filters.

"Perhaps, Michael, while I'm doing this," Tony suggested, lowering his voice "you might see to warming some of your own preferred beverage, and some for Carrie and me as well."

Mike was about to oblige when Carrie came up behind him and, slithering her arms about his waist, said, "You've had the hardest night, Michael; why don't you sit and take a break while I tend to that."

Raowwwww! Kato made an indignant entrance, then leapt up onto Mike's shoulder, pawed at the epaulets with an indignant glare, then settled into his arms instead.

Mew! Mew! Teila greeted Carrie in her still–kitten– like voice, also demanding to be picked up.

Carrie had already dropped her gun-belt and peeled off the tunic of her uniform and dropped both into an armchair, followed by the necktie, and was undoing a few of the top buttons of the uniform blouse, while Teila batted at the buttons and her hand, as if determined to help.

"This is Teila," Carrie explained to Natasha. "That noisy one over there, who clearly thinks his master was gone too long, is Kato."

"How beautiful," Natasha declared, brightening for the first time all evening. "Are they friendly?" she asked as she cautiously approached. "I've heard stories about Siamese cats."

"Teila more so than Kato," Mike explained. "Kato isn't unfriendly, just a bit shy of strangers."

Be good, Mike projected to Kato, who sniffed at Natasha's hand, then rubbed his head against it, before withdrawing back against Mike's chest. Teila, on the other hand, climbed up onto Natasha's shoulder.

"They have amazing eyes," she observed, "but then, so do both of you. I've never seen a human with eyes so brilliant."

"Your own eyes aren't so far from Carrie's in colour," Mason pointed out. "I noticed that almost right away, that first day that you visited my cell."

"Did you now?" Natasha asked, her smile showing disbelief and a hint of coquettishness.

"How do you stand wearing that uniform day in and day out?" Carrie asked her. "I used to complain about the rule of having to wear proper nurses' scrubs everyday, but, while not exactly a fashion statement, they were the ultimate in comfort compared to a uniform like this."

Natasha just shrugged. "For me it was about the indignity of being made to dress like nothing more than a female version of the people who controlled my life. Just when I thought much of the worst was finally behind me, I'd encounter a fresh reminder. Major Grigori Dyatlov was the worst. Whenever I thought sure I'd never hear of him again, he'd reappear, like a recurring nightmare, just to prove he could still intrude on my life. I wish I'd had the courage to just empty my weapon into him last time. He lorded over my review panel when I was in the final stages of approval for my current rank. Thank God for General Kashirin — he encouraged me to apply for the promotion. He noticed Dyatlov sneering, whispered something to him, which, I can only assume was some sort of warning."

Mike set Kato down on the back of the armchair, then picked up Carrie's stuff, set the gun-belt on the floor, then draped the tunic on the arm of the chair. He then pealed off his own tunic and set it with Carrie's, then removed his shoulder-holster harness, and laid it on the floor next to Carrie's gun-belt. He pulled up an adjacent chair and sat, loosened his tie and, within moments, removed both epaulets from his jacket, then, crossing over to the sofa by the window, where Mason sat, exchanged them with the epaulets on the tunic Mason was wearing.

Returning to the chair, he settled in again, Kato coming around the back to lay across the back of his shoulders.

Natasha sat next to Mason, and stared at Mike, her eyes almost bugging out. Mike had just extended a fingernail with a point as sharp as a talon, and picked at the colonel epaulets until all the stitching was removed and nothing was holding the white fabric in place but the stars and the FSB emblem. Before long he'd restored the first lieutenant insignia to its original condition, then reattached both epaulets to the shoulders of her borrowed tunic.

By the time Carrie returned with a warmed mug of O+ and an A+ for herself, he had restored all three borrowed uniforms to their original state. "I think I'd like to smuggle these back into that locker–room," he mused, "before they're missed. Especially if it saves poor Dmitry any grief."

Tony interrupted, setting a tray on the coffee table with two steaming mugs of coffee. "I know you take your's black, Mason, with just a touch of sugar, but there's cream and milk in the fridge, whichever you prefer, Natasha."

"Black is fine," Natasha said, her tone more subdued since her discussion of Major Dyatlov.

Mike sipped at his mug, then took a long swallow, keeping his mouth closed until his fangs receded.

Carrie stood possessively behind him, a hand on his neck, occasionally stroking Kato with a finger.

"Why don't you take your gun and go get changed first," she whispered to him. "I'll help hold down the fort here, and make another drink for you."

Mike took a moment to assess the mood of the room, then adjourned to the bedroom, Kato trailing him. He stored his Walther in the drawer of the bedside table, stripped off the remainder of the uniform, then donned his black Levis, a black turtleneck, and his black Otomix sneakers. Returning to his own identity was a relief.

Kato still shadowing, he returned to the living-room, resumed his seat, Kato resuming his perch across his shoulders.

"Please tell me if I'm out of line with any of my questions, Michael," Natasha hesitated, "but, how do you do what you do?" When Mike didn't answer right away, she added, "You know: The voices in my head, seeming to read my thoughts, whatever you did with the surveillance camera and microphone, and getting Tony out of Lefortovo? I'm sure that, if I went back and checked tomorrow, no one would know anything about it, and there'd be no trace on any surveillance camera. The last bit, I know from your conversation with that man, Nigel, — from what I could decipher of his Cockney accent — that he's largely responsible for — You specifically asked him to scrub the camera data. I presume that means he's some kind of computer expert — *hacker* is the term?"

Mason started to chuckle. "My dear, Natasha, Nigel is the king of hackers. We have such men in MI6, and they are torn between hating Nigel out of unbridled envy and worshipping him as a god."

"But what about you, Michael?" she persisted. "How do you know all that stuff about me — about my father. I've told almost no one about that time in Seoul, during the '88 Olympics. I can understand you being able to learn about my father, Mikhail Trepashkin, and about his former colleague and friend, Colonel Litvinenko — the internet outside Russia is apparently filled with their story, but not *inside* Russia. *Inside* Russia the internet is controlled, many websites banned. If the government doesn't want it known, it will not be known. One TV station in particular was shut down after controversial coverage concerning the '99 bombings.

"Did you do whatever you did to the camera in cell 19 to deal with surveillance microphones in this suite?"

Mike nodded.

"Michael is what some people might call a witch," Mason said. "Remember I told you about the *Scholomance* Castle in Anstruther Scotland?"

"*Scholomance*," she echoed, as if the name was known to her. "The same *Scholomance* mentioned in Bram Stoker's novel, *Dracula*?"

Mike shook his head. "That one is in Romania, in Transylvania. The school in Scotland came into being much later, a few hundred years ago, to counteract the other, which had become polarized toward evil."

"Michael not only studies there," Mason went on with what, to Michael, sounded like a note of pride, "but he teaches, as well."

Natasha wanted to know more about what he taught, but Mike avoided the topic. "Basic martial arts, mostly," was his only comment.

Tony picked up the litany. "An ancestor of Michael's was a Wicca adept who practiced healing, and had a tremendous rapport with animals, traits that Michael has clearly inherited. It seems that, the more he learned about her, and the more he believed in himself, the more his talents expanded and the more new talents he discovered. His skills still grow, to our constant amazement."

Mike rolled his eyes and shrugged. "And Uri Geller could read minds and bend spoons," he said dismissively.

"Uri Geller was a fraud, and it was proven," Natasha declared. "That much you can see on *YouTube*, even in Russia."

"Michael, Tony, and Carrie are special and unique," Mason summarized. "Together they are an incredible team."

"But," Carrie said from the bedroom doorway, "there is no one like Michael."

"*Od's fish*, m' dear, but you just said a mouthful there!" Tony declared.

"Thank you, Lord Dewhurst," Mike said dryly, hoisting his mug in a toasting gesture.

"*Lord* Dewhurst?" Natasha queried. "Nigel called you *Your Lordship*. Is that true? Your accent does reflect the British aristocracy, as do your manners. Are you really an English Lord?"

Mike grinned. "Well, since no one minds embarrassing me, it's your turn, Tony. Natasha: May I present to you Lord Anthony Dewhurst, Duke of Exeter and Earle of Richmond.

"Now, Tony, if you care to change out of that uniform, and, perhaps, find a spare change of clothes for Mason, I'll bag it with all these others. I'm eager to get them out of here — no sense having incriminating evidence hanging around."

20: *Clean-Up*

N atasha Cherninova plied Carrie with question after question as they changed, Carrie offering her her choice of what clothing she'd brought with her.

"*So, Michael's a sorcerer?*" Tasha whispered, "You mean, a real sorcerer, like Merlin or Harry Potter?" She found it all so hard to believe.

"More like Merlin, probably, and less like Harry Potter," Carrie assured her. "It has nothing to do with wands or reciting phrases in Latin, though I sometimes have to use the Gaelic word for fire to help me create it. We're both of Celtic ancestry, so it's probably more psychological — saying it helps me visualize it and make it happen. In the beginning I could only draw flame to me from a fire source, like a candle or a kerosene lamp, then release it to what I wanted to set afire. Michael, though, almost from the beginning, could make fire by converting his chi and spiritual energy into flame. Michael is a Kung Fu master — no kidding, he even lived at a Shaolin temple in some obscure part of China before we met. Then there was all those months he spent with Tulku Anil in Tibet."

Natasha stared at Carrie, wide–eyed. "This chi you speak of: I know about it," Natasha mused. "One of my swimming coaches had studied martial arts in the People's Republic of China, and spoke to me often of channeling my chi into my swimming. And I can sense Michael's power, it positively radiates from him — it's almost like being next to a nuclear reactor!"

Carrie stifled a giggle. "I know what you mean, and it's become even more intense since he met — well, let's just say he met someone of much greater skill and power than himself, and what came of that meeting has increased his power greatly. I sometimes wonder if he, himself, is aware of how great his power is. He's always been in some kind of denial about his abilities. I think it stems from his childhood and having been badly bullied during his early teens. He also had an older brother who insisted on overshadowing him."

Natasha became pensive, musing over a memory of something she'd heard Dmitry Rosikoff quote.

"The noir hero is a knight in blood–caked armour. He's dirty and he does his best to deny the fact that he's a hero the whole time." she recited. "Dmitry — Michael was wearing his uniform — used to read a lot of comic books by an American artist named Miller — some of the darker Batman stuff. "He must have quoted that line maybe a dozen times, until it got stuck in my memory."

"Mike is almost never dirty, but he has been pretty bloody at times," Carrie conceded. "In Uzbekistan and Tajikistan, a man named Aziz kept referring to him as the Archangel of Death. I've been in love with him for so long, and have watched him evolve —" she shrugged, "I guess I still see him as the same Michael I've known and loved, but, the truth is: he and I have both changed almost beyond recognition. The beauty of it is that, through it all, our love continues to grow."

"You are kindred spirits," Natasha pronounced. "I sense that about you as clearly as I sense Michael's powers and your own."

"I think you and Mason might have the same connection as Michael and I," Carrie suggested.

Natasha blushed and averted her eyes a moment, then said, "It's not so easy for me. I've been so tormented throughout my life — I've never been with a man because I wanted to. There's always been either force or intimidation. And yet," she felt suddenly shy, almost afraid to say it, "when I am near him, I can't help but feel that it would be amazingly different — intense, vibrant, and wonderful." Her hand flew to her mouth, as if hoping to keep the words from escaping.

Carrie was suddenly hugging her. "Michael and I have seen how Mason looks at you, too. You go for it, girl!" she declared, giggling.

Moments later, Natasha was also laughing merrily. Then Natasha shook her head, almost overwhelmed. "I used to talk to my mother about everything, but she was killed a few years ago by a hit–and–run driver. I've never had any close women friends I could talk to like this. Thank you, Carrie."

She seemed almost surprised when Carrie's eyes teared up. "You have three new friends, now, Tasha. And, of course, there's Mason."

Then they both started giggling again.

———

Mike was on his third mug of O+, eased back in the corner of the other sofa, when Tony and Mason returned, both dressed in *civvies*.

"You must be tired," Mason commented. "And Michael — you, too, Tony, but, especially you, Michael —" He hesitated. "Well, there aren't words to adequately thank you. I can't even begin to understand what you did to my legs, and how you seemed to reenergize me. When I met you at Heathrow years ago, I knew you were special, but I never would have dreamed — It's all just so unreal, no matter how often you explain what you do."

"Yes, I, too, have the same reaction," Natasha declared. She was just emerging from Mike and Carrie's bedroom, wearing a pink fuzzy knit sweater and a pair of black corduroys, borrowed from Carrie. "It all just seems too far-fetched, like something from fantasy fiction."

Mike smiled. "Hey, don't knock fantasy fiction," he joked.

"Michael is a published author, with at least six fantasy novels to his credit," Tony explained, "— at least it was six when I helped unpack at that Sci–Fi/ Fantasy convention in Austria in 2011."

"Seven," Mike commented *sotto voce*. "The second vampire novel came out last fall. I've been trying to get the third finished, but Charbonneau keeps finding new reasons to interrupt."

"He's hoping to have it ready by spring," Carrie announced, just emerging behind Natasha, wearing a wooly black turtleneck. "He's also outlining a fourth — at least he was when the director of CSIS called to inform him that MI6 was requesting his help in locating and rescuing our dear friend there."

"And all these things you can do, do you include them in your books?" Natasha asked.

Mike was about to ask for an expounding on what *all these things you can do* entailed, when, turning to face her, he noticed Carrie's attempts to make more cute the guilty expression on her face.

"I just lit a candle or two," she said, trying to sound innocent, and showing him a childlike smile.

"A candle or two," Mike murmured, shaking his head, then he let out a sigh.

"It was four candles, Carrie," Natasha corrected, her expression as wide–eyed as a child, then she shot a hand to her mouth, as if to shut herself up.

In less than a second, she and Carrie were both laughing so hard they were clinging to each other, as if to avert falling over. When they finally subsided, Carrie flopped on the sofa against Mike, pulled her legs up, and cuddled against him.

She gave him a small nudge, then, in his head, *Watch them,* drawing his attention to Natasha, who made a beeline for Mason, who was just resuming his former position on the sofa by the window. She sat next to him, so close that, with his superior height, he was obliged to put an arm about her.

She engineered that, Carrie declared in his head. *She confessed to me while we were changing and doing makeup, that she's never willingly been with a man of her choosing — it's always been some form of intimidated coercion, except for her first experience, which was flat–out rape!*

Mike pondered this for a second then asked, *And you're telling me this because...?* He always felt uncomfortable whenever Carrie tried to share with him what he considered girly gossip.

Because part of her wants to 'be with' Mason, Carrie replied, all the while giggling and snuggling harder against him.

I assume by 'be with' Mason you're being euphemistic, and alluding to having to make adjustments for tonight's sleeping arrangements.

She kissed him on the cheek. *Bingo!*

Mike took a moment to go into Tony's head and explain the situation.

Meanwhile, Mike was also keeping an eye on Natasha, who was watching Carrie cuddle against him, and seemed to feel more relaxed about her own position with Mason. As he began probing her thoughts on the subject, he encountered a surprising obstacle. She was frowning, seemingly aware of him in her head, and struggling to push him out. It made him recall noticing her resistance to being made to see false names on name–tags, especially her own name–tag.

Natasha seems to have no appreciation of her own Wiccan powers, he confided to Carrie.

He pushed back into her head, using subtle ploys taught by the *Scholomance*, worked past her resistance, and found a veritable storehouse of memories locked away — locked away because she'd thought them too bizarre to countenance — vicious guard dogs who calmed when she wished they'd stop barking and snarling at her — the household remedies that she seemed to know with no one having taught her — the lights flickering and a garbage can being mysteriously hurled against the wall during the locker–room attack in South Korea.

This last overlapped into another protected area of memory — her history of sexual abuse and sexual harassment under the auspices of the FSB. For every event she'd spoken of or alluded to, there seemed several that she'd buried from her consciousness, leaving her frigid toward relationships with men. It surprised her that, now, into her forty–third year, she was suddenly forcing herself to consider a man in an entirely different light. Then surprise disappeared. Mason, from the beginning, had been the opposite of every man she'd ever met — a strong man forced into a position of vulnerability, yet exhibiting nothing but kindness to her. He was the complete opposite of Grigori Dyatlov. Mike had already sized up Dyatlov as an entitled punk who glorified in the weakness of others, making him feel stronger in comparison. *Just another bully,* he decided, *and I hate bullies.*

She was actually wondering if she might be different with Mason, being with someone who seemed genuinely fond of her, and for whom she felt fond.

He withdrew just enough for her to become aware again of his presence. Once more, the frown, then a grimace as she tried to force him out. *No; like this,* he said in her head, then showed her how to do it, smiling when she adapted quickly and pushed him out. Amused, he pushed back in to give her another chance at pushing him out, resisting the urge to chuckle when she almost hurled him out of her head.

She sat, breathing hard and staring at him wide-eyed from the security of Mason's arms, both of which were now about her — he seemed to have sensed her agitation moments before, and wanted to protect her. *Good old Mason.*

This time Mike connected to Mason's thoughts as well. *It's okay, Mason; she has the gift, and didn't know it.* He showed her all the locked-away memories and explained what they meant. *It's why you felt the buzzing in your head and couldn't read anything on Carrie's name-tag,* he explained to Natasha. *We weren't letting you read your own name, but you were refusing to see a false name.*

"Perhaps *Scholomance* Castle in Anstruther should be moved closer to the top of our eventual itinerary," Mason suggested with a smile.

"Perhaps," she said coyly. "For now, though, I'm starved. If I may, Tony," she suggested, "I'd like to see what else is in the kitchen."

"*Sink me! And scourge me for a bounder!*" Tony declared. "I've been totally remiss! I've been so used to Michael and I, then Carrie, too, fending for ourselves that I..."

"It's okay, Tony," Mason assured him. "No need in carrying that thought further than necessary. I'll help her look. I'm sure we can come up with something."

"Or ring for room service," Mike suggested. Then, fixing Dewhurst with an amused glance, *Honestly, Tony! I thought for a moment you were going to blurt out something about not being used to having to provide food for non-vampires!*

Mason was on his feet almost as fast as Natasha, accompanying her to the kitchen.

Sensing that Carrie was reaching out with her senses to follow them, Mike interjected, *Really?*, then kissed her. He was still kissing her when he felt her reaching out again for a brief sneak, which ended with her hand caressing the back of his neck.

It's okay, she conveyed, still kissing; *They aren't doing anything that we're not doing.*

"So," Tony announced, picking up the phone, "have you decided yet what I should ring down for?"

Mike grinned and relinquished his hold on Carrie. "I'm not sure if they've discovered yet just how bare your cupboards are. It might take another minute or two. In the meantime, how do you feel about giving up your bedroom tonight — after all, we have the cats in ours, and I'm probably going to have to crash at some point. I'm also determined to smuggle the uniforms back into the locker–room at Lefortovo by—" A glance at his watch showed 12:30 AM, "—3:00 AM, at least. Care to ride shotgun?"

"If you're entirely rested," Tony suggested, "we could do it now. Carrie's signed in at the front desk as having joined you, so I'm sure she could take care of whatever Mason and Natasha might require."

Like maybe a box of condoms from the gift–shop? Carrie said in his head, giggling.

Mike was about to frown in disapproval when the sounds from the kitchen made him decide Carrie's assessment was bang–on.

It took less than twenty minutes for Mike and Tony to make their way back to Lefortovo and unburden themselves of the incriminating uniforms. Being the stickler for details that he was, Mike made sure to put everything back in its original locker, and even removed the prison denims from the private's locker. He blurred back down the hall, past the duty desk and

Lt. Rosikoff, manipulated the lock to the door of cell 19, and deposited the denims on the bed, before re–locking the door and exiting the building. Once more, the guards on the door stared in confused astonishment as the door suddenly burst open and something *whooshed* past them in a gust of wind.

Tony had switched to the driver's seat while Mike was in the building, so Mike was able to simply duck into the passenger seat, letting Tony pull away as he was still closing the door.

Mike pulled out his phone to call Nigel and ask him to cover their tracks vis–a–vie traffic–cams.

"Ffey'll never know ffe car lef' ffe bleedin' 'otel, gov'nor!" Nigel declared, "an' ffat includes earlier tonigh', too. So, you actually go' Mason outta blinkin' Lefortovo Prison? Ffat's bleedin' awesome!"

"Yeah, well; we still have to get him, and, by the looks of it, Lt. Natasha Cherninova of the FSB, out of Moscow and out of Russia," Mike reminded him. "About earlier, Nigel; Natasha Cherninova is Mikhail Trepashkin's daughter. From what I saw in her mind, it's possible that he doesn't even know of her existence. So, about getting them out of Russia: Any thoughts on that? I wish you were here to help us rig something with Mason's passport."

"Gimme a mo' to ffink on 'at, Michael," Nigel mused, then resumed telling Mike a horror story about Litvinenko, Trepashkin, the FSB and, ultimately, Russia's President, and a host of witnesses or dissidents who'd disappeared, become victim of hit-and-run drivers, or been gunned down in front of their homes.

"That's a lot to think about," Tony commented as he pulled into the hotel parking lot.

Mike mused about the outrageousness of it all during the elevator ride. "You know, Tony," he commented, "the Russian Federation would like to pass itself off as being so modern and liberal, but it's hardly any different than how I always imagined the Soviet Union was. Putin dresses well, and presents a carefully crafted image before the cameras: fishing, playing with dogs, and all that alpha–male crap, but he's really just a thug."

Tony nodded. "You can sense it all simply by watching him give a speech — well, those of us with the dark gift, certainly. As for being a thug, he actually told an interviewer that, as a teenager, he *was* a thug."

Carrie and Kato greeted them at the door, Kato yowling insistently.

Mike snatched him up immediately. "Hush," he insisted, "before the neighbours complain. *"Jeeze,* Kato; that wasn't even a half–hour, for cryin' out loud!" He nuzzled the cat against his face, letting him get his need to purr over with, then set him down and took Carrie in his arms.

"Thank you," she declared, pretending to pout. "Perhaps I should learn to yowl like Kato," she teased, then kissed him. "How did you manage?"

"All taken care of," he assured her. "What about Mason and Natasha?"

"The lovebirds?" Carrie asked, then dropping her voice to a whisper, "Talk about *Get a Room!* It's unbelievable! They've only known each other for a week! Anyway, I suggested they might feel more comfortable in Tony's room."

"And how were we a week after our first date?" Mike asked.

Carrie looked like she was reminiscing, then gave a grin, which faded almost immediately to a sympathetic smile. "Do you think they have the same type of psychic connection we've always had?" she asked.

Mike shrugged. "They have synergy, just as we do. Each completes a need the other wasn't aware of."

Tony spoke up. "I think we need to find them their own hotel room," he said. "The last thing we need is the VSB searching this suite and finding evidence of two extra occupants on the same night that a prisoner goes missing."

"What if Nigel can remove all traces of Mason from the system at Lefortovo?" Mike asked. "It was Natasha who originally logged Petroff and Mason in. It would be justice to erase Mason and leave Petroff on the ledger. And, while Nigel's at it, he should also erase storage for any cameras that might be in or around the hotel. If this is the only suite with a surveillance problem, it could draw suspicion."

"I'm going to go down and have a chat with the concierge at the front desk," Tony advised. "Continue to ponder your current line of thought, perhaps call Nigel. There may be added value in springing Petroff as well. After all: they came in together. If we make it look like it never happened..."

Mike put an arm about Carrie and was guiding her toward the sofa when she turned and began steering him toward the bedroom.

"Maybe we should do something touristy," Carrie suggested. She was in the process of undressing him, seeming to delight in running her hands over his chest.

She peeled off her sweater, dropped her cords, stood in just her bra and panties, hands on her hips, as if wanting to be admired, then came back and reached her arms up around his neck.

"I'm trying to make my boobs smaller," she commented. "I can will my nails to grow into claws and control the size of my fangs, so why not my boobs?"

Mike puzzled over this, then asked, "Why would you want to?"

"A typical male response," she countered, "but you'd understand if you'd had to carry these around ever since you were fifteen — well, they did get a lot bigger after Jim was born. Anyway, finding a bra that fits has always been a nightmare.

"Anyway," she said between kisses, "I just thought you should know."

"Thanks for the heads–up," he said, returning her kisses, then, as he undid the back clasp and slid a hand up under the loosened cup, he declared, "You're right! This one is already smaller than the other one!" which was all it took to cause them both to explode into gales of laughter as they fell onto the bed.

Later, as she lay with her head on his chest, Mike pondered, "What would we do if we did extricate Petroff? My first thought, after what he and his daughter put Mason through, especially after finding the bodies of the Bandarovsky couple decomposing at their kitchen table, is to push him and his wheelchair off the nearest cliff."

Especially since I know he's responsible for the death of Mason's wife, he added to himself.

"Rolling him down that hill where he shot Mason, making Mason shoot him, might be poetic," Carrie suggested, "especially if it lands him in Finland, where he can be nabbed by the Fins. Would they charge him with being a spy?"

"Maybe," Mike murmured. *Rolling downhill — like a runaway train? There was a major train yard in Vyazma.* His mind was now in gear to come up with a way to get Mason out of Russia. *Belarus is out — it's little more than a mini–USSR, still clinging to the old Soviet pattern of the government owning everything. Ukraine still feels like the way to go, despite Tony's concern about the developing unrest. Train to Kyiv? The British Embassy in Kyiv could then sort Mason out with everything he'd need — MI6 would provide new credit cards, ID, etc.*

"I hear Tony in the living room," he commented.

"Not, yet," she whined in a sulky tone, clinging possessively to him. It made him smile. Then, still sounding sulky and begrudging, she said, "Oh, okay. Your mind is somewhere between out there and random images of trains in train yards, anyway. Sorry; I took a peek. I could almost hear the wheels grinding."

Mike slithered out from under her, got dressed, then went out into the living room, pausing to fetch himself a mug of blood.

Tony was beaming.

"You tell me what you've got and I'll tell you what I've been rattling around," Mike said, quickly warming Tony's mug and passing it to him.

"Cheers," Tony toasted, hoisting his mug, to which Mike replied, "*Slàinte mhath!*"

"Well," Tony resumed, "I got them a modest room one floor down — Having them on the same floor as us felt too conspicuous, too suspicious. I paid the bill in advance for the rest of the term of our stay here." He shrugged. "I used my Interpol expense account, so they'll take care of reclaiming any unused portion if we have to move sooner.

"So, dear boy, what do you have?"

"First, I've been mulling about what you said about Petroff," Mike explained. "I'm thinking we should spring him and return him to Vyazma, put him in that farmhouse with the bodies of his sister–in–law and her brother, and call the Vyazma police from a pay–phone. We can spin a tale about smelling the stench and seeing dead bodies through the window. Let them figure it out. Too bad we can't put the exact gun he used to shoot them in his hands."

"That may be possible; we could always check the other building to see if it's there." Tony suggested. "I could certainly detect residue of Petroff having handled any weapon we might find, and your Wicca nature elevates your vampire senses far beyond mine.

"And the rest? What about our new loving couple? Have you a plan for them."

"Well, first," Mike resumed, "I think Natasha should report for duty this morning at her usual time. It will go toward deflecting any suspicion that might otherwise fall on her. In fact, she can be the one to discover both Mason and Petroff's disappearances." He smiled. "If Nigel can scrub their system fast enough, she can go on record as discovering that: *Funny; there's no record of cells 19 and 36 being occupied. Are you sure the prisoners were ever checked in? But, I remember checking them in myself — didn't I?*" He ended his imitation of Natasha with a chuckle. "Who knows? If we play this right, she might even be rewarded with an extended vacation, giving her an excuse to travel."

Tony frowned. "*Sink me!* It's almost 2:00 AM. Well, here we go again!"

Mike stood and said, "I'd better tell Carrie."

Once again, Tony manned the *getaway* car while Mike worked his magic with the guards and the lock to cell 36.

Petroff, still blabbering and blathering at the ceiling, was oblivious to Mike's presence. Mike finally felt obliged to go into his head and silence his vocalizations, though the lips still kept moving. Sweeping Petroff up into his arms, he deposited him into his wheelchair, noticed a safety strap, and made him fast to the seat, then, on a sudden mischievous impulse, he left the door to cell 36 open, then wheeled Petroff out passed the duty station. He paused on the way past Rosikoff, to plant an idea in Dmitry's head: *Were cells 19 and 36 ever occupied this past month?*

This time, he made a show of shoving the exit door open and whisking through, leaving the guards as astounded as the times before. At the car, he hoisted Petroff out of his seat and into the backseat, got his seatbelt fastened, then folded the wheelchair and stowed it in the trunk.

He grinned as he slid into the passenger seat at exactly 2:30 AM. "Next stop: Vyazma," he said as Tony started the car and pulled away from the curb, then he called Nigel.

"Traffic–cams between Lefortovo and 'e M1," Nigel said, typing away at his keyboard, "ffen all ffe way to Vyazma. You go' it, gov'nor. Ffen, af'r 'at, I'll ge' onto ffe train situation between Russia an Kyiv. *An'* we'll see whot ol' Nigel can pull out of an 'at by way of entry an' exit papers for our frien' Mason. An' yer bleedin' 'otel: I don' know whot smarmy parker ffey used to install all ffeir surveillance gear, bu' none of it works righ' — ffey go' oll kinds o' Barney wiff ffat!" He chuckled. "*Anyway*, good luck widd Petroff."

By 4:15, they were pulling up in front of the farmhouse where Petroff had left the bodies of the Bandarovskys. Mike got Petroff's wheelchair out of the trunk, took it into the kitchen, opened it and parked it at the table with the two moldering corpses, then fetched Petroff from the car, and strapped him into the wheelchair.

Tony, meanwhile, had left the car and gone to the other building. Mike found him in the main room past the front entrance, scrutinizing firearms.

"I think it's this one," Tony said, indicating a .22–caliber Tokarev.

Mike extended his senses, recognized Petroff's scent, and nodded. "That's the one, Tony," he agreed. He wiped his hand on his pants leg, formed a layer of chi around his hand to isolate the Tokarev from trace evidence he might transfer, then picked up the weapon.

Side by side, he and Tony zoomed back to the farmhouse, where Mike looked fixedly at Petroff. "Right–handed or left–handed?" Petroff's right hand twitched. Mike checked the Banderovskys one last time, still finding only one bullet wound each. A check of the clip showed two bullets missing, no doubt the ones he'd removed from Mason's legs. He put the gun in Petroff's right hand, placed Petroff's index finger on the trigger, and aimed the gun to one side. Lastly, going into Petroff's head, he made him pull the trigger, continuing to fire until the gun was empty.

The successive reports seemed to startle Petroff, but, still in his head, Mike locked the fingers in a grip on the weapon that might rival a so–called death grip. Still angered by Petroff's role in the bombing of Mason's car, Mike gave the villain an image of the Devil as judge of his crimes, complete with an inferno, and left him sweating profusely and trembling in abject terror, his right fist clutching steadfast to the Tokarev.

"There. Nothing like a detectable dose of gunshot residue to close a case," Mike commented. "Aside from keeping anyone else from being shot by him, continuing to shoot after their deaths, just seems in keeping with the psycho image.

"Well, it certainly provides a smoking gun, as the saying goes," Tony observed.

They pulled into the town of Vyazma around 4:40 AM. Tony found a pay–phone, dialed *495-933-0077*, and said in Russian, "I need to report multiple murders at the Banderovsky farm, just beyond the outskirts of town. It stinks of death and decay, and I saw bodies through the windows. I also think someone is making drugs at the next farm over — you know? — that stuff that they make from cough syrup? Maybe the drug people killed the people at the Banderovsky place. *And*, I'm sure I saw three or four white vans drive out about a week ago?" Then he hung up.

By 6:00 AM, more than an hour before dawn, they were back at the hotel, with a full tank of gas. Mike stared at the odometer, focused his mind and his chi, and smiled as the numbers clicked back to what they'd been before leaving the hotel to drive to the prison to rescue Mason.

"So how did it go?" Carrie asked when she met them at the door, giving Mike a hug. "I was worried about you," she confided to him. "I keep fearing you'll extend yourself too far and have some kind of relapse of that PTSD–issue you had in Austria after — well, you know..."

"I'm fine," Mike assured her, smiling, "but I do admit to being tired.

"Mason and Natasha: Are they asleep?"

"I should hope so," Carrie giggled. "I think they wore it out 'round about 2:30 AM, maybe twenty minutes after room service finally arrived with food for them — hamburgers, from the smell."

Mike warmed mugs of blood for Tony and himself, then connected to Nigel on FaceTime.

"Oi, Michael," Nigel chirped cheerily. "Wiff 'e ffree–hour difference, it mus' be 6:00 AM ffere. Jus' finishin' up an exciting night o' skullduggery?"

Mike brought him up to date, including their phone call to the Vyazma police.

"Well," Nigel said, typing on his keyboard, "you'll be gratified wiff 'at result — ffe *peelers* sent *la–di–dahs* to each location before ye were barely back on 'e 'ighway. Ffey foun' all 'e bodies, an', from 'e textin' back n' forff between senior detectives, ffey're mountin' an airtigh' case against Petroff for ffe murder o' ffe Banderofskys. Ffe las' note 'as one bloke sayin' it's more likely ffe looney bin ffan porridge, bu' we can always keep our fingers crossed, eh, mate?

"Ffe rest o' ffe carnage at ffe ovver buildin' were bein' chalked up to drug–related bovver, until ffey go' a proper look at ol' Kemedov's factory. Well, matey, lemme tell you, 'e switchboard lit up oll at once, wiff 'at! Nex' ffing ye know it's kicked upstairs to ffe big boys — ffe FSB!

"Ffe 'ole place is a burnout, 'cept for ffe office, which didn't get touched. Anyway, some minnow in 'e pool — maybe a corporal or sommat, sees ffat framed clippin' o' Kemedov, and sings out, 'Oi, ev'rybody, ffat looks like General Kemedov!' Well, didn't ffey drag 'im outta ffere quicker'n *Bob's yer uncle*! I go' mos' of it saved fer ye fer la'er viewin', if ye like. I tapped into ffeir 'elmet cams and microphones, ffough it do need a bi' o' translatin'.

"Anyway, a bleedin' colonel general? — ffree stars on a gold background? — is runnin' 'e show. I ffink 'is name is Kashirin. I'll sen' you a photo and whot file I could get on 'im. Mos' o' ffe squawk seems geared to 'ow ffey're gonna cover it up, bu' I can assure you ole Kashirin don' wan' noffin' covered up. 'E wants ole Kemedov's arse on a bleedin' skewer!"

As Mike took it all in, a slow smile formed, giving him the pieces for the next part of the plan. He recognized the name *Kashirin* as having been some sort of mentor of Natasha's.

"Can you eMail General Kashirin the files I sent you off Kemedov's computer?" Mike asked.

"O' course, gov'nor — a simple matter o' routin' it ffrough a couple o' bogus servers.

"An' *by ffe by*, Michael, ffose files 'e 'ad on Mason an' Petroff: I ffink yer boy Kemedov was behind gettin' Petroff all stirred up abou' Mason. I ffink Petroff on'y did 'xactly what Kemedov wanted 'im to do! My ffeory is ffis: Putin is makin' so much anti–drug noise, mostly to look superior to ffe US, but, wiff whot 'e's up to, ffat had to be makin' Kemedov nervous. So, wiff a ploy like ffis, 'e gets to turn Mason over to Putin and score 'uge brownie points. Putin can drag ou' a mock trial in fron' o' ffe cameras, embarrassin' ffe bloody 'ell out o' Britain an' MI6, 'specially Mr *FaceBook* 'isself — Michael, ye should o' seen ffe cartoons ffey came up wiff to razz 'at bloke!

"O' course, whot we give Gen'ral Kashirin: it's all 'earsay, sor' of, wiffout ffe actual 'ard–drive."

Mike zipped to be bedroom at vampire speed, and zipped back with the hard–drive in hand. "You mean this hard–drive?" he asked.

Nigel grinned. "Good on ye, mate! So, what's it gonna be? An 'andoff in 'e park? A dead–drop? Any park ye like in particular? I'm serious, Michael, Moscow is full o' bleedin' parks. Myself, I fancy ffe Moscow Zoo."

Mike cast a sidelong glance at Tony, who shrugged. "I daresay Nigel has been listening to Mason and I chat over the years, and some of it has rubbed off."

Mike told Nigel: "Someplace where I can talk to General Kashirin might be a good idea. He knows Natasha — she feels he's protective of her. Maybe I can make some kind of special consideration for Natasha, possibly even Mason, part of the price of the hard–drive."

Nigel next relayed everything he had on Trepashkin and Litvinenko, offering to eMail the file.

"In summary, gov'nor:" the diminutive Cockney recited, "Litvinenko, a Colonel on an Organized Crime Task–force, 'ad been given 'e job of assassinatin' Trepashkin. Upon investigating, he decided to stall, an' made lots of excuses, but, in ffe end, he sided wiff Trepashkin, makin' him the lead investigator, then lawyer to a group seekin' justice for the victims of the bombin's. *Ffen*, unexpectedly, Litvinenko 'olds a press conference an' denounces, *no' jus' ffe FSB, but bleedin' Putin!*

"Trepashkin had pointed fingers at 'e upper echelon of 'e FSB, an' wrote a letter to 'is boss, ffe 'ead o' ffe FSB, givin' 'im all ffe lowdown on all ffe Barney 'e'd dug up 'bou ffe bombin's, including 'ow one o' ffe blokes in Ryazan 'ad been in on 'e Soldi Bank fudge–up a couple o' years before!

"But yer boy Litvinenko 'ad had ffe balls to accuse Putin an' ffe FSB, an' in public, no less! 'E were arrested and tried in November o' '99, found not–guilty, ffen rearrested, and, again, ffe charges were dismissed. Ffis time he fled to 'e UK, righ' 'ere in London, where he remained, writin' a couple o' books, until '06, when 'e spotted Andrei Lugovoy in 'e same restaurant. O' course, 'e knew ol' Andrei from 'is KGB days. Ffe Ruskies claim Lugovoy were a bodyguard for 'e KGB, but Litvinenko knew 'im as an assassin. Litvinenko claimed ol' Lugovoy slipped ffe radioactive polonium into 'is tea. I don' ffink 'e lasted more 'n' a few weeks af'er 'at.

"Anyway, Michael, let me shake ol' Kashirin's tree, an' I'll get back to ye."

Then Nigel signed off.

"That's a lot to put into perspective," Tony commented, drawing a sober nod from Michael.

Carrie pulled closer to Mike. "These Russians are a scary bunch, Michael. I can't wait to get Mason out of Russia and head for home."

"Most of that I gleaned from reports in secret files." It was Natasha, standing in the bedroom doorway, clad in a hotel bathrobe. "Did I hear your Nigel mention Colonel–General Kashirin? General Kashirin has been a mentor of mine over the years. I keep hoping he'll get his fourth star and eventually help change things in the FSB."

"He's sympathetic to your situation?" Mike asked.

Natasha wagged her head in an uncommitted gesture. "Sympathetic? Yes. But, sympathetic is one thing; doing something with that sympathy, that's quite another. I believe, however, that, if he can see a way to give me a boost out of all of this, he will do so. That said, he knew about the men's swimming team — of course, he also knew that higher officers than he saw Dyatlov as a rising star among the young men of the KGB, while I was just a woman who swam fast, and could get girls from other countries' teams to talk to her." She shrugged. "It wasn't his fault; there was only so much he could do.

"Anyway, I am going to take a shower, get dressed, and go in to work. I have decided I should be with Rosikoff when the absence of Petroff and Mason is discovered."

"Nigel has erased all knowledge of them from the system," Mike pointed out.

"So, if General Kemedov wants to make a fuss, I am the only one who can confirm or deny their having been logged into the system?"

Mike nodded. "And, thanks to Tony and I stirring up a hornets' nest with the Vyazma Police, who, in turn, called in the FSB, General Kemedov may be very busy keeping himself out of a cell at Lefortovo. The police have Petroff in custody, looking very guilty of at least two murders, while Kemedov looks guilty of murders at the same location, as well as up to his epaulets in the production of methamphetamine. My guess is that Putin might want to avoid negative publicity, especially in these months leading up to the Sochi Olympics. What do you think, Tony?"

"I suspect Nicholai Alexei Kemedov might be taken in one of his own white vans to the edge of a grave in a secluded location, be gifted with a single bullet to the back of the head, then dumped into the grave. Perhaps they'll arrange yet another tragic car crash. Moscow roads are notorious, after all. We saw that, didn't we, Michael?"

21: *General Kashirin*

Natasha had gotten dressed, broken fast, and was ready to go by a little after 9:00 AM. What she needed was a drive back to her apartment to catch her usual bus. "There are surveillance cameras on all buses," she explained. "I always travel on that bus, and it will come to someone's attention if I arrive at work by alternate means. The USSR may be gone, but the paranoia of maintaining power remains, making the Russian Federation little different than its Soviet predecessor. Taking a different bus on your day off is fine. Arriving for duty at an FSP prison on a different bus or from a suspicious location is not fine."

"How do you define *suspicious location*, my dear?" Tony asked.

"That would be any location unknown to the FSB personnel studying the surveillance cameras, *especially* on a day like today, when they will discover an escape from Lefortovo Prison," she replied.

"I'll get the car keys," Mike agreed.

She arrived at Lefortovo the same time as always, yet her arrival was nothing like any other day. Her night with Mason had been amazing. At first she'd been almost afraid that the nightmare images would flash through her mind, but they didn't. Instead, it was magical, ending with her falling asleep against Mason's chest. That Mason was twenty–six years her senior seemed impossibly ludicrous — he had the body and stamina of a man her age. As for his apparent wisdom and sensitivity, he seemed worlds beyond any man she'd ever heard of outside of fiction.

Simmer, Tasha — It would not do for you to come parading in singing and dancing, and acting like — how do the Westerners say it? — like you just got laid. But I did! I just got laid! She suppressed a giggle.

"Dmitry," she greeted, struggling to look serious. "Anything new? You look troubled."

"Just this stupid surveillance system," he declared. "You already know about Cell 19, but 36 went out sometime last night. I checked 19 while Colonel Pitofsky was still here, and don't mind saying: Ever see a lion tamer put his head inside the lion's mouth? Well, it felt like that! But now the problem also seems to be affecting cells on other floors, though the pattern implies a common cause."

Natasha frowned. "What cells on what floors?"

"Well, the same cells on the next floor," he replied. "I neglected to check with floor 3, but floor 2 reports that their 19 and 36 also exhibit signal corruption."

She nodded, then sighed, "Well, let's page a guard and perform a visual check anyway. Our superiors will be a lot happier, which means, if we keep it all strictly by–the–book, *we'll* be a lot happier."

While waiting for the guard, she did a random status check on the computer — Michael had warned her what she'd find, so all she had to do was frown and look puzzled.

"Well, according to the computer, there's no record of anyone being assigned to either of those cells."

"But, that's impossible!" Rosikoff declared.

"You don't need to tell me that, Dmitry; I logged them in myself. Yet, according to the system, there have been no new arrivals to this floor since the middle of last month."

The guard appeared at the desk, but she made him wait while she called Butyrka.

"This is Lieutenant Cherninova at Lefortovo," she announced the moment she had someone on the line. "Do you have a record for the 21st of this month of two prisoners being transferred to here in custody of General Kemedov? None? Not even for one? How about Petroff, Anatoli? No? Mason? No Mason, either? Thank you. No, no problem, just double–checking what may be a glitch in our system."

Her next call, all by–the–book, was to the second floor. "This is Lieutenant Cherninova down on first," she began. "I gather you, too, are having a problem with the electronic surveillance of your cells 19 and 36. Have you conducted a visual inspection? So 36 is vacant, 19 occupied; basically both as they should be. *Spacibo.*"

When the guard unlocked cell 19, she walked in, picked up the folded denims from the bed, then set them back in place.

"You didn't bring him a food tray last night?" she asked Rosikoff.

Dmitry frowned. "No, and I'm not sure why. It's strange — almost as if I felt ordered not to."

It was just as strange at cell 36 — the door was ajar and swung open at their touch.

"You're off duty," she told Dmitry. "You should go home. I'll take care of this. I think I'll call General Kashirin. This is too big for Captain Stepashin, and I don't like Major Dolenkev." She'd lowered her voice to a whisper. "Go on; get! Your wife is waiting," she teased, then dialed the number for General Kashirin.

The General was not in his office, so, at her request, the call was transferred to his cell phone, and he answered on the third ring.

"Kashirin, here. So what's happening at Lefortovo that requires my attention so urgently that my office would call to tell me they're transferring to my cellphone?"

She took a deep breath. *For Mason — and for me!*

"Hello?" Kashirin said when she didn't respond right away.

"Sir," she began, "it's Lt. Natasha Cherninova, Special Wing, First Floor, Lefortovo. We have a troubling mystery."

"For the logical mind, *all* mysteries are troubling," he replied, then chuckled. "Natasha, it has been a while. So, my brave Tasha, what is your mystery?"

"Sir, last week General Kemedov brought in two prisoners, transferred from Butyrka. He had all the forms. One was a Russian named Petroff, the other seemed British, and was described as being a Captain Mason of Britain's MI6."

"Petroff: Would that be Anatoli Petroff, formerly of the KGB's counterespionage section?"

"Yes, sir. I put Petroff in cell 36, and Mason in —"

"Let me guess:" Kashirin interrupted, chuckling, "And now Petroff is missing."

"Actually, sir, they're both missing. Furthermore, according to the system, they were never here. I have yet to verify the presence of the filed paperwork, but I wouldn't be at all surprised if that, too, is missing. Someone with high access could have deleted the entries, but, if the paperwork is also missing, it implies a mole here at Lefortovo."

There was a long pause. "By all means, Natasha, look for the paperwork. If you find it, seal it in a suitable envelope, mark it to me, *Eyes Only*, and keep it in a drawer at your duty station until I can arrange for its collection."

She waited a moment after getting off the phone, then paged for a junior officer. It was five minutes before a warrant officer appeared, straightening his tie and looking anxious.

"I just got off the phone with General Kashirin. I need you to man this station while I go to the records room."

The WO snapped to attention with a brisk salute, which Natasha returned casually, as befitted an officer superior in rank.

She promptly turned and walked to the elevator, where she had to wait another five minutes for the slow, out–of–date device to grind its way down to her. She spent what was usually a tediously slow upward crawl mentally reliving her experience with Mason the previous night.

How is this possible? she began asking herself. *How can I feel so strongly about a foreigner, so soon, just because he has been kind and gentle?* Then she chuckled. She had been trained in the more subtle aspects of interrogation, involving almost pure psychology. *Because, my little Tasha, he is the complete antithesis of that pig Dyatlov, and with more strength and courage than Major Dyatlov could ever imagine. He is what a man should be.*

She then thought back to what she'd observed with Michael and Carrie — clearly madly in love, yet so different in temperament and expression. Carrie was more the extravert in her ways. She'd never seen Carrie's stronger, aggressive side — *of course I have: the part she played here, wearing my uniform.*

And there was something else, something hinted at by her more–brilliant–than–normal eyes. And Michael's iridescent sapphire eyes — they practically glowed with fire at times, a glow he seemed able to extinguish when he became aware of it. But there was another oddity to Michael's eyes: It had been when they all went to the hotel, and Kato had met Michael with such a demanding attitude. The Siamese had settled about Mike's shoulders, his face against Mike's cheek in caressing fashion, his eyes (the same colour as Michael's) glaring at her as a stranger. For just a second, Michael's eyes had looked exactly like Kato's, right down to the vertical pupils! Then, just as she registered the image, Michael seemed to arouse from his state of weariness, there was a slight blurring, and his eyes immediately resumed a normal appearance.

There is something different about all three of them: Michael, Carrie, and Tony, she mused, — *something in the way they seem to be communicating without speaking. Okay; Michael came right out and claimed to be a witch, and Carrie performed that astounding demonstration of lighting candles in the bathroom by merely reaching out with her hand and saying something in a language that I didn't recognize — me who has been trained in most of the languages of Europe — of course not, silly; she said it was Gaelic. So are the three of them witches? Is that it? No, Tony's attitude toward them implies that they differ from him in some way. In fact, the way he spoke of Michael's ancestor having been a Scottish witch — it was like a father proudly explaining that his son is the first in the family to ever go to college. No, there has to be something else. And I'm certain I saw one of Michael's fingernails extend into a claw, long, sharp, and darkly discoloured. Is that related to him being a witch?*

The elevator ground to a halt, interrupting her thoughts. She headed down the hall to the records room, and went straight to the drawer where she expected the transfer papers to be. Sure enough, she had them in less than a minute. She extracted a full–

size envelope from another drawer, which allowed her to insert the pages without folding them. From yet another drawer she removed a red ink–pad and an *EYES–ONLY* stamp. Next to the red stamp pad was a broad–tipped red marker pen, which she used to print *Colonel–General Kashirin* in bold capitals under the *EYES–ONLY*, then stamped another *EYES–ONLY* under the name.

The ride back down was slower than the ride up. *This creaky old contraption seems to fear crashing to the basement!* she thought, then spent the rest of the ride reminiscing on the feel of Mason's tender love–making, the warmth of his kisses, the gentleness of his hands on her — how he seemed to know just how to — She used the envelope to fan her face, feeling the heat of a blush. *This will never do! I can't afford even Dmitry to see me this flushed. How will I explain it? Secret lover? I'm watched too much, under almost constant surveillance, especially by that pig Dyatlov. Oh My God, if Dyatlov finds out about Mason!* Sheer panic almost took over, then she had an image of Michael intervening between Mason and Dyatlov, his hand poised to draw from his shoulder holster, his eyes giving the same challenging, steely glare he'd given last night while posing at Capt. Menkin. *I hope you do get to meet Michael, you pig*, she decided.

Mike sat in the hotel, iPad in his lap, waiting for Nigel to finally get back to him. It was 3:00 PM, — he'd been awake for thirty minutes, sipping on a mug of blood, reading, waiting for the FaceTime interruption.

Finally Nigel's face appeared on the screen, with a prompt to accept or decline.

"Well, *yer Daimyo-ship* — or is it *yer Maha–ka-ship* — *Crikey*, Michael; yer titles jus' seem to be

pilin' up, don' ffey? Oi, I jus' came across anovver one
— *Shinobi* — ffat's Japanese for a covert agent. Ffey
used to call ninjas ffat. Did you know ffat?"

Mike gave a slight smile. "I may have heard the
term," he suggested. "Have you anything of
importance, Nigel? — other than adding to a list of
annoying nicknames?"

Nigel quickly replaced his cheeky grin with a more
sober expression. "Sorry mate," he continued. "It took
a bit o' — well, anyway, I finally got ffrough to
Colonel–General Kashirin — Oi, Whot's wiff 'at? We
go' Brigadier Generals an' Major Generals, so where
do ffe bleedin' Ruskies get ffis Colonel–General?
Anyway, I got 'im on 'e phone, an 'e seemed to know
all about Kemedov's 'ard–drive bein' missin' from
whot were left of 'is computer at ffat burned out
factory you torched, an' expressed great interest in
meetin' wiff 'e man whot nicked it. Ffe weird ffing,
ffough, is: even wiff 'is eagerness to meet you an'
acquire ffe 'ard–drive, 'e took almos' an hour to get
back to me wiff ffe where an' ffe when."

"And that would be?" Mike prompted.

"Ffe Moscow Zoo, jus' like ye asked," Nigel
reported. "An' I know ye wanted 7:00 PM, bu' 'e
countered ffat wiff 5:20." Nigel shrugged.

"5:20 is after sunset, but still the last lingering bit
of twilight," Mike mused. "That's a curiously precise
time unless — but there's no way for him to expect —
do modern Russians even believe in vampires?"

"Don't rule out any possibility," Tony advised. He
was just emerging from his room, and proceeded
straight to the kitchen to warm some blood, continuing
to speak as he went. "Kashirin is a senior FSB officer,
who had an illustrious career in the KGB. He and
Kemedov were both in Oleg Kalugin's section, though
Kashirin spent most of his career in investigations.
Think about it Michael: MI6 has had a dossier on you

since your excursion into China and Tibet back in '06. Your rather spectacular disposal of Stephan Sutu's vampire thugs may have caught the eye of the FSB — remember: Chernin had been low level KGB *and* spetsnaz. Did they know about Borgia and Torok? What about von Strelitz? Rostock is not so far from here, Michael — only Belarus and Poland lie between here and the German border. *And*, the FSB was one of the agencies you had Nigel task with finding women abducted by Mihilache's operation. Then there's your actions before the Summit in Austria not so long ago — not just the cleaning out of Castle Montrachet, but the discovery of that Al–Qaeda bomb–maker. *Identified and apprehended by an un–named operative of the Canadian Security and Intelligence Service* was how the news described it, and there was a Russian representative at that conference, so you know the SVR, maybe the FSB, were there, as well."

Mike pondered this. "Anything else, Nigel?"

"You're to meet 'im at ffe pony ride area jus' norff o' ffe bird pond — which is easy enough to find — I'll send you ffe official map o' ffe zoo wiff 'e location marked." The flippantness was gone from Nigel's manner. "Ffa's abou' it, 'less ye need anyffin' else..."

"Thanks, Nigel. Great job as always," Mike said with a smile, then ended the link.

Tony was chuckling. "Poor Nigel; he just can't seem to help himself with his need to be cheeky."

Mike nodded. "I know."

"But there are times when you jolly–well wish he'd just stay on point," Tony added, as if finishing the thought for Mike.

Mike smiled and gave a nod. "He's decided that *Shinobi* should be the latest to my long list of nicknames," he added, rolling his eyes.

"I'm familiar with the term — I was in Japan during some of the postwar cleanup — the American

Occupation, as the Japanese titled it," Tony acknowledged. "It's actually quite appropriate."

Mike shrugged, then changed the subject: "I think I should plan to make an early visit to the zoo, maybe around 4:30, to give me time to reconnoiter."

Tony nodded. "Smart idea," he approved. "It could even be a trap of sorts. After all, Michael, he is a three star FSB general, about to meet with a Western spy."

Mike frowned at Tony's suggestion of Kashirin knowing he was a spy, but Tony was shaking his head, eying Mike all the while.

"Count on it, Michael. His first instinct would be to have the message traced. His IT people would encounter the usual maze of IP–address–bouncing that Nigel typically uses to throw people off his tracks, and know it had to be a foreign spy, especially when Nigel eventually contacted him to setup the meet, on a phone connection that was equally untraceable."

Mike nodded. "All the more reason to scope out the place ahead–of–time," he said, then smiled. "Maybe I should let you and Carrie tag along. After all, with my cover as a visiting author exploring potential scene locations for an upcoming novel, it makes perfect sense that's we'd examine the Moscow Zoo. Besides, if it gets tense, you and Carrie can offer a distraction — you might blur in and out seemingly from nowhere, snatching someone's weapon —" then, grinning, "— Carrie might even set fire to something convenient, or inconvenient, as the mood takes her."

Moscow Zoo

Colonel–General Kemedov sat on one of several benches along the broad circular pathway that encircled a small grove of trees, using an earpiece transceiver to maintain contact with the eight men he had stationed throughout the area. The pony rides had ended for the season more than a month ago. The sun had just disappeared below the trees to the west, and there was plenty of light left. He'd spent better than an hour studying everything the FSB had on foreign agents, finally, more from gut instinct than anything else, settling on a Canadian agent who'd begun to catch the attention of the FSB when he took it upon himself to focus the intelligence community's attention on the trafficking of young ladies kidnapped for use in the sex trade. The dossier on CSIS Special Agent *Samurai* included some redacted files stolen from MI6, which implied that he'd covertly entered both China and Tibet about eight years ago, ostensibly to perfect already profound martial arts skills, and to acquire whatever mental training a certain Tibetan tulku had to offer. He dismissed the latter as being too fanciful to be real.

Fanciful! Mystical Tulku powers are nothing to the implications of more recent redacted files out of Rostock, Germany, and Northern Transylvania, not far from the Romania–Moldova border. Pfff — There are no such things as vampires! And yet, he wanted to meet here at 7:00 — well–after sunset. But, nonsense or not, it never hurts to be prudent.

Thus, there was still a lingering glow of twilight when he first noted the man walking toward him from the northwest, as if he'd just been to see the mountain goats. He looked to be about 174 cm tall, maybe 78 kg, and extremely fit. He wore nothing more than a blue form–fitting turtleneck sweater over black jeans, and some form of high–tech sneaker. Just looking at him made Kashirin want to shiver. There was a light dusting of snow on the ground, and the temperature hovered just around freezing. The General pulled his greatcoat closer about him and adjusted his scarf.

The only thing that stood out against the approaching man's dark clothing was a circular belt buckle, apparently bronze, with a Celtic knot pattern, and a pewter pendant, also Celtic in design. It was even in the files that Agent *Samurai* affected an affinity for Celtic artisanship, but this man, now that he was close enough, seemed much younger than the late–forties or early–fifties estimated for *Samurai*.

"You have something for me?" General Kashirin asked when the man stopped about two meters away.

"Perhaps," was the cryptic reply. "There are a few things to which you'll have to agree first."

"Advance and surround," he murmured in Russian.

Sure enough, in just a few seconds, eight of his men, all handpicked for unarmed combat skills, converged and formed a semicircle about the man, leaving just the General facing the opening, and he now drew his sidearm.

The stranger smiled, as if expecting this all along.

"I thought you wanted Kemedov's hard–drive," the stranger commented, still looking far too amused and not at all concerned.

"And I mean to have it," Kashirin declared, gesturing with his Makarov. "Agent *Samurai* is it?"

When the man gave no reaction to the name, the General added, "Well, no matter — Whoever you are, you are clearly a Western spy on Russian soil and, as such, are subject to detention and interrogation."

The amused smile broadened. "I'm sure you think so," he replied, then disappeared in a blur.

The General felt the Makarov ripped from his hand. His men seemed to whirl about in a fury of hand– and foot–strikes, and flashing commando knives, then it was over as quickly as it had begun.

His men stood gasping for breath, staring at each other in shocked chagrin. *And no wonder!* Each soldier whose back was to him had a commando knife stuck into the rear of his combat jacket, coming down from above so that the blade passed through the fabric and came out again, with just an inch or so of blade tip exposed at the bottom. One soldier removed the knife from his neighbour's jacket, returning it to that soldier, then, as each man realized what had become of his combat blade, he reached over his shoulder and extricated the weapon, returning it to its sheath.

"*On mog ubit' nas vsekh!*" (He could have killed us all!) one soldier gasped.

There was a sudden *whoosh* of wind, for not even a second, and Kashirin's missing Makarov reappeared beside him on the bench.

"The sooner you dismiss your men, the stranger's voice announced, the sooner we can discuss how you acquire General Kemedov's hard–drive. As you can see, they are of little use against me. You're lucky I didn't set anyone on fire."

To his consternation, a nearby wastebasket, filled with paper cups and wrappers, abruptly burst into flames, rapidly consuming the contents.

Kashirin swallowed hard. He'd read the report on the fate of a Count or Prince Torok in Transylvania. This *Samurai*, along with a witch, purportedly also a vampire, had used mystical powers to cause Torok to burst into flame, from the inside outward. It took but a moment for him to review his options and make the only choice open to him. He dismissed his men.

The moment he could tell that they'd moved beyond hearing range, there was a hint of flame and a shimmering of the air before him, then the man appeared, as if by magic.

Relax, Colonel–General Kashirin, the voice commanded in his head, then the man took a seat next to him. *Remove your earpiece.*

"*What are you*?" Kashirin hissed, pocketing the transceiver. "No human can do what you just did!"

The stranger just shrugged, then drew a computer hard–drive from a back pocket of his jeans, and set it down on the bench, leaving his hand over the top of it. The general felt certain that any attempt to make a snatch for it would be not just humiliating but possibly fatal.

"Your conditions?" the general asked.

"Simple," the man said. "First: Captain Mason was kidnapped and brought here against his will. He needs paperwork to leave the country unmolested. A colleague of mine is working on forging the same, but I think authentic documents would be better." He punctuated it with a thin smile.

"And Second?" the general asked.

"Leftenant Natasha Cherninova has earned a vacation, perhaps a long one. You should issue her whatever is necessary to accommodate such. I expect she'd like to travel a little — get away from some of the memories that still torture her, even now, more than twenty years later. Of course, having to suck up to Major Dyatlov to get her last promotion was despicable."

Kashirin nodded. "I am well–acquainted with her tragic history, as well as that of the reprehensible Major Dyatlov." He let out a sympathetic sigh. *Yes, my poor Tasha, you do deserve more than you've been given — barely more than scraps, as if some mongrel had been forced to beg at the table. If I hadn't mentioned Ryazan to him, he would not have approved your promotion.* "Consider it done," he declared. "I will make both happen this evening. What else? I simply need to know how, where, and when to make the exchange."

"Exchange?" the stranger asked, smiling. He pushed the hard–drive a little closer to Kashirin, removed his hand from it, then, reaching again to a back pocket, pulled out a large envelope that had been folded in half on the long axis.

"She's really quite surprising, your Leftenant Cherninova. In spite of all she's been subjected to, she's retained an indomitable strength. Her tendency to fragility only shows when something triggers memory of the rape and subsequent, less violent recurrences when the charming Major Dyatlov chose to intimidate and dominate her further with his superior rank. Classic symptoms of post–traumatic stress.

"I sensed her concern about leaving this in a drawer at the duty desk, first floor of her building at Lefortovo, so I took the liberty of saving her the worry, and you the trouble of stopping by to retrieve it. You'll also find in there a page I took from one of four FSB sergeants who supervised the drug lab for Kemedov."

"Is there nothing for yourself?" He asked it almost automatically; his mind was racing — *leftenant, not lieutenant — only the British, Canadians, and some Australians pronounce it that way, and his accent clearly isn't British or Australian.*

He suddenly blurted, "You are the Canadian Agent *Samurai*, aren't you? — The existence of whom CSIS insists on denying — well, something to do with a lot of outrageous stories about vampires."

"*Samurai?*" the man asked innocently, his brow furrowed, as if puzzled. "I think the Samurai became somewhat obsolete soon after the Meiji Restoration of 1868."

He seemed to ponder something.

"Coming back to delivering papers to me: There is an obscure Canadian novelist visiting Moscow at present — He writes fantasy fiction. I gather, he, too, is something of a fan of the notion of CSIS having a *Special Agent* tasked with dealing with the dreaded Vampire problem on Canadian soil." He chuckled. "At least, that's the plot of the first two books of his latest series. I much prefer his previous works — an adventurous sort of medieval fantasy. Anyway, he calls himself M.D. Cameron, and he's staying in a suite at the *Raddison Slavyanskaya*. I think his wife recently flew in and surprised him, bringing their two Siamese cats, if you can believe that."

Kashirin was taken aback. "You know this man?" he asked, wheels turning in his mind.

The man Kashirin was now certain was *Samurai* gave an ambivalent shrug. "Only through his writing."

"And you want me to deliver such important papers to a total stranger?" *This is too incredulous.*

The stranger smiled. "No more incredulous than your belief that these papers," he gestured with the envelope, "were safely located in a drawer at a duty station in Lefortovo Prison, or, perhaps Kemedov's notion that Captain Mason and former KGB asset Anatoli Petroff would remain safely imprisoned in their cells at that same facility. No; you just mark your paperwork in care of M.D. Cameron, and I'll take care of the rest. Cameron will never know a thing about it."

"So it was you who got them out. And *you* planted Petroff in that farmhouse near Vyazma?" the general was beginning to see how it all fit.

But the stranger just did another shrug. "I merely returned Petroff to the property where Kemedov found him. I chose the farmhouse instead of the old processing building, because that's where he'd left the bodies of his sister–in–law and brother–in–law — I can only surmise that his own property was in a state of disrepair, and he needed theirs. Not a nice man is he, our Mr. Petroff? But then, on face value, with his crystal–methamphetamine production, and his efforts to corrupt Russia's youth for his own profit, I don't think much of General Kemedov, either."

"Kemedov is a corrupt disgrace to his uniform," Kashirin snarled, "though he is not the only one." *The reforming of the KGB was nothing more than a name change*, he thought, feeling anger and disgust.

The stranger smiled his little smile again. "Once more, West and East find something upon which to agree," *Samurai* commented. "You know, General, I think you and I might be surprised at just how much we might be in agreement on several issues. Natasha's father, for instance. It's a damned shame what Putin and the FSB upper echelon did to *him*."

He knows that Trepashkin is Natasha's father! How could he know that? Only her mother and I...

Samurai looked him in the eyes and shrugged.

"Now, if we ever need to disagree on something, there's always hockey. For example, in the upcoming Olympics at Sochi, you probably are hoping for a Russian gold in hockey, but you can't forget that Team Canada will have the goalie for the *Montreal Canadiens* in their net." This time a sparkle of mischief was in the eyes, the smile more broad.

Kashirin couldn't resist a subtle smile of his own. "M.D. Cameron?" he checked, then pulled out a smartphone, typing as he continued to speak, knowing that the note would almost immediately appear on his office computer, reminding him of what was required. "I'll mark the envelope to M.D. Cameron, and have it left at the front desk of the *Raddison Slavyanskaya*, tomorrow, probably by 3:00 PM," he promised. "It will contain vacation orders and, I think, some funds for Natasha's vacation, as well as the necessary travel documents for Mr. Mason of MI6."

"Don't worry, Cameron will never see the envelope," the man he thought was *Samurai* reiterated. "And, I can also assure you that the last thing Petroff's daughter saw before she died was Kemedov's face and the Makarov in his hand."

"So, how did you manage to —" He was about to ask how *Samurai* had gotten Mason out of Lefortovo, and how he could possibly know what Petroff's daughter had seen.

There was an audible *whoosh* and a rush of air. Kashirin looked about in consternation, but he was alone on the bench. The man whom he'd decided was Agent *Samurai* of the Canadian SIS was gone.

22: *Kemedov*

Mike sat in the living room of the suite, Carrie next to him, (Kato and Teila on their laps), with Mason and Tony seated opposite. Mason had him repeat parts of the story several times.

"Sounds like our bloke Kashirin no' only 'as ye pegged as our intrepid *Agent Samurai*," Nigel said from the FaceTime screen on Tony's laptop, "but 'e's gotta be ffinkin' yer a vampire."

Mike shrugged. "As long as he can't track me, what he thinks is irrelevant. Tony and Carrie made sure neither Kashirin nor any of his people knew they were in the area. Carrie even embellished on my theatrics with hints of flame in places."

Carrie interjected: "After all, Michael, you're the one who made the remark about him being lucky you didn't set any of his men on fire. I just felt inspired to add a hint of flame to your appearance, just to remind him. Besides, according to Tony, he was even thinking about rumours he'd heard about that villain Count Torok's destruction."

"It isn't criticism, dear; just clarifying the facts for Nigel," Mike assured her, then gave her a one armed cuddle and kissed the top of her head. "But you did get a bit theatrical with that trash can."

That made Carrie laugh. "*I can't believe I actually did that!* In fact, I was so shocked at how well it worked that I almost screamed! But, since you're clarifying the facts, tell him what you told the general about hockey at the Winter Olympics."

"I wanted to end our conversation with an aspect of levity, and that was all I could come up with at the time," Mike confessed, punctuating it with a shrug.

"You an' 'Is Lordship asked me to come up wiff a route to get our man Mason an' 'is lady leftenant outta Russia. Well, whot I come up wiff is a train trip from Moscow to Minsk to Warsaw. O' course, wiff whot ffe general's promised, ye can probably fly 'mos' anywhere, but, meself, I'd feel safer wiff a train."

Mason seemed to ponder this, then commented, "I agree. Even with the elevated security at all train stations, post 9-11, it's still remarkably less paranoid when compared to airport security."

"But, with an aeroplane, Mason," Tony interjected, "there is the added advantage of knowing that, once you're in the air, you're safe."

"You mean once you're in the air and clear of Russian airspace," Mason countered. "And, Tony, don't forget, it's that very fact that makes security personnel, especially folks like the FSB, perform at an ultra–paranoid level before the airplane is even boarded. I've seen the Russians order a plane back to the airport. With a train, there's always the notion that they can keep looking once the train is underway. I like Moscow–to–Minsk–to–Warsaw by train, and I can't think of any objection Natasha might have, but she and I will certainly discuss it when she gets off duty and returns here."

"My dear Mason," Tony chuckled, "I'm sure the lovely Ms. Cherninova will approve of anything that successfully liberates you both from Russian territory."

It was after 11:00 PM when a breathless Natasha Cherninova entered the suite. She wore a dark parka–style coat with heavy fake fur trim. When set down a shopping bag containing her uniform, and then removed the parka, Mason let out a whistle. She was wearing a simple vermillion–coloured knit top, but the accented V–neck showed just enough cleavage to capture Mason's attention. "You wouldn't believe the elaborate lengths I went to to make sure no one could track me here," she declared.

Or the elaborate lengths I went to to make sure she looked sexy, Carrie projected to Mike, winking when she caught his eye.

Mike made sure his face remained expressionless.

Natasha went on: "I took the bus back to my apartment, changed my clothes, — Imagine my surprise at finding my closet entirely cleaned out, leaving nothing but the parka I wore here and this change of clothes that I'm wearing, as if whoever moved my belongings had decided how I should look when I got here."

She looked about the room, then her gaze fell on Carrie, who seemed trying not to look too guilty, and she smiled warmly. "I trust you brought everything here," she said, then continued with her narrative.

"After my apartment, I walked four blocks, hood up, head down, to avoid presenting anything recognizable to any of the many surveillance cameras, until I could catch a tram to within a block of here."

Mason then explained about General Kashirin's agreement with Mike. "Can he be trusted?" he asked.

Mike could see that he was watching Natasha's eyes closely as he awaited her response.

"Where I'm concerned, yes," she replied, nodding slowly. "He's been a sort of guardian angel for almost as long as I can remember, especially after I was indoctrinated into the KGB, which more or less became the FSB the moment the USSR dissolved and the Russian Federation came into being. He knew my mother, but I think he must have also known my father — well, of course he did — he transferred to the criminal investigations unit right after General Kalugin's defection. So, since my father was a lieutenant colonel, and Kashirin was a general, he had to have been one of my father's superiors.

"But, the main answer to your question is: yes. Kashirin would never knowingly do anything to put me in danger. I also know him to be a profound believer in fair play — an oddity in the FSB." She frowned, a decided sadness overshadowing her features. "How he must have tried to warn and discourage my father from his course of action, knowing how corrupt the hierarchy around him was — all either corrupt, steadfastly loyal to Putin, or too afraid of Putin to do anything other than toe the party line. He's made it quite plain since becoming President that, *he* is the one who truly runs the FSB. He runs everything, even Gazprom — Gazprom's head is ex–KGB and owes his position to Putin.

"But, Michael, when did you take the transfer papers from the duty station drawer?" Natasha asked. "I was at the station for the rest of the shift."

Mike smiled. "Except for your bathroom break, when you had the guard stand duty for you for — what was it? — about four minutes?"

"Did you mesmerize him somehow?" Natasha pressed. "He did look oddly vague and confused when I returned. I just figured he had things on his mind."

Mike's smile broadened. "The guards at the interrogators' door by now are convinced that the door they guard is either incredibly defective or haunted. The least little breeze seems to blow it wide open"

"How do you do all this?" Natasha exclaimed.

"Maybe someday I'll explain," Mike offered, "but, for the time being, let's get you two safely out of Russia and into some territory that's at least part of the EU, and, hopefully, NATO. I've been watching events unfolding in Ukraine, and getting more and more concerned — I have this image of Putin brewing something along the lines of his nefarious plot of 1999. I think he's planning a takeover of the Ukraine — engineering a scenario where certain factions in that country will beg him to do it."

Alarm showed on Natasha's face. "I think you're correct. I've been sensing something like this for weeks. There's even been whispering among certain officers, as if they know something. I even overheard that a Dept. S sniper is on his way to Kiev, to that plaza where they're protesting against Yanukovych."

"So, my dear," Tony put in, "you understand why Michael feels a need to stay focused on our current situation and all its associated parameters — at least until we're all removed to more secure locations."

"One of these days," Mike added with a reassuring smile, "when Mason is ready to take you on his promised tour of scenic places — I do recall some mention of Anstruther — I, myself, can arrange a guided tour of *Scholomance* Castle; perhaps even a chance for you to explore your own innate talents.

"So, coming back to arrangements:" Mike summarized, "Sometime tomorrow a packet of essential papers will be delivered to the front desk downstairs. In the meantime, I'm sure you're in need of some rest. You've had a stressful day, if only from your own hyper–anxious temperament all day. Tony has arranged new accommodations for you on the floor below us — I think a room or two to one side of this, but he knows better than I."

Tony grinned and held up a key card, wiggling it back and forth. "I'm sure, my dear, that you and Mason would like some time alone," he interjected, handing her the keycard. "You'll find the rest of your missing wardrobe in the closet. Carrie and I took a few liberties this afternoon, while Michael stood guard at the car, trying to look like a tourist snapping photos of the local architecture, and all before he had to keep his appointment with your General Kashirin."

Carrie added, "Your framed newspaper clippings of Colonels Trepashkin and Litvinenko — I know from Michael that Trepashkin is your father — are in the suitcase, which is in the closet with your clothes. I did my best to arrange the closet the way you had things in the closet at your apartment."

Natasha arose, ran to Carrie and hugged her, then abruptly fell to sobbing on her new friend's shoulder.

Carrie wrapped her arms about Tasha and held her, insisting. "It's nothing, Tasha, — just something good friends do for each other."

Natasha, still weeping, released Carrie, only to grab Mike in a similar embrace. Abashed, Mike stroked the back of her head, and assured her, "It's like Carrie said, Natasha. Besides, aside from taking a liking to you ourselves, you have the added perk that we've become inordinately fond of Mason over the years, ever since that day at Heathrow Airport when we were on our way to Afghanistan — my first actual mission for CSIS — when he arranged for me to have my MI6–issue Walther PPK."

Mason joined them, placing arms about Mike and Carrie's shoulders. "I dare say, Tasha, darling, that, while you'll, no doubt, meet many new friends once we put the Russian Federation behind us, these two and my lifelong friend Tony Dewhurst are the best friends one could ever have."

Lefortovo Prison, Moscow
Sunday, Nov. 31st, 9:50 AM

General Kemedov watched out the side window as his unmarked car pulled up in front of the interrogators' entrance at Lefortovo. He was eager to deal with Petroff — *the stupid fool — how dare he shoot Mason in the legs, just for his own warped sense of revenge.* But, if he could break Petroff enough to negate any possibility of his contradicting the devised plan, then that was all that mattered. As for Mason, well, he'd only question Mason as a matter of protocol — in order to keep up appearances. He chuckled.

Putin might be cracking down on drugs — *So what's that all about? When did he become so self–righteous? No, it was the Americans — their country is so overrun with narcotics that Putin wants to hold Russia up as a shining example in comparison. It's the same with his new obsession with homosexuals being some kind of subversive Western abomination. He's obsessed with Americans, ever since that clown from Texas, Wilson, conned the American Congress and the CIA into backing the Mujahideen in Afghanistan. We bankrupted ourselves trying to hold onto that hellhole.*

He snarled, the snarl deteriorating into a ripple of laughter. *Russia a shining example of a drug–free society? What nonsense! Our colonels were trading medical supplies to the northern Afghanis for opium! We're a country of raging alcoholics! Drunk driving is so rampant that it's not even safe on our roads!*

His interrogator, a stern–looking captain, opened the door to the car and said, "It is time, sir."

Kemedov smiled, feeling ready for what lay ahead. "So it is, Captain, so it is." And he exited the vehicle.

The guards at the door snapped to attention, and didn't even ask for ID before holding the door open and ushering him into the FSB prison.

He almost marched as he strutted toward the duty station at the V of corridors that led to the more elite cells. He'd been hoping to find that busty beauty, Lt. Cherninova, on duty — ah, here she was, just coming along behind him. He was about to wait for her to catch up, but the duty officer at the desk seemed unduly nervous.

Of course, he thought, *even if the interrogation is scheduled, he'll be nervous. I'm a General, and I've made a point of maintaining an intimidatingly nasty reputation.* He decided to proceed and take some pleasure in the man's discomfiture while awaiting the arrival of the lovely lieutenant.

"Lieutenant — Rosikoff —" he read the name–tag. "I am General Kemedov, here to interrogate two prisoners. My 10:00 AM appointment is with Anatoli Petroff, formerly of the KGB. He is in cell 36, I believe. Let's have him wheeled to an interrogation room, shall we?" But Rosikoff, sweating profusely, continued typing at the computer, looking anxiously at the screen.

"Take your time, Lieutenant," Kemedov said with a sneer. "After all, I'm a General — I have all day, and an abundance of patience." He put as much intimidation into the tone of the last bit as he could manage.

"I'm sorry, General," he said, "but I find no record of an Anatoli Petroff in the system."

Kemedov scowled. "Impossible!" he blustered.

"Are you sure, Dmitry?" Kemedov didn't have to turn to know it was Lt. Cherninova, finally catching up. "I checked two prisoners in for General Kemedov more than a week ago."

Rosikoff seemed to relax with the arrival of the first lieutenant, who struck Kemedov as being uncharacteristically calm, while Rosikoff, staring at the screen, continued to shake his head. "No, nothing."

"But this can't be!" Kemedov declared. "There must be something wrong with the computer. Someone has made a mistake."

"I can't imagine how," Rosikoff stated. "The computer records indicate that —"

Lieutenant Cherninova brushed Rosikoff aside, taking his place at the computer. "Let me, Dmitry," she murmured. "May I have the two names and cell numbers again, please, General?" she asked.

"Petroff, Anatoli, and Mason, Bruce, MI6 Captain; cells —" he took a moment to recall the cell numbers, then added, "— 36 and 19, respectively."

Cherninova typed, she, too, now shaking her head.

An outer door opened and closed, then the sounds of several sets of footsteps approached.

"No Mason and no Petroff," Cherninova stated, "and, according to the computer, cells 19 and 36 have not been used in several months. In fact, General, according to the log, there have been no new prisoners since October."

From seemingly out of nowhere, Kemedov and his adjutant were surrounded by a squad of FSB soldiers armed with AK–105s.

"The error, Nokolai Alexei, is yours, but it is one of judgement, not misinformation," announced an authoritarian voice that Kemedov recognized.

Kemedov wheeled about–face, then raised his arms in surrender when the Kalashnikovs all jerked in warning.

"General Kashirin," he struggled to suppress his alarm and sound innocent, "what is this?"

"What it is, Kemedov, is the end of the line for you," General Kashirin declared. "I have your transfer papers from Butyrka to here. And it's plain to see that you had someone erase all records of them having been to Butyrka — but we do have camera footage of them being paraded in the front door and out a side door. So what exactly was your game, Kemedov? What leverage did you use to convince Petroff to orchestrate the kidnapping and smuggling into Russia of a senior MI6 officer — little more than an administrative official these days, and about ready to retire, from what I hear? Were you planning to parade him before President Putin, hoping to distract the President from your illicit drug factory in Vyazma? Or did you get nervous when you realized that Petroff was holding Mason too close to your methamphetamine laboratory?"

Kashirin cocked his head and raised an eyebrow, as if expecting a reply. Kemedov felt the cold fingers of panic creeping up his spine. He cast about for a path of escape, but the young men surrounding him had the hardened steely eyes of trained killers.

"I don't know what you're talking about," Kemedov stammered. "I know nothing of a drug lab. I've never been to such a place, so I can't imagine how you could possibly connect me to it."

"I have it all, Kemedov," General Kashirin assured him. "I even have the hard–drive from the computer you left behind when you torched the building."

Stepping to Kemedov's side, he pulled Kemedov's Makarov from its holster, immediately pulling the clip and extracting the chamber round, which he inserted back into the clip. He sighted the view of the bullets in the clip, smiled, then handed the weapon and clip to his own adjutant.

"Even if you habitually keep a round in the chamber, Nikolai Alexei," he stated, "you're two rounds short. If either of those rounds prove, through ballistics, to be in one of the bodies at the Banderovsky property, then we have your weapon present at the scene of a small–scale massacre. My guess is that we'll find one of your bullets in the head of the late Brendu Petrova, alias Brenda Peters, daughter of your lost prisoner, Anatoli Petroff.

"We found him, by the way, at the farmhouse on the same property, muttering like a deranged fool about hellfire and the Devil."

He glanced at the lieutenant of his soldiers, and said, "Place the General in handcuffs, Lieutenant, then, since I see no point in taking him back to Lubyanka, turn him over to Lieutenant Rosikoff, who will, I'm certain, assign him to one of the two clearly vacant cells. Isn't that correct Lieutenant Rosikoff?"

"Yes, sir!" Rosikoff asserted, "unless you'd prefer First Lieutenant Cherninova to see to it."

"Lieutenant Cherninova?" General Kashirin repeated in surprise, then seemed to become aware, for the first time, of Lt. Cherninova as she stepped away from the computer. "But what are you doing here, Natasha? I was given to understand that you were on vacation — and a lengthy one at that. In fact, I have some of the paperwork right here. I was going to drop it off after leaving here." He paused, seeming to ponder the matter, then added, "I can't imagine my recent acquaintance objecting to you delivering it for me."

He reached inside the tunic of his uniform and withdrew an envelop that, from it's thickness, held a number of documents. She stepped up next to him and he placed the envelope in her hands, cocking his head as he looked at her. "Are you happy Natasha?"

She nodded her head in tiny rapid motions, then whispered, "Yes, sir. I am — very happy."

General Kashirin smiled, then placed a hand on her wrist, leaned in and whispered, "Cling to that, Tasha–*Myshka*; there is so little true happiness in the world these days, and you have been denied your fair share for far too long. Besides, I fenced a little with Mason, back in the day, when it was more as if we were just players on opposing teams. He was a worthy opponent, and always impressed me as a man of honour, with his British sense of fair play."

Then, wheeling back to Kemedov, he demanded, "Are you still here?" Kemedov still hovered on the sidelines in handcuffs. "I thought you'd be looking at the backside of a cell door by now. Let's make it cell 36, shall we, Lt. Rosikoff? I have a feeling that cell 19 might be far too comfortable."

Then, turning to the lieutenant commanding the soldiers, he added, "I think you can release General Kemedov's interrogator. I can't imagine the man did anything more than follow his general's orders."

The last thing Kemedov saw before they carted him off to cell 36 was General Kashirin taking Lieutenant Cherninova by the arm to escort her out of the building.

23: A Major's Obsession

Moscow, Hotel Raddison Slavyanskaya
Sunday, Nov. 31, 2013, 10:30 AM

Mike looked up from his iPad screen, disturbed by the sound of a brisk tattoo being knocked on the door to the suite.

"Hold that thought, Nigel," he said to the IT wizard with whom he'd been conversing on FaceTime.

"Michael, Tony, Carrie? It's Mason and Natasha." The voice was Mason's.

He reached his left hand in the direction of the door, mimed the turning of a doorknob, and the knob on the door to the suite responded.

"Come in, you two," he said. "But I thought you'd gone to work, Natasha."

Mason seemed about to say something, but Natasha seemed unable to restrain herself, so Mason just smiled. "By all means, my dear; this is your story."

Natasha took a breath, then, "General Kemedov is jailed in Lefortovo! General Kashirin arrived shortly after me, had his men surround handcuff and Kemedov, then delivered a scathing rebuke for all his crimes. He even instructed Dmitry to put him in cell 36, Petroff's former cell, stating that 19 was too comfortable!

"When he saw me, he seemed amazed that I should be there, claiming that he'd heard I was on vacation! And next thing I know he's giving me this packet — Mason and I already looked through it, and it contains full travel documents for him — he doesn't even need his passport! — a waiver on the lack of entry card or entry stamp in his passport, and an authorization for me for vacation travel *outside of the Russian Federation! And there's even an envelope full of money! I didn't take time to count it, but it's American hundred–dollar bills, and there must be close to fifty!*"

Mason smiled, then teased, "Natasha, is this any way for a first lieutenant of the FSB to act?"

She sobered immediately, but for barely a second, then broke into a grin. "But, you must understand, Captain: I've never been free to travel before, and I've never been in love before. Can you imagine how it must feel for me knowing that, not only are you free to go home, but I can now leave with the one I love?"

Mason smiled. "I don't have to imagine."

Mike left for a moment, then returned, stating: "I found this in a desk drawer when Tony and I searched your apartment," then handed Mason his passport.

Mason's mouth opened as if to say something, then he just smiled.

"Perhaps we should look into putting you both on a plane as soon as possible, before someone higher than Kashirin takes exception to his decisions," Mike suggested. "He has to have left some kind of paper trail." He held up his iPad, displaying Nigel's face.

"Hello, Nigel," Mason greeted. "What do you think? Airplane or train as originally considered?"

"Well, Capt'n," Nigel observed, "ye can jump off a train wiffout an 'ole lo' of attention — an, should I mention: on a plane, ffat firs' step is a doozie."

"But they can create a checkpoint and stop a train to be searched at any time," Mike mused. "Officials can just as easily force a plane to land — even turn it around and order it back to Moscow." He shrugged. "It's really up to the two of you, but my gut instinct still leans toward rail travel — and, if we're making this about my innate intuition, then I'd say the sooner the better. And that includes the rest of us."

Mike's instincts were working overtime, and all in the negative. It wasn't panic, but he felt like some force greater than himself was trying to push him toward an immediate departure.

"Nigel, what can you do for Mason and Natasha either today or tomorrow?" he asked. "Then see what you can come up with for Tony, Carrie, and I."

"Ffe bes' is still ffrough Belarus to Poland," Nigel replied. "It's a train whot makes a regular run from Moscow to Minsk to Warsaw. No need for reservations, just show up an' buy a ticket."

Mike focused his Wiccan senses on the issue, nodding slowly as he sensed no immediate danger to Mason, just a vague cloud over Natasha. Carrie and Tony seemed in the clear, but the sense of danger to himself felt more imminent. "No reservations means no chance of anyone spotting it in the system. Too bad it can't work for us."

"But why not?" Natasha asked.

"The cats," he replied. "The paperwork that got them into Moscow will get them back to London, but Belarus or Poland would require more paperwork." He made a rictus of a smile and shrugged. "Our best option is to stick to the original plan and simply fly back to London."

He raised a hand to his head, fighting off a surge of lethargy. "We'll talk later, Nigel," he said abruptly.

"Rightee ho, gov'nor," Nigel chirped, and disappeared from the screen.

Mike tossed the iPad onto the chair, turned with a tense smile, and gripped the back of the chair.

"Good Lord, Michael," Mason suddenly exclaimed; "I had no idea of the time — I'm so sorry — you must be about ready to —"

A wave of vertigo forced Mike to dig his fingers into the top of the chair back. He gave a quick nod. "It's okay, Mason. The turn of events took you and Natasha by surprise. You will have to excuse me, though."

Mason nodded, turned, and herded Natasha out the door. As the couple continued toward the elevator, Mike could hear Mason cooking up a lame explanation of how Mike had to have been up all night making plans and assessing the situation. He then heard Mason insisting: *Natasha, Michael's eyes and ears looked perfectly normal to me — Cat's eyes? You mean with vertical pupils? Pointy ears?* Then the sound of Mason chuckling. *I'm sure it's all related to how exciting your day has been...*

He barely made it to the bedroom, darkened by the thickness of the drawn curtains, and composed himself on the bed next to Carrie, before his muscles began to go rigid, as if *rigor mortis* was setting in. Even his heart slowed noticeably, as if it might actually stop once he was in vampire sleep.

Raaa–aaoow! Kato blatted out a yowl, seemingly reprimanding Mike for making him wait so long. He was perched on Mike's pillow, glaring at him with impatient eyes.

Mike settled back on the bed, got his head on the pillow, felt Kato's fur against his face, then lapsed into oblivion.

———————

Arms and legs immobilized — Head thrashing back and forth — Not the immobility of vampire sleep — Flood of water in his face — Instinctive panic —

The monster within, mindless predator, furiously determined to escape!

Mike's eyes snapped open, his fangs extended, even his claws had extended. Kato was complaining in a low moan that was almost a growl. Mike felt his own urge to snarl, but he forced his fangs back to normal, then glanced at his hands, forcing the claws to become normal fingernails, then raised a hand and stroked his friend's neck with the backs of his fingers, but the cat refused to settle. A glance at Teila showed her staring at the door, her eyes widened in alarm, looking huge.

Kato repeated his moaning growl.

Mike thought about the images and sensations that had intruded on his rest, now knowing them for what they were: premonition, warning.

He reached out with his senses and became immediately aware of four intruders in the living–room, moving things around, opening and closing drawers.

I know; he projected to Kato, *we're not alone; there's someone in the suite who doesn't belong — out in the living–room.*

He slid out from under Kato, easing him down onto the bed, but the cat immediately arose, rumbling an angry snarl, clearly meaning to follow Mike.

Mike fixed him with a stern glance. *NO, STAY. Stay here and guard Carrie. Guard Teila.*

He made sure his Walther was secure in the nightstand drawer, then reached out to Tony's mind. Tony was still in the depths of the coma vampires called sleep. He glanced at his watch: 2:12 PM — Tony wouldn't awaken for another half–hour.

He moved silently to the bedroom door — he'd left it ajar, but it was now closed. Someone was searching through the living–room and kitchen areas. *Burglars?* He tuned into thoughts. *Russian. Damn; and Tony's not available for translation.* Something about them felt

official — They seemed unconcerned; there was none
of the anxiety one might expect from a routine burglar
who feared being caught.

FSB. It came to him like a revelation. But why
would Kashirin muddy the waters after getting all the
evidence on Kemedov that he so clearly wanted. Was
this a further effort to identify or contain *Samurai*?

Mike glanced at his reflection in the mirror over
Carrie's boudoir table, watching as the image blurred
and altered: the eyes became dull, a sprinkling of grey
in the hair and mustache, the hairline more receded,
age lines about the eyes and neck. In about a second–
and–a–half his apparent age went from under thirty to
over fifty.

He opened the door, stepped out into the living–
room to find four men, all in uniform. Three wore the
epaulets of lance corporal. The fourth — wavy blond
hair and the smug expression of someone who felt he
had the world by the balls — wore the epaulets of a
major. Mike didn't need a name–tag; he'd seen the face
in Natasha's mind — Major Grigori Dyatlov — now in
his mid–forties, former boyish good looks sagging into
middle age. He still had the same wavy blonde hair, but
clearly struggled to look younger, right down to the
carefully hidden cosmetic surgery scars. Vanity? —
No, Narcissism — ruthless narcissism, with not a trace
of empathy in his soul.

From the images in Natasha's mind, Mike had
expected him to be taller — at least 6–feet, more likely
as much as 6–foot–3, but the real Grigori Dyatlov was
barely 5–10. The rock–hard muscles of his swimming
years had softened, and his open jacket displayed a
layer of flab projecting past his belt. Resentment
seemed to flare in his eyes as he eyed Mike's trim,
much harder musculature.

*He's enough of a narcissist to hate me for being in
better shape beyond fifty than he is at — what — forty–*

five? Forty–six? This guy's pathetic, and all the more dangerous for it.

"Perhaps, if you tell me what you're looking for, I can help you find it more quickly," Mike said, maintaining a frown, and keeping is eyes, indeed all his senses, focused on the major.

The major smiled. "Nice iPad," he commented. "You seem to have a lot of notes on Moscow — interesting buildings, observations on how the streets look at night as opposed to in the daytime — you've even captured the fact that we have a problem with our dog population, though it certainly keeps the number of stray cats to a minimum. Your reading tastes are also extremely — what is the word — eclectic? Not as many apps as one might expect from a Westerner. Perhaps you aren't as reliant on technology as some Americans."

Mike shrugged. "I'm Canadian."

"Yes, of course. And you are here researching a location for parts of your next novel?"

Mike decided not to answer.

"That was a question," the major snapped, as if needing to intimidate him.

Mike remained calm. "No doubt you read that from whatever the officer at the airport typed into the computer. Yes, I am considering Moscow as the site of my next book. I write fantasy fiction with an espionage twist." He shrugged. "Moscow, especially the old Moscow of Soviet days, is almost a cliché staple for spy novels. After Christmas I'll visit Prague — same reason."

"So, no interest in Sochi? Not even with our upcoming Olympics? As a Canadian, I'd expect you to be a hockey fan — *Montreal Canadiens*, maybe. Their goal tender will be net minder for the Canadian team."

How could he know about my parting comment to Kashirin? Mike shrugged. "I might watch some of the skiing, the odd luge event, but I'm not a huge sports fan. I've always been more of an academic."

"Yes," the major mused. "You have degrees in science — medical biology, math, some physics — you even taught for a while, in Bermuda. That must have been nice. So tell me, Mr. M.D. Cameron, why don't you live in Bermuda? Why Chester Basin in Nova Scotia? I would have thought, with your interest in sailing, Bermuda might be more suited, especially considering the climate."

Mike replied in a deadpan voice. "I like the change of seasons. The Bermuda–Azores High reduces Bermuda's summer winds to ten–knots or less. The Chester area has superior sailing conditions, even if the season is shorter."

Dyatlov scowled, clearly resenting being wrong.

"So, tell me, M.D. — what do the initials stand for? Melvin Douglas? Martin Desmond?"

"Since my passport was scanned and logged into your system, you must know that it's Michael David," Mike said, deciding it was time to add a cautious touch of irritation. "I usually go by *Mike*, though my wife and my uncle call me *Michael*."

"So how do you know Agent *Samurai* of CSIS?" the major asked point–blank, keeping his eyes on Mike's, as if watching for a change in expression. "And what did you do to the listening devices installed in this suite?"

Mike recognized one of the corporals as having been in Kashirin's group at the zoo, in fact, he was one of the first that Mike had skewered the back of his jacket with his own combat knife. He seemed to be thinking in English, *This suite? The surveillance system is out for the entire hotel!*

Mike frowned and shook his head. "Listening devices?" He shrugged. "You came all the way over here to check on faulty electronics? Why not just send a technician? He could have claimed to be a telephone repair man.

"As for this CSIS agent you mentioned, I don't know him at all. In fact, I know next to nothing about CSIS. I have a cousin, retired RCMP, who used to liaise with CSIS on security issues, and advises me on certain technical stuff. As for an Agent *Samurai*? That sounds like a codename. I had no idea CSIS used codenames."

"But it's in your vampire novels," Dyatlov said.

Mike shrugged and smiled. "So are about half–a–dozen or more vampires. Didn't know them, either. It's fiction, officer, — none of it's real."

"That's *Major*," Dyatlov hissed, his smile tight and icy. This clearly wasn't going the way he wanted.

"This *Samurai* character instructed an FSB general to leave a package at the front desk downstairs, in care of you. One might naturally assume that he knows you. Did you pick up the package? It's not there; the concierge insists no package was left, but they are not reliable," he stated, agitation plain in his tone.

Mike shrugged again. "Sorry. Can't help you."

"Can't or won't?" Dyatlov's demeanour was now antagonistic in the extreme.

"I can't tell you what I don't know," Mike insisted. "I've been a scientist for most of my life; I prefer facts over guesses."

"So do I," the major hissed; "but you're not giving me any facts. Perhaps you'd prefer to come with us to FSB headquarters at Lubyanka."

Mike sighed. "Major, do you really think intimidation is going to suddenly provide me with knowledge that I don't have?"

"Bring him along," the major commanded. Two of the lance–corporals moved to either side of him, the third taking up a position just behind him. He felt the presence of a gun at his back.

Mike's brain went onto overdrive, rapidly processing his options, and he decided to go along quietly. He could have killed or incapacitated all four in seconds, but then he'd have to dispose of the bodies. By cooperating, he could learn more about what Dyatlov was after, how best to deal with him, possibly even General Kashirin, assuming the general had anything to do with this. His gut told him that Dyatlov had his own private agenda — supporting what he'd seen in the general's mind about FSB corruption.

They took him downstairs and out of the hotel, past the front desk, where the concierge seemed helplessly embarrassed and quickly looked away. The corporals escorted him out to a marked car, got him into the back seat, one on either side, each now pressing the muzzle of a Makarov into his ribs, while the third got in on the driver's side and took the wheel. Dyatlov took the passenger seat. Then they took off, driving eastward, toward the center of Moscow. They crossed over a bridge, then, after several more twists and turns, came to a stop before what Mike recognized, from movies and prior research, as Lubyanka, the former headquarters of the Soviet era KGB. Once through the front doors, Dyatlov flashed his ID to an armed attendant, then led the way as they took him down into the basement, and back in time to a world of dingy cells, dingy smells, and faded paint discoloured by accumulated grime.

This is a far cry from how Mason and Natasha were hoping the day would unfold, he thought. *But it sure substantiates the foreboding that's been plaguing me. I can't imagine what this guy hopes to learn. Could Kashirin have put him up to this after all? No. This prick is on a mission of his own making.*

How did he even know about General Kashirin's meeting with Samurai? *And how could he know about the plan to drop things off at the hotel front desk?*

Natasha! This bastard has a flag on Natasha in their computer system. — A brief scan of Dyatlov's mind showed that he'd studied computer science. *Whenever her name comes up, he gets notified. Is it because he led the gang rape on her or because of some lingering fascination?* He rationalized further — *He knows about Natasha's travel papers, but does he know about Mason? That corporal was in Kashirin's crew — Planted by Dyatlov?*

He was just making his way further into Dyatlov's mind when they took him into a stark cell, pushed him into a strangely designed chair, and used wide nylon straps with heavy buckles to immobilize his arms and legs against the arms and legs of the chair.

Dyatlov pulled on close–fitting leather gloves.

"Seriously, Major?" Mike said. "Are you hoping to beat it out of me? I'm fifty–three years old, a Canadian citizen, a former teacher, turned novelist." He shook his head, trying to look nervous and apprehensive.

"I know all that from your biography," Dyatlov stated blandly. "I have even been to your website, so I also know of your martial arts background, though, I presume that was many years ago. Perhaps you can still take a punch. Do you have a strong constitution — *Mike* is it? Can you stand up to a good beating, Mike, or would you prefer water–boarding like the CIA used on prisoners in Afghanistan?"

Mike was about to delve further into Dyatlov's mind for his obsession with Natasha when the first blow landed, followed almost instantly by one from the major's other fist.

Pain — Intense, almost agonizing pain.

The major stepped back, clutching at his fists alternately, glaring with hateful resentment at Mike. He blurted something in Russian, but Mike knew it had to be something about how hard Mike's jaw had seemed or how much Dyatlov's hands hurt. Mike had barely felt the blows, but the major was picturing broken bones in his hands.

Mike wished he could make his mouth bleed but, even if he bit into his lips, the bleeding would only last a few seconds before the wounds closed, his vampire constitution refusing to allow an open wound. *I guess we'll be switching to water now*, he thought.

He began probing Dyatlov's mind for thoughts of Natasha. *She's his obsession.* As a teen she'd ignored his advances. Mike decided it was out of shyness and some aspect of demureness, but Dyatlov had felt it was something else — she thought she was too good for him? No girl had ever rejected him. He'd been entirely successful — with his good looks, his sculpted swimmer's physique, his fame as a national athlete, and then his status as a member of the FSB — the latter had helped greatly, especially when his fame as an athlete began to fade. He'd struggled, especially after thirty, to maintain his physique, but, by forty, even that was requiring more and more work. Now he felt disgust when he looked at the flab that insisted in forming over his once rock–hard abs. Just last year he'd resorted to liposuction, then laser treatments on the *crow's feet* about his eyes. And his neck — lately the skin toward his throat was trying to fold up like an accordion!

Mike felt sick. *This clown is so in love with himself that he just can't fathom Natasha not being in love with him, nor any woman, for that matter! He rapes her, intimidates her into further nonconsensual sex, and expects her to fall in love with him?*

Okay, you sick creep, how did you know about Kashirin's meet with me? Then he found it. Kashirin had dared to interfere on Natasha's behalf at her promotional meeting — *Ryazan* — Paranoid, Dyatlov had been keeping Kashirin under surveillance. One of the soldiers in the park with Kashirin had been his man, the same who'd thought in English at the apartment, the one who had strapped him into this chair. Even now that corporal was pondering how Mike and *Samurai* were the same height, same build. Mike ended that line of thought by locating that memory in the corporal's brain, and popping a blood vessel.

The corporal frowned, the frown deepened, then he let out a groan, his eyes widened, and he shot hands to both sides of his head as the mini–stroke came and went.

"Let's try one of these," the major was saying. There was a selection of syringes on a small table to one side.

"Sodium pentathol?" Mike asked. "Sodium amatol? Scopolamine perhaps? Scopolamine won't work on me — at least it didn't have much effect in the *Transderm* patches I wore during an ocean crossing."

"You've done your research," the major complemented. "Then, let's try a blend of all three."

He felt a needle go into his arm and heard what he assumed was a Russian expletive from the major. *I guess he had trouble piercing my skin. Hmm — feels kind of warm but — yep — it never gets to last for very long. It's like that first hint of a buzz from a good Scotch, like Glenlivet; the moment it starts to work, my system goes to war and processes it out. Oh, well, I guess my liver needs something to do, since the only protein in my diet is already digested.*

"So, where is Natasha going? My Natasha is going away on a vacation. Where is she going? The paperwork was marked to come to you."

Mike shrugged. "Who is Natasha? I think I had a student by that name once — No, that was Natalia."

"*Natasha!*" Dyatlov snarled in his face.

"No good. Sorry," Mike said. "Don't know her. Want to try beating me some more? You must have a few unbroken bones left in your hands. You know;

back in the late '70s or early '80s, I did *kumite* tournaments, full–contact martial arts, for three years, and never got knocked out once. Could this have something to do with that? I'm sure I must have gotten hit a few times."

The major gave Mike's chair a shove and it tilted back, placing him in a head–down position, at about a forty–five–degree angle. He placed a thick cloth over Mike's face, picked up a water hose, and turned it on to a slow stream. The whole idea was to make Mike think he was drowning. But Mike had almost drowned at least twice in his life, and wasn't frightened.

Then, when he was twenty, earning his original SCUBA certification, he proved he could hold his breath for three minutes at the bottom of a pool. Over the next few years, in Bermuda, doing underwater photography until his tank ran out, he'd lie still on the bottom until he'd finished a roll of film, then perform an emergency free–ascent to the surface, proving he could last close to five minutes. Now that he was a vampire, he had no idea how long he could go without breathing.

The major kept up a steady flow for five minutes, then stopped, pulling the cloth away from Mike's face.

Mike lay there a moment, then hacked out a series of gasping coughs, sputtered a lot, then gasped for air, thrashing his head back and forth when the cloth reappeared above his face. He kept mumbling about how he didn't know anything about CSIS or an agent with the codename *Samurai*. But the cloth spread out over his face anyway.

I'm soon going to tire of this, he decided, but he wasn't sure how to proceed. *This is what I saw as I was waking. The monster inside me won't tolerate this for long. Get what you can out of Dyatlov's head!*

He probed deeper, but it was a struggle. Stored memory images were no problem, but the associated thoughts were in Russian. He could trigger a thought and force Dyatlov to express it in English, but that was tedious. Then, with almost no prompting, Dyatlov was thinking in English. *Of course! The KGB had drilled it into him during his spy training — If you're ever caught by the Americans, even thinking in Russian will betray you!*

Okay, you creep, what are you really after?

Natasha — the rape — more nonconsensual sex, coerced through intimidation — but it was Grigori who was afraid? — Yes — The bully dominating his victim to keep her from reporting him, yet constantly fearing that she might inevitably find the right senior officer to hear her complaints. But, the more he got away with it, the bolder he got, seemingly convincing himself he was untouchable. Yet, even years later, he couldn't let her be. He was obsessed with her. She was the woman he couldn't have, the woman who didn't want him. He couldn't accept that a woman wouldn't want him.

The face of Mikhail Trepashkin surfaced. Why do you fear Natasha talking to her father?

Ryazan.

Kashirin whispering the word in his ear at Natasha's promotion review.

Okay, Grigori, what the hell is Ryazan?

What came was a shock.

Sept. 22, 1999 — Ryazan — small city less than an hour from Moscow — Reading street signs: Novosyolov Ulitsa, then numbers on buildings — 14/16 — There was a store next door. Parking in front and being there for any length of time won't create suspicion. The leader, a woman, gets out and checks the basement. "All clear; you can unload," she says.

Dyatlov obeys, hefting, one at a time, two white 50–kg bags from the trunk of a white Zhiguli into a basement. His partner — Dyatlov thinks the name: Romanovich, Vladimir Romanovich — dark–haired, square–jawed, mustache, wearing glasses — helps the woman carry the third into the basement of an apartment building. "Hey," he points out, when Dyatlov comments on him not carrying the sack alone, "I'm used to manning electronic–surveillance in a van, not lugging this shit about like a warehouse stooge!"

Mike couldn't figure out what he was seeing. Then he saw the stacked white plastic sacks as a whole, in an isolated area of the basement, right up against what he judged to be the building's main support. *Dyatlov thinks: When this blows, it'll bring the whole building down!*

The basement seems flooded, all except for this bricked off area — water elsewhere all over the floor, two– or three–inches deep in places. This was the only dry area in the basement.

Dyatlov makes eye contact with Romanovich, who nods, turns and reaches a hand toward the woman, who passes him something, then he passes it on to Dyatlov. In his hand, Dyatlov has what looks like three D-cells bound by electrical tape, a digital watch, and a shotgun shell, all connected by wires. Dyatlov sets this on a sack, then takes out a knife, flicks open the blade with a thumb, shifts the top bag, cuts an opening into the middle bag, exposing a yellowish substance — Mike likens it to fine dried pasta, like spaghettini, chopped into small bits, finer than rice — *He sets the detonator pack into the opening, inserting it into the contents of the sack, wiggling it until it settles into place in the material, then shifts the top bag back into place over the bag with the detonator.*

The woman giving the orders says something in Russian, calling him Lejtenant Dyatlov — Lieutenant Dyatlov. He could sense Dyatlov saluting and departing the building to wait outside.

He was interrupted by the flow of water again. This time he blocked it out, focusing instead on the major's memory — *an apartment building in Ryazan — 1999 — the infamous Russian bombings of September, 1999, this last attempt discovered before it could detonate, and eventually declared by the FSB to have been a training exercise! So, major, you were a flunky? And why would they want you, a lieutenant, to do the heavy lifting on that job? Because you had the muscles? But why pick a lieutenant? And who was your superior, who told you you could go back outside?*

They already had the rape complaint, but they wanted more to hold over you. And you had done it all before — six days before on September 16th — parking a truck outside — explosives in the truck — Volgodonsk.

But who else knew? Who at the top of the FSB? Kemedov! And, to whom did Kemedov report? Who was this Patrushev, and to whom did he report? Come on, Grigori, you know — It took a moment for the familiar face to appear — *Putin, — Prime Minister Vladimir Putin, head of the FSB until Yeltsin appointed him Prime Minister, and Putin appointed Patrushev.*

Then — Trepashkin — the criminal investigator uncovered the FSB involvement — Notes in General Kashirin's computer — Kashirin knew Trepashkin was Natasha's father! One more reason to keep Natasha under control. If she ever communicates with her father — if her father knows who the third officer in the basement was — Natasha — so lovely, yet such a threat — Fear me, Natasha!

The water now seemed to insist on going up Mike's nose and into his sinuses. He coughed and snorted, forcing the water away from his lungs.

The images flashed in his mind, unbidden, uncontrolled, unwanted.

Struggling to breathe, his face wet — extremely cold — his face in snow, held in the snow, the tight grip on the back of his neck forcing his face deeper and deeper into the snow. Back–and–forth rocking motion grinds icy particles into his face, into his eyes, up his nose, even into his mouth — That awful suffocating feeling — Then the kicking starts.

This isn't real. That was grade 6, his mind insisted, knowing Earl Miller was dead. It had to be a flashback related to deep–seated post traumatic stress. But the knowledge did nothing to stem the flood of helplessness and anger forever tied to that trauma.

The monster within refused to be contained any longer. The snarling rage had begun.

Enough of this shit! No more! Mike snarled. Rage built up and burst out of him, into Dyatlov's head, like a bolt of lightning. In his mind he saw the major's eyes widen as he dropped the hose and grabbed at his head with both hands, his palms against the temples.

Mike focussed on the wet cloth, pushed outward with more chi, forcing it away from his face, until it fell to the floor.

No one in the room was paying any mind to him. Two had rushed to assist the major, easing him into a chair. The third lance–corporal was still holding his hands to his own head.

Mike sent part of his consciousness out of himself enough to see how he was fastened to the chair. He tried undoing the buckles, then, as fury at Dyatlov got the better of him — fury for Dyatlov's behaviour toward Natasha, his involvement in the bombing plots of September, 1999, and fury at Dyatlov's intolerable personality —

The monster snarled and lurched forward, snapping one nylon band, and bursting buckles apart — pieces flying across the room as he hurled himself out of the chair, lashing out with hands and feet. He struck all four men several times, dropping them to the floor, including the major, who had struggled to rise out of the chair into which his men had set him.

"Not you," The monster snarled as he snatched Dyatlov and kept him from falling. The major's intrusion into the suite had interrupted Mike and kept him from feeding. Being subjected to torture only exacerbated his need for blood. He had no real sense of how long he'd been subjected to drugs and water–boarding — he'd been too busy with all he'd seen in the major's head.

"You bastard!" he snarled. *"My wife was asleep in the bedroom when you hauled me off! I know what you did to Natasha! I know what you did in Volgodonsk and in Ryazan!"*

He could barely vocalize beyond a snarl. The inner monster, once crucial to vampire survival, was unleashed.

"You wanted *Samurai?*" he growled. "Well, you've got him. Do I know *Samurai?* I *am Samurai!* But I'm more than that — more than you bargained for! You think you can do anything — *You are FSB!* Well, Major, you've unleashed the monster, you narcissistic, spoiled, entitled —" he couldn't find a worthy epithet.

He saw it all in Dyatlov's terrified mind: vertical cats-eye pupils, extended fangs, exaggeratedly pointed ears — the face of the monster — Dyatlov's nightmare — then he tore into Grigori Dyatlov's throat, inhaling more than a quart of blood before letting the body drop to the floor and finish bleeding out — he'd made no effort to leave enough saliva to close the wounds.

For a moment he watched the major writhing in hysteria, only making his heart pound faster, making himself bleed faster. The blood had sated the monster enough to get it back into its cage.

Good strong heart — must be all those years of swimming. Then he corrected himself — *strong heart. There wasn't anything* good *about Dyatlov's heart.*

He rifled the major's pockets and located a flick–blade knife that looked to be the same one he had used to cut into the bag of explosive. He flicked it open and used the serrated portion of the blade to saw at the puncture wounds in Dyatlov's throat until they were obliterated by the jagged cuts, then, with one deft slice, cut Dyatlov's throat almost ear–to–ear. *No sense letting some superstitious fool get the notion there might be vampires in Moscow,* he decided, then excised the lacerated remains of the punctures and used his Wicca talent to incinerate them.

As he looked at the destroyed throat, an idea came to him: a way to create an even bigger mystery and stir up some panic among certain factions in the FSB.

He turned off the water hose, seized Dyatlov and used him to mop up and disperse the worst of the puddled water on the floor. Then, dipping two fingers into the blood welling from the wounds, he wrote on the concrete floor next to the body, dipping his fingers several more times, until, standing, he surveyed his handiwork with grim satisfaction, hoping that someday the residents of the controversial apartment building in Ryazan and survivors of other bombings, in other cities, even Moscow, would hear of it, and feel vindicated, and, hopefully, feel that those who hadn't survived the successful bombing actions had finally been avenged.

Volgodonsk, Sept. 16, 1999
— Avenged at last —

14/16 Novosyolov, Ryazan, Sept. 22, 1999
— Vindicated —

Satisfied, he turned his attention to the wide–eyed lance corporal who still seemed mystified by the pain in his head. *You,* he projected, then snatched the man off the floor. *How's your English?* Then he recalled that the man had thought in English back in the hotel suite. He ordered him to locate and take the car keys from the one who'd been the driver.

The other two corporals were dead: One from a powerful blow to the heart, the other from a reverse roundhouse kick to the head. Mike shrugged it off to vampire speed and strength, pushing any remorse into the back of his mind. After all, they'd been willing participants in the major's water–boarding of an apparent tourist, simply because he wasn't supplying the major with the information he wanted. *Don't dwell on it*, he insisted. *They felt obliged to follow orders; I felt obliged to survive. Blame it on the FSB.*

The surviving corporal was the one who, on Dyatlov's orders, had infiltrated General Kashirin's advance team. He now escorted Mike out of the building and back to the car. Recalling traffic–cams, he had the corporal drop him a block before the hotel.

Now drive to the nearest hospital and tell someone you think you've had a stroke. In the meantime, work on forgetting everything that's happened to you since you got out of bed this morning. Remembering any of it will probably trigger another stroke.

He blurred forward, coming out of vampire speed at the entrance to the hotel. Just inside, in the lobby, he found a large mirror and, after a moment's study of his reflection, decided that, once he licked lingering blood trace from around his mouth, he looked reasonably presentable.

An ornate clock told him it was 3:35. He'd been gone for maybe an hour. *Tony will have been up for a while, and Carrie might be waking soon,* he calculated, then summoned the elevator and ascended to the floor of the suite. *Bastard didn't even let me grab a jacket,* he growled in his mind, noticing for the first time that his arms felt mildly chilled.

"Ah, Michael; at first I thought you might still be resting," Tony commented as Mike entered. "Then I noted that the place seemed in a bit of disarray. Were you looking for something before going out?

"I smell blood — Michael, there are blood stains on the first two fingers of your right hand."

Mike glanced at his fingers, then went to the kitchen to wash them. "We had a visit from a nosy FSB major — Nothing to worry about now. Seems the late Grigori Dyatlov was trying to keep tabs on General Kashirin. He even planted one of his men among those the General took along when he met with me. He'd placed a marker on Natasha so that the computer system would alert him anytime someone accessed anything about her. He was also hacking into Kashirin's files, which gave him Kashirin's note on delivering documents to *Samurai* in care of me, here."

"And did you say *the late major*?" Tony prompted.

Mike nodded. "I spent the last hour in the basement at Lubyanka, being punched, drugged with disinhibiting narcotics, and water–boarded."

"*Good Lord, Michael!*," Tony exclaimed.

"I'm okay," Mike assured him. "I had time to explore his thoughts and memories while he thought he was torturing me — he was looking for proof that I know Agent *Samurai*." He flashed a hint of a smile. "He was determined to head off Natasha getting those documents, in a panic to know where Natasha was going — perhaps he thought he could join her on her vacation. He really was a sick narcissistic pig. Anyway, it was his own fault for not giving me a chance to have breakfast before insisting on dragging me out of here. I'm afraid the monster got loose. What troubles me is that I saw a glimpse of that monster in Dyatlov's mind: except for my hair and skin colouring, it looked a little too much like Torok. Torok embraced the monster and became it." Mike shook his head to dispel the image.

"And, Tony," Mike pulled a chair up next to Tony's, sat down, and explained, "Dyatlov was a lieutenant in '99 when he parked a truckload of explosives outside an apartment complex in Volgodonsk, and carried bags of explosive into the basement of an apartment building in Ryazan — the one where the FSB changed the story from having foiled another bombing to it being a training exercise. Why they picked him is beyond me. Making an officer carry heavy sacks into a building seems highly demeaning. He did insert the detonator into the middle sack, but another officer, superior in rank by the way she was giving orders, was carrying the detonator, and only passed it to the third, to pass to him, when it was time to cut the bag and put the detonator in with the explosive material."

"But it made him involved, and guaranteed his silence and cooperation," Tony explained. "No doubt, it's a bit like the old Mafia expression about *making your bones*, and becoming a *made man*. Once they have you involved in something incriminating like that, they own you, and know you can be trusted.

"Did you see any evidence of sugar? The authorities insisted that the bags were filled with harmless sugar."

Mike shook his head. "The bags may have looked like large sugar bags, and were stamped with some kind of factory label that I couldn't read or recognize." He projected an image of what he'd seen of the bags and their labeling to Tony.

"Are you sure it wasn't sugar?" Tony asked. "The labeling you showed me said, *Cherkessk Sugar Plant*." Tony frowned. "Cherkessk is a strange place to process and package sugar; it's in the Caucasus, almost on the border with Georgia, and not too far from Chechnya. A bag labeled as coming from Cherkessk might be useful in pointing a blaming finger at Chechnya."

"No sugar, Tony; it looked like dry spaghettini or angel–hair pasta cut into 2– to 3–mm bits. And any lingering sugar would have flashed just as dangerously as flour, increasing the blast and making fire spread."

"That sounds like *RDX*," Tony mused, then he nodded. "So, can we also infer from your adventure that Kashirin is clean and above reproach?"

"He knew about Ryazan, but, presumably, all the higher officers did. My gut says that he's ethical, and against the corruption in the FSB, hence his desire to bring down Kemedov." Mike replied. "Dyatlov learned of the labeling of the packet to me — his man among the soldiers might have overheard, but the major also had the general under surveillance, and he made a note of the info I gave him on his phone. If it's like my system at home, the moment he made the note, it was on his office computer, and Dyatlov was clearly hacked into Kashirin's computer."

"Does this mean we're free to depart?" Tony asked. "I've never been terribly fond of Moscow, and, I can't say that the city has become more endearing."

Mike nodded. "I'm definitely ready to get out of here, but, before we can make our escape, there are details to arrange. Natasha deserves to know about Dyatlov, as well as his link to what her father had been fighting to prove. And, Tony, Dyatlov found out, somehow, that Mikhail Trepashkin is Natasha's father. Since Trepashkin had come so close to exposing the FSB involvement at Ryazan, Dyatlov used that as another excuse to keep Natasha *in line* — that's from *his* twisted perception. Over the years, it grew into an irrational obsession! It started as lust — I guess she had a remarkable figure for sixteen?"

Tony frowned and nodded. "Speedos, with their flimsy fabric, don't exactly leave much to the imagination," he mused.

"But," Mike said through clenched teeth, "the more he tried to break her, the more the sick bastard became determined that she love him. He even referred to her as *my Natasha*, and commented that she was leaving without him. I know, from her thoughts and what she's said, that he put her through hell over the years, but I had no idea he was so sick."

Tony leaned over and rested a hand on Mike's shoulder. "It's over, dear boy. And you're right: Tell Natasha that it's finally over."

24: *Last-Minute Details*

M ike leaned forward, watching Natasha's face as she took in the significance of what he was saying.

"He's dead? He's really dead?" she asked. "So I'm finally free of the beast?" She shot a hand up, fingers covering her lips — "Oh, my God, Michael! When I was getting the paperwork for General Kashirin, I had a vision of Dyatlov trying to interfere between Mason and I, then one of you drawing your handgun so incredibly fast, and I actually wished for him to have a run–in with you. Oh, Michael, I'm so sorry!"

Mike laughed. "Natasha, surely you don't think you wished him on me and made that happen!"

Her fingers still covered her lips, but she withdrew them slowly, and smiled an embarrassed smile. "I suppose, in a way, I did think that. But he was such a beast..."

Beast, Mike thought, knowing it was *the beast* who had truly ended Dyatlov.

"He's dead, Natasha," he assured her. "As for being free of him: that's up to you and whether you can get beyond how he's demoralized you."

"So, not only was my father correct, but Dyatlov had a hand in some of it?" she asked. Anger and disgust seemed mixed with surprise. "Mikhail

Ivanovich knew about Romanovich — I'd seen it in his notes before they were destroyed — but knowledge of the third culprit always eluded him. Then Romanovich got conveniently killed by a drunk driver. Of course it was Patrushev's fear of Romanovich being identified as FSB that made him come up with the whole absurd *training exercise* lie. From gossip I've heard, some officers thought Patrushev arranged for Romanovich's hit–and–run accident, to prevent him ever being questioned about Ryazan."

Mike nodded. "I can only verify the incidents in Volgodonsk and Ryazan, especially Ryazan. Romanovich passed the detonator to Dyatlov. It looked authentic, and the contents of the sack Dyatlov cut into was not sugar. Sugar is white, with nearly–cubic crystals. These weren't crystals; they were oblong, more pale yellow than white."

Natasha frowned. "From my limited training in the subject, you seem to be describing hexogene."

"RDX, is the most common trade name," Mason interjected.

Natasha hesitated, — "And you say he was afraid I'd eventually report him to someone who'd actually do something? For the longest time I thought General Kashirin might be the one, but, as more time passed — well, I think he was walking a tightrope of trying to stay clean in an increasingly corrupt job and concern for drawing undue attention or disapproval if he were to champion my cause. Everyone fears Bortnikov because Bortnikov is Putin's puppet."

She shook her head. Mike sensed a blend of frustration, sadness, and disillusionment.

"No one was ever prosecuted," she murmured. "How many Chechens died needlessly? And the most senior of the villains, Patrushev, that arch–liar, got another star from Putin and then actually got promoted to Secretary of Russia's Security Council."

"So Kashirin's hope of using Kemedov to expose Putin is just a pipe–dream?" Mike asked.

"*No one* associated with the FSB has ever been prosecuted," Natasha sighed, "Just innocents like my father and Litvinenko, who were falsely charged, and, again, by the same FSB. The true villains were almost always rewarded in some way — some, like Patrushev, got promoted."

Mike shrugged. "I still think that Kashirin is biding his time to go after the big man."

"You mean Putin?" Mason asked, frowning.

Mike nodded. "I saw it in his mind that day in the park. What he whispered in Dyatlov's ear that day was the word *Ryazan*. He knows the truth about a lot of things, and I had a definite sense of him waiting for something — perhaps something that he thinks might be about to happen — this mess in Ukraine, for instance. If Putin is stirring things up somehow, creating unrest and fanning the flames —"

"Yanukovych," Mason mused.

"What about him?" Mike asked.

"He's so pro–Russian and pro–Putin that ethnic Ukrainians hate him," Mason continued. "If the people were to rise up and oust Yanukovych, and Putin chose not to recognize the followup interim government..."

"Czechoslovakia," Mike murmured. "In 1938 Hitler fostered unrest, then moved in the troops to 'protect the rights of the Germans in Czechoslovakia'."

"The eastern edge of Ukraine is predominantly Russian," Mason pointed out, "and so is about 60% of Crimea. Would he really dare to plan that?"

Mike shrugged. "He's slipping in popularity. I doubt if even Olympic success will make much difference. Either way, I'm sure he'll wait 'til after the Sochi Olympics to make any kind of move.

"But Kemedov is still a problem, one that probably shouldn't wait."

"What are you going to do, Michael?" Mason asked. "I think you should, as Sam might put it, 'Get out of Dodge' while the getting is good."

"Do you really feel comfortable leaving Kemedov behind?" Mike asked. "He had files on both you and Petroff in his office computer at that meth–lab, within a stone's throw of where Petroff was holding you. I'm serious, Mason; I think he orchestrated this whole mess. Think about it: If you were still active in the 00–Section, what would you do?"

Mason looked pensive a moment, then nodded and said, "I'd eliminate him."

——— —— ——

Mike composed himself on the bathroom floor, surrounded by candles. Carrie and Tony were seated nearby, keeping watch.

Moments later his consciousness was hovering just below the ceiling, looking down on his still form and the vigilant forms of his beloved wife and his best friend and ancestor. He pushed through the wall and off to the east, over the now–darkened streets of Moscow. Trying to cross the river, with the slipstream of air flowing above it was nigh onto impossible, but attaching to a car traveling across a bridge made it easy. Soon he was at Lefortovo, then heading down the hall to Cell 36.

Kemedov was seated on his bunk, looking disgruntled and hard–done–by.

He went into the general's mind and marveled, aghast, at what he found — Kemedov's plans — Putin's plans — *waiting until after February's Winter Olympics to parade Mason as a British spy caught in Russian territory — Kemedov suggests 'catching' him in East Ukraine, stirring up trouble in the pro–Russian regions of Kharkiv, Donetsk, Mariupol, and Luhansk.*

Putin nods — 'We have a man in Donetsk who can handle that. After reclaiming Crimea, then Odessa, we can take back the rest of what Khrushchev so misguidedly gave away, and blame this British spy as being the catalyst.'

My God, Putin means to redraw the Russian border — He's had it all planned ever since he first made a move against Georgia in 2008, becoming more fully committed last year when —.

He's been blaming unrest in Ukraine on Western intervention stirring up anti–Russian sentiment in pro–Russian regions, just like he did in Georgia. So Kemedov comes up with the plan to hijack Mason, leaving Petroff as scapegoat in the unlikely event that something went wrong.

"Sorry, General," he snarled, "but Mason is going home. You, on the other hand, are going somewhere much hotter."

Still in the general's mind, he summoned images of an inferno of raging flame, and said: "Welcome to Hell, General. It's your punishment for the drugs your people cook, for all the people you've killed — and whose deaths lie at your door — and for your complicity in the plots to reshape this part of the world, not for the people of the region, but to suit the ambitions of what might very well be an egomaniac. Maybe you should say a prayer."

Still maintaining the image of flames, he reached down into Kemedov's cardiac muscle and made it work harder to pump cooling blood to the over–heating brain. Harder — harder —— Then he wrapped his energy round that heart and squeezed.

At 11:23 PM, Sunday, Nov. 31, General Nikolai Alexei Kemedov died of a massive coronary infarction, though Mike was certain that his body would be 'found' somewhere more suited to someone whom the papers would call a Hero of the Russian Federation.

FSB HQ, Lubyanka Square, Moscow
Monday, Dec. 1, 2013, 11:00 AM

Lieutenant–General Sergei Smirnov picked up the receiver of his ringing telephone, listened a moment, then slammed the phone down, snarling a curse.

He thought a moment, then snatched the receiver and punched a button on the multi–buttoned phone.

"Get me Colonel Kalugin, Department S," he ordered, then, once that man was on the line, "Kalugin, my office, right away," then he hung up and waited. It took less than four minutes before a knock and an immediate opening of the door.

The newcomer stepped in, snapped to attention, and saluted. He was tall, over six-feet in height, with the burly physique of a wrestler, yet he moved with the grace of a dancer. His dark brown hair was buzzed to a crewcut.

"Take a seat," Smirnov beckoned, indicating the chair before his desk. "We have a problem," he began, not even waiting for the colonel to sit. "First, Kashirin unearthed sufficient evidence to order Kemedov's detention in Lefortovo. No matter," he added when Kalugin's eyes widened, "he was found this morning, dead of an apparent heart–attack. Kemedov had assured us that Mason and Petroff were both safely ensconced in Lefortovo, but they aren't.

"There is no record of Mason — no record at all. Petroff, on the other hand, was found, as mad as Rasputin, at his brother– and sister–in–law's farm, gun still in hand, both of his wife's siblings in advance stages of decomposition, having been shot by Petroff, according to ballistics and paraffin tests. So the President's plan for parading Mason as a British agent captured in the act of subverting Ukrainian nationals seems in the toilet."

Kalugin frowned, and seemed about to comment, when Smirnov continued.

"We have a bigger problem, Kalugin. What do *Volgodonsk, Sept. 16, 1999* and *14/16 Novosyolov, Ryazan, Sept. 22, 1999* mean to you?"

Ilya Kalugin's frown deepened. "Aren't those two of the apartment complexes we targeted during *Operation Firestorm*? When Ryazan was exposed, and the sketch artist produced a likeness of our man Romanovich, Patrushev tried to explain it away as a training exercise."

Smirnov rolled his eyes and grumbled, "A stupid idea at best, one that just got even more stupid the more Patrushev tried to stick to it. I can't believe the President promoted him to the Security Council.

"But that's not the point. Those places and dates, along with the phrase, 'Avenged at last' and the word 'vindicated' were found written in blood on the floor of an interrogation cell seven floors below us. The blood belonged to Major Grigori Dyatlov, found lying in a congealed pool of it not one half–hour ago. Evidence suggests he was interrogating someone, but we have no idea whom.

"He apparently left sometime yesterday afternoon, accompanied by three corporals, but they're of no help. Lance Corporal Uri Yazmenov was hospitalized for a stroke, which erased areas of memory. The other two are dead. One took a blow to the head that created massive fracturing of the parietal-occipital bone, but left no discernible impact mark — the forensic people refer to it as a tool mark. A forensics specialist suggested it was as if he'd been kicked by a large plow horse wearing sneakers. The other has severe bruising to the sternum in the shape of a fist, the outline of the knuckles actually impressed into parts of the bone."

When Smirnov concluded, Kalugin said, "So, kicked and punched by someone able to achieve velocity and impact beyond that of our best martial artists." He sighed, then cocked an eyebrow, "I'll have a team examine traffic cameras to see where Dyatlov went when he left here. I'll also have the car's GPS examined, but it could be early tomorrow before we learn anything useful. — Sir, wasn't Dyatlov part of the *Firestorm* teams at Volgodonsk and Ryazan?"

"So you see the significance of the message in blood on the floor," Smirnov commented, then ordered: "Make this investigation your number one priority. If it leads to a suspect, I don't think we want to question so dangerous a person. You used to be one of the KGB's so–called *bodyguards*, so I want you to personally handle this assignment."

Kalugin nodded. "Yes, sir; I'll move on it the moment I know something conclusive."

Monday, Dec. 1, 2013, 11:00 PM

Mike, Carrie, and Tony watched the crowds at the Moscow station as Mason and Natasha boarded the train to Minsk, Natasha with her large grey suitcase. Mason was wearing a suit Tony had bought for him that afternoon.

Mike scanned the minds of all those milling about, especially anyone who looked official, but no one seemed interested in either of the two passengers.

"I detect nothing," Tony declared.

Mike nodded and mused: "I think they're safe. If anyone would have scoured to find Natasha, it would have been Dyatlov. I can only imagine the commotion that must be going on at Lubyanka with the discovery of his body in that basement cell, especially with the cryptic message I left next to the body. Let them think it was a retaliation against guilty FSB personnel.

"Kemedov, of course, died of natural causes."

"So, what now, my love?" Carrie asked, clutching his arm possessively.

"We have the rest of the night to kill," Mike pointed out, "and most of tomorrow, since the flight doesn't leave until evening. I was thinking of one last tour of Moscow — remember, I'm still gathering last minute inspiration for the next book. How about a look at the imposing front of the Lubyanka Building at night?" He smiled, noting the concern on Carrie's face.

"Michael, isn't that pushing things a bit?" she asked. "Risking being seen outside FSB Headquarters the day after killing that awful major?"

Mike frowned, feigning puzzlement. "Major? What major? FSB Headquarters? — I've never been near the place. Besides, in a modern spy novel, Lubyanka is a must — former home of the KGB, you know.

"Hey — I wonder if they give tours. We need to check on that! And we also need to get some photos of the Saint Basil's Cathedral lit up at night. I still say they reflect some Moslem influence, at least in their shape."

Tony chuckled, "Just don't let a Russian hear you suggest that. And, for God's sake, don't call them minarets within the hearing of a Russian, or they just might try to cart you off to prison."

"As long as it's Lefortovo — I'm actually starting to feel like I know my way around *that* place," Mike joked. "Butyrka, on the other hand, is hell hole. Even Lubyanka is a Four Star Hotel compared to Butyrka."

25: By Rail to Warsaw

Train to Minsk; Monday, Dec 1; 11:10 PM

A lone at last," Mason sighed as he escorted Natasha to their seats. Natasha kept insisting that he lean on a cane to spare his injured legs a little of the effort, but he found he was managing remarkably well. He kept fresh gauze dressings over each bullet wound, mostly to keep Natasha from noticing how far the healing process had progressed, the wounds now closed over as pale pink scar tissue.

If she keeps pressing me for how Michael knows what he knows and can do everything he's done, especially escaping four FSB personnel and a cell in Lubyanka, I may soon have to tell her about vampires, and the fact that I'm technically not entirely human.

"This kind of reminds me of the movie *From Russia With Love*," Natasha whispered, her voice jarring him out of his revery.

"Hopefully without the advent of Robert Shaw's character," Mason teased.

She smiled and kissed him. "No, we certainly don't need him. And I can't wait to see the last of Moscow. I'll be marking off every landmark, every milestone of the journey, especially once we cross the border into Belarus."

The compartment reminded Mason of the interior of Mike's sailboat. Technically it was Natasha's compartment; he had a seat out in one of the many coach cars. Both he and Natasha had feared looking like they were traveling together until they were beyond Belarus. Belarus, in many ways, was more like the old Soviet Union than Russia, still clinging to the outdated system of the government owning everything.

"The ticket agent informed me that there won't even be a border stop to check passports," Mason commented. "We might even sleep all the way to Minsk."

Natasha slipped off her coat and tossed it onto one of two tiny chairs against the wall opposite the narrow bed, a slightly oversized single bunk. "I don't know about *you*, Captain," she whispered, her voice sultry, "but *I'm* not planning to do too much sleeping right away," and she began helping him out of his coat and loosening his tie.

"You seem to have something in mind, my dear," Mason observed, smiling.

"I may have," she teased.

Moments later they were naked, under the covers, and celebrating the hope of soon being free of the confines of the Russian Federation.

The knock on the door jarred Mason back to consciousness.

"Excuse me," a man's voice said in Russian. "We arrive in Minsk in less than an hour."

Mason smiled, amused at his reaction to the knock — *Steady on, old man! Were you expecting the cossacks to burst in? Okay, admit it; you were.*

Early morning sunlight was coming through the shades, and the urban sprawl of outer Minsk was evident the moment he opened them.

"Time to wake up, Tasha," he said, kissing her cheek, until she turned, and then her lips, whereupon her arms slid up around his neck. "Seriously, Natasha," he insisted, "We're almost at the Minsk Station. It's time to gather our luggage, exit the train, and be ready to present our travel documents."

Train to Warsaw; Tuesday, Dec. 2; 10:00 AM

"**Well**, that was entirely painless," Natasha declared as the train pulled out of Minsk. "Even the document check was amazingly fast. I think they were impressed with my Russian FSB credentials. Too bad we had to change trains. I liked that sleeper compartment!"

Mason grinned and took Natasha in his arms. "I'm sure they were eager to change the sheets," he teased, making her blush. He kissed her, making her giggle before kissing him back.

"Right here in the corridor?" she teased. "Don't you think we should find our compartment first?"

"If you insist, Leftenant," he replied, then kissed her again. This time she clung to him longer, prompting passing passengers to say *excuse me* a lot, as they were forced to squeeze past them in the confines of the passageway. "Since you have the tickets, you navigate and I'll tow the luggage."

Moments later Natasha found their compartment and, with a small cry of accomplishment, opened the door, then took her case from him. She studied his face searchingly, looking for traces of him having exerted too much.

"You should have used a porter as I asked," she admonished. "Are you sure you are alright?"

Mason rolled his eyes. "Honestly, darling, you worry too much. The bally thing's on wheels; I just tow it along. I'm fine," he insisted, giving her a charming smile. "I must say; being ticketed as traveling together does guarantee a more spacious sleeping car. Is that a double bed?" He took her in his arms.

Natasha gazed into his eyes, seeing only confidence and love, no sign of pain or undue fatigue, and began to relax.

"I'm starved," she declared in a whisper, "but, before we find a dining car, perhaps we have time for — well, we could make sure the bed is comfortable."

She noticed Mason's smile take on a roguish aspect. "My dear, whatever your heart desires."

Natasha felt she could have spent the day in the compartment. They had two swivel chairs slightly larger than those of the previous train, but, after a slow and extremely attentive session of Mason's lovemaking, they agreed to opt for facing window seats with a table, in a public car, so they could enjoy brunch while taking in the scenery of cattle farms and grain fields, while the train rumbled smoothly along on its westward journey.

This leg of the trip was expected to be almost the same duration as the previous, with an anticipated arrival in Poland's capital at ten o'clock that night.

Tony's man, Nigel, had already arranged reservations at a posh hotel: the Hotel Bristol. *Bli'me, ye can't go wrong wiff a name like ffat! Ev'ryffing is Bristol–fashion at ffe Bristol, eh gov'nor?!*

Natasha smiled, recalling how laughable had been her efforts to decipher the Cockney's crippling of the English language, as well as how proud of himself Nigel had seemed. *Good Lord, he's a talker, but there's something endearing about him.*

After dinner, they adjourned for a while to the sleeper car, but both wanted to watch out the window as the train eventually passed through the city of Brest, just a few miles before the Polish border.

"We've done it!" Mason declared the moment the train had crossed the border. "We're now officially back in NATO territory. Tomorrow we'll take a taxi to the British Embassy, and I can get in touch with MI6 and assure them that I'm safe. I may as well give *C* my notice at the same time."

"Are you sure you want to do that?" Natasha asked, feeling a sudden pang of anxiety. "I don't want you to feel like you have to quit for me."

He looked into her eyes, then shook his head. "Not a single doubt," he assured her. "It's probably overdue. I was under age when I joined, and I continued on long past retirement age."

"But you seem so young; I just can't believe you're as old as you claim!" She stared at him.

"Michael and I sort of share some of the same blood," he finally admitted. "He got all the outrageous talent, but we both heal with astonishing speed — well, he heals *considerably* faster than I — and we both look younger than we actually are — for example, would you guess that Michael was fifty–three last August?"

Natasha was astounded. "Are you kidding? — No; it's clear from your expression that you're not. So, does that mean that you and Michael are related?"

"It's complicated," Mason said. "It also kind of connects to Tony in a way — well, actually, we're both connected to Tony in a way that's —"

"Complicated?" Natasha suggested, smiling at Mason's awkwardness. Then she shrugged and kissed him. "I'll just settle for that and not over–examine a good thing. What's the Western expression about looking a gift horse in the mouth?"

Mason smiled and kissed her back. *How did I get to be so lucky?* he thought with a sigh.

Warsaw, Poland; Tuesday, Dec. 2; 11:42 PM

Mason stood at the window of their room at the Bristol Hotel, glancing out over the city. He'd been here years before, when it had been part of the Soviet Union. *Water under the bridge, old man,* he reminded himself, knowing that part of him would always miss his spy days, but it took only a glance at beautiful Natasha to suppress any regrets he might have about leaving the Service. Moving to the side table, he picked up the phone and called down to order up a first class meal to be served in the room. While awaiting its delivery, he called the British Embassy.

"Yes, Captain Mason," the night attendant assured him, "we were notified to expect both you and Ms. Cherninova — would she prefer to be called *Ms* Cherninova or *Lieutenant* Cherninova? Anyway, congratulations on your escape. We'll expect you in the morning. Is nine o'clock tomorrow morning fine with you, Captain Mason?"

"Your name wouldn't be Pennington–Smythe by any chance, would it?" Mason asked, thinking of the over–eager and mildly annoying MI6 analyst.

The Embassy man *hemmed and hawed,* puzzled, even flustered, but Mason just plowed ahead. "Mark us down for 11:00 AM. We'll want two tickets on the next available flight to London, and enough funds for some new clothes for both of us. We've been managing on borrowed wardrobe since my departure from Lefortovo and my erstwhile FSB hosts. I'm also looking forward to a first class meal in an exclusive restaurant."

"Certainly, Captain. I already have an MI6 credit card in your name right here, as well as a replacement for your SIS credentials. You'll have a flight tomorrow night, British Airways, first class. The dining room in your hotel has an excellent reputation, but I can also recommend *Restaurancja Polska Rozana*, just a few blocks from The Bristol. And, Sir, it's Faversham, not — what was that name you suggested?"

Mason grinned. "Very good, Faversham. See you tomorrow at 11:00 AM."

26: *Dodging the Storm*

FSB HQ, Lubyanka Bldg, Moscow
Tuesday, Dec. 2, 3:20 PM

Colonel Ilya Kalugin frowned as he studied the report for the third time. Surveillance camera footage showed Major Dyatlov's car pulling up in front of the *Radisson Slavyanskaya,* a major airport hotel for Domodedovo, and that was only confirmed by a lucky camera from a business diagonally across the street. After the major and his men exited the car, there was nothing else: The hotel's surveillance system seemed entirely defective. Kalugin wasn't sure if it was a coincidence or something more suspicious. The next camera to pick up the car was at the emergency entrance to a Moscow hospital, where Corporal Yazmenov got out and staggered in, still gripping his head.

Dyatlov arrives at the hotel, then no more Dyatlov. But Dyatlov was found dead in the basement of this very building, with the ominous message, written in blood on the floor next to him.

What about cameras in the atrium? He brought up the security feed from the main entrance. Sure enough, there was Dyatlov, showing his ID to the attendant, then proceeding to the basement stairs, and there were the two corporals, dragging a prisoner between them, with the third bringing up the rear *and blocking the camera's view of the prisoner!*

Ilya had instructed the forensic techs to test Dyatlov's fingers with *Luminol*, thinking that Dyatlov might have written the message himself while dying, but the tests proved negative. Dyatlov's killer had written the message, and Dyatlov must have picked up his killer at the hotel and taken him to Lubyanka.

"So, Grigori, what were you doing at a designated tourist hotel?" he mused, then continued to reread the followup report by the captain who led his investigative team. "You inquired at the concierge's desk about a package left for an M.D. Cameron.

"Let's see what your files have to say, Grigori," he mused, then used his superior rank to over–ride the major's security and access his computer files. He had to tread carefully — his uncle, a former KGB general, stationed in the US, had been declared a traitor, and taken asylum in America. Ilya suspected that his uncle had been framed by a greedily ambitious inferior, but that didn't offer any solace for being left permanently overcast by the cloud of suspicion he'd left behind. *No, he told himself, only an excess of conscientiousness and success can wash away that stain.*

He turned his attention back to the screen.

"Still obsessed with stalking your busty swimmer, Grigori?" he mused, shaking his head. "In a world of top–rank female swimmers, you have to fixate on the only one to actually grow a pair of tits. *Tsk, Tsk, Tsk.* So your flag on her in the system alerted you to the fact that General Kashirin had ordered travel documents for her, valid for six months. And you were also monitoring Kashirin's activities? The plot thickens. So, Kashirin, what are *you* up to? Is this a reward or some sort of balm for the long–suffering lieutenant? Since there was also a cash dispensation, I suspect the latter."

Further reading told him that there had been a clandestine meeting between Kashirin and a western spy with the codename of *Samurai,* and the general had promised to drop off papers at the hotel desk, marked for pickup by this M.D. Cameron. *So, Dyatlov, you implanted your Corporal Yazmenov among the general's commandoes, and he reported back to you, went with you, and ended up in the hospital, allegedly from a stroke, with almost no memory of the past week.*

There was no M.D. Cameron in the system, just Border Control noting his arrival, purpose of visit, etc., but there was an Agent *Samurai.* "The Canadian Security and Intelligence Service," he mused aloud. "More like MI5 than MI6. So why would this capture your attention so, Grigori.

"Of course," he muttered, nodding to himself. "Kashirin was using this *Samurai* as a courier to deliver travel documents, and you feared your precious Natasha would finally give you the slip? How pathetic of you, Grigori. *And how pathetic of you,* General Kashirin, using a foreign agent to help you emancipate your — your what? She's too young for you, Kashirin, and yet you stole five–thousand American dollars from the special projects fund to give to her. I'll have to keep an eye on you, Kashirin. As for you, Grigori, The Russian Federation is probably better off without you. Still, there must be more to this. M.D. Cameron is Canadian, an obscure author, over fifty, married, has a history of martial–arts involvement..."

A few more keystrokes brought up Cameron's immigration information, passport photo, and statistics — age: 53, height: 173 cm; weight: 79.3 kg; hair: dark brown/greying; eyes: blue; build: athletic.

Agent *Samurai*: No photos, but — age: estimated at 25 to 30, height: about 173 cm; weight: about 79 kg; hair: dark brown, almost black; eyes: brilliant blue; build: lean and athletic. Known associates: None confirmed, but speculated as knowing Anthony Dewhurst of Interpol, Samuel Larkin of the CIA, and Bruce Mason of MI6. Special skills: Advanced martial arts training, and, seemingly an expert with swords, most notably the katana or Samurai longsword.

He glanced at his own brown–hilted katana, in a lacquered stand on his desk — an authentic 15th–Century piece, made by an outlawed swordsmith, awarded to him some years back.

"Well, Mr. Cameron, if not for your age, you'd be a fair match to the mysterious Agent *Samurai*, and, by an astounding coincidence, you just happen to be traveling with your uncle, Anthony Dewhurst.

"Was it you that Major Dyatlov was really after?"

He continued to read — in northern Romania, this *Samurai* was alleged, aided by a witch, if one can believe such drivel, to have caused one Count Gregore Dragomir Torok to burst into flames. But then, most available witnesses insisted that Count Torok was a vampire and a monster. *Isn't that a bit redundant,* he pondered with a chuckle, *Aren't all vampires monsters?*

The system next told him that Cameron, his wife, and Dewhurst had confirmed a late flight to London, moving the date of their scheduled return up by eight days. "Finished researching your book already, Mr. Cameron, or did *Samurai* conclude his mission sooner than expected?"

He picked up the phone and called surveillance, to learn that the cameras and microphones in Cameron's suite had become defective soon after his arrival, then the hard–drive was inexplicably fried, destroying what little data had been gathered, with just a few printed photos and a scant few pages of uninteresting transcript remaining — just a day before the entire hotel system went out.

He punched another button on his phone. "Anya, get me the front desk of the *Radisson Slavyanskaya*."

"I'm sorry, Colonel, but Mr. Cameron and his party just checked out, leaving the London address of Mr. Dewhurst as a forwarding address. Mrs. Cameron said something about wishing they could have had one last evening tour of Moscow before taking the train to the airport. They had all their luggage with them, including the cat carrier with two Siamese cats."

"I don't give a damn about Siamese cats!" Kalugin declared, slamming down the phone. "What kind of moron goes on a spy mission and takes his cats?"

His eyes returned to the katana, and his lips pulled back in a sneer. *I will find you, Samurai. Perhaps it will come down to you and I seeing just which of us is the superior kenjutsu–ka.*

Domodedovo Airport, Moscow
Tuesday, Dec. 2, 7:58 PM

Mike spotted the Border Control officer watching him, and smiled. Getting Carrie and Tony's attention, he projected, *It's our old friend Sergeant Cherninov. I think he spotted us and remembers us from arriving, Carrie in particular*, he added, noting how Cherninov was grinning in Carrie's direction.

"Sergeant Cherninov," Mike greeted.

"Mr. Cameron," the sergeant replied cheerfully. "The first of your vampire novels was very thrilling — I finished it last night. I trust you had a productive visit, and found inspiration for the next one."

"Extremely productive, though there were a few surprises," he responded, jerking his head indicatively at Carrie, then set the cat carrier on the counter.

"Yes, I met your wife and your blue–eyed cats upon her arrival," the officer commented. "Your early departure, suggests that she came to bring you home."

"And brought the cats to help make her point," Mike added with a smile.

"So, will you soon be ready to write the next book or have you already started?" Cherninov asked. "That first one consumed my attention until I finished it. I promise to read the others, and will be watching for the newest one."

"Thank you," Mike replied. He tapped the side of his head and added, "There's a lot up here and maybe a hundred photos to sift through. It could be a month or more before I get started, but, once I do, I expect it'll just pour out. Some days I can't type fast enough."

The officer's eyes widened in fascination. "I can't imagine — but," he let out a hearty laugh, "if I had your imagination, I would be writing books, instead of this mundane day–after–day duty." He shrugged and looked about, as if fearing having been overheard.

Then he froze, staring at the screen.

Mike went into his head immediately, calming him, and reading the screen through his eyes.

Stop and detain Michael David Cameron and Anthony Dewhurst, by order of Colonel Ilya Kalugin, Department S, Moscow FSB.

Mike wished he could reach into the system and delete the info the way he did with the surveillance cameras.

Tony? Can you get Nigel to do something about this? I wouldn't want them to ground the flight.

Tony tapped into Mike's view of the screen, then pulled out his iPhone, called Nigel, and had him on the phone almost immediately.

"Sure ffing, yer Lordship," he chirped. "I'll 'ave 'er done in a jiff."

Mike pictured the diminutive hacker typing in a fury, then the flashing notation disappeared.

He made a quick gesture for Carrie and Tony's passports and departure cards, passed them to Sergeant

Cherninov, flashed a smile, *We're good, here, Pavel,* he said in Cherninov's head, and — *Stamp, Stamp, Stamp* — they were through. He hadn't even scanned their luggage, and Mike's Walther was in Carrie's bulkier suitcase, rather than his almost insignificant kitbag.

"It's been a pleasure meeting you, Pavel," Mike said as they were leaving for the departure lounge.

The frown of puzzlement on the sergeant's face amused Mike. *How did he know my name?* he read in the officer's mind.

Mike had a sudden mental flash — *danger!* — *a group of uniformed FSB soldiers, commando–types, pushing their way through the crowds, trying to converge on their location.*

Then, from out of nowhere, blurs of movement — Soldiers thrown into walls, disarmed, their weapons tossed beyond their reach.

One soldier manages to stab an assailant in the chest with his commando knife — Mike recognizes Aleksandr Nicholaiovitch — Aleksandr pulls the knife free and buries it in the commando's chest, then seizes him by the shoulders and tears into his throat.

It triggers greater violence on both sides, but the alarmed FSB commandoes can't even see their attackers! Blood sprays against a wall!

Then, clear and strong in his mind, — *Your vay is clear, Michael Cameron. Have a safe journey home.*

Mike smiled and projected, *Thank you, Aleksandr Nicholaiovitch. You are a good friend. If ever you need me...*

In less than an hour the plane was airborne and on it's way to London.

"I'm sorry, sir," the very British first class steward said, "we don't have *Glenlivet*. Will *Glenfiddich* do?" He was in his mid–twenties and seemed nervous.

"New at the job?" Mike asked, to which the steward gave a rapid nod. Mike was about to explain how the two brands were almost indistinguishable, being made in the same region, their water coming from the same river, but he just smiled and said: "*Glenfiddich* will be fine."

He and Carrie were in a central three–seat spread in the business class area — Mike decided he detested the one– and two–seat cubicles. Kato and Teila's carry case sat on the seat between them, door open, and Kato had just ventured out and onto Mike's lap. Teila was in the process of seeing peeking out, then, with a quick *mew?* to ask permission, made a scurry to Carrie's lap, where she began kneading — *making bread*, as Carrie called it. Kato had hardly settled on Mike before he began his pathetic tug–of–war for Mike's thumb.

"I'm sorry, sir, but — *oh, my, how cute!*"

Mike looked up to find a prissy–looking attendant, her eyes darting back–and–forth between the two cats, mostly watching Kato's determined effort to suck Mike's thumb.

"They just need a moment to feel reassured, then they'll go back in the carrier with minimal objection," he assured her.

She continued to frown, shaking her head. "I'm sorry, sir, but it *is* against regulations. Besides, I have a cat, and know how impossible it is to get *him* into a cage. I assume that yours, being larger, is a male."

Mike frowned. "Wow. Male bashing extends to cats, too? Don't listen to her, Kato. Just show her how well you behave." He fixed a glance on Kato, catching the attention of the eyes that were so similar to his own, when he wasn't using glamour (like now) to disguise that fact, and gave a sharp snap of his fingers.

Kato muttered a complaining grumble, arose, turned, gave his tail a swish, and entered the carrier, turning to glare with baleful disdain at the attendant.

"You, too, Teila," Mike said.

"*Mew*?" she asked.

"Yes, you, too," Carrie replied, and she followed suit, huddling into a crouch just in front of Kato.

"Well, I'll be —"

"— Ignoring these two exceptionally well-behaved first class passengers?" Mike finished for her, raising his eyebrows.

"Well, I'm sure they won't be a problem," she conceded, looking just a tad glassy-eyed, then walked on to continue her rounds.

You compelled her, Carrie said in his head.

Mike cracked a smile. "Just a little," he admitted aloud, then snapped his fingers just enough that Kato took it as an invitation to resume position on his lap.

"*Mew*?" Teila asked.

"Yes, you can come out, too, Teila," he added with a hint of a chuckle.

"What's Tony doing with his laptop over there?" Carrie asked.

Mike glanced over at the single cubicle, which hid all but the barest glimpse of his great-great-great-great-grandfather. Mike could hear Nigel's voice and it's Cockney-crippling of the English language coming from Tony's headphones.

"He's FaceTiming with Nigel," he explained.

"How can he do that?" Carrie queried. "We're on an airplane!" Her expression bespoke bewilderment.

"I'd heard something about certain first class flights having WiFi," Mike told her, and gave a shrug. "I can only assume that this is one of those flights."

Mike spent most of the flight collating notes on his iPad, while Carrie watched what Mike liked to tease was a *Chick's Movie*. He felt almost brain-dead from excessive mind–linking with Tony to update him on everything he'd gleaned from Kemedov, as well as his own instincts on what might be about to unfold concerning Russia and Ukraine. The cats were curled up in their carry–cage, asleep, looking for all the world like one cat with two tails and two heads.

Before long, Mike put his iPad away, leaned his head back, and let his mind reach out throughout the giant airplane. All seemed peaceful. Most of the travelers were tourists, a few traveling on business. There were several Americans, returning from pre–Olympic tours of Sochi. None were FSB or SVR.

Well, that's a relief, he decided.

He then tried experimenting with an astral excursion, but that was almost terrifying. He'd barely left his body when he felt himself being hurled backward toward the rear of the plane at what he estimated was about 300 knots!

He immediately latched onto the back of a seat, using spiritual energy and chi to maintain his grip. Then, reaching out to the seat back in front of him, he took a grip, let go of his current hold, and pulled himself forward. He soon found he could reach ahead several seats and, by the dint of this tedious method, finally made his way back to his body, feeling immense relief once he was back inside himself.

He was chuckling in embarrassment when a steward stopped to ask if he required anything.

"Yes; a double *Glenfiddich*, neat."

"Very good, sir. If I might suggest, sir; we also have a premium 25–year–old *Glenmorangie*."

Mike smiled. "Sold," he said. "And deliver a single to my friend in the cubicle across the way, with my compliments."

27: *In Warsaw*

British Embassy, Warsaw, Poland

Mason grimaced and rolled his eyes. "No, sir; I'm afraid my mind is made up," Pulling the phone away from his ear, he let Sir John Sawers, *C* of MI6, ramble on, trying to convince him to remain with the Service, then interjected: "Sir, I've considered it for years, the last eight in particular. And, yes, of course I'll stay on for at least a month into the new year: time enough to train a new man for the position, but I will need extra time over Christmas. We have a trip planned — No, sir, to Scotland. I have no interest in returning to Europe at the moment; we're, frankly, focused on getting *the hell out* of Europe."

He heaved a sigh. "Yes, sir, I'm sure I can manage at least one media interview. Yes, sir, I can just imagine the field day the opposition had with this, especially with the liberal press stretching negative speculation to the limit. No, sir, I'm positive that *Samurai* doesn't care about getting credit. If you think he's some sort of glory hound, then I'm afraid you've missed the mark entirely with *Samurai*, which won't help you any should you ever feel in need of his assistance again."

He grinned suddenly. "Really, sir? Not just Pennington–Smythe, but Harry Potter *and* Ronald

Weasley? Yes, sir, as a matter of fact, I do find it amusing. It has Nigel, Tony's hacker friend's, mark all over it. No, sir, it's intended to make a fool out of the *Daily Examiner*, not the Service. Besides, sir, Samurai told me he'd warned you about this right after he had Nigel prepare the fake copies."

Mason rolled his eyes, pulled the phone away from his ear again, looked at the clock on Faversham's wall, then said, "Yes, sir, — the moment I'm back in London, at least, as soon as it's business hours."

Natasha Cherninova was biting a hand to keep from laughing.

"*Thank God that's over with!*" Mason declared as he hung up the phone. *M* at least had been a field agent, with some years as a *double–0*. Guess what you get when you cross a scientist with a diplomat, then post him to a job as a bureaucrat." He rolled his eyes one last time, knowing it would make her erupt into gales of laughter, which it did, until tears were rolling down her beautiful face.

"The good news," he announced, "is that I was still earning my salary during my time of captivity, plus an over–sized bonus — somewhere between danger pay and injury compensation. I think it's a bribe to head off any future claims for damages — half of our soldiers who came back from Iraq or Afghanistan have PTSD."

He took her by the arm. "My dear, I say we start with lunch, then go shopping. I need a new suit and a new watch. I'll be needing a new cellphone, too, but that'll have to wait until I'm back in the UK. Then there's you: I've seen your wardrobe, Tasha. You have a few lovely things, but, it's clear that you spent too many years in uniform, and on far too oppressed a budget. Today's mission: something fetching to wear to the best four– or five–star restaurant in Warsaw." Turning to Faversham: "What was the place you recommended over the phone, old man?"

Faversham smiled. "That would be *Restaurancja Polska Rozana*, sir. I'll write it down, along with the directions, but any cabbie will know where it is."

Two hours later they were walking along the sidewalk in Warsaw's most fashionable shopping district, Mason wheeling a new suitcase by it's extended handle, most of the results of their shopping stored inside the new piece of luggage, as well as the clothes they'd worn when they set out that morning. The other results of their shopping excursion were reflected in their fashionably–dressed appearance, right down to Mason's new *Rolex Submariner*.

Mason paused, smiling, then drew Natasha's attention to something in a window display.

Still pretending to chuckle, he said in an undertone, "Tasha, darling, we have a tail — you can see him in the window's reflection, across the street, in the doorway of that older building. Two decades ago I'd have called him KGB, so I'm guessing he's SVR. Do you know him?"

Natasha studied the man in the reflection, then Mason felt a shiver run through her. "He's FSB: Major Bryutin of Dept. S — *special assignments*, headed by Colonel Ilya Kalugin."

"Kalugin," Mason mused. "Any relation to General Oleg Kalugin, formerly of the KGB?"

"A nephew, and eager to please the Kremlin," she affirmed. "ever since his uncle defected to the West."

"Actually, my dear," Mason corrected, "that's the Russian version, or, more specifically, his underling, Kryuchkov's, version. Kryuchkov set him up, and accused him of treason. A lot of his contemporaries went to their graves insisting that he was fiercely loyal to the KGB, but, when Kalugin stayed in the US and took up a teaching post at a university, the Kremlin decided it confirmed his treason.

"As for Kryuchkov's alleged loyalty to *Mother Russia*, after becoming the head of the KGB, he orchestrated the 1991 coup attempt.

"But, of greater concern to us is: to prove his own loyalty, your Colonel Ilya will be ultra–zealous in any assignment given him. Well, let's stroll on a little further and see just how much of an assignment we are to our current shadow, Major Bryutin."

They continued along at a desultory pace, laughing a lot, stopping to peruse window displays. Then, at a shoe store display, Natasha stopped and pointed.

"Those shoes would be perfect with the evening dress I just bought," she declared, taking a two–handed grip on his arm.

Mason smiled. "Since the dress is for tonight's dinner," he suggested, "we certainly can't have you enter the most posh restaurant in all Warsaw barefoot!"

Moments later: "Now where did our man Bryutin get to?" Mason asked when they exited the store, black lady's pumps added to the contents of the suitcase.

"I see him," Natasha murmured. With a burst of feigned laughter, she pointed to something at an angle across the street, then added, "twenty degrees left of where I'm pointing."

Mason followed the line from her fingertip and angled the necessary twenty degrees left, then spotted Bryutin in what might be the recessed doorway to private apartments above a store. He had his right hand to his ear, and his lips were moving. *Talking on a cellphone? Talking to whom?*

The next store specialized in shoes and purses.

Mason smiled as an idea took shape — Moments later he and Natasha were inside the shop, and Natasha was looking excitedly at purses — "*FSB officers don't fuss over purses,*" she imitated. "*especially candidates for promotion to second class lieutenant* — or so I was once warned by a nasty colleague."

"Well, my dear, why don't you take your time and browse. I'll rejoin you in a few minutes."

Her face snapped back to his, her eyes locked onto his in an intent gaze.

"Trust me, Tasha; I feel fine. This is just something I need to do." He felt like she was struggling to probe his thoughts — not so much how it felt when Michael raided his brain, but perhaps the beginnings of the same talent.

"Don't worry," he assured her. "I promise to be gone no longer than ten minutes."

The moment he saw her gaze relax, he turned to the sales lady and asked if there was a back way out of the shop, and was soon in a back alley, following it past the neighbouring shop until he found another break, little more than a walkway back to the street. In fact, the lane continued across the street beside the building from where the FSB man was conducting his surveillance.

Mason flattened himself against the side of the shop, just a foot from the sidewalk. Traffic was minimal, pedestrian traffic almost nonexistent — it had been that way all day, Mason assumed because it was the middle of the week.

Bryutin was still staring at the front entrance of Natasha's shoe and purse shop. Then, he pulled out his phone once more, studying the screen. *Identifying an incoming call?*

Mason leaned his cane against the brickwork, and made his move. In a burst of speed that surprised and amazed him, he tore across the street and into the continuation of his narrow lane, flattening against Bryutin's building, just shy of the sidewalk.

"No, they're just shopping. You'd think they were on holiday," Bryutin was saying in Russian into his phone. "I have no idea who the man is; I've never seen him before, and haven't been able to get a picture of him.".... "Okay, — Yes, I've got it."... "Yes, I'd say that's him, at least it looks like him. If the surveillance subject is a top–level MI6 supervisor, why was he in Russia, and how did Lt. Cherninova come to know him?"... "I see. So what do you want me to do?"... "Yes, Colonel; I will continue to watch. If anything occurs, I will call. Yes, Colonel, I will not allow them to escape. Please repeat that Colonel. Yes, sir: Terminate rather than lose contact. Both of them, sir? Lt. Cherninova as well? Yes, sir."

Mason strained to hear more, but Bryutin seemed to have put his phone away.

He frowned. *Time to act.* He reached his hand just past the corner of the brickwork and snapped his fingers twice in quick succession. It got exactly the response he'd planned: Bryutin stepped out to the corner, looking about suspiciously. Mason grabbed him, spun a three–quarter turn, and slammed him against the brickwork, bracing his left forearm against the Department S man's throat.

Immediately, Bryutin pulled a Makarov PM, Russia's inferior copy of the Walther PPK.

Mason's right hand shot to Bryutin's hair, the left hand found an inverted grip on Bryutin's throat, and the right hand yanked the head toward Bryutin's shoulder.

"Drop it or I'll —" Bryutin went limp; the Makarov clattered to the asphalt.

"... Break... your... neck," Mason voiced the rest of his sentence, puzzled by what had happened.

A rapid survey of his surroundings verified that there were no witnesses. He felt for a pulse, found none, then confiscated the pistol and rifled Bryutin's pockets for any ID, finding a wallet and an FSB ID, which he pocketed. After a few more rushed moments, he'd stripped off Bryutin's coat and relieved him of his shoulder holster, then shrugged off his own jacket to don the holster, holstered the Makarov, then pulled his jacket back on.

Let's hope I can make it back to the opposite alley as fast as I just crossed the street, he thought, then amazed himself again by how fast he could move over a short distance. It worried him — he was recalling Michael's recount of his experiences in 2008, during the months before an assassin's bullet through his heart forever changed him.

Steady on, old man — let's not forget, Michael was still in the eighth grade when he exceeded the high school record for the hundred–yard dash, and that was thirty years before irrevocably changing. Surely my speed crossing the street wasn't much faster than his talented sprint back then. As for breaking Bryutin's neck, yes, that was more than my usual strength, but it was probably as much due to human adrenaline as any vampire influence.

"At least, that's what I'll keep telling myself — for now," he muttered, forcing a roguish smile.

Reclaiming his cane, he made his way to the alley behind the shops, then to the back of the shop where Natasha awaited his return. He entered, and found Natasha admiring a small black evening bag, though she seemed distracted. One glance told Mason it would fit in perfectly with the black evening dress and stylish dress pumps she'd just acquired.

"I'd say that's perfect," he announced, the sound of his voice causing her head to jerk in his direction.

Her face reflected a mix of shock and relief. Purses seemingly forgotten, she ran into his arms, burying her face into his chest. He could feel the dampness of free–flowing tears.

"It's alright," he assured her in a whisper. "Surveillance has been discontinued for a time."

She looked up, sniffed a few times, then tried to wipe her eyes. Mason forestalled her by whipping out a brand–new handkerchief, and blotting her tears before allowing her to take the handkerchief in her hand. She immediately burst into a radiant smile.

"But how?" she began.

"That, my dear, is a tale for over lunch. There must be a restaurant near–by; perhaps your clerk here can advise. And, I see she's holding a larger, more practical, purse for you."

He turned to the clerk and, flashing his roguish smile, pulled out his wallet, extracted his new credit card, and announced, "We'll take them both. Perhaps you can recommend a nearby restaurant where we can grab lunch. I do declare, I'm suddenly famished — positively ravenous."

Natasha objected immediately, hissing, "Mason, you know I have money from General Kashirin —"

"And, as soon as we're safely back in England and you're settled in, you can deposit that in a bank," he insisted. "You are starting a new life, Tasha; you don't want to burn through your windfall in the first week."

She smiled a sheepish smile. "There is so much I'll have to get used to," she sighed, "so very many good things, now that I'm with you and out of Russia."

As it turned out, the recommended restaurant was just past the end of the block. They took a table by the front window, affording them a broad view of the street, and Mason gave a synopsis of his exploits with Bryutin, let her glimpse the Makarov he'd appropriated, then passed her the FSB ID.

"We can't be carrying those about," she cautioned him, then, "I'm sorry — of course you know that. Forgive me, Mason, it's my anxiety and irrational fear of the FSB. It's the same fear the KGB drilled into me as a young woman. You have no idea: They rule the public through fear." She forced a smile.

Mason felt the waves of butterflies and warmth racing through him. *Steady on, old man*, he told himself. *Even her forced smiles illuminate her face. It's a good thing you're retiring, old chum; you'd be useless in the field with her on your mind all the time.*

He turned his attention back to the menu. "I could really go for a rare steak," he declared, "but, in light of tonight's plan for The *Restaurancja Polska Rozana*, I think I'll settle for a small roasted chicken breast and a salad."

Natasha smiled. "Just the salad, for me."

"Dressing, ma'am?" the waiter asked. "We have an excellent Russian dressing, as well as our own house vinaigrette, which is very popular."

An air of mischief coloured Natasha's smile. "I'll have the vinaigrette. I think I'll be avoiding anything Russian for some time."

Mason disassembled the FSB ID into its component parts, pocketing them, planning to dispose of them separately, then began to do the same with Bryutin's wallet. He ignored the Rubles, but pocketed a considerable wad of Euros.

Moments later the sound of sirens announced the arrival of the Polish police — the body had been discovered and reported. *Unidentified man found dead in an alley in a fashionable Warsaw shopping district*, Mason imagined the police report, knowing they'd puzzle over the broken neck and lack of other signs of violence on the body. *No ID — no way to even trace the nationality — his fingerprints aren't in the Polish system. Perhaps we should forward the prints to Interpol.* It all made Mason smile.

"Do you think we have time to walk back to the hotel?" he asked Natasha, "Or should we flag a cab?"

Natasha pursed her lips in what Mason decided was a kissably endearing manner, wagged her head slightly, then said, "I think we can walk, especially after the size of this salad! — That is, unless your legs are bothering you any."

"My legs are remarkably good, considering that, until less than a week ago, they were each carrying a bullet from that assassin's weapon Anatoli fired at me." He frowned, recalling how he'd dashed across the street in — what? — three seconds? — two seconds? — then shrugged. "I'm fine, and I still have my cane."

They had nothing to do but enjoy the pleasant stroll back to the hotel. Six blocks from the site of the incident with Bryutin, Mason began tossing bits of the Russian assassin's ID into separate trash receptacles, sometimes making use of storm drains, until all that remained was the wallet and the Makarov. The wallet went to a trash receptacle, having been thoroughly wiped of prints. Mason decided to keep the Makarov.

"So much for Major Bryutin," Mason commented with a smile. "I doubt Colonel Kalugin will be hearing back from him any time soon."

He pondered it all — Bryutin following Natasha and him — *How did he get on our trail? Why would — Of course! It's Me he was after! Michael may have erased the camera data at Lefortovo, and Nigel scrubbed the system, but Dyatlov knew about Natasha's travel documents, so he must also have known about mine, and he knew about* Samurai *having met with General Kashirin. Could they be trying to find Michael? I need to warn him!*

But, surely he and Tony know Dyatlov's death will not have severed connections to Michael and Samurai, *even though the only survivor, the corporal who'd been planted in Kashirin's tach group for that day, has had his memory compromised.*

"I think we should flag the next available cab," he confided to Natasha. Then, seeing her look of concern he added, "Don't worry; it's not my legs; I need to make a call to Nigel. If all went according to plan, Michael and Tony will, hopefully, be landing back in London sometime today. It occurs to me that Michael may have been the main focus of FSB interest, and not you, though, it may also have been me, to some extent."

He'd barely spoken when Natasha stepped off the curb, threw up her arm, and a cab swerved in and screeched to a halt in front of them.

"Your cab, sir," Natasha said, her eyes twinkling with mischief. "It's all the the posture," she joked. "I think I was just into my twenties when I discovered how easy it was for me to stop a taxi."

"You may have been in your twenties when you first *tried* to stop a taxi," Mason teased with a grin, "but I'm sure you were stopping traffic a few years before twenty."

28: London

Heathrow Airport, London
9:15 AM, Tues., Dec. 3

Mike scanned the crowd as they made their way to the luggage carrousel, reaching out, sensing for evidence of danger. It could have been someone watching too intently, following covertly, or just something that decided to nag his sixth sense for danger. *Sixth sense*, he mused. *How many people out there give credit to their sixth sense, not realizing that's it's an innate clue to their own witch skills, evidence of Wiccan ancestry.*

I think we're good, my love, Carrie said in his head. *I can't find a hint of anything out of the ordinary.*

Nor I, dear boy, Tony chimed in. *In fact, I can't even find a trace of anyone from MI6. I half expected Nigel to be here — even Wentworth Pennington–Smythe would be a welcome sight at this point. Of course, either of them would have been forced to wait beyond the quarantine zone around Customs.*

Mike just shrugged it off. He wasn't eager to encounter anyone from MI6 just yet. As far as he was concerned, the mission wasn't over until he met up with Mason and saw him safely to Vauxhall Cross. The mission was to rescue and successfully return Mason to

MI6, not rescue and abandon him in Moscow. He still felt guilty about that.

They breezed through Customs and Immigration, partly on Tony's Interpol ID, though largely from Mike compelling the agent.

Nigel met them just beyond the quarantine area.

"Can I stop 'oldin' me breaff now?" he joked. "I kep' picturin' some bloke tryin' to garrote you on 'e plane, an' you 'avin' to go all Bruce Lee over 'im!"

Mike gave a half smile and thanked Nigel for coming to meet them.

"Yes, old man," Tony added, giving Nigel a clap on the back, "I dare say, I dreaded the prospect of *C* sending Pennington–Smythe to meet us, if *C* even knows we're coming."

"Oh, ye can believe Mr. FaceBook knows yer arrivin' t'day," Nigel announced. "Mason, it seems, 'ad a lengffy chat wiff 'im from Warsaw, so he 'as to know yer on ffe way.

"Anyway, I go' a van ou' fron', and I'm sure yer anxious te ge' back to ffe flat."

———

The moment they were inside Tony's flat, Mike set the cage down and opened the door.

Ra-a-owww! Kato announced his displeasure at having been confined, while Teila just took off at a dash, looking for the litter pan. Kato leaped up into Mike's arms, pushed the top of his head into Mike's jaw, then dropped to the floor to pursue Teila.

"Well, I gotta be 'eadin' back to ffe office," Nigel announced. "I go' Gregory 'elpin' wiff tracking 'e movements of anyone suspected o' bein' SVR, FSB, or former KGB spooks."

"And I'll call *C*, just in case his feathers need smoothing," Tony offered.

Mike shrugged.

He was just settling back on a sofa, Kato pestering for his thumb, when Tony took an unexpected FaceTime request from Nigel.

"Mason jus' 'ad a bi' of adventure wiff 'e Ruskies. Polish coppers jus' foun' a body in an alley, in whot ffey're callin' *a fashionable Warsaw shoppin' distric'*. Looks like ffere were a bit of a dust up, maybe fifteen minutes ago, involving one Drago Bryutin, a major in 'e FSB's Dept. S — ffat's ffeir special assignments department 'eaded by Colonel Ilya Kalugin, made up mos'ly of assassins. Polish Intelligence identified ffe stiff, since someone — an I'm gonna put my money on yer boy Mason — made off wiff 'is ID, an' 'is sidearm — I'm guessing: Makarov PMM. *AN'* Yer Lordship, ffere weren' a mark on ffe body, jus' a broken neck."

"Natasha may have recognized Bryutin and identified him for Mason," Mike mused. "The broken neck is easy enough to explain, though Mason's strength could be escalating."

He stepped up beside Tony, and saw his face come into view on the screen. "What about Mason's flight?" he asked.

"It were booked by ffe Embassy, an' leaves tonigh' at 11:30, arrivin' on 'e tarmac at 'Eaffrow in 'e wee earlies — 'bou' 2:00 AM. Anyffing else, gov'nor?"

Mike glanced at his watch — 10:18 AM, London time — a little over fifteen hours until Mason and Natasha's flight was due to arrive.

"Look for suspicious arrivals here in London and anyone out of the ordinary on their flight. Start with known assets from Major Kalugin's section."

"Kalugin," Tony mused. "Nigel, check on a connection between your Major Ilya Kalugin and former KGB General Oleg Kalugin."

More typing. "Go' it, Yer Lordship — 'is nephew, an' it looks like ffey're watchin' 'im like an 'awk."

Tony nodded. "Oleg and I have considerable history," he confided to Mike. "He was conscientious and loyal, though it always felt like a friendly chess match with Oleg. He got set up by an ambitious and jealous underling — framed. Since he was already in the US at the time, there was no reason for him not to stay. That only made the hardliners more convinced of his guilt. The main issue is, his nephew will be out to prove his loyalty, and, if Bryutin is any indication, brutally ruthless in his efforts."

"For Mason dealing with Bryutin like that, he must have felt pressed," Mike suggested. "So, were they after him or after Natasha?"

"Well, dear boy, since Natasha had leave to be on vacation, I'd say they were after Mason," Tony suggested, his voice showing signs of extreme fatigue. "Mason being in Russia was orchestrated. How embarrassing would his escape be on top of that?"

"Embarrassing enough," Mike offered, realizing that he, too, was starting to fade. "If Bryutin spotted Natasha with Mason, he might have decided that she helped him escape, which doesn't bode well for her. Putin will want them both back, but especially Mason. He has a plan in place, and he's not known for abandoning plans willingly. Whatever he's got in mind for Donetsk, Luhansk, and Kharkiv, he'll be determined to find a way..."

Carrie crept up behind him, gave him a feeble cuddle. "I'm done — going to bed," she murmured groggily, then departed for the stairs leading up to the bedroom, clinging with both hands to the rail as she ascended.

"I dare say we're all on our last legs," Tony said. "I suggest we all give it up until after the void."

Tues. evening (Warsaw Time)

Mason finished straightening his tie, it's navy blue standing out in stark contrast against the crisp arctic white of his shirt, then did up the buttons of his vest, navy blue with pale grey pinstripes. He was just pulling on the matching jacket of his new three–piece suit when Natasha made her entrance.

Mason could only stare in wonder as she emerged from the bathroom, where she'd been closeted for close to an hour. The 'little black dress', as the sales clerk had called it, fit her as if she'd been poured into it. *No, he decided, still staring in awe, 'sprayed on' is far closer to the mark.* The cut of bodice showed just enough décolletage to be distracting.

Her black dress pumps, polished to a high sheen, had ankle straps and just enough enclosed toe to cover her toes. The medium heels added another couple of inches to her height. Finishing it all off was the tiny evening bag — *a clutch on a tether,* the clerk had joked — which hung from her shoulder. But most amazing was how much the subtle touches of makeup had transformed her — barely more than a hint of blush on her cheeks, some lip gloss, some bronzing on her upper eyelids, and cautious use of mascara.

Then he realized: The time she'd spent applying her look, while studying herself in the mirror, had allowed her to get in touch with her femininity, so long repressed by being forced to wear a military–style uniform. For what may have been the first time in years, she had seen herself as being beautiful, and, feeling beautiful, it came glowing through.

Her hair, always healthy, now shone with a resounding luster, and even exhibited a subtle hint of waviness he'd never noticed before, cascading over her shapely shoulders in ripples. He could only stare, amazed and enthralled.

"Tasha, you are —," he breathed, almost in a stammer, "Well, dearest Tasha, I can't find the words to describe how beautiful you are. And your hair, —"

"I know," she declared. "All I could do was brush it, but, after the hot shower, the more it dried, it just seemed to want to pull back into waves, no matter how hard I brushed it. My mother had —" Natasha paused, a look of sadness coming over her. "My mother died suddenly, struck by a car, hit–and–run, probably a drunk driver — Russia, is rampant with them." She forced her frown back into a smile. "She had incredibly wavy hair, claiming that she'd gotten it via an ancestor who was a Romani gypsy, one of those *Szgany* of the Carpathian Mountains in Transylvania."

"Michael and Carrie will want to hear about that," Mason breathed, barely a whisper, as he continued to stare, abruptly aware that he was fighting back tears. He blinked away the moisture, then added awkwardly, "They spent a few months in the Carpathians, among such Romanian gypsies." Then, in a deep breath, he declared, "Your hair, like the rest of you, Tasha, is exquisite. I want to take you in my arms and positively smother you with kisses, but I dare not spoil this masterpiece you've created."

Natasha blushed and flashed a smile. "Later," she whispered. "And, you look — how would a British lady say it? — positively dashing."

"Well," Mason extended his elbow, "if we're both ready, then I suggest we depart. The doorman can hail a cab for us, and, well, dammit, the sooner we get to the restaurant, the sooner I can begin admiring your pulchritude from across the table."

"Pulchritude?" Natasha queried with a puzzled smile. "Language training never taught us that word."

Mason smiled. "It comes from classical Latin, and refers to unearthly beauty. But, since the clock is ticking, I suggest we get that cab, enjoy our dinner and our evening, then adjourn straight to the airport. The sooner we're in the air, the sooner we'll be in London, and finally safe."

"My suitcase is all packed," she assured him, "and I see yours there by the door already."

———

Mason was reasonably certain his dinner had been first class, but he had no idea what he'd eaten. All he could remember was gazing across the table at the breathtakingly ravishing Natasha Cherninova.

Hours later, thirty thousand feet above the ground, with a view of the stars through the window next to Natasha, Mason gripped her hand, smiled his best and most roguish smile, and said, "We're on our way, dear. By breakfast we'll be in London. And, I checked: There's no sign of anyone who might even remotely look like ex–KGB or FSB."

Natasha smiled and nodded. "I know. I, too, checked — on the way to the washroom, I scanned almost every face. Besides, I have an inexplicable feeling that, if an FSB asset were aboard, I'd somehow know it." She shrugged. "I've always had weird instincts about things." Some of the colour drained from her face. "That awful day in Seoul, I felt a terrible dread, then, on the way to the locker room, actually felt sick to my stomach. And, the day of my mother's tragic accident, I'd had an awful foreboding: that someone was out to get her, in connection with my father, Trepashkin. It had been five years, to the day, since his release from prison."

Mason frowned, nodding. "Perhaps, the first stop on our romantic tour should be Anstruther," he suggested. "I'm sure, if we can arrange for Michael and Carrie to meet us there, that you'd learn a lot more about your instincts and how to develop them."

"I shall look forward to that," she assured him, leaning her head against his shoulder, "but, since I'm still in my evening dress, and you're still in your new suit, I'm hoping our first stop will involve some hangars, and a nice big, comfortable bed. Didn't you say something earlier this evening about wanting to smother me in kisses? I think it's extremely important that you keep that promise soon, like as soon as we're on the ground — well, as soon as we're at your apartment. It wouldn't look to good if we did it in the airport. What would the *Examiner* make of that on top of your recent scandal."

London

Mike's eyes snapped open at 2:50 PM. *Jet lag?* he wondered, *or just a need to catch up after too much stress?*

He could hear Tony just beginning to move around in his room on the floor below. Carrie, on the other hand, would be at least an hour before emerging from the void of vampire sleep.

Reaching up, he gave Kato a gentle scratch along his jawline, causing the Siamese to stretch extravagantly, pushing his forelimbs out across Mike's chest, his furry face rubbing against Mike's cheek.

"Let me up, buddy," Mike murmured, whereupon Kato retreated fully onto Mike's pillow. As Mike launched himself upright and out of the bed, he spotted his holstered Walther on the chair, along with the clothing he'd removed before getting into bed. He was about to put the blue turtleneck back on, then made a face and extracted a black one out of his kitbag, as well as his other pair of black Levis. *I can't wait to be home and back to the rest of my clothes*, he thought with a frown. Once dressed, he pulled on the harness for his gun, shrugging it into place before securing the hold-downs to his belt.

He crept quietly down the stairs to the kitchen, and had just warmed a mug of O+ and was making contact with Nigel when Tony made an appearance.

"There's a warm mug of blood for you on the counter, Tony," Mike announced, sensing Tony behind him. Tony placed a hand on his shoulder and murmured thanks.

"What is it?" Mike asked, sensing a strange vibe from Dewhurst.

Tony shook his head. "Not sure. I may have been unduly restless during sleep, but I can't imagine why. Something feels unfinished."

Mike nodded. "I won't feel completely at ease until I see Mason safe and sound." He sighed and shook his head. "I should have sent Carrie and the cats back with you, while I shadowed them on the train."

"Water under the bridge, dear boy," Tony soothed, gripping Mike's shoulder. "Let it go."

Just then Nigel's face appeared on the computer screen. "Oi, Michael, an' I 'ope 'Is Lordship is ffereabouts some'ere — Well, firs' off, gov'nor, yer Russian vampire friends created some serious Barney at ffe airport 'e day you lef'! Ffey a'mos' shut ffe place down! Two o' ffe buggers whot was after you got jus' abou' drained o' blood! Ffe 'ole ffing as been 'ushed up — I 'ad to dig deep, goin' af'er *Eyes–Only* reports.

"Luckily, ffere were no such similar incident involving Mason, but ffere is one ravver pissed Colonel Kalugin on 'e missin' list. I 'ad to dig for whot fake IDs 'e migh' 'ave, and, lo an' behold, one o' ffem arrived at 'Eaffrow jus' minutes ago."

"He'll make contact with whatever SVR agents might be planted here in London," Tony suggested, taking a gulp from his mug, "though, I dare say, there might be a few deep–cover KGB assets still lingering. I can't imagine Kalugin himself would go in for anything so crass as a firsthand termination — not with Lugovoy still wanted by Special Branch for Litvinenko's murder."

"Oi, I wouldn' be placin' any doh–ray–me down on ffat wager!" Nigel interrupted. "Kalugin were one of 'e KGB's *bodyguards,* an' spent four years stationed in Tokyo, devotin' all 'is spare time to masterin' ffe samurai sword, as well as some kind o' karate. An' Michael, when I say *mastering,* ffat's 'ow ffe Japanese put it. Seems 'e were some kind o' prodigy, not unlike yerself, gov'nor. Ye didn't 'appen to bring yer own samurai sword along, did ya?"

Mike shook his head. "Nope. I'll just have to rely on speed and magick. Can you track his arrival on security cameras and send me a screen–capture?"

"Go' it righ' 'ere, mate!" Nigel chirped, "Textin' it to ye spit–spot."

Mike studied the face on the screen — tough, hardened features, grim of expression, with stoney sharklike eyes that seemed devoid of human emotion.

Tony's hand came down onto Mike's shoulder. "That's the cause of my unease, Michael. That's the face of a ruthless killer."

Mike cracked a half smile. "Worse than Sato Satsuo?" he queried. "I assure you I'll be as careful as always. I never take anything for granted, Tony. You should know that by now. Besides, if he was something to worry about, I'd be getting my own premonitions."

Dewhurst's grip on Mike's shoulder tightened. "I know that, Michael. Still, I'm your great–great–great–great–grandfather. I'm allowed to worry."

"What do you have on possible local assets?" Mike asked Nigel.

"Well, Michael," Nigel put in, "if it were as easy as askin', MI5 would'a' rounded 'em all up, wouldn' 'ey?

An' 5's system's go' noffin' but files on 'oo ffey already rounded up."

"Can you continue to track his movements?" Tony asked. "What about attempts to contact local agents? Can we tap into any phone calls he might make from public call boxes? Does he have a cellphone with him? Can we tap into that?"

"I go' 'is cellphone info — Russian phones — well, gov'nors, privacy ain' 'xac'ly priority–one in 'e Russian Federation, is it? Gimme a sec — yeah — ffere I am! Go' it! I jus' cloned 'is SIM card, an 'ave a virtual simulation o' 'is phone goin' on my desktop. Ffe minute 'e rings anyone, I'll 'ave a transcrip' for ya, quick as Bob's–yer–uncle.

"An', I go' ffe GPS data off 'is phone, too. Now oll I need is for ffe bugger to show up on 'e network. I ffink 'e's go' 'is phone turned off. If it were a Bri'ish phone, I could force ffe bloody ffing to turn on, bu', well, i's a bleedin' Ruskie phone, i'n' it?"

"We've still got the rest of the day, Nigel," Mike reminded him. "Relax — just keep track of it and wait for him to activate his phone."

After signing off, he focused on the picture on his phone, wondering if there were some way to reach out and find Kalugin using his Wiccan powers. *Time to light some candles and experiment*, he thought. *If only I had some sense of Kalugin's mind beyond what I get from this picture.*

After a half–hour of out–of–body searching, questing over the city, he withdrew back into himself and gave up, almost exhausted.

Carrie was kneeling next to him, blatantly anxious.

"Michael, you can't keep doing this to yourself," she declared. "You didn't even use the heat of a hot bath to aid you."

He nodded, knowing the truth of her assertions. "I just feel a bit desperate, knowing that Kalugin is out there somewhere, with Mason on his way, not knowing what might be ahead, waiting for him."

"You think this Colonel Kalugin will try to retake Mason and smuggle him back to Moscow?" Carrie asked. "After all we went through to get him out of that prison, and all you went through to find him before I got there — well, I can see why you'd feel desperate. Could part of his plan be to retaliate against Natasha? So, what do we do?"

"We find Kalugin," Mike replied.

"Here," she said, turning on the hot water tap and closing the tub drain. "You soak in the heat and reclaim your spent energy. I'll warm up a supply of blood, and have Tony check with Nigel. Maybe our conniving little computer wizard has found something."

By the time the tub was full of steaming water, Carrie had returned with an entire bottle of warmed blood. "I already shook it enough to re–suspend everything," she assured him, as he took it and quaffed off a quarter of its contents.

He eased down into the tub, lay back against the curved back of the Victorian claw–foot, and closed his eyes, sucking in the heat of the water. His sense of humour, even at so serious a time, conjured the image of a lizard basking on a rock heated by the sun, absorbing what was needed to elevate its body temperature to levels that improved oxygenation and enabled better movement.

More blood to the brain, more heat for my Wiccan nature to feed on, he mused, casting a glance at the banks of candles crowded onto tables about the tub.

He took another pull from the bottle, then another, and passed it back to Carrie, mouthing a *thank you* as he closed his eyes again.

The blood, the heat of the water, the flames of the candles — it all helped to rejuvenate his senses. Soon he was off, this time at a greater altitude, exploring over the incredible sprawl that was modern London.

He knew Tony's apartments were in an older section, across the river from Vauxhall Cross, but he didn't realize how far they actually were. *Drivers measure distances in time more than actual distance,* he reminded himself — *Chester Basin is ten minutes from Chester, twenty–five minutes from Bridgewater, forty–five minutes from Halifax. I guess Pennington–Smythe and Nigel were maxing out the speed limit to get us here.*

In fact, Tony's flat was just a few blocks south of the region of old London known for Piccadilly Circus (actually just a traffic interchange) and Trafalgar Square, all a few miles north of Vauxhall Bridge. Two bridges north of Vauxhall was the huge ferris wheel he'd seen in movies. *When and why did they decide to build that?* he wondered, then shrugged it off.

He could sense the numerous swarm of London vampires just stirring as the sun began to set. A few — very few, he'd come to realize — were already up and about. He and Tony seemed a rare distinction among their kind. Even Jonathan, enigmatically, was more of a late riser — well, later than Mike and Tony — but then, he usually pushed well beyond sunrise when the pathology lab was busy.

Perhaps the vampire network can help me, he pondered. Focusing on this thought, he sought out the web of threads, noting how many silvery threads there were, and how few approached the hints of gold he associated with older vampires like Jonathan. *The Great Fire of London must have killed off a lot of older vampires,* he speculated. He began touching on the minds of more powerful vampires, whose threads to the web were silver or tinged with gold, showing them Kalugin's face, and explaining who the man was. Who Michael was seemed to require no explanation. Every mind he touched on seemed to know all about him. Tony, of course, was royalty among them, but they also knew about Myrddin — Merlin — and Michael's connection to the ancient druid.

The response of the London vampires was both instant and cooperative: *We will look, child of Lord Dewhurst,* came the replies. *He might hide his sword from mortal eyes, but our eyes will not be so easily deceived.*

He continued to prowl, now hovering lower, moving faster, hoping against hope to pick up the *swish* of a katana blade cutting the air as Kalugin practiced with his blade — Michael would have devoted at least a half–hour to ritual kata before embarking on a planned battle.

He tried tourist hotels in the heart of the city, humble guest houses, pubs with upstairs lodgings, cheap hotels, posh hotels — all yielded up nothing, not even a glimmer of hope.

He was beginning to feel the strain. Reluctantly, he returned into his body, to note that the tub water had gone cold — not even tepid. The candles had also burned down to puddles of paraffin. With a bit of a splash, he got his legs under him, and stood. He reached out to a towel, using chi to levitate it off the rack and float it to him. It dropped to the floor just a few feet shy of him.

He leaned back against the wall, did a few cycles of Qi–Gong or Chi–Kung power–breathing, his arms and hands moving through the ritual motions — the hand mirror, the downward press, the upward lift. Reaching out, he successfully levitated the towel from the floor and into his hands.

Once dry, he pulled his clothes back on, situated his shoulder–holster harness, then spotted the remains of the bottle of blood on the counter. It was cold but, as spent as he was, it didn't bother him. He set out to find Carrie and Tony.

"Michael!" Carrie cried out in alarm, "You look awful." Then, "Good lord, no wonder! Look at the time! The water must have gone freezing!"

"And the candles burned down to nothing," he confessed with a nod. "I scoured the city, found a host of older vampires willing to lend a hand — Seems I'm not as obscure as I usually hope to be."

"I suspect I'm not the only one who's been extolling your praises to the vampire community," Tony confided. "Both Jonathan and I get the feeling that Merlin has been making the rounds, especially on this side of the ocean. I think that, in his own way, he seeks to establish some kind of vampire spy network to aid you in your travails."

He pulled an armchair up behind Michael, sat him into it, then adjourned to the kitchen, where Mike soon heard him going through the motions of warming yet another bottle of blood.

"Nigel still has nothing to offer," Carrie said. "He thinks he's narrowed possible suspects for imbedded sleeper agents down to the four most likely, and has MI5 watching them. He also tried tracking Kalugin's alias to a hotel, but suspects that, once he was through Customs and Immigration, he switched to yet another alias. He's trying every known alias, even backtracking other official Russian passports that have pictures that in anyway resemble Kalugin."

"What about Belarus or Ukraine? Ukraine might be at odds with the Russian Federation now, but they weren't always," Mike murmured.

Carrie nodded, then checked a list in her hand. "He also checked other so–called breakaway republics. He's got a few hopefuls that he's trying to track. He promises to check back with us by 1:00 AM."

Mike checked his watch and frowned. 12:20. *No wonder the water was cold and the candles spent.*

Tony pressed a warmed bottle into Mike's hand, then pulled up two small tables, one to each side of his chair. Moments later he'd placed a large kerosene lamp on each table and lighted it, adjusting the flame until wisps of black began sputtering against the chimney. The flames seemed to pull toward Mike.

Mike swallowed a mouthful of blood, drew in the warmth and magical feel that blood always imparts to a vampire, then focused on drawing energy from the lamps, exaggerating the one–sided leaning of the flames. He continued to drink, relaxing, allowing his energy reserves to be replenished, rather than doing anything to deplete them again until he felt more himself.

He began to pick out sounds from the street — someone mounting the steps to Tony's flat, the front door opening, then the sound of footsteps on the stairs.

"I think we'll be hearing from Nigel in person," he commented with a slight smile, just as the door to the flat opened and shut.

"'Allo, 'allo, 'allo," the Cockney sang out. "I see ev'ryone's oll gavvered abou'," he announced, then, *"Cor Bli'me, Michael! Wotcher done yerself? You look toasted! Kick me down ffe ol' Kent Road!"*

"He's been exhausting himself trying to find this Kalugin character," Carrie declared. "He used to claim that, since Merlin's infusion of blood, his need for blood had lessened to about half, but that was before he started pushing himself beyond reasonable limits. Please tell us you've found something."

"Wha' I've found," Nigel replied, "is two blokes whot ffe MI5 lads is 'oundin', waitin' for 'em to make jus' ffe slightest move. An' I got Gregory workin' on tryin' to trigger 'e smarmy bugger's phone to turn on. In 'e meantime, I can watch for ffat from 'ere, an' give you firs' 'eads up ffe moment I know someffin'. Beyon' 'at —" He shrugged, looking as hopelessly frustrated as Mike felt.

29: Excitement in *London*

Heathrow Airport, London
2:35 AM, Wed., Dec. 4

Mason beamed as he took Natasha's hand and led her off the plane into the flow of bodies making their way through the corridors that led to Baggage Claim, then Immigration and Customs. He paused briefly to take her into his arms, kiss her warmly, and say, "Welcome to London, Tasha."

She hugged so hard against him that he could feel her heartbeat through her heavy wool coat. "I can't believe we actually made it this far," she breathed.

Mason glanced about. "I suppose I won't feel truly home again until I'm out of Heathrow and back on the streets of London," he commented, once more scanning his surroundings, his ever–vigilant eyes questing for evidence of danger, and finding none.

"MI6 should have a car here for us, but I suddenly think I should just hire a car and drive us myself. Last time I was in London, I was in my own car, with my assigned driver, and that didn't work out so well — especially for him."

"I guess your Aston Martin is in a garage somewhere?" Natasha queried, grinning. "Don't all MI6 agents drive an Aston Martin?"

"Only those chronicled by the late Ian Fleming," he answered with a grin of his own.

"Oh, Mason, look!" Natasha cried, pointing to a newspaper rack.

The headline of the previous day's *London Times* proclaimed:

EXAMINER HAS EGG ON IT'S FACE.
MI6 EXPECTS AN APOLOGY!

"Well, I'll be —" Mason declared.

His SIS ID got them through the official screening process almost effortlessly, and they were soon on their way to the rental counters.

They were just leaving the Hertz counter, keys in hand, when Mason paused; he'd spotted a man off to the side, seemingly reading a copy of the *Times*, but peeking furtively over the top at them.

Tasha tightened her grip on his arm.

"Is that someone from MI6?" she asked. "He seems too interested in us. I have an anxious feeling."

"I agree," Mason said. Reaching inside his topcoat and suit coat, he unsnapped the securing strap and loosened the Makarov PM in its holster, then opened both his coats a bit more. *I wish I had my PPK instead of this damned Makarov*, he thought, but said, "We'll just maintain vigilance, and make our way to the car."

They were exiting the motorway exit into metro London when Mason spotted the same man in his rearview mirror, at the wheel of a following vehicle. He tried to pull away, then, as he stopped for the first red light, another car pulled up beside the one tailing them. The former newspaper reader gave a slow nod to the newcomer, who nodded back.

It was just after three, and traffic was minimal. Mason gunned the accelerator, took off, running the light, and roared eastward toward the heart of London.

He was about six blocks from Vauxhall Bridge when the first car pulled out and overtook him on the right, pacing him alongside, while the other car pulled up close behind.

In a coordinated move, the rear car hit them from behind on the outer corner, while the car abreast of them swerved and sideswiped, forcing them up onto the curb.

"Brace your hands against the dashboard," Mason instructed, and swerved further left, up onto the sidewalk, accelerated, just missing a lamp post by a couple of centimeters, then made it another ten meters before crashing into the first car, which had just swerved up onto the sidewalk in front of them and slammed on the brakes.

Mason immediately threw his door open, grabbed Natasha's arm, and pulled.

As if by some instinct, she pulled her legs up onto the seat, making it easier for her to slide across the console between the seats, behind and clear of the gearshift, got her feet swung around and ready, so that she hit the ground running with Mason.

"That was amazing!" Mason declared. "Alas, your lovely shoes aren't going to help much," he added, frowning as she almost rolled an ankle.

They made it past two more buildings before the first spitting sound occurred. There was the scream of a bullet ricocheting off a lamp post, just centimeters above Mason's head.

He spotted an alley, dodged left, and steered Natasha down it, pausing just long enough to pull the Makarov. Experience had taught him how disheartening it could be to discover in the heat of action that the last bullet had been fired. He ejected and pocketed the chamber round, then fired a series of shots at the two men now pursuing them on foot. The staccato *crack* of the reports was still echoing off the walls when the chamber slide stopped in recoil position, announcing that the magazine was spent. His fusillade was answered by what Mason decided must be at least seven or eight silenced shots from the two in pursuit. He tried to keep track of their shots fired, but couldn't be certain. He took the bullet from his pocket and loaded it into the Makarov, then holstered it.

Natasha made a tearing gesture at one foot, threw her shoe behind her, then divested herself of the other in the same manner. "I hope there's no broken glass," she said, then increased her pace.

Mason, for his part, found he had to focus on not running too fast for her.

"*Aww!*" she cried out, then staggered. "I should have kept my mouth shut!"

Bollox! Glass in her foot! Mason mentally castigated, as if it were somehow his fault, then swept her up into his arms and took off at his best sprint — Until the brick wall before him announced that he'd just run out of alley.

Setting Natasha on her feet against a sidewall, he drew his weapon, chambered the one remaining round, and waited for their pursuers to get close enough for a sure shot.

The pursuers caught up, stopped just long enough to take aim, and —

A dark figure dropped from above, into the path of the two gunmen.

Both muzzles flashed repeatedly, making their iconic spitting sounds. The unknown intruder seemed to jerk in response to the impact of bullets, then staggered and fell. Mason thought Natasha screamed, then realized the scream was from higher up, on a rooftop above them.

Tony's Flat, London

"Finally!" Nigel declared. "I ffought ffe bugger'd never turn 'is bleedin' phone on. 'E's 'eaded, well, *Bli'me* if 'e ain't 'eadin' in ffis direction! An', bugger me if ffose two blokes whot gave MI5 'e slip aren't in a'mos' 'e same place. I ffink 'e's on 'is way to catch up wiff 'em, an' in a bi' of an 'urry, too."

Mike stared at the screen. It was just after 3:10. *Mason's plane will have landed by now*, he thought, then, something prickled at the back of his neck.

"Light those lamps again, Carrie, — I don't want to spare the energy."

As soon as Carrie and Tony had each lit a lamp, he reached out to scan the area in the direction of the flashing dot that represented Kalugin's cellphone's GPS signal.

"He's only six blocks from here."

"And he seems to have stopped," Tony added.

"I've got him," Mike declared. "He's got his katana with him. What's he plan to do with that in the heart of urban London?"

He launched to his feet. "It's an alley about seven blocks away. The other two are chasing after Mason and Natasha on foot."

He glanced at his jacket, shook his head, and was out the door.

"Not without me, you don't!" he heard Carrie declare as he headed for the roof at vampire speed.

He dashed eastward toward the river, leaping from rooftop to rooftop, building up enough momentum to leap across the intervening streets to rooftops on the other side.

We caught two running toward the two chasing your friends, the voice of a London vampire said. *They are dead in an alley. We cannot reach your friends before you, Lord Michael.*

From up ahead he heard a series of reports from a Makarov, then the spits of two silenced weapons. He counted four shots each from the silenced weapons. *If they're older Makarovs, they'll each have four shots left*, he decided, *unless someone fired more shots before I came within hearing.*

Then a woman's voice cried out, "*Aww! — I should have kept my mouth shut!*" the tone reflecting both pain and anger. He recognized Natasha's voice.

One more burst of speed and he skidded to a stop just as Mason was trying to position himself between Natasha and their assailants.

Mike dropped into their midst, braced himself, then summoned enough chi to form a forcefield in front of him. The two Russian sleeper agents emptied their Makarovs at him.

He heard Carrie scream from the roof above.

He felt the faint impact of four slugs from one, then three from the other. The two ejected their clips and were about inject replacements.

The first four of the slugs clattered to the pavement, their momentum absorbed by his projected chi, but the other three didn't. He felt them tear into his chest. *Newer bullets, better powder*, he decided.

He snarled, and blurred forward before they could insert the new clips and shoot again. He grabbed one and hurled him head–first into the stonework of a building. There was a sickening crunch as the head slammed into the brickwork.

The second had just clicked his magazine into place when Mike blurred to him. He struck the weapon aside with a crane–wing block, then zipped behind him. Seizing him by one shoulder, he grabbed a handful of hair atop the assassin's head, then gave a wrench that made the thug's ear smack against his own shoulder. Mike sensed the life–force fading from the corpse, and let it drop to sprawl on the pavement.

Mason was just helping Natasha to her feet as Carrie dropped from above, to the obvious consternation of both.

Mike collapsed against the building, pulled the flask from his back pocket, and quaffed a mouthful before putting it away and turning his attention to the three bullets in his upper right chest. Using his left hand, he summoned chi and pulled at the bullets. Within a second they pulled free and fell to the ground.

"Damn!" he muttered, "That turtleneck was a *McGregor*; I really liked that shirt."

"Michael, are you okay?" Carrie demanded, alarm in her voice. "I saw you get shot. Do you need more..."

"Carrie? Is that you? Michael?" It was Natasha, in Mason's arms, one foot dripping blood.

"I'm okay," Mike assured Carrie. "And thank you for refilling my flask."

A Slavic–accented voice spoke out behind Mike, from closer to the entrance to the alley. "Well, well; what have we here? Mason of MI6, the wayward Lieutenant Cherninova, and, can it be? — the incredibly annoying Agent *Samurai* of CSIS, all in one place? How lucky for me!"

Mike turned to face the newcomer, recognizing the face from the airport security image.

"Colonel Kalugin," he said, keeping his eyes on the other.

"I'll happily shoot him for you, Michael," Mason declared, "I managed to retain one bullet."

Mike shrugged and eased Carrie back behind him.

"He's probably wearing *Kevlar* under his coat, but I think Kalugin has another weapon in mind than firearms," he commented to Mason. "Carrie, you should probably take a look at Natasha's foot. She has two shards of glass in her right foot, possibly some smaller slivers, as well."

"Are you sure?" she asked, keeping her eyes on Kalugin.

Mike smirked, and said, "I'm sure I want you to check Natasha's foot. And, yes, I'm reasonably sure I can handle the colonel here."

But he frowned when Ilya Kalugin opened his long coat, and, sure enough, there was evidence of a ballistic vest under his clothing. Kalugin drew an ancient katana from its *saya* in a specially–constructed inside pocket. From the workmanship, Mike decided that it's maker may have been a student of *Muramasa*, if not the great *Muramasa Sengo* himself. From the way Kalugin twirled it with both advanced precision and speed, there was no doubt that Mike faced a master. However, he was equally sure of his own vampire speed and the Wiccan powers.

Kalugin moved, katana lashing about him in figure–eight whirls, then his left hand pulled a Makarov PM.

Carrie screamed and launched a ball of energy that fell about Mike.

Mason and Natasha shouted simultaneous warnings.

Kalugin fired four rapid shots.

Caught off–guard, distracted by Carrie's scream and the energy she'd launched, Mason and Natasha's shouts, Mike felt the four slugs enter his chest, then tore forward in a blur.

Pain! Fiery fierce pain in the chest!

Just do it — No fancy shit — Simple — What you've known for years — But FAST!

The blur stopped next to Kalugin.

Mike's right hand came down on the katana, just back of the *tsuba*, tearing it loose from his grasp, sending it clattering to the pavement.

He zipped behind Kalugin — Right hand taking his throat in a pincer grip — Left hand sliding down the left shoulder — hardened fingertips compressed nerves exiting the rotator cuff — then down the arm, wrenching the wrist, shattering the radius and ulna. The Makarov jerked free and dropped to the ground.

Mike maintained his grip on the colonel, blocking his airway and blood flow to the brain, knowing Kalugin would pass out in minutes.

Massive pain in his chest!

He felt his canines expanding. The monster smelled the blood oozing from his chest, and sensed the throbbing, coursing blood just beneath the surface of Kalugin's throat, within the carotids and jugulars suppressed by his fingers and thumb.

Carrie's projected energy hadn't stopped the bullets. In fact, it still hovered as a glow about him.

He stretched his mouth wide, his fangs fully extended, and voiced an involuntary aspiration that was part hiss, part snarl.

Mason was staring in fascinated understanding.

Carrie stared in alarm, her face reflecting her own worried horror for his safety and his sanity.

Natasha just stared in horror, seeing a monster.

As the image of his face in Natasha's mind permeated his consciousness, Mike took a deep, cleansing breath, willed himself to relax, and felt the fangs recede. His energy was all but spent. He had nothing left to exude the glamour necessary to disguise his eyes.

Reaching out, he pulled Carrie's cloud of energy into himself, absorbed it, then focused on the bullets, and pushed. Slowly the four slugs emerged, falling inside his cotton turtleneck. He pulled his shirttail free, allowing the bullets to tumble to the ground. *Well what do you know — that was barely harder than pulling them out!*

He let go of Kalugin, who collapsed to the pavement, almost on top of his own bullets.

Carrie rushed to Mike, looking aghast, tears streaming. "Michael! Are you okay?"

"I think so," he sighed, enveloping her in his arms. "I need a drink, and a major sleep."

Carrie hugged him back and uttered a nervous laugh. "I'm sure you do," she agreed. "Here." She pulled his flask from his back pocket, uncapped it, and held it to his mouth long enough for him to drain it.

"Michael, I don't know what to say," Mason began. He approached, helping Natasha as she tried to compromise between hopping on her left foot and just placing the ball of her right foot on the ground. Natasha, though, seemed to want to hang back, as if she wasn't sure about Mike anymore.

"It's okay, Tasha," Mason assured her in a low tone. "It's Michael. He just showed up out of nowhere in time to save us. It's another part of what he does — what makes him so amazing."

"Chto, i to chto on vampir," Natasha murmured.

Mike frowned, then pulled, *That, and the fact that he's a vampire* from Mason's mind.

He fixed his eyes on her, and projected. *Yes. So now you know why I'm so fast and why my Wiccan powers are amplified beyond what is possible for a normal human.*

Tony arrived on the scene a moment later.

As he placed handcuffs on Kalugin, Natasha stared at him, then at Carrie, then back and forth between Carrie, Michael, and Tony.

"I was just about to finish getting the rest of that glass out of your foot," Carrie said, and tried to get Natasha to sit on the ground.

Natasha started to recoil away from her, then, looking puzzled, she suddenly shook her head, smiled, then hugged Carrie. "You're a vampire, too? But you're still my friend?" she stammered.

"It's complicated," Carrie replied.

Natasha cast a glance at Mason. "Complicated?"

Mason shrugged.

With lights flashing, an unmarked car pulled up to the curb, and two men leaped out, brandishing Walther P99s. They looked as if they were planning to take everyone into custody, but Tony forestalled them, showing his Interpol ID, whereupon Mason smiled and commented, "Thanks, Tony, but I dare say mine trumps yours," and showed the men his MI6 ID.

The taller of the two heaved a sigh of relief. "Good to have you back safely, Capt. Mason," he said. "I'm Saunders, MI5." Turning to Tony, he added, "Since you're Lord Dewhurst, sir, does that mean that this gentleman is *Samurai* of the Canadian SIS?"

Mike gave a nod and nudged Kalugin.

"This is Colonel Ilya Kalugin of Department S of the Russian FSB. He entered the UK on a false passport. That's his firearm. The sword was also his, but, I'll keep custody of that," whereupon Mike located the *saya* from the inside of Kalugin's long coat, picked up the katana, and sheathed it.

"By the way," he added, "Kalugin should regain consciousness in another minute or two — Cerebral hypoxia. He'll have a hell of a headache, but he deserves it."

Saunders frowned, then glanced at the katana in Mike's hand, as if about to argue it's custody, but Mason stepped in.

"Thanks for the mop–up, as always," he said. "MI6 will handle the rest from here, including reporting to Vauxhall Cross." He punctuated the sentence with an arched eyebrow, daring Saunders to challenge it.

Saunders looked at Mason then at *Samurai*, who cocked an eyebrow himself.

Saunders just nodded, and helped the other MI5 man frog–walk Kalugin to the car and install him into the backseat.

"Are you ready to report to *C*?" Mike asked Mason.

"Not until we've had a sit down and a bite of breakfast," he retorted. "And, I dare say you could do with a bit of something yourself."

"I dare say, that means heading back to my flat," Tony suggested. "Well, *Sink me* if this isn't Nigel's van pulling up in time to give us a lift."

"Hopefully we can stop on the way and retrieve our luggage from the abandoned car hire."

———

"**I** never saw either of you eat, and you were always drinking something from warmed mugs — using the aroma of strong–brewed coffee to mask whatever aroma it might have given off. — But I've seen you in daylight," Natasha argued, as if that would somehow undo what she'd just said or what she'd seen: Mike surviving four bullet wounds to the chest, his fangs extending, the vertical pupils of his ancient, nocturnal eyes.

"I saw glimpses of those eyes when you were tired, back in Moscow, and pointy ears, too, I think." She shook her head, still somewhat in denial. She seemed to be trying to find a way back to her previous attitude toward him and Carrie, though she kept studying each of them, as if trying to see through them.

Mike explained: "The few of us who seem capable of being awake during daylight hours can move about in sunlight, as long as we use sunscreen, and make an effort to protect ourselves from direct ultraviolet exposure. But I'm different. Because of my sorcery — my ability to make and handle fire — I was able to survive most of a day in the sun a couple of years ago. It darkened my skin somewhat and, ever since, I seem more tolerant. Carrie, though, being much younger as a vampire, must avoid even minor exposure to ultraviolet rays."

"So there are more of you? And very few are monsters — predators? So how do you all feed? Blood bank blood? Surely there's not enough. I hear advertisements all the time asking for more blood–donors, claiming that there just aren't enough."

"Years back," Tony explained, "scientists found they could clone blood, but there was an outcry against anything to do with cloning. So, while the world at large let the notion slip their minds, the vampire community took over the whole thing, funded the work, developed a series of networks for distribution in various countries, including Russia, which is how we had an ample supply while in Moscow."

"So what else do you teach at this *Scholomance*?" Natasha asked Mike. "You mentioned teaching Kung Fu and aspects of Qi Gong, what you call Chi Kung."

"I also lecture on the nature of vampires — teaching the facts, and dispelling the myths," he explained. "Certain *Scholomance* members dedicate themselves to keeping track of vampires suspected of being predatory monsters."

"But doesn't that put you in danger?" she argued. "I mean, all those powerful people — do they call themselves witches? — knowing what you are, and you teach them more or less what works and doesn't work should they determine to kill you?"

"Tasha, Michael has killed more vampires in the past five or six years than there are students at the *Scholomance*." Mason interjected over a mouthful of toast and orange marmalade, then took a sip of tea. "He's the most successful vampire–hunter since Van Helsing — more successful, really. I know firsthand: Tony and I were doing our best in a crypt in Rostock, Germany — and our best wasn't terribly good — when Michael showed up and took over. It was like a scene from a bad John Carpenter movie. They were flying at us from opened coffins — if it hadn't been for Michael and his speed and skill with a katana —"

"So," Natasha summarized, "vampires have been peacefully among us for a very long time. And you sort of sort out the evil ones, though you are a vampire yourself." She shook her head, as if still puzzled.

Mike nodded. "Criminals are human; so are the police. I don't just protect innocent humans; I protect innocent vampires from being exposed — predatory vampires draw attention to the existence of all of us."

Tony came around and faced Natasha, forcing her to look him in the face. "My dear," he said in his kindly tone, "I am the original Lord Anthony Dewhurst who, along with my dear departed friend and cousin, Sir Percival Blakeney, became fictionalized by Baroness Emuska Orczy in her *Scarlet Pimpernel* series. After helping Percy rescue French Aristocrats from *The Terror* during the late 18th century, I spent much of the 19th working with Scotland Yard on difficult cases, including dealing with Jack the Ripper in covert fashion, keeping it off the books, so to speak, because, he, too, was a vampire.

"In the early 20th century, I met a man named Georgi Rosenblum, who talked me into joining the Foreign Office as a spy, where I met Mansfield Smith–Cumming, the original *C*, who's service eventually became MI6, though, before the Second World War, I also did some work for MI5. So you see, Natasha, it's somewhat normal for many of us to contribute our special talents to making this world a safer place. And, for a compulsive knight–errant like Michael, it's second nature."

Mike cracked just a hint of a smile. "I probably inherited such urges from my Great–great–great–great–grandfather," he said, casting a meaningful glance at Tony, who responded with what seemed a blush.

"That's far too long a story for today," Carrie cut in. "Let's just leave it that Tony's true love, Michael's maternal ancestor, was a Wicca."

"Which gave Michael no' jus' an 'ead start on 'e 'ole vampire ffing," Nigel decided to interject, "but a considerable 'elpin' o' whot ye migh' call 'e family juju. An', ffrough it oll, *I* seem to 'ave become ffe family record–keeper." He beamed as if extremely proud of the self–assumed role.

Mike drifted to a sofa with Carrie, letting the others continue to talk while Mason and Natasha finished breakfast. He need a moment of peace and quiet, and felt Natasha wasn't quite ready to watch either him or Carrie imbibing blood, though Carrie was doing just that via ceramic mug.

"How is your chest?" she asked, gently brushing featherlight fingertips over the skin just under his clavicle. She had her eyes closed, but Mike could sense the glow of Wiccan power and feel the tingly current of electrical energy coming from her fingers.

He nodded. "The wounds have closed. I never thanked you before for hurling that energy at me. I thought you were trying to shield me. Then I realized you were hoping to feed it to me."

"You wrote that in the third book of your fantasy series," Carrie explained. "I figured, if the heroine could pour energy into her man, then so could I. And you can thank me later," she added, a mischievous twinkle in her eyes.

"So what's with the katana?" she asked. "Adding it to your collection? How many does that make?"

Mike picked it up from where he'd set it beside the sofa, and examined the hilt. It hadn't been as carefully preserved as his *Yama Kaze*, but the similarities were unmistakeable. In fact, it looked as if someone had created a twin of *Mountain Wind*, wrapping the hilt with twists of brown cloth instead of black.

He stood and carried it to the kitchen, searching through drawers until he found tools that would serve to tap and push the bamboo pins out of their purchase, allowing him to slide the parts of the handle off of the tang. The ubiquitous half smile formed as he recognized Muramasa's *Kanji* ideogram.

"I can't say if it's older or younger than *Mountain Wind*," he told Carrie, "but it's definitely a sister blade. Only Master Tekaga could say for sure."

"Is it valuable?" she asked. "I never asked about *Mountain Wind* — I know it has huge sentimental value for you, being so old, and having belonged to you back when you were Yakura Tomomatsu. I suppose it must be worth several thousand dollars."

"Perhaps a million," Mike corrected, "which leads me to wonder how Kalugin ever came by it. I can't imagine even an over–indulgent master awarding this to a student. There are people who would kill for this."

"Perhaps he did," Carrie commented, frowning.

It passed through Mike like a shiver — a shiver that emanated from the katana and passed upward into his arms. "I think you're right," he murmured.

"You said, Mason, that you and Michael were somehow related, in some complicated manner, that was connected to Tony," Natasha was saying. "Does that mean that you are somehow part vampire?"

Mike sighed. "I guess I'm the best one to explain that," he suggested, then told the tale of how Tony had saved Mason's life, and the medical consequences, including the limited probability of him ever becoming a vampire.

Natasha looked up into his eyes, then smiled. "No wonder you said it was complicated, and didn't want to expound. And you only learned of this when they came to get you in Lefortovo?"

Mason nodded.

"And you've been worried about it ever since?" she asked.

Mason shrugged. "Worried a little for myself, but mostly worried about how you'd react."

Natasha continued to look into his eyes, then kissed him, a slow, drawn–out kiss. "No wonder you seem so young. How could I ever fault you for something that's kept you alive, and was never of your own choosing?" And she kissed him again.

30: Mission Accomplished

MI6 Head Quarters, Vauxhall Cross, London
Wed., Dec. 4

When he'd heard the full story from Michael and from Mason, with supplementary input from Tony, Carrie, and Natasha, Sir John Sawers, *C* of MI6, fell silent, seemingly dumbfounded by it all.

"I don't know where to begin," he hesitated. "*Samurai* and, of course, Lord Dewhurst, but, you, in particular, *Samurai*, well, it's just remarkable. *Good Lord*, the file will be so redacted they might as well just find some white ink and write out what few sentences they can on a black page!

"As for Colonel Kalugin," he smiled, "well, Mr. Putin will be aghast when he sees his man on the news. Of course, he'll be tried for espionage and attempted assassination. I dare say, this new fellow, Sergei Lavrov, will be working overtime to deny it all — No doubt inventing some role for him that implies diplomatic immunity.

"And then there's this Islamic State group — Of course we've been monitoring them in Syria for a while, but they've never done much — Your incident on the flight here from Halifax is the first.

"Anyway, *Samurai*, The Service is immeasurably indebted to you, and to you, as well, Mrs. Cameron."

"And, Captain Mason: Of course, welcome back and all that, but are you truly determined to stand by the resignation you tendered over the phone?"

Mason just nodded. "I've been in the harness long enough — longer than most." Taking Natasha's hand in his, he smiled and added, "And now I have a reason to begin taking it easier." He handed *C* an envelope.

C took it in his hand, looked at the envelope without opening it, and nodded his understanding. "Of course, you understand our need to debrief both you and Ms. Cherninova. There is a wealth of information she can provide us about the FSB and it's workings. And, needless to add, there'll be the odd nay–sayer who insists she's an SVR plant. However, I, for one, trust your judgement, Captain. And then, there's *Samurai* vouching for her, which, with his uncanny gifts, certainly settles it for me."

Then, turning to Natasha, he extended his hand, adding, "If your father should ever feel the need to escape Putin's grip, we can offer assistance.

"And, *Samurai*, that's an astonishing wealth of intelligence you've provided us. I'll be briefing the PM and the Defense and Foreign Ministers later today. They'll be wanting to be brought up to speed on this Ukraine situation. It's just mind–boggling. Of course, we knew from Litvinenko himself about the bombing scandal, but to have it confirmed so dramatically by you, *Samurai*, why it's truly mind-boggling.

"Of course, both you and Lord Dewhurst will be covered for much more than your out–of–pocket expenses, and remunerated at usual danger rates for a *00*–mission.

"*Good God, man!* Walking Mason out of Lefortovo under the very eyes of FSB guards! And escaping Lubyanka after — *Good Lord, man* — but, of course, there is your — well — you do represent a truly unimaginable skill–set — both you and Lord Anthony, and, of course, your charming wife." He favoured Carrie with a warm smile.

C looked back at Mike, seemed to hesitate a moment, then, as if steeling himself, drew in a breath, — and hesitated yet again.

"You know, *Samurai*," he finally said, "I've had our legal staff look into your records. Technically, both your certification in marine celestial navigation and your captain's license were done through offices that fall under the auspices of the British Admiralty."

Here we go, Mike thought, but kept quiet, waiting to hear *C* say his piece.

"If you were a UK resident and we were at war, you'd be offered a commission in the Royal Navy as at least a second leftenant, if not first leftenant. And, after the incredible success of this mission, you'd most certainly have been promoted to leftenant commander, if not full commander."

Mike couldn't resist a rictus of a smirk. "My director already grinds his teeth whenever he hears of JTF2 personnel referring to me as *Commander Cameron*. 'There are no Commanders in CSIS,' he once growled at me."

C smiled patiently. "There are, however, commanders here at '6, most notably in the *Double–0* Section. And you do seem to have spent considerable time over here in the last couple of years, well, at least in Scotland."

"Are you asking me to quit CSIS and join MI6?" Mike asked. "Wouldn't that require a change of citizenship?" He shook his head. "I don't know, sir — I've been Canadian my whole life. Even when I was away, I was yearning to return; and we just built a new home in the place where I'd been dreaming of living for years." He concluded with an ambivalent shrug.

"And yet you travelled for at least two years on a British Dependent Territories passport issued in Bermuda — that is, until your sailing vessel foundered between Bermuda and the Bahamas.

"Seriously, *Samurai*, you could be both: dual citizenship, working for both the Canadian SIS and the British SIS. I'm sure the use of those initials in the name of your organization is meant to be indicative.

"And, by the way, did you know that Fleming's model for James Bond, aside from Lord Dewhurst here, was actually Canadian? Well, he was former SAS, and working as a lumberjack somewhere out in your Canadian west when the service tracked him down and recruited him, but the fact that'd he acquired Canadian citizenship didn't matter a bit."

Mike remained silent for a whole minute.

"It's a lot to think about," he said finally. "If forced to respond today, I'd have to say *no*."

"Then don't respond today," *C* rebutted with a smile. "Take all the time you need. Who knows, in a month or two, once Putin has had his fun with the Sochi Winter Olympics, we may be looking to borrow you again, depending on what skullduggery he decides to pull in Ukraine. Are you sure he's hellbent on destabilizing that region? He's always seemed so bloody reasonable compared to some of the hardliners that came before him."

Mike frowned and shook his head. "That's how he wants to be seen," he said. "He's rather devious in crafting his image. Gather up all the media clips he's endorsed and get a professional psychological assessment. You might even have your people read Masha Gessen's biography."

Mike was starting to fume as the further debriefing went into its third hour. Is wasn't just MI6 officials; he also had to acquaint representatives from State and Defense, as well as other unidentified bureaucrats, with all he knew about Kemedov's activities, what he'd gleaned about Ukraine, and Dyatlov's and the FSB's involvement in Russia's September Bombings of 1999.

What vexed him the most was that he still had to establish Mason's innocence in his own kidnapping, but he sat back patiently while Tony told them about the forger, Boronovich, and how he'd invented Brenda Peters out of Brendu Petrova.

Mike decided that one of the interrogators must have been a bureaucrat from a department constantly under scrutiny from the media. The annoying man demanded repeated explanations of the alleged phone calls from Mason's cellphone to Brenda Peters, and especially to Kemedov.

"*Really?*" Mike queried. "Are you still stuck on that? The head of Quartermaster Branch explained that to me before I even set out for Russia. Maybe you should ask Q. I guess you're not with SIS and haven't been briefed, but it certainly isn't my job to explain internal MI6 intelligence.

"Beyond that, since you'd still have to *prove* Mason guilty before a judge and jury, I'd suggest that his very presence here, with a former FSB officer to verify his story, is proof enough of his innocence."

The bureaucrat went florid in the face, began to bluster, then blurted, "The fact that he's returned with a Russian woman might be seen by some as evidence that he hopes to reinsert himself back into MI6 as a double agent."

Mike's failing patience expressed itself in a tight smile. "It's a shame that his recent notice of retirement to *C* bursts that bubble," he snapped in fine irony. "Of course, the *Examiner* did make an ass of itself, suggesting that Harry Potter worked for MI6, not to mention Ron Weasley. Mind you, Pennington–Smythe *is* an SIS analyst, but he's *hardly* a *double–0*." The ripple of laughter was not shared by the pompous bureaucrat.

"And *that*, by the way, was my doing, if you need to blame someone. Once I learned from the night cleaner, who had stolen the file from Mason's desk, that he'd turned the file over to that editor at the *Examiner*, I rescued the file, sent photos to our IT tech, and had him create a new, fake file, which I put in place of the stolen file. I figured, since the *Examiner* was so determined to print something, let's give the country a chance to laugh at *them*. If your so hell-bent on lynching someone, why not go after the one institution that had no qualms about displaying what was assumed to be classified information all over the pages of their rag?"

He fell silent, glaring about the room, then, with a glance at Tony and Mason, announced, "Gentlemen, I've had enough. I'm afraid my tolerance for bureaucratic bullshit isn't what it used to be." And, with that, he stood up to leave.

The MI6 and Ministry of Defense people merely nodded and thanked him for his time and his service, but the argumentative bureaucrat launched to his feet, still blustering, though it was all but inarticulate.

Mike wheeled on him, ignited a glow of Wiccan energy in his eyes, and focused them on the blusterer. *Calm Down, and Sit Down,* he commanded, *NOW!*

The man, who turned out to be a Deputy Under-secretary of State for Foreign Affairs, swallowed and sat down abruptly. The MI6 people about the table didn't even try to hide their smiles.

"That went well," Mason declared, laughing. "Michael, it was almost worth what I've been through to see you slam Braithwaite so thoroughly. He's always been a pompous sod, but I think he gets worse with each birthday. Maybe a good laxative would help.

"Anyway, I say we collect Carrie from wherever she went — Can you believe Braithwaite wouldn't even let her in the room? But, of course, he made Natasha wait outside for most of the session. However, getting back to what I was about to suggest, I think a celebratory dinner is in order, though Nigel, Natasha and I will be the only ones eating. Perhaps aged Glenmorangie? But, be that as it may, dinner is on me."

Mike drew Mason aside, and confided, "Mason, you can have closure on your wife's death; it was Petroff who orchestrated the explosion, using one of the KGB *bodyguards*; I saw it all in his mind. I took revenge by frying his mind before leaving him, smoking gun in hand, for the Vyazma police to find."

Mason took a grip on Mike's arm and smiled. "Now I can truly lay that chapter to rest."

Just then, Carrie appeared from around a corner.

"I have to thank you," Natasha said, taking Carrie's arm. "My foot feels as good as new, and I can't believe you found my shoes!"

Carrie laughed, "We girls have to stick together, Tasha, especially when it comes to shoes! Besides, it was Michael who really fixed your foot."

Natasha frowned. "Are you sure? It was you who removed the glass and cleaned out the wounds. No, offense to you, Michael, but all you did was run your thumb along the cuts after Carrie did her work."

"It's all in the spit," Carrie whispered. "Michael's saliva is better than mine or any vampire's, with the exception of Merlin's."

"Merlin? *The* Merlin?" Natasha queried in disbelief. "You're joking — aren't you?"

"If you keep hanging around us," Carrie assured her, "you'll meet him sooner or later, especially if you come with us to *Scholomance* Castle in Scotland.

Michael and I are planning to visit for maybe a week before going home, hopefully in time to set up for Christmas, though, at this point, having Christmas in Anstruther might be easier."

Natasha looked studiously at Carrie's face, then at Mike, who just shrugged and smiled. "Merlin?" she repeated, "Seriously, *The* Merlin?"

"Well, he's Michael's friend, and, in terms of vampire bloodlines, sort of an ancestor of ours," Tony explained, "but, yes, *The* Myrddin Embrys, Sorcerer to King Arthur. He seems quite fond of Michael, but then, aren't we all." Tony beamed as he added the latter, then Mason chimed in.

"Well, I for one — no doubt one of many —" he declared, "am extremely fond of my rescuer and miracle–worker."

Mike's half smile faded to a frown. "Actually, I'll need to be a miracle–worker to get Carrie and I, her luggage, *and* a cat carrier back to Chester Basin in a Pontiac Solstice. Taking a two–seater with almost no trunk seemed like a good idea when I left home and headed into Halifax to meet Tony, but in retrospect, I should have taken the Cherokee."

For More Information on Agent Samurai,
and the other works of D.C. Rhind,
or to view the video trailer for this and other books,
Visit *www.DCRhind.ca*

References & Bibliography:

Putin's Dark Rise to Power
Scott Anderson
GQ Magazine, September 2009

Blowing Up Russia
Alexander Litvinenko & Yuri Felshtinsky
Encounter Books, March 7, 2007
ISBN: 978-1594032011

The Man Without a Face, The Unlikely Rise of
Vladimir Putin
Masha Gessin
Riverhead, March 6, 2012
ASIN: B00BUW7I6Q; ISBN: 978-1594486517

A Portrait of Putin
A Video–Portrait by Neil Macdonald,
CBC News Correspondent
Aired on CBC's *The National*, April 9, 2014

Lightning Source UK Ltd.
Milton Keynes UK
UKOW03f0236231014

240526UK00001B/5/P